THE MEMORY COLLECTORS

THE MEMORY
COLLECTORS

KIM NEVILLE

WHEELER PUBLISHING
A part of Gale, a Cengage Company

Wheeler Publishing Large Print Hardcover.
The text of this Large Print edition is unabridged.
Other aspects of the book may vary from the original edition.
Set in 16 pt. Plantin.

LIBRARY OF CONGRESS CIP DATA ON FILE.
CATALOGUING IN PUBLICATION FOR THIS BOOK
IS AVAILABLE FROM THE LIBRARY OF CONGRESS.

ISBN-13: 978-1-4328-8748-3 (hardcover alk. paper)

Published in 2021 by arrangement with Atria Books, a division of Simon & Schuster, Inc.

Printed in Mexico
Print Number: 01   Print Year: 2021

To Shane,
for always believing

PROLOGUE

The air beneath Evelyn's paper mask is hot and damp, and even though a shaft of sunlight from the open barn door reveals swirling sawdust, she pulls the mask up to her forehead and allows herself a breath. She rarely gets a moment alone in her father's workshop, so she pauses briefly to enjoy the grown-up feeling of it, her boots rustling the shavings on the floor, the smell of cut wood and lacquer, no one around but the old headboards and mirrors hanging on the walls, the maze of chairs, wardrobes, dressers, and end tables that stretches all the way back to the darkened doorway leading to the shop floor.

Sunday is Evelyn's favorite day of the week. On Saturdays, Daddy's store is open and strangers come in and out of his workshop all day to purchase antiques or to ask him to restore old pieces of furniture, and Evelyn has to stay inside with Mama and

Noemi. On Sundays, the store is closed. In the early mornings, her father goes out to garage sales. When he gets back, he brings his finds into the workshop and he and Evelyn sort through them together. After that, they work side by side. Now that she is eight, he has been showing her how to use his tools. She's not strong enough to work a plane yet, and she's not allowed to use the drill or handsaw. But she knows how to use a hammer, a scraper, a screwdriver, and a hand sander. Daddy especially likes her to help with detail sanding because her small hands are good at getting into tight places.

The square of sandpaper she's been using has grown creased and worn. She lightly traces the bumps and curves of the chair leg she's working on. The armchair stands naked on top of the worktable, the fabric cut from its seat and back and all the stuffing pulled out. Soon Daddy will dress it again. He showed Evelyn the fabric he's chosen, a rich green velvet the color of the ferns that grow along the fence in the backyard.

A gust of wind rattles the barn doors. The morning was sunny, but clouds have blown in and the sky is darkening. She can hear Noemi talking to herself in her nonstop baby chatter, which means Mama is still in the garden. She hears footsteps coming up the steps to the workshop, Daddy with the last boxes from the truck. He huffs as he places them on the worktable and then comes around to see how she's doing.

"How does it feel?"

"Warm," says Evelyn. "Happy."

"Yes." She hears the smile in his voice. "I think it's time you come out to the sales with me on Sundays. Would you like that?"

Evelyn nods. He places his hand on the top of her head and scratches gently, like she's a kitten.

"Feel this." She catches his fingers and moves them along the chair leg, first on the bottom, where she hasn't yet worked, but where Daddy's coarse sandpaper has scrubbed off the old white paint, leaving the wood rough and scratchy. Then up to the top, where Evelyn's finer sandpaper has worked its magic, turning the surface satiny and soft.

"Beautiful work. I have something for you." He pulls the boxes closer and opens the flaps of the top one, pulling out a smaller battered box covered with masking tape. Daddy pulls the tape away and shakes out the pieces inside. Evelyn picks one up. It's made of the lightest material. It looks like wood but feels like cardboard.

"It's balsa wood," he tells her. He fits the pieces together into the shape of an airplane. Evelyn cups it in her hands.

"It's plain," she says. It doesn't feel like anything.

Her father laughs. "It's not for the shop, it's for playing. It's very old but it should still fly. Go on. Before it starts raining."

Evelyn takes the airplane outside. Four-year-old Noemi sits at the edge of the garden, digging with a stick. She's covered in dirt. When she sees her sister, she cries out.

"Evin! I made a hole. What's that?"

Evelyn turns slowly until the wind is at her back. She points the plane's nose up to the clouds and throws. The wind catches the plane and it glides through the air for a moment before spinning down into the tomato plants. Noemi squeals with delight.

"Again!"

Evelyn runs to collect the plane, but before she can get to it, it's up once more, floating, hanging in space with the wind pushing against it. She glimpses her mother's grinning face between the leaves of the tomatoes. Behind her, Noemi screeches. The plane wobbles downward and settles on the grass. Evelyn and Noemi both race for it. Noemi snatches it up.

"Careful." Evelyn puts her hands around Noemi's to make sure she doesn't crush the soft wood. "It's delicate."

Noemi strokes a wing, leaving a dirty smudge behind. "Nice birdy."

Evelyn is about to correct Noemi, but then she sees her mother smiling at them, standing now, with a spade in one hand, wind fluttering the ends of the scarf holding back her hair. She remembers what Mama says about being a good big sister, and how just because she's older and wiser doesn't mean she always needs to be right. "You are Noemi's sun," Mama always tells her. "Keep her warm."

"It is a nice birdy." She shows Noemi how to throw the plane. Her sister drives it straight into the ground and stares at it, frowning.

"Is it broken?"

"No. Look." Evelyn throws it again. It curves up high and gets blown toward the big oak tree. Noemi chases after it. She picks it up and runs to Mama, who shoots it back at Evelyn. The wind calms, and the plane arcs far over Evelyn's head. She spins to follow and sees Daddy behind her, diving for it. A few raindrops hit Evelyn's head but she ignores them because now they're all playing, throwing the plane as hard as they can and chasing after it. Noemi stays in the middle, spinning in circles and clapping.

The rain picks up. Daddy throws the plane low and fast and Mama dives for it, skidding right into Noemi's dirt pile. Noemi sees her chance. She grabs the plane and tries again, pointing the plane right at the oak tree. The wind picks it up; it glides beautifully right into the lower leaves of the tree, where it gets stuck.

"I did it." Noemi looks so proud Evelyn decides not to be mad. Besides, it's raining hard now. All of them are muddy and wet. Daddy takes Mama's hands and pulls her to her feet. Laughing, they all run inside together, leaving the plane to be rescued another time.

Harriet grips the battered glider between two fingers, although she has no intention of letting it fly. Instead, she basks for a few sweet moments in its glow. Though it is warped from rain and missing its tailpiece, it speaks to her of simple joy, of playfulness and family harmony. Her heart is torn, one half grateful for this evidence of happier times for the family whose history she has plundered, the other half miserable, for the little airplane only proves how much has been lost.

The miserable half wins. She places the toy back in the box where she found it, along with the other objects she has no right to own. It's too late. For better or worse, they belong to her. She feels the flutter of her panicked heart as the shadows gather around her, the memories caged here, piled one on top of another. The enormity of it overwhelms her and she can think of nothing else but her need to run away. She presses down the flaps of the box and edges outside into the cool, early evening air, closing the door on all of it with an air of finality.

1

Ev squats on a heap of garbage, one hand on the edge of the dumpster to keep her balance, and listens for ghosts. Something inside this bin has a sweet stain. It's strong enough that she could sense it when she skimmed past on her bike. Feels like love, or close enough that people will pay good money for it. It doesn't matter if the stain belongs to a wedding band, an old photograph, or a doll with matted-up hair. Ev's gonna find it.

She yanks the broken seat of a vinyl kitchen chair out from underneath some bags. A hint of resentment clings to it, muted but still sour. It's been buzzing against her boots, rattling her nerves and interfering with the hunt. She chucks the seat over the side of the bin. Down the alley she hears Owen's voice calling out to her. She ignores him, focusing on her prize. *Where are you?* There's still something blocking her, causing confusion, and making it hard to concentrate.

"Evelyn?" Owen knocks on the side of the bin. The sound reverberates in her ears.

"Quit it. You're giving me a headache." She feels ill, in fact, but she's too close to give up.

"Find something good?"

"Maybe."

"Whatever it is, I bet I've got better."

"Hey, can you take these?" Ev dangles a six-pack of empty beer bottles over the side. She feels the weight of them ease.

"Got 'em."

Ev digs deeper, tossing out the occasional empty as she works. She grabs the knotted top of a plastic grocery bag. It's heavy, with the soft lumpiness of used cat litter. *In here.* Ev tears into the bag. Flamingo-colored sand spills over her gloves, along with shards of broken glass and five pearly sea-shells that radiate a solid vibe: affection, longing, and tenderness. They hold a bitter note at the end — betrayal — but it only lends the rest of the stain a satisfying poignancy.

Jackpot. She picks the shells out of the bag and drops them into a lead-lined pouch belted at her hip. She can sell them for ten bucks each. She grabs hold of the edge of the bin and vaults her body over, landing in

16

a squat, boots slapping on wet pavement. A wave of dizziness clouds her head. She stays put and inhales deeply through her nose. She's mastered the shallow mouth breathing required for this kind of work but could be she was in there longer than she thought. Sometimes she loses track of time when she's on the hunt.

The feeling doesn't pass. If anything, it gets worse, a low-grade fuzz scrambling her brain and turning her stomach upside down.

Owen's voice floats past. "Are you all right?"

She tries to nod but it only shakes things up more. Her head is a snow globe, a blizzard of glitter, a thousand tiny plastic flakes reflecting too many colors for her mind to track. She closes her eyes and waits for the settling.

"Ev, honey." Owen puts his hand on her arm and she's too sick to shrug it off. She retreats further, finding that empty place inside. The quiet spot in the center of the globe where the snowman stands alone. She breathes into it. She is the snowman.

"Why are you laughing?" asks Owen.

"I'm a snowman."

Keep the dirt out, Evelyn.

The intrusion in her mind knocks her off balance again, makes the nausea rise. She clenches the muscles in her face, tightly curls her arms around her body. Squeezes the voice out. When she opens her eyes, she sees the jar. A mason jar with a dented lid. It sits at Owen's feet, filled to the top with buttons. Brass buttons. Plastic buttons. Satin-covered wedding dress buttons. A blue button with a Dalmatian puppy painted on it. A gold button in the shape of an anchor. Every one of them stained.

Each button contains a unique set of emotions imprinted upon it by a past owner. They are, all of them, tiny ghosts, carriers of desire, sadness, lust, and pride. None of them radiates particularly strongly, but the overall effect is similar to watching two hundred television channels simultaneously. No wonder she feels like puking.

"Here." Owen presses a stainless-steel bottle into her hands. She takes it. The water tastes soapy, but she drinks anyway. It gives her time to center herself. Owen has taken the refundables she found and lined them up against the side of the bin, offerings left for the next binner who passes through.

As she regains control, questions begin to flood her mind. *Who collected those buttons? How? Why? What are they doing in the garbage?* This isn't a jar of odds and ends, spares kept in a sewing box. Someone went through the trouble of tracking these down one by one. It wouldn't have been easy. Ev knows this well, having just spent twenty minutes knee-deep in dirty diapers and greasy week-old chow mein for the sake of five seashells. It takes a serious emotional connection for an object to get stained. Most trash is just trash.

Someone built this collection over time, button by button — someone who can feel the stains attached to each one. In twenty-two years, Ev has only known one other person who could sense stains like she can. She's not ready to meet another.

She points at the jar. "Where'd you get that?"

"Eighth and Woodland. Alley out back of an apartment building." Owen rubs his salt-and-pepper beard as he regards it. "Wonderful, isn't it? I think I'll make a mosaic."

A fucking mosaic. Sure, it'll be gorgeous, like the rest of Owen's work, but it won't sell. It'll end up on the wall of some café in Kits, its eight-hundred-dollar price tag collecting dust and espresso stains. Ev can earn a couple hundred dollars off those buttons if she packages them right. Owen would give her the jar if she asked. But she won't ask.

"Did you find anything else?"

"This. I thought of you." He pulls a handkerchief out of the pocket of his jeans and unwraps it. Inside lies a stone, smooth and flat, the color of bone except for one black splotch in the middle that resembles a bird perched on a hilltop. The stone fits neatly in Owen's palm. It has a soft, comforting energy. Protection. Peace. He smiles at it, crinkling the skin around his eyes.

"It seemed like an Evelyn thing to me," he says. "All the things seemed like Evelyn things, but this one especially."

Ev disagrees. The stone is an Owen thing. She's tempted by it. It would be a nice weight in her pocket, a thing to carry with her always. When he offers it to her, she pinches it delicately and drops it immediately into her pouch. The stone will sell in a heartbeat at the market.

"How much more is there?"

"Three boxes. I tucked them behind the recycling bins, but that was an hour ago."

Ev's throat dries up. That much stain gathered in one place equals a psychic bomb waiting to be triggered. Also, the potential for a lot of money. She studies Owen's face, thinking. He doesn't know stains, but he's done enough salvage missions with Ev that he's gotten good at guessing at the kinds of things she likes. If she gets her hands on three boxes of stained goods, she could take some time off come winter. At the moment business is good. The Night Market is thriving this year after a couple of dead summers. Ev won't need to set foot in the stuffy chaos of the flea market until September. But the weather has turned wet and cool over the last few days, a reminder of what picking trash during the rainy season feels like. Bloated cardboard that falls apart in your hands. Water mixed with rust, mud, stale beer, and rotten fruit seeping under your gloves. Oily puddles. Soggy, lipstick-stained cigarette butts.

Some cash in the bank to ride out the cold months is awfully appealing. Appealing enough to quell the fear that rises every time Ev wonders who the hell is out there in her city collecting stains. If it's been an hour, by now the boxes have probably been picked over. Still, if there's anything left . . .

"Show me," she tells Owen.

2

Harriet runs her fingers over the belly of the velvet monkey. He's horse-muzzle soft and the color of smoke. His stitching has come undone at the tail, and his black button eyes are glued on crooked, but of all the plush animals on display, he's the only bright one. He's the only bright thing Harriet has found all week, and since she's already given him a name — Frédérique — she will have to take him home.

"Can I help you find something?"

The shopkeeper has snuck up on her. His words are deferential, but his eyes tell a different story. He's sizing her up. He's letting her know he's watching. Harriet knows he only sees a bag lady. She doesn't mind. It's a camouflage she has cultivated for many years. She finds the invisibility a comfort, for the most part. And, when required, she can still muster up a decent measure of haughtiness, draw back the cloak, and show a glimpse of her former self. She straightens her spine so she can look down her nose at the shopkeeper and gives him her most condescending smile.

"Thank you. I've found exactly what I want."

She doesn't normally shop in stores such as these, cheap ones full of new, vacant things. Retail stores disturb her, rows and rows of empty objects. Products with no souls, no energy, people buying and discarding them before they have the chance to take on any kind of life, the world growing more cluttered and at the same time more barren every day. Harriet only entered this store because she caught sight of Frédérique while she waited out the rain. Sometimes Harriet finds treasure, and sometimes the treasure finds Harriet.

Normally at this time on a Wednesday she would be home from her morning errands and fixing a cup of tea. But the afternoon had turned windy and wet while she walked to the bus stop, forcing her to stop and take shelter in the mall. She bought a cup of bitter coffee at the food court. Then she found a bench under a skylight where she could wait for the clouds to take a breath. The monkey had caught her eye as she sat. She could feel the gentle brightness on him. She could sense that he wanted her to take him home. Who could blame him? Harriet wouldn't want to live on a cardboard shelf on the edge of a dollar store either.

The shopkeeper eyes Harriet's shopping cart and the oversized bag spilling over its rim.

"Just the monkey?"

"This is the only thing." She turns away from his insinuation and marches as best she can toward the cash desk. Navigating the cart between boxes of discounted gift-wrap and disposable dishware makes it difficult to effectively march.

Taped to the side of the cash register is a school photo of a boy no more than six. She imagines him finding Frédérique and loving him alive. It would have to be some fierce love to brighten him so quickly, but children have that magic, the ability to love so hard, undimmed by the fear of loss. She imagines this man, now huffing to the register like he's put out about taking her money, snatching poor Frédérique from the child and stuffing him back in the sale bin. Harriet skips pulling out her wallet and instead makes the effort to stoop and extract a damp, tacky bill from the emergency stash she keeps tucked inside her knee-high stockings. A side of calf sweat for her stingy shopkeeper.

She tucks Frédérique in the pocket of her coat, both to keep him dry and so that she can stroke his soft tail from time to time.

Outside, the rain has subsided. She makes her way to the bus stop. Wet weather causes her hip to ache, and not for the first time Harriet wonders why she still makes this damp West Coast city her home. If she left Vancouver, no one would miss her. The answer is simple, of course. Only her bright things — her shining treasures — tie her here. Would that she could move them to California. But she'll never leave them.

The bus windows are still fogged up from the damp. Harriet leans her head on the vibrating glass of the bus window and listens to the city music — tires on wet pavement, horns and bells, the mingling of conversations in several languages. The world smells of wet hair and exhaust.

She draws lazy spirals on the slick glass. The bus shudders to a stop, releasing several droplets. One runs down the middle of her design and settles, with a cool tickle, in the space between the pad of her index finger and her nail. Harriet imagines the droplet as a water sprite. Better yet, a tiny universe, and Harriet the elephant tasked by fate with protecting the life encapsulated within. She

25

holds her finger upright, watching until the droplet vanishes, the universe evaporating from her skin.

The bus driver is one of the conscientious ones, lowering the front so she can get herself and the cart onto the curb with a measure of grace. She takes comfort in this bit of decency. It warms her almost all the way home, right up to the point when her building comes into sight. There are vagrants in the alley, rooting through some boxes that have been left next to the dumpster. Except these are no ordinary boxes. Brightness leaks from them. Her heart freezes. The boxes, they are her boxes. Those are her books piled up on the pavement, soaking up moisture. Those are her linens in a pile beside the dumpster. Her antique wooden building blocks and shopping bags and woolen hats. Her bright things, torn and wet and scattered halfway across the parking lot.

The space in front of Harriet's eyes turns spotty and then black, and her skin turns cold. She leans on her cart until she can breathe. Distantly, she registers a car honking at her. She stands in the middle of the alley, unmoving. The vagrants have stopped pawing her belongings and are staring at her. One, a white man, runs toward her.

Harriet fumbles for her keys, jamming them between her fingers in case she needs to jab him.

"Ma'am, are you all right?"

He reaches a hand out. His long, graying hair is pushed off his forehead by a blue bandana, allowing Harriet to clearly read the concern in his big eyes. It only pisses her off more.

"Those boxes don't belong out here. They're mine."

"It's okay. Let me help you off the road."

Harriet shakes her head, and pushes forward with her cart, forcing him to step aside.

"Get that girl away from my things."

A car swerves around her, gunning it down the alley.

"Hey," shouts the man after the car. "Show a little respect."

His partner in crime is a young Chinese woman, dressed for the job in mud-splattered yellow rain pants and industrial rubber boots, her hair pulled back into a tight knot. A red chiffon scarf trails from the girl's gloved hand. Harriet's red chiffon scarf. She stands frozen, staring at Harriet like she's a ghost.

"Put that down." Harriet rasps the words as she labors forward. She waves the girl off, except at some point she's pulled Frédérique out of her pocket. His arms, legs, and tail wobble.

The scarf floats to the ground.

"That's my stuff. It's not garbage. You hear me?"

The girl nods, the tiniest of motions. She hasn't blinked.

"It's not trash," Harriet repeats.

"I know," says the girl, a question in her eyes.

She *knows.* Harriet feels it with sudden certainty. That girl can sense the brightness on Harriet's things. Harriet's breath catches. She's not just another vagrant. She's a bright-sensitive.

Who are you?

The man comes bustling around in front of Harriet, blocking the girl from view.

"I'm sorry we distressed you." He has a wrinkled shopping bag in one hand; the other he holds raised, palm out, to show he means no harm. "We didn't know. We thought they were free for the taking."

"They aren't supposed to be out here."

It's that fussy bitch in 102, has to be. She's always complaining about fire hazards. Sometimes Harriet has to put a box or two in the hall while she shifts things, makes room. Never occurs to anyone to offer some

28

help to a senior citizen. They've only been outside her door for a few days, a week at most. Haven't they?

She remembers a voice mail from the landlord. Maybe two. She never checked them. A sudden fear grips her. What if there are more things missing? He can't go into her apartment, not without asking. But would he? He'd love an excuse to get in and root around, find a reason to evict her. She's torn between the need to check, to make sure her things are intact within, and the need to find out more about the girl. Another bright-sensitive is a discovery beyond measure, the shiniest of treasures, even if questions about the girl's identity twist at Harriet's insides.

"Ma'am?" The man puts a hand on her cart. She jerks it away. "Okay," he says. "It's all right. Look, here are all the things I took." He places the bag gently in Harriet's basket. "If you want, I'll even help you pack up your boxes and bring them inside. Evelyn will give back her things too. Right, Ev?"

They both look toward the girl. She's halfway to the other end of the alley, her bike swaying from side to side as she pedals madly away.

3

Ev shoves open the door to the underground
parking garage and shoulders her bike and
trailer through, legs wobbling after the effort of pumping hard all the way home. Her
hands are curled stiffly from gripping the
handlebars and her throat burns from suck-
ing back lungfuls of air. Inside, the noise of
the city falls away. She rests for a moment,
leaning against the concrete wall to catch
her breath. It's not only the ride that has
left her shaky.

The stuff in those boxes out in the alley.
Every single item stained. Ev knew it before
she even saw them. She knew it when Owen
turned into the alley, ringing the bell on his
old, wide-handled gold cruiser, because she
could feel the vibrations. Not from the alley
boxes. Those were drowned out by the
vibrations Ev felt coming from inside the
apartment building, radiating out through
the walls. The soft, scrambled buzz of

30

thousands of stains. Her hunch was correct. The old white lady with the monkey is a stain hoarder.

Ev has never come across another person who feels stains like she does. Other than her father. And that old hag, the Stain Hag, with her possessiveness and panic and that wild light in her eyes when she waved the stuffed monkey at Owen, she reminds Ev a little too much of him. Especially at the end. But the worst thing, what keeps crawling up and down Ev's spine, is the look the Stain Hag gave her. The sudden spark of recognition in her eyes. Ev knows she hasn't seen the last of her.

She squeezes her eyes shut, counts her breaths. *In for one, two, three, four.* She hears the numbers in Noemi's voice, as she always does. She can almost feel the pressure of her little sister's hands against hers, their breath whispering out in unison. She ignores the tightness in her chest and lets Noemi count her down until she can think again. *Four, three, two, one.*

What would Ev's sister say about the Stain Hag?

Only three people have ever known about Ev's sickness and the way it makes objects speak to her. Two of them are dead. Noemi is the only one left, the only person Ev can talk to, but Noemi's been gone six months. *She doesn't want to talk to you anymore.*

Even Owen doesn't know exactly why Ev chooses her particular pieces of trash, why she ignores the copper piping the other binners prize, the tools and the refundable recyclables, in favor of a plastic children's watch or a faded denim jacket. Owen doesn't ask too many questions, and for that she's always been grateful. Maybe he accepts her idiosyncrasies because as an artist he has his own odd scavenging agenda. They work well together because of it, both of them happy to leave the scrap metal for those who need it. Since he works as a bike courier by day, she tips him off when she finds good materials for whatever art project he has on the go. In return, he feeds her, and occasionally borrows his roommate's car to help her haul some of her larger finds.

Every now and then, when they're sitting on Crab Beach with a container of agedashi tofu between them, watching freighters ease toward the port, she thinks about telling him everything. He's the closest thing Ev has to a friend. But she can never find the words to start. She considers it now, trying to explain to Owen why she ran away from the Stain Hag, why the woman turned her skin clammy and her throat dry.

No.

Not Owen. She needs her sister. But Noemi's not here in the dark underground parking lot. She's far away. So, if Ev wants her sister, she'll have to fall back on memory and imagination.

The parking garage gate begins to lift and an Audi's headlights flash at her. Ev rolls her bike clear of the driveway, heading toward the storage units.

She imagines swinging in the rope hammock that nestles in the upper branches of a big old cedar on a median strip near the south end of the city. She and Noemi, feet tucked up under them, listening to the rush of traffic below. Noemi with a big stick in her lap, in case someone thinks to climb up after them.

Ev burrows further into the memory — has it been six months since the last time they climbed? She imagines Noemi into the tree, as though she didn't finally drive away the only person who halfway understands her.

"This woman," she tells imaginary Noemi. "She knows I can feel stains. I could see it in her eyes."

Noemi's eyes would grow round, not with fear but excitement. "That's so cool. Did you talk to her?"

33

"No. And I'm not going to."

"Did you ask her if she knows any others? I thought you were the only one. Oh, we should totally spy on her!" By now Noemi would be waving her stick around, wobbling the hammock and letting loose a shower of cedar tips.

"No."

"Maybe we can get our hands on some of her loot."

"Noemi."

"I know, I know, no stealing. But we could tail her. Maybe she knows some good places to find stuff."

"I'm worried."

"Why?"

"Because she's batshit crazy. You should've seen her, all draped in costume jewelry, white curly hair poking out of a floppy hat. She came rolling at us, ready to run Owen down with her shopping cart, waving this monkey around —"

"She attacked you with a monkey?"

"A stuffed monkey."

Noemi whoops. She has the laugh of a person twice her size. "She's an eccentric old lady. What's she gonna do?"

"I don't know." *That's the problem.* Noemi doesn't remember. She doesn't understand how the sickness works. How important it is to be vigilant, to protect one's mind at all times. How the stains can turn a person, even a small, weak person, into a monster.

Noemi nods, laughter gone as suddenly as it erupted. She has a way of hearing the things Ev never says.

"It's okay." She taps her stick gently against Ev's knee. "We can take her."

Ev catches herself rocking forward and back with her hands tucked between her thighs. She sits on concrete in a dark parking garage, not in a hammock. Alone. She straightens her spine and drops her shoulders. The market starts in an hour. She needs to focus.

It would be faster to bring her bike upstairs, but she won't. She hates to be late for the market, but she sticks to the routine anyway. No stained items ever go up to her apartment. She has to maintain a clean living space. The bike, the trailer, and its contents have to be stowed in Ev's storage unit. She unlocks the door that leads into the storage room. She can feel her stains from down the corridor, a mild tingling against her skin, not unpleasant. Some of the other residents' storage lockers contain stained things too. Those other lockers are all floor-to-ceiling packed with boxes and furniture, most of it clean but not all, so she walks quickly, letting the vibrations wash past her like a breeze, not pausing to allow any of them to distract her. She's had years of practice at this, at shutting her mind, protecting it.

It's harder to find that empty space today. How does the Stain Hag do it, live 24/7 in all that noise? She has to be at least seventy, maybe older. How long has she existed this way? And her neighbors, they must be ill from the contamination oozing through the walls. She needs to get upstairs and clear her mind. Meditation helps. Ev usually sits twice a day for twenty minutes; on market days, a full hour. She doesn't have time for that today, but she can at least try to make some space inside. Empty mind, quiet and buffered, cradled in an inward smile. She turns up the corners of her mouth as a reminder.

She stops under the number nine and unlocks the padlock, swinging open the wooden gate. There are only three boxes in Ev's locker. The blue Rubbermaid tote that she tows to the market in her trailer. Next to that, a second tote for overflow goods. The third, in the back, she never opens. Along one side of the storage space is a wooden shelving unit for the few larger objects that don't fit easily into the totes.

Currently, it's home to a hula girl lamp, a large silver platter, and a golf club.

She clicks the padlock into place, stains contained. As the elevator door closes, she realizes her head is pounding. Her muscles ache and she feels skinless, every nerve exposed. Too much stain exposure today. Her body and her mind ache to be at home.

The elevator stops at the lobby and a man in a suit gets in. He scans Ev up and down.

"Can I help you?" he asks. He has his finger on the button that keeps the doors open. This happens to Ev a lot. She gets it. She's been crawling around in garbage. Her coveralls are splattered with mud and she probably reeks. It still pisses her off.

She jingles her keys at him. "I live here."

The man raises his eyebrows, but he lets the door go.

The problem with needing an unstained home is she has to go new. And new in Vancouver means expensive. She doesn't exactly fit in with her neighbors. She tries to keep a low profile around the building, and she makes sure to pay her rent on time, even if the other bills get neglected. It means no cable, no Internet, and knowing where to scavenge for free food. And dealing with assholes like elevator guy. But so far, she's managed to hang on to her tiny haven.

Even so, the place has gotten a little too comfortable. Even through the gloves she can feel how her key speaks to her as she unlocks the deadbolt. It whispers *home* and *solace.* She needs the safe space but can't get too attached to the particularity of this apartment. She's grown used to the shape of the room and the cool blankness of the walls, to the rounded matching light fixtures that poke out of the ceiling like a pair of glowing breasts, the crack in the ceiling shaped like a shooting star, the diamond pattern in the kitchen tiles. She'll have to move again soon.

She pulls off her boots, socks, and rain gear at the door and heads straight for the bathroom. Her bare footsteps echo through the room. Ev loves that sound. Even the tiniest bachelor suite can seem palatial when essentially empty. A visitor might think she'd moved in two days ago, not last year. If she ever had visitors. Only a single bed, neatly made, a dresser, and a desk and chair interrupt the space. No art on the walls. No papers on the desktop. No lamps. No television. It looks like an abandoned college dorm room. It's just how she likes it. Clean. Unstained.

She checks the time on her pay-as-you-go flip phone. Half an hour. She heads straight into the shower to scrub off the grime as quickly as she can. All the while breathing in space, breathing out the mental clutter she's collected from her day. Emptying. By the time she gets out, she feels strong again. Calm. Her cell phone buzzes at her from the table by the front door. She ignores it, no time. The market opens in five minutes. Ev's wares aren't popular enough to allow her a night off.

She grabs a pair of jeans and a T-shirt from the closet. Clean and dressed, she slips on a fresh pair of white cotton gloves before heading out. A momentary twinge of anxiety flutters in her stomach as she wonders whether the Stain Hag will come looking for her at the market. She holds on to imaginary Noemi's words. *We can take her.*

While waiting for the elevator, Ev remembers the phone call. Her phone doesn't ring often. Most likely it's Vivian, wondering why she hasn't shown up at the market yet, but when she flips her phone open, she doesn't recognize the number. Ev glides into the elevator, hits the button for the ground floor, and punches in her voice mail code.

"Ev? It's me."

The voice, sweet, tinny, and echoing,

slams into Ev's eardrum, exploding her calm and scattering it into a million glittering fragments.

"I'm back in town. Call me?"

Noemi has come home.

4

Against her better judgment, Harriet pulls open the glass door leading to the dimly lit lobby of her apartment building and allows the bandana man — a stranger — inside. What choice does she have? None of her neighbors are going to volunteer to help clean up the mess out back. The man seems harmless enough, with steady eyes and clear skin, none of the outward signs of addiction that would act as warning flags for her. Mid-forties, or a more weathered thirties, and skinny, but strong enough to lift boxes two at a time.

She's certain the woman across the hall — Melissa? No, Melanie — complained to management. That sly sack of bones has probably been enjoying the alley show through the blind slats in her bedroom window. Sure enough, as she heads down the hall to her apartment, her transient thief-turned-rescuer following with one of

41

the salvaged boxes, the woman's door creaks open. The scent of patchouli and vitamins wafts into the hallway. Melanie steps out, draped as always in organic cotton and judgment.

"Excuse me?" She wears her *namaste* smile. She even has her hands, with their clickety acrylic fingernails, in prayer position. The posture doesn't fool anyone. Her tone of voice is as brittle as always.

"I hope you don't plan on leaving that in the hallway again," she says. "I would hate to have to place yet another call to John."

"I'll bet you would."

There's an envelope taped to Harriet's door. She pulls it off quickly, stuffing it into her cart before anyone else notices. Her hands shake as she unlocks the dead bolt.

"Don't worry," the man with the bandana says confidently. "We'll find a place for all of this inside."

The woman snorts. "Good luck with that."

"I like your earrings." Harriet can hear the goofy smile in the man's voice. "Amethyst is wonderful for mental clarity and calming the nerves. Have you ever tried it for headaches?"

She hears the woman's door click shut. *Ha! The flake outflaked.*

He places the box on the floor. "I'll be

right back with the rest."

The rest. What remains of it. Everything's out of order and half of it is missing. Who knows how many hands pawed through it before Harriet came home? Where is the silver water pitcher, the yellow rubber duck? They were only able to refill two of the three boxes. Perhaps some of it has gone into the dumpster. She considers the logistics of climbing inside to check. Harriet's head begins to ache. Then there's the matter of the letter. She doesn't need to open it to guess what's inside, but she looks anyway, while she's still alone.

Not a letter but a form. *One Month Notice to End Tenancy for Cause.* The backs of her eyes prickle, and the words blur. She knows the rest, knows the Tenancy Act thoroughly. Once upon a time, she was a landlord. She has ten days to dispute. If she does, she needs to prove that she shouldn't be evicted. If John's gone so far as to serve notice, he will already have collected evidence. Photos of the boxes she's left in the hallway for days, weeks, sometimes months at a time. Written complaints from the neighbors. Does she have a defense?

And if she accepts the eviction, then what? Where does she go?

Home.

She brushes the intrusive, pointless thought aside. She can't go home, not as she left things. This apartment began as a temporary fix, a convenient hideaway, but she's been here for twelve years. This is home now.

Was.

Already she knows she will have to leave. A dispute might buy her some time, but not much. John has cause enough. He will win. Unless. She could bring it to the family lawyers. They'd find a way. But is it worth it? It could bring her situation to the attention of her cash-hungry cousins back east. They'd use it against her, evidence of mental decline. No. They've been waiting years for an excuse to sweep into town and collect her inheritance. They care nothing for her collection, only the property and cash. They'd clear out everything, sell it or worse, trash it. She can't allow that to happen.

So now what? Another apartment? She'll have to hire movers. The thought of strangers in her space, boxing up her treasures, touching and jostling and breaking, makes her heart and head pound. She would weep except her helper will be back any second, and she doesn't want to appear weak. She's not buying his altruistic act quite yet.

As if summoned, he appears at the end of the hall with the second box. The panic fluttering in Harriet's chest rises into her throat. Her hand clenches the paper. She stuffs it back in her cart. The door is cracked. She will have to let the man in and find a place for the boxes. It seemed simple enough when they were outside. It always does.

He puts the box on the floor in the hallway, next to the other.

"Do you need some time to sort out where you want them? I can wait here."

"Please." Harriet slips inside. She feels for the light switch. A dim yellow glow illuminates the ceiling of the foyer, casting shadows across the path that leads back to the kitchen. Harriet's stomach sinks as she views her living space through a stranger's eyes.

Her bright things line the hallway from floor to ceiling, stacked on shelves that she acquired carefully, one by one, at various garage sales. Even her shelving is bright. At one time she used a stepladder to access the top shelves, to grow the collection and find a home for each of the things she brought back here. She doesn't do that anymore. She's grown too nervous about climbing the ladder. There are boxes now in front of the shelves, stacked as high as she dares — no more than shoulder height, so that in the event of an earthquake she has a fighting chance of digging her way out.

The living room is worse, where the shelving runs three or four bookcases deep, shelves in front of shelves, so that she can no longer touch her porcelain figurines, or her dolls from around the world, or any of the books that she collected between 2009 and 2014.

Perhaps she can ask the man to put the boxes on the table behind the couch, if she moves the newspapers piled there? Or maybe he can stack them in that space next to the television, if she shoves it a few inches farther into the corner? Of course, the boxes have gotten wet, so they won't stack nicely anymore. Maybe she can leave her cart in the hall and put the boxes in the spot she keeps reserved next to the door.

"Are you okay?" He speaks through the crack in the door.

"No," Harriet snaps. Then, dammit, the tears start. "You wouldn't understand," she tells him.

"I might."

He gently pushes the door open and sticks his arm in, offering Harriet a wrinkled cotton handkerchief. Harriet wants to be

46

disgusted but her eyes and nose are running, and the handkerchief appears to be clean, so she takes it.

"You have some marvelous treasures."

His use of the word *treasures* softens Harriet enough that she doesn't protest when he slides the rest of his body inside her apartment. She still has her keys clutched tightly in one fist, in case she needs to go for his soft parts, but he has her attention.

To his credit, he does not appear shocked or appalled at the state of her house. His eyes do not grow round. His gaze, curious and probing yet nonjudgmental, settles on a dusty corner next to the sofa half-obscured by stacked boxes.

"That's a stunning Tiffany lamp."

"It's a knockoff," Harriet lies.

"Of course." He squints further into the gloom. Harriet shifts uncomfortably. "Market price is a narrow conception of value, anyway. That's not why you collect, is it?"

"No," says Harriet, drawn into the conversation despite herself. "It's not."

"Every item here is meaningful. Every scrap of fabric. Every slip of paper." There's that goofy smile again. He ducks outside and returns holding her jar of buttons. "I'm so taken with these. I'll bet each button in this jar has a story. Reminds you of a person or a particular day or a story or something?"

"Who *are* you?"

He sticks out his hand.

"Owen Riley. I collect things too. That's why I was going through your boxes. I'm an artist, actually. I take found items and transform them. Sculpture, mixed media, that sort of thing."

Owen is growing on Harriet. He may be a flake, but he's a perceptive flake. It goes deeper than that, of course. Her bright things are more than stories. Every item in this apartment contains a piece of Harriet's soul.

She takes a chance. Points at a button in the jar.

"That brass one I found at a yard sale on Alma Street. 1995. Sunny day. Afterward, I went for a slice of pie."

Owen grins wide enough to show his crooked teeth. "A museum of memory. That's wonderful."

She lets the words *museum of memory* settle on her tongue. A lovely turn of phrase, rich as sugared blueberries tucked into pastry. She considers the button, a vintage uniform button, Royal Air Force. When she first held it in her palm, it spoke to her of loss but also pride, loyalty, and duty. Its clean nobility impressed her. How did such a button find its way onto a yard sale table scattered with children's toys, plastic tiaras, beads, and feathered hair clips? That day in 1995, she ate her pie with the shiny button in front of her, imagining its journey from the wreckage of WWII France into the hands of a Canadian widow. A uniform jacket folded neatly and tucked into a cedar chest until the button's thread rotted and set it free. Years later, the lid opening, and the jacket lifted out, allowing the button to tumble out and roll into some dark corner of an attic. More and more years passed until it was discovered by some curious child, who secreted it away in a satin-lined jewelry box.

Harriet wishes she could glean the true stories behind each of her treasures, but she enjoys daydreaming about them almost as much.

A noise interrupts her train of thought. Owen, clearing his throat politely. "I thought perhaps I could fit these boxes next to the window."

Harriet follows his gaze.

"If you can get in there." He'll have to move two bookcases full of china pieces. Harriet's skin grows clammy at the thought of them falling over. "Oh. I don't know."

"I think I can manage it without damaging anything. I'll have to shift those boxes to the left, then pull the shelves out a few inches. I'll move everything back into place, so you still have your pathway. If you don't mind me in your space for an hour or so."

Harriet suddenly feels exhausted. Bright things continue to find their way into her life, and she has nowhere left to put them. She's avoided the truth by keeping people out of her apartment. But she knows damn well she's one hip fracture away from an embarrassing intervention on some reality show. She's been in protective mode for so long, aware of her increased vulnerability as she ages, worrying that she'll be deemed unable to care for herself and lose control, not only of her collection but also her independence. Over the years, Harriet has grown ever more fearful of asking for help.

"Please," she says, and then, "How much should I pay you?"

That goofy smile. "I know you're not going to part with those buttons. So perhaps a cup of tea?"

"Tea is a splendid idea."

Owen presses his fingers to his temples. "I don't suppose you have chamomile? I have a bit of a headache. Must be a pressure change coming."

The headache isn't weather-related.

There's a migraine epidemic in the building, and her neighbors are looking at her, grumbling about mold and toxic fumes. They're right to blame Harriet, but they don't know why. There's no mold problem. There's nothing rotting in here. It's the brightness that scrambles their brains, like too much time spent in the sun. It's a problem. A problem she has ignored too long.

A problem she is now poised to solve. An idea begins to form in Harriet's mind, seeded by Owen's words. A *museum of memory.* An audacious, frightening, and utterly fabulous idea. She always thought she would use her collection to help people. She had plans, grand but vague, to build something that would outlast her, to curate her treasures in a way that fostered healing rather than harm. One day, she promised herself, she would sift through her collection, separate out the hurtful objects, and contain them safely, and thus allow those with positive energies to shine fully. Instead of giving people headaches she could surround them with love and joy. She imagined a space where her best treasures could be displayed. She would advertise it as an art exhibit or a museum of curiosities, but secretly it would work its magic on visitors as they soaked up the energies within. They would gravitate to the objects that held the emotions they most needed, and without even realizing it, they would be filled up. Changed.

Year after year, Harriet failed to make this happen. Her collection grew beyond her capacity to manage alone, and her vision slipped ever more out of reach. It was simply too big a project for one person — until now. With the help of another bright-sensitive and a salvage artist with an appreciation for found objects, she could make it happen. Perhaps the eviction isn't a disaster after all, but the beginning of something new.

She'll need the right space. And she'll need the girl. Harriet very much wishes to speak to the girl again. Something needles at the back of Harriet's brain, an almost connection. She can practically taste it, an inky, musty tang on the tip of her tongue. If she ponders it long enough, she is sure it will come to her.

"You know," says Owen, again jolting her from her thoughts, "if you need ongoing help, say, to give you a hand getting more organized, I am available for odd jobs."

"Indeed," she says, chewing on her lip thoughtfully. "I may have some work for you. On one condition."

"What's that?"

"Tell me where I can find your friend."

you. On one condition."

"What's that?"

"Tell me where I can find your island."

5

Friday evening at the Chinatown Night Market, barely six o'clock, and of course Hangdog is Ev's first customer. She sees him making a beeline for her table before she's even finished setting out her goods. She arrived minutes before, breathless and frazzled, weaving her bike between the street blockades to Ken and Vivian's tent. Vivian waved hello but Ken looked past Ev when she greeted him, a pointed if silent commentary on her lateness. Another strike against her. She doesn't work for Ken and Vivian — she only sublets a table at their vendor booth — but Ken likes to pass judgment on her behavior all the same, to remind her that she only has a table at the market due to his generosity. They both know Vivian is the generous one, but Ev has to do her best to stay on Ken's good side all the same.

She hasn't called the number Noemi left.

She hasn't figured out what to say to her. Ev's cheeks burn with the memory of their last conversation, of Noemi's angry words and the sting of her sudden slap.

Liar.

Ev doesn't know what to say to the Stain Hag either, if she comes looking for her. She needs time to process these developments. She isn't ready to haggle with Hangdog, but she'll have to fake it.

The strings of lights that crisscross over the open-air market aren't yet lit, and only a few shoppers drift between tents. Behind her, Ev can hear Vivian barking instructions at her husband as she organizes her bins of brightly colored socks. Once in a while, she can make out a familiar word, like catching a snowflake on her tongue: nǐ hǎo, *hello;* xièxiè or m̀h'gōi, *thank you.* On quiet nights, Vivian sometimes teaches Ev basic words and phrases, both Mandarin and Cantonese, although Vivian and Ken speak Cantonese to each other.

"It's good for business," she tells Ev. "A nice Chinese girl like you, people expect you to speak a bit of the language."

"Half-Chinese," Ev always reminds her. She doesn't tell Vivian that the first words she ever spoke were Cantonese. That she used to know many words, but she's lost them all.

Hangdog's chin is wonton greasy. His gaze makes it as far as Ev's chest before lowering back to the table. He doesn't speak to her, never does except to bargain, which suits Ev fine. His fleshy fingers slide over her objects. Ev charges Hangdog triple, partly because she finds him gross but mostly because she can. He thinks he drives a hard bargain, but he's no good at hiding his need. Ev knows she shouldn't cater to his tastes, but he once paid her half a month's rent for a dented brass vase she bought at a garage sale for a dollar.

Most of Ev's objects are stained with love or nostalgia. Those are the easiest sells, both for Ev's wallet and her conscience. She has pocket watches and pendants, fishing reels and baby rattles. Some of them vibrate with longing — a compact mirror, a dog-eared copy of *The Sun Also Rises.* She always has one or two items stained with lust. This week it's a shooter glass with a chip in the rim.

Ev could find customers for every kind of stain if she wanted to, even the ones she refuses to collect. Tonight, she has one item that will be of interest to Hangdog. It's no brass vase. It has a weak stain, just enough to attract his attention. It's one of two items

56

she took from the Stain Hag. She almost feels guilty about it, seeing how upset the lady got about her stuff. Not guilty enough to give it back, though. Stain Hag has too much.

As for Hangdog, he'll grumble that she has nothing good, but he'll buy the item anyway. She doesn't bother to point it out. He'll find it. He always does.

Ev watches his fingers creep closer as she sips water. They stop at a brooch, a set of gold antlers around a piece of amber glass. There. It's fascinating to see how regular people perceive stained objects. Stain still affects them, but not at the same level. It's a gentler influence. People at her table behave like flowers turning their pretty heads toward the sun, slowly, slowly homing in on that one object with a buzz that gets their attention. Different people gravitate toward different emotions, though they don't know why they're attracted to one item over another. Hangdog's hooked on her wares, but he probably has no idea why. He only knows *this. I need this.* But Ev — Ev knows *why* he wants what he wants. The brooch, the vase, every single object he's purchased from Ev carries the same tired vibration.

A kinder person might wonder why Hangdog craves shame, but Ev can't afford kindness. She'll take his money, as she always does, and let him carry his shame away. She tells herself she won't let him take too many things. That she won't let them gain a critical mass and take over his life. That would be irresponsible of her. Profitable, but irresponsible.

His eyes glaze over as he picks up the brooch.

"How much?"

"Twenty-five."

"Bitch."

Ev is used to Hangdog huffing and snorting and grumbling, but he's never sworn at her. His face turns red. He leans over the table, getting too close. Ev glances left and right, trying to catch the eye of one of the two security guards who work the market.

"It's a piece of shit," says Hangdog. "I wouldn't give you a dollar for this."

"Then don't."

"I'm tired of you robbing me blind." His voice grows louder. He clasps the brooch tightly in his fist. Ev jingles the string of ceramic bells that dangle next to the tent pole between her table and Vivian's. Ken is busy with a customer, but he raises his head in Ev's direction. She nods at Hangdog.

"May I take a look?" she asks smoothly.

"Perhaps for a loyal customer, I can reassess the value."

Hangdog's fingers twitch. For a moment she thinks he will refuse. Then he releases the brooch to the table like a dog dropping a wet ball from its jaws. Ev snatches it up. She draws it close to her face, close enough that she can feel, fully, the effects of the brooch's stain. It contains clear undertones of anger. Not strong, but enough to affect a man poisoned by too much stain. How did she miss it? She must have been overwhelmed by all the emotions sloshing around in those boxes. Sloppy.

Quickly, keeping her face composed, she drops the brooch into the bin at her feet.

"I am sorry, that one is not for sale." Hangdog's face twists. Before he can protest, she continues. "I apologize for the error. You are correct. It is a piece of shit."

"Evelyn." Ken stands beside her. He says something in Cantonese, more sharply than necessary. She pretends to understand, nodding and shuffling aside, glancing down the aisle to see if there is a security guard nearby. There usually isn't, hence, the bells. Ev makes a point of not using them often. It was Vivian's idea. She knows Ken would prefer not to be her protector.

Ken turns to Hangdog.

59

"How can I help you, sir?" Ken is not a large man, but he's perfected the grumpy vendor stare.

Hangdog says nothing. He seems to be processing, like he's deciding how pissed off he should get. Pinpricks of fear travel down Ev's spine. When too many seconds have passed, Ev knows he's missed his chance. She smiles at Hangdog.

"Come back next week, sir. I will have excellent bargains for you." She glides to Vivian's side and helps her sort braided leather belts until Hangdog drifts away, mumbling to himself.

"I don't like that guy," mutters Vivian. "He's rude. And he smells like a cupboard."

"I'll make sure he stops coming around."

"How are you going to stop him?" asks Ken. He waves his arms around. "We're outside." He pushes past Ev, banging around in the overstock boxes.

"I'll stop carrying the products he likes."

"You should be calling security, not me. That guy is twice my size."

Vivian ignores her husband. She pats Ev's shoulder.

"You call us if he bothers you again. Those security guards are useless. Too busy flirting with the Egg Puff girls."

"I'm sorry, Ken," Ev says. She can't afford to get on his bad side. Ev has applied for her own vendor booth three years in a row, but the Market Association keeps turning her down. Ev's business doesn't look good on paper. The Night Market is a place to buy cheap electronics and fashion accessories and eat fried potatoes on skewers. Vendors like Ev are encouraged to stick to the flea market, where people expect to find junk recovered from the trash. Ev only has a table at the Night Market because Vivian convinced Ken to let her sublet. It's worked out so far because against all odds, Ev attracts customers.

It's been a long time since Ev has made a mistake like picking up that brooch. And Hangdog. She let him accumulate too much and it's made him sick. She's poisoned him. She's not supposed to let that happen. No matter how lucrative the guy might be, she can't let greed cloud her judgment. It's too dangerous. Ev might sell shame and lust and even occasionally fear, but she doesn't sell anger. Not ever. She has to be more careful.

6

Harriet fiddles with the feathery tips of the red chiffon scarf at her neck as the taxi rolls toward Chinatown and the girl with the bright touch. The scarf is a good one to wear on an evening like this, a proud warrior. In another life it was highly valued. It gave some woman, somewhere, a feeling of power. A job interview scarf, perhaps, something to wear in the boardroom or at the podium. It's the scarf of a woman with something to say. Harriet discovered it at a goodwill shop a few weeks ago. Now it radiates a soft reflection of that strength back to Harriet, an anonymous gift from its previous owner. She understands why the girl was attracted to it. It might be frayed on the corners, but it has good magic.

For over sixty years, Harriet has been alone. She's traveled the world, been to the greatest cities on Earth, but has never come across anyone whose sensitivities match hers. There have been a few over the years, collectors with a knack for sensing a bit of brightness on an object, but they've always possessed a diluted and unconscious version of Harriet's gift. For a time, she had a lover in Istanbul who had enough sensitivity to attract great wealth to himself. She stayed with him for a year before she tired of his shallow grasp of his potential. He could only see one side, one facet among the endless refracted rays of his bright objects. Too dull for Harriet, in the end.

She suspects her mother's ability once rivaled hers, but by the time young Harriet discovered her talent, her mother's was stunted by grief and depression, and remained so until her death. Harriet grew up surrounded by a wealth of bright objects accumulated by a woman Harriet never had a chance to truly know. "Find another interest," her mother always told her, waving away her questions. Harriet always had too many questions, showed too much curiosity, attempted to glean too much information from the objects that fascinated her. Until the end, the subject of their shared sensitivity was off-limits, a secret her mother made clear was less a gift than an impolite intrusion on the privacy of others.

To find someone — in her own city, no

less — who might understand. Someone to talk to. Someone who can appreciate what Harriet has built over the years. This girl may be the one person who could help Harriet carry out her vision to turn her treasures into a public exhibit, and might even, perhaps, become the heir to her collection. Who else will care for it after Harriet is gone? She has no one. But she's getting ahead of herself. First, she must learn more about her shiny little sister.

"Ma'am. Are you all right?"

Harriet blinks. The taxi idles curbside next to a tea emporium. Somehow, she missed the driver pulling over, getting out, and placing her cart on the sidewalk next to her door.

"Fine, thank you." She passes him the bill she's kept rolled up inside the sleeve of her cardigan. "Keep the change. You'll have to forgive an old woman her ruminations. It's often more interesting in here" — she taps her head — "than out there."

Through the rearview mirror, she sees the skin around the driver's eyes crinkle with a smile.

"You don't look so old to me. My grandmother, she turned ninety-three this year. Lots of pickpockets working that market. Keep an eye out."

Although it's not far from her apartment, Harriet doesn't go to the Night Market. She wouldn't have guessed someone like Evelyn could be found here. If she feels up to battling crowds, Harriet would rather visit the flea market, where the wares have a little more history, a little more depth.

The weather has cleared up, so the streets are already filled with people. Harriet squints at the tents. So many heads bent over tables and bodies weaving from stall to stall, but she will know Evelyn. She'll know her by her treasures. Harriet feels a twinge of panic or longing or both. How does she do it? How can she let her things go? Harriet can't imagine. She's spent her life recovering bright things. Cherishing them. She could never sell them. It's too sad to consider.

Harriet notices, as she moves through the market, that the crowd jostles her less than usual. Must be the scarf. It draws Harriet's spine and chin upward. Others must also sense it. Subtle, but magical, nonetheless.

The girl's table calls to her. She follows the glow that speaks to her heart. The girl locks eyes with her at the same moment that Harriet spots her. She's cleaned herself up. Long bangs sweep across one cheekbone, and a shimmer of gloss on her lips draws

Harriet's eyes to their plumpness. Paired with a square jawline, her wide mouth gives her face a sullen boldness despite the composure in her expression. Her eyes reveal nothing. She's been expecting Harriet.

Compared to the other vendors, Evelyn's display is spare. She doesn't fill every square inch with kitsch. She has maybe a couple dozen items total. She leaves space, lots of it, where her black satin tablecloth shows through. And yet, her table is by far the most full. Her things all bright. Harriet wants them. Even the tin plate that bleeds queasy anxiety. Even the spiteful teapot.

Evidently, the girl wants Harriet to speak first. Fine.

"Who are you?" Harriet has her own suspicions, of course.

The girl hesitates, her gaze flicking up and to the right as though she's thinking up a lie. Then she thrusts a business card at Harriet. Harriet takes it from between the girl's fingers. She wears white cotton gloves. Interesting.

Miss Cellany, the card reads. *Purveyor of Restored and Refurbished Goods. Contact ev@misscellany.com.*

"Cute," says Harriet. "But it doesn't tell me much."

"Who are you?" Ev shoots back.

"Your new best customer. How much for all of it?" Stupid. The girl could fleece her. But Harriet can't resist. It's all so fabulously bright.

Ev shakes her head. "No," she says. "I won't sell to you."

"Why not?"

Harriet catches a flash of fear in Ev's eyes before she composes herself again.

"You're dangerous."

"I don't understand," Harriet replies, although she can't look Ev in the eye when she says it.

A young girl approaches, cooing over a silver pendant with a hopeful glow, drawing Ev's attention away while Harriet puzzles over her words. The girl spins, gathering her long hair at the back of her head so that Ev can fasten the clasp around her neck. Harriet clenches the handles of her cart as money exchanges hands, and the girl and pendant melt away into the crowd.

"My name is Harriet Langdon," she tells Ev, trying a less belligerent tone. "I'm a collector."

"I know."

"Your goods are extraordinary."

"I know."

Harriet watches the girl for a moment.

The girl watches back. "Why do you say I'm dangerous?"

"How many 'extraordinary goods' have you collected?"

"A few," Harriet lies.

"I was at your apartment building, remember? You've got all kinds of energies built up there. I bet all your neighbors are sick. It's irresponsible."

Harriet has to glance away. It's hard to face the truth in those words. She knows she's hurting her neighbors. It's only headaches, mental fog, confusion, but it's wrong, all the same. And hasn't she done worse? How easy it is to slip from irresponsible to dangerous. She knows it better than anyone. Except maybe this girl, if Harriet's suspicions are correct.

"That's why I need you."

"What you need is to get rid of all that stuff. If you had any decency, you'd burn it."

Harriet recoils — a monstrous thought — but Ev is serious. Harriet has a sudden vision of the girl torching the building as Harriet sleeps. Fear tightens the bands around her heart. Perhaps it was a mistake to come here, to draw attention to her collection. But if anyone can help Harriet fix the mess she has made, Ev can.

"Listen to me." She grabs the girl's hand. Perhaps too hard. The girl jerks away roughly, her face gone hard, a decision in her eyes.

"I've known people like you before. I don't want you to come around here. Go."

"I want to offer you a job," Harriet says. The words spill out of her dry mouth like sand. What happened to treading carefully? She has no reason to trust Ev, yet she can't stop herself. Brightness sparkles all around them, making Harriet's skin tingle, making her weak-kneed with want.

"I don't want your job."

"Please. You must understand how significant this is, you and I meeting this way." Ev shakes her head, a frown creasing her forehead. Her hands, encased in white cotton gloves, curl into fists. Harriet's losing her.

"I have money," she adds. "I'll pay double what you earn here."

Ev reaches to her left and tugs on a leather cord attached to a string of pretty bells with leaves impressed into the clay. They clatter cheerfully, an odd juxtaposition to the girl's scowl. "I told you to go."

An older Chinese woman bustles over from the table next to Ev's.

"Hey Ev, you okay?" She glances questioningly at Harriet.

"Can you cover for me for a minute?" In a lower voice she whispers something at the woman. Then, louder, she says, "This lady was just leaving. I have nothing for her to buy." Ev turns to leave.

"Wait," Harriet cries. "Please, one more thing."

The girl stops, looks over her shoulder at Harriet.

Harriet leans forward to make herself heard over the crowd. "You said you knew others like us. Is that true?"

"Just one. Another . . . collector."

"Can you give me a name?"

"He's dead," Ev replies, just before she swings around and stalks away. "There are no others."

7

Ev weaves through the crowd, catching her breath, doing her best to vanish from Harriet's sight. It doesn't take long. It's the first clear evening in a week and the market is packed. The rows of tents blink and flash with string lights; plastic pennants flutter against a pink-tinted sky. The air smells of incense and fried food. Laughter and pop music jangle behind the chatter of buying and selling. She dodges backpacks and elbows and wooden skewers full of meat, making her way toward the food tents at the market's heart.

A job handling mountains of stains all day. What a nutjob. All that talk of collections and treasures. Her father thought the same in the early days. But he learned. They all learned to know better.

Keep the dirt out, Evelyn.

No. Think about something else. Ev fingers the change in her pocket. Think about curried fish balls. How long will the line be at Ah Fei? She's about to skirt around to the sidewalk to check, when she sees Hangdog. He stands outside the market, leaning against the window of a convenience store. Arms crossed. Watching her.

Ev switches direction, moving back into the middle of the crowd and toward the Egg Puff truck. Vivian's right. One of the security guards stands there, an elbow on the counter next to the napkins, scanning the crowd. The crabby one with the round head. He sees Ev heading his way and lifts his chin in greeting. His eyes travel up and down her body like she's a deep-fried potato on a stick.

"How's business tonight?"

"Problematic. See that guy in the Godzilla T-shirt? He's been hanging around, giving me the creeps."

The guard looks Hangdog over. "He's not in the market. I can't do nothing about him."

"He was at my table earlier, getting aggressive. Could you keep an eye on him?"

"Long as I can keep my other eye on you."

Security. Helpful as always. The guard sees Ev's scowl and grins, not in a friendly way.

"Kidding, kidding. I'll watch him."

"Good." Ev turns to head back to her table.

"Hey." The guard's voice turns sharp. "Why don't you ever smile? I watch out for you, the least you can do is act grateful."

"It's your job to look out for me."

He mutters something under his breath as she walks away. She doesn't stop to find out what. Surrounded by assholes. Might be time to call it a night.

She spots Owen behind her table when she returns. Vivian has let him take over. He's chatting with a trio of girls. Drunk girls, judging by the loudness of their voices and the way the blonde one leans on the table to keep her balance. It's getting to that point when more of the passersby are on their way to the bar than thinking about shopping. Sometimes those are her best customers — the drunk, impulsive ones more likely not to let logic get in the way of spending ten dollars on an ugly necktie.

But she's tired. She's sold half her stock already. Maybe she should pack it in early. She wants to get that brooch off her conscience. She's already decided to bike along the seawall on the way home and toss it into the inlet.

"Everything okay?"

A bag sits on Ev's chair, probably containing yam tempura rolls and wakame salad. Owen lives across the street from a sushi restaurant. He also has a thing about feeding Ev.

"Fine. That woman from the alley came looking for me. She offered me a job."

"Harriet? She's fascinating, isn't she?"

"I don't like her."

Two of the drunk girls have moved on and are trying on plastic beads at Vivian's table. The blonde one hangs back. She has a tiger's eye ring in her palm and a glazed look in her eyes, that expression people get when they find something special on Ev's table. It's like watching a toddler discover a feather, the way the rest of the world falls away and only one thing exists in that moment. A polished rock with a perfect white ring around it. A speckled robin's egg. She thinks of Noemi suddenly and the phone call she hasn't made.

Owen edges around to the outside of Ev's table.

"You leaving already?" Ev bites back her disappointment. Between the Stain Hag and Hangdog and her sister, her nerves are shot. She could use the company.

"I'm painting tonight. I just wanted to drop that off." Owen nods at the takeout bag. "Bet you forgot to eat dinner."

"Thanks."

"See you tomorrow?"

They sometimes comb yard sales on weekends, but Ev still hasn't returned her sister's call.

"Maybe next weekend. I've got something else I need to take care of."

Ev turns back to the girl and the ring. One more sale, a sure thing, and then she'll get out of here.

"How much?" The girl waves the ring at Ev, overemphasizing each word. Ev can't tell if she's using her ESL voice or if she's too drunk to talk.

"Twenty dollars."

The girl digs through her purse with her free hand, frowning, and then pulls out a credit card.

"You take card?" Definitely ESL voice. Ev stares the girl down.

"It's cash only. There's an ATM next to the front gate."

"Oh," says the girl. Sober enough to notice Ev's lack of accent, to have the decency to look embarrassed. She studies the ring for another moment. Enough time passes that Ev thinks she's having second thoughts. Then the girl swipes at her eyes with the back of her hand. She's crying. Dammit. She tries to hide it but she's smeared mascara onto her cheek.

"I'm sure I have a twenty in here some-where." She sounds more hopeful than sure. She thrusts the ring at Ev. "Can you hold it for a minute?"

Ev takes the ring. She can feel its stain, an uncomplicated love. First love, the grade school kind that's all hand-holding and awkward kisses.

The girl empties her purse one crumpled piece of paper at a time. No bills, just flyers for upcoming shows and balled-up receipts.

The girl's sweater has come unbuttoned at the top and fallen down one shoulder, revealing a row of faint scars along the insides of her plump white arm.

Ev grabs one of the crumpled-up papers the girl dropped on the table. *Jesus forgives you,* it reads. She wads it up in her hand.

"There's your twenty," she says. "Take it."

The girl slides the ring onto her finger and smiles at it, stroking the oblong, polished stone as she stumbles away.

"Jesus isn't gonna pay your bills." Ev's head jerks up at the familiar voice. Hang-dog. "It's not like you to give shit away for free."

She cranes her neck for a glimpse of the security guard. He watches from across the lane, arms crossed and a hint of a smile tugging at the corners of his mouth.

"What can I do for you?"

She says it loudly and stiffly, hoping to catch Vivian's attention without having to ring that damn bell a third time. But Vivian isn't at her table and Ken keeps his back turned.

"I want that brooch."

"I don't have it."

"I saw you put it in there." He eyes her bike trailer, his jaw working.

"You need to leave." She waves at the guard. "Excuse me," she calls. He doesn't move.

Hangdog ducks suddenly, scrambling under the table to get at her trailer.

"Hey! Thief!" she yells. "Can I get some help over here?" Hangdog's hands clutch at the trailer. Ev ducks down, yanking the trailer backward, but Hangdog has a firm grip. As she struggles to pull it away from him, she hears more yelling from the other side of the table. Hopefully that jerk security guard is doing his job. Ev jabs at Hangdog's white knuckles with her fist. He lets go with one hand, catches her ankle and pulls, knocking her off balance and onto one hip.

The trailer rolls under the table and out of reach. Ev scrambles after it, crawling under the tablecloth. All she can see is a confusion of feet, black boots and dirty sneakers, and Hangdog's red face. He has his arm inside the trailer. Ev punches his arm but he doesn't react. She punches him again. Hangdog's eyes widen suddenly and he cries out. He starts sliding backward, back under the table. He lets go of the trailer, and Ev drags it to safety behind the table.

The guard has finally made it over. She can hear him yelling.

"Enough. That's enough."

Ev stumbles to her feet. A crowd has gathered around her table. The guard waves them back from the spot where Hangdog lies. She glances behind her, where Ken watches with cold eyes, unmoving.

"I'm sorry," she tells him, but he says nothing. A flash of pink catches her eye. The tablecloth slides suddenly, yanked downward, spilling her products onto the pavement. A china plate shatters. She scrambles over the table, trying to save the rest of her stuff from being pulled to the edge. Her elbow knocks Vivian's bells, and she hears another smash that sinks her stomach. But there's no time to check the damage, because that's when she sees that the flash of pink belongs to a pair of pigtails. A bony back arches over Hangdog, knobs of a spine curving beneath a tight white tank top. A girl is punching Hangdog in the face. Ev chokes back a laugh, half-shock, half-delight. This is probably the wrong moment to be giddy.

"Get off him."

The guard sweeps down and pulls the girl off Hangdog, holding her arms behind her back like she's the criminal. Hangdog sits up, glassy-eyed, defeated, fat lip even fatter than usual and bloody besides.

"Don't mess with my sister, asshole," shouts the girl. And she turns to grin at Ev, brown eyes shining, like this is all a huge, hilarious joke. Like all is forgiven, and not a day has gone by. Beautiful Noemi, skinny, bruised, perfect.

Ev lets the laugh tumble free.

8

Ev chases Noemi down the sidewalk, winding around clusters of people, muttering apologies as she bumps into shoulders and calves with her bike, craning her neck to keep her sister in view. She moves fast, beating a hasty retreat from the market. They've left behind a crowd of ogling shoppers, the smirking guard, a dazed and bloodied Hangdog, Ken's frown, and Vivian's creased forehead as she picked up the shards of her broken bells. Ev knows there will be fallout from tonight, but it's easy to push that to the back of her mind as Noemi's pigtails bob ten feet ahead of her. Ev jogs to catch up, her trailer bouncing up a curb with a clatter. She's half-afraid that her sister will turn a corner and vanish for another six months.

She catches up with Noemi outside a restaurant with steamy windows and a neon sign that reads *Got Dumplings?* One of many trendy, overpriced spots that have invaded Chinatown.

"Let's get noodles," she says. "I'm starving." There's a lineup outside but that doesn't faze Noemi.

"We'll sit at the bar," she tells Ev, reading her mind as usual. It seems a noisy place for a reunion, but Noemi has her by the arm, and Ev, dazzled by her solid, warm presence, lets her sister pull her toward the door.

"Wait," she says, "my bike." While Ev chains it to a signpost, Noemi ducks down and unzips the trailer, where Ev has stuffed the tablecloth with all her unsold goods wrapped up inside. Noemi gathers up the bundle and slings it over her shoulder. Even with the hobo sack and a bruise forming on her cheekbone, she has no trouble gliding to the front of the line, and after she puts a hand on the hostess's shoulder and exchanges a word or two, they perch at the glossy black bar. This meal will cost Ev all the cash she's earned at the market tonight, but she doesn't care, not right now. They order lemongrass sodas, Noemi's with gin.

"This is my long-lost sister," Noemi yells at the bartender, beaming like she's showing off a new toy. "We're recently reunited."

Noemi was the lost one, Ev thinks, but

81

she plays along because the bartender smiles and because, if she's being honest with herself, the attention feels nice.

"In that case, first round's on the house."

Ev feels a poke in her ribs as the bartender leaves. Noemi bends her head close to Ev's. She smells like peaches and wet bark. Freckles dust her nose as they always do in summer.

"He likes you."

"It's not me he likes." It's never Ev.

Noemi tilts her head and regards Ev for a long moment, lips pursed.

"When was the last time you got laid?"

How easily they fall into the same old conversations. The restaurant seems a better idea now, a safer place. Alone, it's harder to dodge Noemi's questions. Ev rolls her eyes in reply.

"That's what I thought. We have to fix that, stat."

"Can we eat first?"

Without warning Noemi throws her arms around Ev, squeezes tight, and purrs in her ear.

"I missed you."

"I missed you, too," says Ev. *Where were you? Why didn't you call?* She knows better than to begin with these questions. She swallows, drawing up the courage to say the words she's been practicing since Noemi ran off. But as always, Noemi's quicker than she is.

"I can't believe I'm here. Two days ago, I was up in the mountains cleaning rooms at this shitty hotel outside Revelstoke."

"Revelstoke."

"Ugh, yes. I planned to work in Banff for the summer, but I only made it halfway into the mountains, long story. So there I was on my knees, wiping some stranger's pubes off the toilet seat, probably about to be fired because I'm too slow, and I thought, *Noemi, what the fuck are you doing here?* So I got up, grabbed my shit, and walked out of there. Walked straight to the highway and hitched a ride back to the city with this nice old German couple."

"Wait," Ev interrupts. "You spent six months in Revelstoke?"

Noemi whoops. "Hell, no. I would've died. I've been to Winnipeg, Kansas, New Orleans, Mexico City, Portland, Montana . . ."

"A road trip."

"An epic road trip. Except for that last shitty part."

"Where does your boyfriend fit into this?" Ev braces herself for a reaction. The boyfriend was a point of contention between them before Noemi left. But Noemi waves the question off.

"Jonathan? Ex-boyfriend, you mean. We parted ways in Mexico."

"Sorry," says Ev, although she doesn't mean it.

"Anyway, that's a whole other story, and I haven't told you the most important thing."

Ev tucks into her noodles. Once Noemi gets rolling, there's no putting the brakes on. Ev lets the cadence of her sister's voice wash together with the bass pounding from the speakers and the shouted snatches of conversation all around them. She watches her sister wind up further, throwing her body into her words, projecting loudly enough to capture the attention of anyone within ten feet. Noemi loves an audience. Ev doesn't have to participate. This is a performance, not a conversation.

"So, then we were cruising through the Valley, and I had this plan to crash at Joan and Mikey's place for a few days and then head north, and I wasn't even going to call you because I was still mad . . ."

Ev draws in a sharp breath, but Noemi flaps her hands in protest, still talking.

"And then we stopped at a gas station off the highway. We were just about in the city. The German guy, he had to pee like every six miles, and his wife was addicted to gum.

She bought a pack every time we stopped, I'm not even kidding.

"Anyway, I saw this big tree across the road from the gas station. And something was hanging from one of the upper branches, tiny and white and glowing. This was last night — did you see how the sky was clear and the moon so huge? And this little thing, it just seemed to float in the sky. It looked exactly like a paper crane. Like the ones you used to make me. Remember?"

Ev remembers. She loved the way a fresh sheet of paper felt beneath her fingers. Clean, crisp, safe. She would fold other things for Noemi too. Hopping frogs, heart-shaped boxes, and penguins.

"You used to write secret messages inside."

"Knock-knock jokes."

"Yeah, goofy stuff. I loved that. And I had this sudden certainty that a message waited for me in that crane. So of course, I had to climb the tree. It was a big cedar tree, like the one we climb up by the park, the one with the hammock? Most of the lower branches had fallen off. They look like eyes, those spots, you ever notice that? I had to jump to reach a solid branch. But I got up, and I climbed until I could see what was hanging there."

Noemi's eyes have gone dark and glassy, like she's back there again, seeing it. Ev can't help but lean toward her.

"I shimmied out onto the branch. And the Germans had found me by then, and they were down at the bottom of the tree, yelling at me, cursing in German. I guess they thought I might jump or something."

Noemi laughs, downs the rest of her drink, and waits for Ev to ask.

"Okay," Ev says. "What did it say?"

"Nothing. It wasn't even a crane. It was an old GiantMart receipt. But that didn't matter. What I realized is I'd been thinking about you all the way back to the city. And not only that, you'd been with me all along. It was like I had this imaginary Ev living in my head.

"Don't laugh, it's true. Every funny, amazing, stupid, or shitty thing that happened, I would tell imaginary Ev about it. I might've left you, but you never left me. I kept pretending all along that I wasn't coming back to the city to see you, except it was a lie. It wasn't just the tree and the crane that wasn't a crane. Everything reminded me of old times with you. Whenever we'd stop for another pack of fucking gum, I'd think about how we used to buy cream soda slushies and red licorice at the gas station in the summertime."

"And we'd ride our bikes down to the river." During the years of Joan and Mikey.

"Yes! And try to skip stones, except we were never any good at it."

"So, we'd just throw them at the logs floating past."

"Oh, and when we drove through the mountains, I kept thinking about that big boulder in the backyard at the red house. We dug a hole next to it and pretended we lived in a cave, remember?"

"You buried treasure in there." That was foster home number two.

"My plastic frog collection and that crabby lady's chicken salt-and-pepper shakers. And you never told on me. Also, the Germans made me cheese sandwiches like you used to. And of course, every time I saw a big cedar tree. Everything kept circling back to Noemi and Evelyn. So when I saw that paper crane that wasn't a crane, I knew I had to come home."

The noodles in Ev's bowl blur together. She tries to think of what to say. She has to say the right thing, to show Noemi it matters that she's here. Noise swirls around them.

"I am always with you," she manages. "No matter what."

"I know that."

Now. She has to tell Noemi.

"When you left . . ."

"It's okay." Noemi leans her head on Ev's shoulder. "You don't have to say anything."

"I do. I'm sorry I hid things from you. It's not that I couldn't remember. I didn't want to."

"Of course you didn't. I was an asshole for trying to make you relive all that old shit."

"I don't want you to leave again. So I'll tell you what I know."

"Ev."

"I mean it. I will. But please be patient with me?"

"Yeah. Okay."

A silence draws out between them as Ev struggles to find more words. She's never imagined the conversation beyond this point. Noemi saves her.

"Ugh, enough of the heavy stuff. How are you? What's new? How's Lisa?"

"I haven't seen her."

"Why not?"

"She's not our caseworker anymore." The girls are grownups now, both of them. At least, that's what the law says.

"So? She loves us. What about Joan and Mikey?"

"It's always about church with them."

"Ha. I guess. What else is going on in your life? Besides raging customers attacking your bike trailer."

"Actually, this thing happened today." Until now, the Stain Hag — Harriet — has been pushed out of her mind. "This weird thing." But Noemi isn't listening. She stares at Ev's hands, chopsticks pinched between white cotton.

"What's up with the gloves? You wear those all the time now?"

"It's easier that way."

The light drains from Noemi's face. "You've gotten worse."

"I'm managing my environment."

"The gloves, no dating, cutting off contact with your friends."

"Caregivers. Not friends."

"The way you're acting all scared of your stuff." Noemi gestures at the tablecloth bundle wedged under her stool.

"I'm not."

"You are. This is why I was called back to you. You need me."

Ev knows better than to argue. She hides her hands under the table and tries to think of something to talk about that won't draw any more attention to poor, weird, broken Ev.

"I'm sorry." Noemi squeezes her arm. "We can talk about this stuff later. I interrupted. You were about to tell me something that happened today."

"It's nothing," says Ev. "Forget it."

AFTER

Ev makes a mountain fold to meet its twin in the center of her waterbomb base. She has an animal origami book from the library, and she's learning every animal, page by page. It gives her something for her hands to do. She can't use tools anymore. She asked Jack, her foster dad, if she could build a birdhouse in the garage or even just hammer some nails into a board, but he said no. He waved his hand with the missing third and fourth fingers in the air and said, "This is what happens when kids get around tools," and added that carpentry isn't a hobby for a ten-year-old girl anyway. So instead, she sits in the gazebo in the backyard, creasing and folding. The gazebo is quiet, and the paper is clean and empty, a safe escape for her hands. Above all else, Ev must keep her hands safe, so that she can also keep her sister and herself safe.

Noemi, as always, is running around the

yard, singing, dancing, and getting dirty. She's given up trying to get Ev to play tag or hide-and-seek with her, although she can sometimes convince her to climb the cherry tree. When she has tumbled all of her after-school energy out, Noemi hops up the gazebo's three steps and sits across from her at the table. Ev makes her last fold and flips the form over, pushing it to Noemi.

"Crab," she says.

Noemi wrinkles her nose. "Looks like a frog to me."

She's right. The shape is too simple. Ev makes a mental note to find a more challenging book. She flips the page. Next up is a crane. She picks a sheet of purple paper, Noemi's favorite color. While she folds, Noemi strokes the crab absently.

"Did Mama do origami?"

Ev feels a hot jolt, as she always does when Noemi brings up their mother. It's like being poked with a live wire.

"No."

"I think she did. She made crabs and put money inside."

"You're thinking of the red envelopes for Lunar New Year." A memory intrudes, of kneeling on the plush green rug on her bedroom floor while Mama presented the red envelope with both hands and a little bow, oh-so-serious except for the bright warmth in her eyes. Ev pulls her hands away from the paper she's folding and clasps them tightly between her thighs.

"Oh." Noemi falls quiet but Ev stays on guard, her body tense. She can see by Noemi's frown that she's absorbing this information and formulating new questions. Noemi is six now, and she's starting to forget things from before. In some ways, it's easier that way. She doesn't cry for Mama at night anymore. But she asks questions. They come when Ev isn't expecting them, and they always hurt.

Maybe Ev should have given Noemi a red envelope this year. If she doesn't keep up family traditions, they will be lost. The trouble is that while Noemi struggles to remember, Ev has been working hard to forget. She has packed her old life away in a box in the back of her mind and does her best to keep it there. It's too hard to separate the good stuff from the terrible stuff. One always leads to the other, and all of it feels bad. So, for the last year and a half, she has been practicing, telling everyone who asks, "I don't remember." Caseworkers, therapists, nosy foster parents and teachers, rude kids who've heard the rumors, even Noemi. *I don't remember, I don't remember.* Until they stop asking. Until it's true.

Before Noemi can ask more about the red envelopes, Ev begins to fold again, talking as she works.

"When we're grown up, we'll live together in a big white house." A new house, clean and perfect.

"Will we have our own rooms?"

"If you want." They share a room at Jack and Elsie's. Many nights, Noemi ends up sprawled out in Ev's bed, squishing Ev up against the wall.

"I want us to be in the same room."

"Okay." She folds a neck, then a tail. "And we'll have lots of trees in the backyard."

"And a tree house!"

"Yep." She forms the crane's head. If she keeps her hands busy, it's easier to say the words Noemi needs to hear. "We'll live together forever. I'll always take care of you."

"No. We take care of *each other*," Noemi replies with conviction.

"Yes." She folds out the wings and presents the purple crane to Noemi. "We do."

Her sister still claps her hands when she's excited. Ev hopes she never stops doing that. She's relieved to see the frown has vanished from Noemi's face as she makes

the crane swoop and dive through the air.
I'll always be your sun.

9

"Are you sure you don't want to come?"

Noemi combs her fingers through Ev's hair, gathering another lock into the tight braid that winds around the nape of her neck.

"I gotta work."

"Joan's making spinach lasagna."

"You know I can't on weekends. You'll be back on Monday?" Ev can't hide the anxiety that tightens her throat, making her voice higher than usual. She'd like to ask Noemi not to go at all, but she knows that's silly.

"I promise." There's a smile in Noemi's voice. "No road trips for a while." She fastens the end of the braid. "Well, at least you'll look stunning. Do I need to worry about any ruffians attacking you tonight?"

"No," says Ev. She hopes. When she unwrapped her market bundle at the end of the night, the brooch wasn't there. Either it got lost during the struggle or Hangdog got his hands on it after all. She suspects the latter. At any rate, she doesn't think he'll show his face again tonight, not after the job Noemi did on it. Her bigger preoccupation is Ken. She knows there will be consequences for last night's fight.

Back on her bike, alone and heading toward Chinatown, she can't avoid her anxiety any longer. It's not the first time her table has attracted trouble. At the beginning of the summer, two customers got into a shouting match over a conceited watch; and only a week later, a drunken tussle broke out over a passionate satin slip. The slip tore, security was called, and Ev has been extra careful ever since. She knows Ken only lets her stick around because Vivian likes her. She also knows Vivian pulls a lot of weight in that partnership. So, while she expects she'll have some apologizing to do, maybe even some groveling, she's not expecting what she finds when she arrives at the market. Her usual table isn't empty, waiting for her. Vivian's covered it in rhinestone-encrusted cell phone cases. Her heart sinks. She knows what this means. She rolls up, bicycle gears clicking as she coasts to a stop in front of Vivian.

"Hey." Vivian keeps her head down, pretending to focus on counting her cash float.

"Viv, what's up?" The woman's hands pause halfway through a fanned stack of fives. She glances at Ev with a twist in her thin brows. Ev's heart sinks further.

"Talk to Ken," Vivian says. "Sorry, Ev."

She finds Ken unloading boxes from the back of his pickup. He turns to Ev with his hard face on, the one he usually reserves for belligerent customers.

"I can't rent you space anymore. Your business brings us too much trouble."

"I'm sorry about last night. It won't happen again."

Ken shakes his head. "Security's given us two warnings. I can't risk it."

Ev glances back at Vivian. She's pretending not to listen. Heat flashes across Ev's eyes, and sour bile rises in the back of her throat. She tamps down the anger.

"I paid you for the season," she says.

Ken pulls a wad of twenties from his pocket and thrusts it at her. Vivian doesn't look up again. She keeps her head down until Ev turns her bike around and walks away. She wheels through the crowd, clenching the cash, scanning the other vendor tables. Maybe someone else will sublet space to her. *Keep breathing,* she tells herself.

The sound of scratchy radio static alerts

her to the security guard keeping pace to the right of her. Same guard from last night. Same smirk on his stupid round face.

"I'm going to have to ask you to move on," he says, as though she's some lurking shoplifter. She wants to punch that smug little smile.

"This is a public space. I'm not doing anything wrong."

"Sure, sure." He puts his hands up in mock supplication. "Just so long as you're not selling. The Association has banned you. If you make any more trouble, I'll have to call the authorities."

"I get it." She pushes past him with her bike. As soon as she passes the street barricade, she swings her leg over her bike and starts pedaling. She rides without thinking, out of Chinatown, across Hastings, over the railroad tracks and down to the waterfront, rolling over the grassy lawn at Crab Park to the beach. Not a big beach, but it's enough; a bit of open space for her to breathe in.

She sits for a while, kicking at the sand, building a little pile of good skipping stones. She's still not great at it, but she's improved since those afternoons at the river with Noemi. On a good day, when the park is quiet and the ocean is calm, she can usually get in a few triples, maybe even a quadruple skip. She pulls her shoes off and rolls up the cuffs of her pants. It always seems to work better when her feet are in the water. She works on skimming her pile down, one stone at a time, and breathing her way calm.

Owen finds her as the sun begins to sink below the high rises. She's collecting another pile of stones when she sees his silhouette, spine straight, big handlebars, round helmet, bumping over the tracks. He's got something large stuffed in the crate on the back of his bike. A paper bag dangles from one handlebar, and her stomach rumbles. She picks her way over the wet pebbles with her shoes in her hand, finds a log to sit on, and waits for Owen to join her.

"I thought I'd find you here." Owen sits down, passes her the bag. "Croissant?"

The bag is greasy and crumpled and stuffed with pastries. Ev breathes in the butter scent. She plucks out an almond croissant with a smushed corner and takes a huge bite.

"So good," she mumbles.

"Castoffs, courtesy of Faubourg. What happened at the market?"

"Vivian didn't tell you?"

"She was avoiding me. Ken said you don't work there anymore."

"I'm too much trouble." Ev stuffs more croissant in her mouth and chews, considering how much to tell Owen. "My sister came home."

"The one that ran away from foster care?" That's as much as Owen knows about Noemi. Except Noemi didn't run away from foster care. She ran away from Ev.

"She's eighteen now. She wants to live with me."

"Will you say yes?"

"Of course. She's my only family." Noemi is the only person who understands Ev, who truly knows her. It's strange. When Noemi was gone, Ev got used to being alone. Now that she's back, Ev can see she survived by numbing herself to how shitty she felt. She doesn't want to go back to living that way. Besides, Noemi doesn't always realize it, but she needs Ev as much as Ev needs Noemi. They look after each other. They always have.

"What's she like?"

"Loud," says Ev. "Gorgeous. Impossible to ignore."

"Is that why you look so tired?" She can hear the smile in his voice. "I look forward to meeting her."

"I need a job."

"What about Harriet? You said she offered

you a job."

"No."

"She's quite interesting."

"No."

"Well," Owen continues, unruffled, "what about the Richmond Night Market? It's much bigger."

"They don't want me."

"There's always the flea market."

"I know." Ev sells at the flea market in the winter. "But the money's not as good."

In truth, she makes a fraction of what she could get at the Night Market. The flea market takes place in a big red warehouse next to the train station. People mostly go there for cheap deals on old tools and computer parts. At the flea market, everyone wants to haggle. They come in sharp-eyed and pass by Ev's table of oddities without even looking, intent on their mission. It's outside of the downtown core, so it doesn't attract the wandering tourists and half-drunk suburban partyers who are Ev's bread and butter.

"I could put in a good word for you at Hitoe. Mikko was just telling me they need another server. Do you have any restaurant experience?"

Ev doesn't have any job experience. She only knows trash. She looks away. Owen's bike is parked beside hers. The thing in the back is a torso. A half-mannequin with long red hair.

"Nice find," she says.

"There's a bin full of them near Granville and Nelson. I might go back with my trailer, see if there are any left." He glances wistfully at the mannequin's head.

"I've got a trailer," she tells him. "Let's go."

There's another binner trundling down the alley when they arrive, a guy Ev's seen before. He wears a wool blanket tied over his shoulders like a cape, and he's always muttering to himself. His shopping cart is piled high with garbage bags stuffed with cans and bottles.

"Hello, Eddie," says Owen, because Owen knows everyone by name. Eddie grunts in response.

"All the good metal's gone," he mumbles as he passes. Ev peers down the alley. Some store must be renovating. A long, low bin is piled with wire shelving, wood scraps, and occasional limbs. Another helpful scavenger has cut the chain on the bin's padlock, and the lid is propped open by a chunk of drywall. Ev doesn't even have to climb in to hook an elbow and yank out another torso.

"Eddie looks well," says Owen. "He's not

limping anymore. I wonder if he received some medical attention for his arthritis."

"How do you know these things?"

"I talk to people."

"Right. I'm terrible at that."

"You're better with objects," Owen concedes.

"People make no sense."

People hide their feelings. They obscure and deceive. They change in a moment from one emotion to another. People are too complicated for Ev, always have been. Ev knows Owen is as complex as any other human, but he doesn't act that way. She knows he has an ex-wife and son who don't talk to him, although he's never burdened her with the backstory, and she's never asked. She only knows about the family from an offhand comment another binner made once. Probably there's a motive behind the way he looks out for Ev. He's compensating for his shitty relationship with his kid or something. But he doesn't force his complicatedness on her like other people do, with their unspoken expectations and needs that she can't decipher. Hanging out with Owen is easy.

By the time their recovery mission is completed, darkness has settled on the city. They've stuffed three torsos into Ev's trailer and tied one more onto her front basket. As they head toward Owen's house, a breeze raising gooseflesh on her forearms and legs, Ev catches herself smiling. A good find, even if it's not for her, always cheers her up.

Owen lives in an old house with peeling paint. On the wide porch, with its sagging patio lights, a couple slumps into each other on a worn sofa, legs tangled together. Owen's roommates rotate regularly. Ev has never been able to keep track of them. The couple waves as Ev and Owen approach.

"You want to come in?" Owen asks as they untie his bounty.

Owen's house is full of junk. Art junk, but still, there are bound to be plenty of stains. She doesn't have the energy. Two years she's known Owen, and she's never been inside his house.

"Maybe another time."

"Well. Thanks." He watches her for a minute. "I'm sorry you lost your table at the market."

Ev nods. "Me too."

"You'd be a good bike courier, but the money's not great anymore." Owen used to courier full-time, but over the years his hours have been cut to less than half that.

"It's okay. I'm not sure I'm cut out to be anyone's employee."

He pauses. "I started working for Harriet, you know."

"That's a bad idea."

"It's temporary. I'm helping her with a special project." He pauses again. "She asks about you a lot."

"I don't trust her."

"If you're worried that she can't pay you, don't be. Despite appearances, she seems to have plenty of money. She bought a space to store her stuff and get organized. An old bank."

"She bought a damn bank?"

"Just the building."

"Still. She's never heard of self-storage?"

"Oh, she has plans beyond storage, something about a museum. I'm going to help her clean it up and move her things in. She won't even consider getting rid of some of the junk that's in there. She pays well. She's good people, Evelyn."

"How do you know that?"

"You get feelings about objects. I get feelings about people," Owen says. He holds the pastry bag out to her until she reluctantly takes it. "I know the good ones."

10

The intercom buzzes a second time. Harriet pauses in her work, her hands submerged in soapy water, considering how long it will take to get from the kitchen to her front door and the likelihood that whoever buzzed will still be outside by the time she gets there.

"Let them rot," Harriet says to her kitchen witches. The witches, all ten of them dangling from the window frame on a piece of twine, bob on their twig broomsticks, riding the breeze from the cracked window. Their pointy felt hats wobble as if in agreement. So be it. Harriet's knees are still stiff from walking around the market the other night and she's tired. Anyone who actually needs her would call her cell phone, which is always on her body. It's probably the local courier, or that woman in 301 has lost her keys again. Both of them are in the habit of buzzing every damn unit until someone lets them in. Harriet continues washing her mugs.

She has a dishwasher, but since she only prepares tea in her kitchen, she never has enough dirty dishes for a full load. She's long since filled it with bright things, little objects that like the dark and the quiet and don't want to be disturbed. They sleep in rows, safe as babes in their mother's womb. Once a week or so, Harriet fills her sink and washes the accumulated mugs and spoons. They live on a tea towel laid out on the counter next to the sink, because the cupboards are full of bright things too.

As she washes, she hums, and worries at the problem of the girl. Bright-sensitive humans are apparently more complicated than bright objects. She needs more information about Evelyn before she tries again. Owen remains close-lipped and annoyingly loyal to his friend. If he does know her background, he feigns ignorance. Harriet will have to dig deeper to confirm something she's not sure if she hopes or dreads. After she'd visited Ev, she wallowed in queasy shame for hours, dwelling on their argument and the look of disgust Ev had shot at her before she stormed off.

Today she's optimistic. She took action and put an offer on a building she's had her eye on. She thinks it will work. It will be her new home and more, much more. She believes her treasures can do good in the world, even if Ev doesn't, yet. Owen has agreed to help with the moving. He suggested more helpers, some other scavengers he knows who could use the cash, but she can't allow it. Hard enough to trust one stranger in her apartment. She feels reasonably certain that Owen will treat her collection with respect, pack it with care. He promised to return this evening to begin. A month is enough time. She hopes.

Harriet's scalp tingles, that feeling one gets when one is being watched. Has Frédérique gone wandering? She found him in the bathtub this morning, though she could swear she left him next to her pillow. She's never figured out how it works. Do the objects move of their own volition, or are they responding in some way to the humans in their orbit? Countless times over the years, Harriet has attempted to deliberately influence her treasures, staring at them until her eyes water, willing them to come alive at her command. Never with success. Maybe she tries too hard or wants it too badly. If it happens, it's always when she's just looked away, or when her attention is elsewhere. But every time, it gives her a thrill.

She looks behind her. No movement, no sound. No monkeys. Perhaps the witches, then. Harriet turns back to the sink and drops the teacup in her hand. It breaks at her feet. A face peers into her kitchen window. It is not the woman in 301.

The window shudders in its wood frame as Harriet shoves it open another few inches. There's no screen, but the bars on the outside divide Ev's face into three pieces.

"Do you want to come in?"

Ev shakes her head. She gazes past Harriet into the kitchen, taking it all in. Harriet doesn't often think about the state of her kitchen, but she sees it reflected in Ev's numb gaze, how the table in the corner hasn't a spot for a single mug. How the bright things gather on the chairs, too, and under the table, and in the corner in boxes all the way to the ceiling. Then there's the pantry and the space on top of the pantry and the boxes in front of the pantry. In truth, little more than a narrow corridor runs from the door to the sink and that little patch of counter where the mugs and spoons live. Harriet supposes it might be overwhelming to a bright-sensitive child.

She can't very well blame the girl for her slack-jawed silence.

"I'll come out, then." Harriet shuts the window and stoops to pick up the shards of broken teacup. She lays its pieces on the tea towel, side by side. Somewhere, she has a tube of super-glue to mend it with.

Ev waits for Harriet on the front steps. She's left her hair down and she's dressed plainly in jeans and a T-shirt. She still wears the white cotton gloves. She leans against the iron railing, arms crossed, shadows gathered under her eyes.

Harriet sits on the top step, saying nothing. She's learned not to come on too strong. She stays quiet and moves slowly, avoiding eye contact, as though she's trying to befriend a stray cat. Phlox blooms in the pots on the landing, purple and white. She runs her fingers along their soft petals, bending to breathe in their sweet scent.

"Owen told me you're not as horrible as I think you are, and I trust Owen." The words come out in a rush, almost angrily. "I guess I wanted to see . . ." She breaks off. "Mostly, I came to return this." Ev holds a stone in her outstretched palm. A special stone, Harriet's stone. Harriet takes it, strokes the little black bird on its smooth surface, drinks in its sweet glow.

111

"Thank you."

"How can you stand it?" Ev explodes suddenly. "Being around all that stuff?" Her tone is rude, defensive. She doesn't want to be here. Which means she sought Harriet out because she wants something. Or needs something. Harriet answers carefully.

"I've built up resistance. Too much containment and you become vulnerable." Harriet glances meaningfully at Ev's gloves. "Those make you weak, oversensitive."

Something flickers across Ev's face. Annoyance, but also uncertainty. She wants to argue, but she stops. Harriet has her attention. She goes with it.

"You're right, though. I've been thinking about what you said about my treasures spreading sickness. About the danger of them. The energies in my apartment have become increasingly unstable. They're no longer contained. It's wrong of me to be affecting others. That's why I need your help."

Ev doesn't bolt, so Harriet carries on.

"I have a plan. A plan to redistribute and stabilize the collection. Make it safe — better than safe, if we do it right."

"Owen mentioned a museum."

"Yes. What if we could use these objects for good? To heal, rather than hurt? To spread the good energies — love, joy, peace?

Hope? A place people could visit to experience the best that my treasures have to offer?" She doesn't mention the eviction, hasn't told Owen, either. She's not going to let on that she's being forced into the change. Harriet hesitates, decides to take a chance. "Will you do something for me?"

Ev shrugs, stubbornly giving away nothing, but she doesn't leave.

"Tell me what you think of this." Harriet pulls an object out of her pocket. A wooden top, small enough to fit in the palm of her hand. Ev reaches for the top. "Without the gloves," Harriet adds.

"No." Ev pinches the top between two cotton-gloved fingers and frowns at it. After a moment, she says, "I think I could sell this for five dollars. Ten, if the right person comes along."

"That's not what I meant."

Ev narrows her eyes at Harriet. "It's stained," she says finally. "A mid-range vibration. The predominant emotion is longing."

Stained. Interesting.

"I won't help you add to your collection. You have too much already." Ev takes a last look at the top and passes it back to Harriet.

"That's not what I want," she tells Ev. "I

need a curator."

"What would I be doing?"

"Sorting. Organizing." Ev is already shaking her head. "Caring for the artifacts."

"I can't."

"It would pay very well." She pauses. "Your friend Owen is helping, but I need you, too. Only you can help me choose the right items. Together, we could create a truly transformative space."

Ev paces the sidewalk in front of Harriet. "I don't mean I won't. I mean I can't. I can't be around all those things. I'd get sick. How do you not get sick?"

"You talk of stains and sickness." Harriet pulls a single phlox bloom from its stem and tickles her own chin with it. "That's not how I experience bright things."

"Bright."

"Infused with life. They're beautiful. They bring me joy. They always have."

"Beauty. Joy." Ev stops directly in front of Harriet. "What about the things that aren't bright? What about the ugly, dark ones?" She gestures toward the top in Harriet's hand. "That top, it's not just tainted with longing. There's some love in there, sure. But there's also pain and resentment and bitterness and even a little hatred. And it's old, but it's strong. It's got a lot of emotion

114

for such a small 'bright' thing.

"You wanted to know what I think about that top?" To Harriet's surprise, tears spring to Ev's eyes. "I think the child it belonged to was unforgivably betrayed by the person who gave it to her."

Harriet clenches her fist around the top, turning her gaze back to the phlox. It takes a few moments to gather her thoughts. The girl's sensitivity is much stronger than hers. With time, Harriet may be able to identify the specific emotion of longing, but not the others. Never with such certainty. And Harriet knows Ev is right on every count. The top was a gift to Harriet from her father.

"The brightness I sense on objects is not that precise," she admits, wishing her voice wouldn't tremble as she speaks.

"I feel it all. I can't even imagine being in a room full of objects screaming their emotions at me. I'm sorry," she says, and Harriet can hear Ev's genuine disappointment. She needs this job. "I know you think I'm the right person to help you, but I'm not. I can't."

"What is it? Religion?"

"Excuse me?"

"What's got you so scared?" Harriet pauses to collect her thoughts, careful not to say too much, push too hard. She nudges her speculation forward. "You talk about objects like they're full of sin. Is that it? Your parents told you your gift was an abomination? Made you fear what God gave you?"

"Something like that." She turns her face away.

Harriet softens her voice, backs off. "Listen. What kind of a mind do you think you have?"

"What's that mean?"

"You're a strong young woman. With a strong mind. Why do you act like these things can hurt you?"

"I've seen them hurt people. I've seen them turn people's minds."

"People hurt people too, but you can't spend your whole life living in fear of them." Harriet cringes as she speaks the words. *You old hypocrite.* She abandons that argument. "Yes, people can be influenced by objects. But it doesn't have to be that way. You don't have to live in fear. You can be free."

Ev stares at her, hard. "I want to believe that you're not insane."

"Do I sound insane to you?"

"No. But . . ." She breaks off, shakes her head. "It's too dangerous."

"It's only dangerous because you're afraid. We train, a little at a time." Harriet pulls another object from her pocket, a dried bougainvillea blossom. Three magenta petals around a white stamen, dried, so a little wrinkly and a little brown at the edges, but otherwise as lovely and as softly kindness-bright as when it was given to her ten years ago. A good thing to begin with. Pure and uncomplicated brightness. No dark layers hide in this little treasure.

"The danger is in too much too soon, and in handling too much of the wrong kind of brightness. The more you understand it, the stronger you get. And you're already strong. You just don't know it." Harriet nods at Ev's gloves. "Take them off."

"Nope. No way." She starts backing up at the very suggestion.

"This is a gentle object. It won't hurt you."

"I can't," she whispers, but she peels one glove off even as she speaks. She tucks it in the front pocket of her jeans, where it hangs in a limp wave.

"You can." Harriet places the blossom in the middle of Ev's small, sweaty palm, hoping it won't get damaged too much. But she has to keep going. She almost has her.

"Now. Just let the brightness in."

Ev stands still. She keeps her eyes squeezed shut. Three seconds, then four, then five. What happens next makes Harriet's breath catch, makes her clutch the metal railing to keep steady. The blossom, dead and dried as it is, slowly begins to uncurl its papery petals.

Ev's eyes snap open. "What just happened? I felt something strange."

"You were communicating."

Her eyes widen when they flick down to the blossom and see its petals unfurled. Her nostrils flare out.

"No."

"It's extraordinary." Harriet can't keep the awe, the giddy excitement, out of her voice. Forget what she can teach Evelyn. What can Evelyn teach Harriet? "You're a very special girl."

Ev's hands yank away. The blossom floats to the ground as Ev bolts down the sidewalk at a dead run. Harriet watches her go, but she doesn't worry this time. She stoops to pick up the little flower, cupping it gently. The girl came to her. She'll be back. Harriet is certain of it.

11

Ev squeezes her fingernails into her palms as the elevator lifts her up and up. If she presses hard enough, it dulls the crawling feeling that's been haunting her since she felt that flower react to her touch. The sensation of the petals curling against her palm brought a new memory to the surface. A thick, knobby stick tracing lazy circles on a wooden floor, moving on its own like a magic wand. Ev's hair falling in a curtain around her face as she focuses all her attention on it. Wonder and dread swirling around in her gut. The slow scratch of its pointy tip reaches across the years, raising the flesh on Ev's arms and neck.

My special girl.

And Harriet's words. They brought another memory. A dusty Christmas bauble dangling from a large hand. His other hand a gentle weight on the top of her head.

He wipes away the layer of grime on the

surface. Inside is a pristine scene — white cotton snow, little pine tree, tiny plastic fawn with tiny white spots.

"This is how your mind has to be, Evelyn. Like this baby deer, safe and protected. The glass keeps the dirt out. Keeps the inside safe and clean. My special girl."

She leans her head against the mirrored wall, grateful for a solo trip to her floor. She wants to sleep for three straight days, right after she washes the stench of Harriet's mess from her skin. Looking in the window of that apartment, she realized the woman is something entirely unfamiliar to Ev. She's surrounded by garbage, boxes and plastic bags stuffed with more plastic bags, shelves lined with empty containers and dusty jars and stacks of newspapers. And stains, hundreds, thousands of stains. Their vibrations bleed through the walls. They infect the building. Harriet lives in the middle of an emotional swamp, and yet Ev spied her through the window, placidly humming into her soapsuds, white hair frizzed out around her plump face like a halo. Content. Happy.

How can it be?

A third memory surfaces suddenly, a flash of green velvet, a woman's smile broadening as she strokes the back of a chair, Ev watching as the effects of happiness spread from the woman's manicured fingertips, flowing up to soften her face.

Sometimes stains help people. She's seen it at the market. She witnessed it as a child. Harriet's idea isn't terrible. Ev just isn't the right person to help her execute it.

As the doors glide open, she hears the muffled jangle of rock music in the hallway. It's coming from her apartment. Noemi. She pauses for a moment before opening the door, half-grateful, half-wishing she'd headed to the beach instead.

Her sister has all of her clothes spread out on the bed. She wears nothing but a lacy bra, a feather boa, and a tutu. She sits on a pile of dresses, painting her toenails pink to match her hair.

"Where were you?" Noemi shouts. "I wanted to go for Sunday pannekoeken. Do you *ever* answer your phone?"

Ev cuts the volume on her laptop. "I wasn't expecting you back so soon."

"Joan and Mikey have a baby now."

"Noisy baby?"

"Crack baby. All he does is scream. I got like two hours of sleep."

Ev sits on the floor at Noemi's feet, shoving aside her sister's backpack. It gapes open, a tangle of socks and underwear spewing from its mouth. A matter of hours and already Ev's countertop is littered with crumpled papers, makeup, and disposable razors. How can one small human create so much chaos?

"Want some licorice? Under the feathers."

Ev lifts the end of the boa to reveal the bag. She tears off two pieces.

"Thanks. So? How are they doing?"

"Same. You're right about the church thing. I almost went with them. I like the singing." Noemi sucks in her bottom lip, pretending to be absorbed with her left pinkie toe. Ev knows what she's thinking.

"I went over there for dinner once," she tells Noemi, "a few months ago."

"Was it weird?"

"Yep."

"Mikey said I could come over anytime, for a visit, but I can't sleep there anymore." When Noemi looks up, her eyes are bright. "I thought I could go away and you'd be okay. You know, not lonely, because you have family here."

"They're not our family."

"They care about us," Noemi says emphatically, almost fiercely.

"I know. But we're adults now." Officially out of care. "We don't need support anymore."

"Everyone needs support."

"I'm your support." Never mind that she can't afford to feed Noemi. Ev's stomach growls, as if to emphasize the point.

"Pannekoeken, Ev. Three o'clock is not too late for breakfast."

"I can't." Ev looks toward the kitchen, willing food to appear in her cupboards. She has rice and ketchup, and the small wad of cash Ken gave her yesterday. But she needs to make that last until she has a plan.

"Come on. There's plenty of time before the market starts."

"We can't afford to keep eating out. Walk with me to the store. I'll make the lentil curry you like."

"What was that look? What's wrong?" Ev blinks at Noemi. "That look you gave me just now," Noemi persists. "You're upset. What happened?"

"I lost my table at the market."

Noemi stops fanning her toes and drops her head into her knees. "Because of me?"

"No. I mean, yes, that was the last straw, but Ken's been waiting for a reason."

"That's fucked. They can't just take your table away."

"Actually, they can. The Association never wanted me there to begin with. They rejected my application this year and last. Ken and Vivian let me sublet. But I'm more trouble than I'm worth."

"Assholes. What are you going to do?"

"I don't know. Flea market, I guess?"

"Gross. That place smells like old shoes. And anyway, no one goes there to spend money."

"I know." Ev studies the floral pattern on her sheets, tiny roses and forget-me-nots. She found them, along with the rest of her bedding, in an alley in the West End. "I'm going to have to get a real job."

Noemi cracks up. "Omigod, remember the time you worked at the pizza place? That lasted, what, three days?"

"That was bad." Ev can't share Noemi's amusement. A family-run franchise, the kitchen oozed marital discord from every surface. Ev shudders, remembering the hot stabs of anger that assaulted her every time she picked up the phone to take an order, the taut cords of disgust and frustration that ran through the razor-sharp slicer. Bile tickles the back of her throat at the memory of laying her hands on that piece of machinery.

"I have to be careful, is all. Pick a cleaner environment." She would never have taken that job if she'd known what the kitchen felt like.

"You gonna roll out pizza dough in those

gloves?"

"I can do it." Noemi's teasing has turned her sour. Ev doesn't sound convincing, even to herself.

"You'd be miserable. Aw, honey." Noemi rolls off the bed and crawls over to her. She rubs Ev's shoulders. Ev tries to relax under her touch. "We'll figure something out. It's summer. You can put a blanket out on the Drive, over by the old post office. Save up for a street vending license."

"In the meantime, how are we going to pay the rent?"

"I can work too, you know. I'll start looking for waitressing jobs tomorrow."

Noemi should be going to school. She's smart enough and she doesn't have Ev's stupid affliction. She doesn't have to spend her life scraping by. But that's an argument for another day, and Ev doesn't want to goad her sister into another road trip quite yet. She pulls off her gloves, examines the angry red lines her fingernails have left in her palms.

"There is another option." Ev hesitates. She realizes she's afraid to tell Noemi about Harriet. She knows what Noemi will say, and she's not sure she wants to hear it.

Her stomach rumbles again. If Noemi weren't here, Ev would boil rice and dump ketchup on top, then ride over the bridge to see what she could dig up in the bins out back of the bakeries and produce stalls of Granville Island. When it's not a market day, she and Owen often meet there at closing time to fill their baskets with the day's castoffs. Ev isn't ashamed of this. It keeps her belly full, and it amuses her to feast for free on the same cranberry-pecan sourdough loaf that the woman loading the trunk of her Mercedes a few feet away has just paid eight dollars for.

But it's different with Noemi here. They've never lived together as adults. Ev transitioned out of care three years ago, and Noemi stayed on with Joan and Mikey. She visited Ev on weekends, and they made plans for after, once Noemi had finished high school. But when it was Noemi's turn to leave, she went in the opposite direction, away from Ev.

Living together has been only an idea until now. And now, looking at her mattress on the floor, her scavenged bedclothes, and feeling the twist of her hunger, Ev knows she wants more for Noemi than she wants for herself. She doesn't want her to eat for free because she has no other choice. She wants Noemi to have choices.

"I was offered a job today," she says. And

she tells Noemi everything. Everything about Harriet, from the jar of buttons to the possibilities Harriet opened up to Ev on the steps outside of her apartment. She tells Noemi all of it, except for the part about the flower blooming at her touch. That part freaks her out enough, she doesn't feel ready to put it into words.

Noemi reacts exactly as Ev knew she would. She leaps up from the bed as Ev speaks, and paces the room, interjecting with questions, shaking the boa so that she leaves a circle of pink feathers in her wake.

"I can't believe there's someone else out there like you. Has this ever happened? I thought you were the only one."

"So did I."

Noemi stops moving for a moment, chews her lip furiously, staring at the floor intently as she thinks.

"What is it?"

"Nothing," Noemi says. "What if there are others? I bet there are others. How cool is that?"

Not cool at all.

"When can I meet Harriet? You're taking the job, right?"

"I don't know."

"Omigod, you have to take that job!"

"It would make things easier," Ev agrees.

127

"Not because of the money, dimwit. You need Harriet. She's going to help you get better."

Ev doesn't want to agree, and yet she can't suppress a tiny thrill of excitement. *You can be free.*

"Ev, this is amazing. You know this is going to change your life, don't you?"

"There are risks involved."

"Everything worth doing is risky."

"You don't understand."

"Of course I don't," Noemi snaps. "You won't let me." Tension crackles in the air like the sudden onset of a summer storm. The old argument, the same one that split them months ago, rolls in heavy and dark over their heads. Noemi may have brushed it off at the noodle house, but Ev knew it would intrude eventually. Still, even with the months of brooding over it, of rehashing and promising herself she wouldn't mess up again, Ev's not ready for it. Maybe she'll never be ready. Maybe there won't ever be a right time.

"You know what happened with our father," she stalls, preparing herself. Her stomach clenches, hunger turned to queasy anxiety.

"I know what any ass who can use Google knows." Noemi launches onto the bed face-first, burrows her head into Ev's pillow. She sounds as tired as Ev feels of the familiar script.

"You're right. I promised I'd tell you, and I meant it," Ev says. "I'm not going to make excuses this time."

Noemi stills. Moments pass in silence, neither of them moving. Ev steadies her voice. "I need to show you something."

BEFORE

Evelyn draws stars and spirals in the margins of her exercise book while she watches her father at work in the shop. This side of the barn is tidier than the workshop side. Here, the floors are regularly swept and the furniture dusted. It's still a jumble, but the pieces are fully refinished, all shining wood and plush new fabric. On top of every available surface sit lamps, vases, and decorative odds and ends, except for the big desk at the back where Daddy does the books, and where Evelyn now sits on an old stool with a seat that spins. On quiet days, he lets Evelyn stay with him after school so that she can finish her homework without interruptions from Noemi. There have been more quiet days lately, so Evelyn has been spending a lot of time behind Daddy's desk, even when, like today, she doesn't actually have homework. She spreads out her exercise books along with worksheets she's already completed, and pretends to be busy.

Daddy is finalizing the sale of the green chair. He finished it last weekend, and just as he predicted, it was only on the shop floor for a few days before it captured a customer's attention. A woman with red hair and a bright floral blouse is gushing over Daddy's expert restoration. She runs her fingers along the green velvet, and Evelyn can see how the happiness in the chair soaks up into the woman's fingers and makes her eyes soft. That's how happy the chair feels. Sitting in it is like curling up with a litter of sleeping puppies. The woman doesn't know she's soaking up the happiness, but it makes her want the chair more. That's why Daddy puts the objects with feelings at the front, or anywhere else he wants to lead his customers. It's funny to watch people drift around the shop, unconsciously touching the things Daddy has carefully placed to lure them deeper inside. Mostly, he chooses items that bring smiles to faces, but he has a few tricks, too. Inside a vase next to the door he has hidden a deck of cards. The cards have a strong rushing feeling that Evelyn doesn't have a word for. Daddy says it's a gentle encouragement for his customers to spend more money.

Evelyn knows the chair will have a good

home, but still, she is sad to see it go. She would like to run over and say goodbye, but she has promised never ever to interrupt Daddy when he's with a customer. She wishes they could keep the chair, even though she knows they need the money from this sale. Her parents don't talk about money around her, but she's not dumb. She knows what it means when there are too many quiet days at the shop. She's seen how Mama is more careful at the grocery store, taking the time to compare prices, pulling coupons from her wallet at the checkout. They don't stop for ice cream on the way home anymore. Evelyn notices these little things.

She keeps her head down while he runs the woman's credit card. She doesn't let her tears fall until he has picked up the chair to follow the woman to her car. Daddy's humming to himself when he returns. When he meets Evelyn's eyes, he stops.

"Evelyn. What's wrong?"

She shakes her head. "Nothing."

"Is it the chair?"

She shrugs. Her father puts a finger to his lips, thinking, and then he pulls a small wad of tissue from his pocket.

"Here, I found this for you."

She unwraps the tissue. There's a tiny

ceramic kitten inside, holding an even tinier ceramic ball of blue yarn. She holds it in her palm.

"Love," she says.

"What else?"

She waits, letting the love sink into her skin. "A mother."

"That's right, maternal love. Well done." He bends and kisses the top of her head. "You can keep that one."

"Thank you, Daddy." She places the kitten on the papers in front of her. She can tell by the way he lingers nearby that he has more to say.

"You mustn't cry over a chair," he tells her.

"I know."

"This is the work we do. We find old things that are no longer wanted. If necessary, we make them beautiful again, as beautiful on the outside as they are on the inside. And then we find them new homes."

"But I'll miss it." It feels like losing a friend.

"Nonsense," says her father. "Remember, the object only reflects a feeling that came from a human. It holds a story from where it came from, but it's not alive." As if he's reading her mind, he adds, "The chair is not your friend. It is only a chair."

Evelyn sighs in frustration. She knows the chair isn't her friend. She knows it's not alive. She wants to explain better, but can't find the right words. It's a happy-sad feeling, like when they read *Charlotte's Web.* Daddy read out loud while all of them snuggled in the big bed together. Afterward, when Mama was wiping her eyes, Evelyn tried to explain that she shouldn't be sad because spiders aren't supposed to live very long, not like people. Mama said, "It's not that. I'm crying because I loved the story, and now it's over."

This is how Evelyn feels about the chair. Mama would understand.

"You love objects, too," she points out. She knows she sounds pouty, but she can't help herself.

"I do." He smiles. "But not as much as I love you, or Noemi, or your mother." He strokes her chin until she smiles back at him, shaking her head and pulling away because his touch tickles her. "People matter most, Evelyn. Not things. Never forget that."

12

Harriet enters the library with a bubble of joy in her chest. What a miraculous place. Seven floors of heaven, hundreds of thousands of books, and so many of them singing out their own tiny souls, brought to life through the hands of strangers. She can't hear their individual voices, but they hum all around her like the distant frog song she used to hear at night coming up from the riverbanks when she was a child. Back when there were still frogs.

She hasn't been inside the library in years. Too difficult. She borrowed too many bright books in earlier days, books she couldn't bring herself to return. They're a source of shame, kept for so long she can no longer pretend they are on loan. She can feel her palms itching, eager to touch stories. But she mustn't get distracted, not today. She has research to do.

Somewhere in her second bedroom there

lives an old laptop, a Christmas gift from an ex-lover. She kept it as a reminder of his misdirected thoughtfulness. He always felt Harriet should be keeping up with modern technology. She appreciates this, but she could never muster up much interest in computers. Why get one's information from a dead box when there are living books to glean from? Facts are only a part of the truth. So much can be learned from books beyond what can be found in the words printed on the page. A properly bright book will tell a story far more multifaceted than any poorly edited web page. Harriet finds little appeal in a cold screen full of text.

Of course, finding the information one needs in books is more difficult than plugging one's question into a search engine, but that's part of the wonder of it. It's a treasure hunt, an intricate dance through a paper maze, moving from one book to the next in search of nuggets of information, and what untold diversions might be discovered along the way. She's lost entire days in libraries, forgetting why she came in the first place.

No forgetting this day. Evelyn's story awaits her. Harriet pushes aside the shadow that follows the girl's name, a wisp of worry that's been haunting her since they met.

Never mind that yet. She takes the escalator to the third floor and stands next to the community bulletin board, momentarily lost. The reference desk is gone; in its place stands a directory, color-coded by floor, and a telephone. That's something, a telephone complete with a handset and a cord — how quaint. It's not a live human, but it beats a computer. Presumably, she will reach a live human if she picks it up.

"Hello? Hello?" She punches the number on the laminated card tacked above the phone.

"Information. How can I assist you to-day?"

"I need assistance. Send a person. A real person, please."

"Of course. If you look to your right, you'll see a directory. Are you looking for popular fiction or magazines?"

"No. I'm here for research. People still do research at libraries, do they not?"

"There are several computer workstations on the third floor. If —"

"I can see that. I don't need a computer. I need a person, a real person."

A light touch grazes Harriet's elbow.

"Do you need help finding something?"

A young man stands next to her, long-haired and wearing a pink T-shirt that reads

137

This Is What a Feminist Looks Like. Harriet has to look way up to find his smile. He has exceptional posture for a child of his generation.

"Are you a librarian?"

"I am a librarian," he says. He sounds both pleased and surprised. "My name is Raj. How can I help?"

Harriet puts the phone down. "I need to track down an old newspaper article. Local paper, the *Sun.* Early 2000s, I believe."

"Splendid." He says it like he means it. "We'll have to dig into the microfiche reels. This way, please."

Harriet follows Raj up two more floors on the escalator. Now that she's chosen Ev as the heir to her collection (an idea that, once sprouted, has taken root in her mind and grown into a stalk so strong and tall, she simply can't shake it loose), she needs to know who she's dealing with. Ev has a story, for certain. It bubbles to the surface in the panic she displays at every hint of darkness in a treasure. Harriet doesn't mind secrets. They're necessary for survival in this world. She suspects Ev's, but she needs to find out for sure before she opens her life to this strange, startling, powerful child.

They pass a row of small meeting rooms and a cluster of computer workstations, making their way toward several rows of putty-colored metal file cabinets, where the microfiche and film collections are kept.

"Right here we have copies of every issue of the *Sun* from 1912 on. Have you ever used microfiche reels?"

"I prefer the real deal." Harriet knows she has an original of the issue. She can visualize the stack it lingers under, long buried and useless to her. If she closes her eyes, she can almost see the grainy front-page photo.

You have more than just a newspaper, don't you?

No, never mind that. Not yet.

"Don't worry, I'll help you get started." The librarian grabs a red plastic bin from the top of the filing cabinet and pulls open a long, shallow drawer, revealing rows and rows of small white cardboard boxes with neatly typed labels.

"Any chance you can narrow down your dates a little? Each reel's got about ten days of papers. One year's going to be thirty-six of these little guys." He pats the tops of the boxes.

"I've got time." Anyway, she only has to look at the front pages.

"Right. Starting with January 2000, then." He begins to fill the bin.

Harriet has little to go on besides intuition. The only details she was able to pry from Owen are that Ev is twenty-two years old, with a younger sister and no parents. These tidbits, plus Ev's aversion to bright objects, were enough to give Harriet's memory an unpleasant jog.

They sit side by side in front of a large screen. Raj demonstrates the process of loading and winding the reels and the various knobs for twisting and pulling, to rotate and to focus.

"Now, I might be able to make this easier for you if you'll let me search online to narrow down your dates. If there's a particular story?" Raj fixes her with an expectant gaze.

"There is."

"I'd need a search term."

"Murder," says Harriet.

He pauses only for the briefest moment. "That's not going to narrow it down much, I'm afraid. A name would be more effective."

It would be, if only the family name weren't eluding her. "Thank you. I can take it from here."

"As you wish." He bows his head as he speaks, a slight smile on his lips, before unfolding from the chair. "I'll come check on you later."

She spins the knob, watching not for words but for photographs. The need to look at only the front page story makes for quicker work. The scrape of the film under the glass as the images spin past sets Harriet's teeth on edge, but she keeps spinning. Her fingers grow grimy with dust from the reel boxes, as though she's been sifting through old records at a garage sale, and she closes her eyes often against the glare and motion of the screen.

Twenty-five boxes pile up one by one on the return tray. Pages and pages whir by, the film making a flickering sound as it winds onto the take-up spool, *click, click, click.* Then, when she gets to the end, the film winds back again, faster this time, *click, click, click, click, click.* Twenty-six boxes. Harriet's eyes grow sore, and she begins to feel nauseous. She looks away, watches a homeless woman lay newspaper on a chair nearby, stack her plastic bags of bottles and cans on the table around her, sit, spread more paper neatly in front of her, lay her head down, and fall asleep.

She returns to her work. *Click, click, click.* Twenty-seven. And then there it is, so startling in its reality that she feels an electric jolt run through her body at the sight of it. She sits for a long while with her hand frozen on the knob, library activity buzzing distantly all around her, reading the terrible words of the headline over and over again.

Valley Horror: Two Dead in Apparent Murder-Suicide.

The photos, the ones her mind has been reaching for, are right below the headline. The murky, yellow-green screen makes it difficult to see the images clearly. They seem to float beneath brackish water, revealing only the wide planes of cheekbones and brows against a dark background, the eyes black sockets. They look dead already. The first photo shows a man standing in front of an antiques store. *Allan Marchand, local antiques dealer,* reads the caption, *killed his wife and himself last night.* The second photo is a close-up of a woman. *Neighbors told the* Sun *that Chunlan Huang and the couple's two children had not been seen in several days.*

Harriet doesn't want to read it. She remembers the awful story well. The details were splashed all over the news for days during a hot summer. Two dead in a rural area just outside of the city. A woman stabbed until her body was unrecognizable, and one man, covered in blood, found dead in the backyard. Her throat tightens as she connects this locally famous horror with the haunted girl she met only a few days ago. Worse, though, is the nauseating shame that rises, turning her stomach to acid and flaming her cheeks, as she remembers her own connection to the story.

"Ma'am? Are you all right?"

Her librarian is back, hovering to the right of her seat. Harriet realizes her cheeks are wet.

"Fine, dear. I'm old. Everything makes me tear up these days. Human suffering. Sentimental advertisements. Dust." Harriet pulls a tissue out of the roll in her sleeve and dabs at her eyes.

Raj touches her shoulder gently. "Can I call someone?"

Harriet waves him away. "Not necessary," she mutters. Still, the boy hovers. "Lovely watch," she says, falling back on an old trick, half-gleaned from the brightness on the watch and a half-wild guess. "Your father loves you very much, even if he doesn't call."

"I know," says the librarian, unperturbed.

Usually the psychic act throws people off-balance long enough for her to make an escape. At least the boy seems to sense her desire for solitude. He touches her shoulder again, pointing in the direction of the periodicals. "I'll be right over there if you

143

need me."

She returns to her work, the work of remembering. She owes it to Ev. The worry shadow has returned, has draped itself over her shoulders, weighing her down. A doubt shadow has joined it, a hulking, lumpy shadow, rough-textured, with roses woven into it. Covered in a white sheet, heavy with fear. Spindle dining chairs stacked in oppressive towers. Harriet's gut clenches, a familiar clamminess dampening her palms. It feels like home. For the first time, she considers if perhaps acquiring Ev is a very bad idea.

No motive for the killing was ever uncovered, although people who knew Allan Marchand spoke of increasingly erratic behavior. Explosive anger, refusal to sell items to customers, and, in the days before the tragedy, the unexplained closure of his shop. No one knows what happened in the last forty-eight hours, when Allan and his family were at home, isolated, alone. The bodies were discovered after a neighbor awoke to frightened cries outside. She opened her door to find an unnamed four-year-old girl huddled on her doorstep. And out of the woods next to the driveway emerged another girl, no more than eight, her feet bare, and the hem of her nightgown bloody.

Harriet doesn't need their names to know those girls are Evelyn and her little sister.

13

The box is nestled inside a small wooden crate with handles, gray splintered wood with *HELMS CO.* stenciled on either end in large block letters. Layers of packing tape at least ten years old hold its flaps down tight. Ev has moved this box three times without ever opening it, afraid less of stains than of the more ordinary pain of remembering.

"What is it?" Even Noemi's whisper echoes down the hallway of the storage room.

"It's our history." Ev backs into the corner of the tiny unit so that Noemi can come inside. The moisture has vanished from her mouth, her tongue clicking against her teeth as she speaks. "It's all that's left from the house."

Ev hears Noemi's intake of breath even though she's turned away, crouched next to the crate.

"I didn't think there was anything left."

"This is it. Only . . . personal items. Photographs. Papers . . ." Ev trails off.

"How do you know what's in here if you've never opened it?" Noemi begins picking at the edges of the tape. "Seriously, Ev. What if there's a . . . a property deed in here, or a key to a safety deposit box?"

"There's nothing like that. Lisa would've told me." The house and its contents were sold to pay off their father's debts. Of which there were many. Noemi knows this as well as Ev does. Only a few personal things were saved, held by the public trustee to pass on to Ev on her eighteenth birthday. Nothing of significant value, Lisa told her. She gave Ev an itemized list as well, but Ev dropped that in the trash on her way out of the building that day. The box she saved, but only for Noemi.

"What if there are family contacts?"

"If we had family contacts, we wouldn't have ended up in foster care."

Ev doesn't know why they have no information on their extended families. If they have grandparents, she's never met them. She remembers only that their little family unit existed as if in its own universe. She remembers how her mother nurtured a strong bond between Ev and Noemi, how important it seemed to her that they were

147

close, and the sadness that sometimes flickered across her face when she watched them at play.

Ev startles as Noemi pulls the first strip of tape off, the tearing sound loud and jarring in the tiny space. Wedging herself in the corner against the shelf, Ev sinks to the floor, wraps her arms around her knees, and covers her ears while Noemi works.

"How long have you had this?"

"Four years."

"Asshole."

Maybe. But this is why. Noemi's known about the box for less than a minute and already she's folded back its cardboard flaps and stuck her nose inside. Ev's stomach lurches.

"It's mostly photos. Omigod," Noemi breathes. "Look at this." She lifts a small, framed photograph out.

"Please don't." Ev turns her face away, swallows. "I'll answer questions, but I don't want to see."

Noemi doesn't reply. After a moment, she sets the frame on the floor, out of Ev's view. Ev's shoulders drop slightly. So far, she hasn't been assaulted by vibrations from any stains. A low-level energy radiates from inside the box, but it doesn't feel threatening, more like the usual washed-out mix of nostalgia and love that accompanies any normal family's memorabilia.

Noemi slides a photo album out, black with gold script on the front. *Our Family.* The stiff pages crack when she opens it. Ev gets busy studying a daddy longlegs making its shambling way up the side of the bookshelf.

When Noemi's echoing voice breaks the silence, Ev flinches.

"What was he like?"

Ev knew these questions would come, knew she'd have to provide answers, from the moment she received that voice mail from Noemi two days before. She told herself it was worth it to have Noemi back, to have her stay. In the far corners of her mind, she's been preparing, thinking what to tell her, planning how much she will need to say in order to satisfy her sister.

Still, the words stick in her throat. There are so many answers to that question. Her mind gropes, settles on the script she's been silently rehearsing in the months Noemi has been away. She begins to speak.

"He was an antiques dealer. He had a shop; this old barn on the property beside our house, and it was full of beautiful things. Mostly furniture. He restored a lot of it himself. Some of them were stained, some not. I used to help him track down stained items, once he realized I could feel them like he did."

My special girl.

"We went to estate sales together, or I'd hang out in his workshop and help him restore furniture." The workshop flashes in her mind. White flaking paint, tiny square windows, and a single bulb hanging from the roof, weak yellow light casting shadows on exposed beams. The *scritch scratch* of the stick sliding across the floor.

Stop making that sound.

"He was fascinated by the darkness in things, drawn to bad stains. It . . . got worse over time."

"Stop it." Noemi glares over her shoulder. Her eyes are glassy.

"What?" Ev snaps. "You wanted to know. You asked." *You're the reason we're down here.*

"I said 'she,' Ev. What was *she* like? Jesus."

Heat flares in Ev's cheeks as if she's been slapped. In Noemi's lap lies the photograph. Ev catches a glimpse, a sweep of black hair that leaves her dizzy. Their mother.

"I can't remember," she mumbles, the same words she's been grasping at reflexively for years. "Only a little," she admits.

"I'd settle for a little."

150

"She wore a blue sweater." Woolen and nubby, the color of fresh blueberries. "She made us steamed eggs." Ev sees her mother's hands setting the cups of frothy egg into the steamer, light filtering through red checked curtains onto a countertop flecked with gold. Her throat constricts. It's hard to breathe. She hears the air whistling through her windpipe, counts herself down.

"You look like her," Noemi says. "More than I do."

Ev doesn't argue, although she doesn't agree. Noemi's eyes may be rounder than Ev's, and her skin a trace paler, but when Ev looks in the mirror, she only sees her father's full lips and heavy jaw.

"Maybe if you looked at some of these photos, it would —"

"No!" The cry bounces off the walls, harsh and ragged. Ev lowers her tone. "Not yet." She squeezes her eyes shut, tries to breathe the shaking away. She feels Noemi's hands on her knees, gentle pressure.

"Okay. Okay." A quiet voice. "Go upstairs. I'll be down here for a while."

Relief washes over Ev, turning her limbs wobbly. She nods. "Take as long as you need."

"But I want you to answer one question first." Noemi tightens her grip on Ev's knees. Ev can't meet her eyes. She knows the question.

"Were you there? Did you see him do it?"

She still sees it. Not every time she closes her eyes, like when she was younger. Not anymore. But some nights when she lies alone in her bed, or when her eyes catch on the wrong news headline, or when she handles sharp objects, or when she hears a male voice raised in anger, or when she sees certain cuts of raw beef at the market, or a certain shade of stain on a beige carpet.

There is no safe place.

"Yeah," she tells Noemi. "I was there. I saw."

She pushes herself to standing, squeezes past Noemi to the door. Noemi doesn't speak until she's stepped out into the hallway.

"You're not him, you know."

"I know." *But I could be.*

"He became a monster because he was weak. That's not going to happen to you."

"Because I protect myself."

"No," says Noemi. "Because you're going to learn how to be strong. You're going to let that woman teach you."

14

"You sure this is where you want to go?"

The cabbie makes eye contact with Harriet through the rearview mirror. The taxi idles in front of a building with cardboard in its windows and a padlocked iron gate in front of the door. A *For Lease* sign leans against the bars of one window. Most of the city block consists of more empty spaces like this one. The only populated storefronts hold a wholesale Chinese florist and a bottle depot. When Harriet was young, this was a bustling, thriving neighborhood. Over the years, it's become a between place; a place to drive through on your way somewhere else. Which makes it perfect for Harriet's purposes.

"This is it." Harriet hands the driver a folded bill. "Home sweet home."

An unremarkable building, but that's the point. Once upon a time, it was a bank. Hints of its past remain in the two stories of gray, sooty, dull concrete. Faux-Roman columns stretch up either side of the doorway, although at some point the doors themselves have been replaced with a standard commercial glass entry. The street number and building name are etched into the arch above, and traces of gold paint still cling in spots: *663 E. Montgomery St., The Woolston Building, est. 1910.* Above that, a plexiglass sign has been fixed to the stone, a red dragon painted on it and the words *Szechuan Dragon Chinese Restaurant. Open Late.* Someone has thrown a rock through the dragon's head.

She smiles. Harriet's very own between place. She pulls a manila envelope out of her purse. It contains all the keys, picked up first thing this morning at her lawyer's office. The gate scrapes on pavement as she pulls it open. Empty coffee cups and cigarette butts gather outside the door. She pushes them aside with her foot. The metal door handle cools her fingers. The dead bolt slides open reluctantly, and the building holds its breath as Harriet enters. She puts a hand on the wall and eases herself to the dusty floor to wait for Owen. She's come early to allow herself and the building some time to settle into each other.

Harriet chose the Woolston for several

reasons, but the most important is its particular brightness. Not all buildings are bright. If they are, people often accuse such structures of being haunted. A truth, of sorts. You infuse a building with enough emotion and it takes on a life of its own. Harriet's new building isn't that kind of bright, not over-bright. It won't interfere. Its ordinariness is part of its magic. No tragedies, angers, or sorrows have been steeped into its walls. Instead, it speaks of gratitude and protection. It holds the old bank layer of security and authority. But it has the other, too. The restaurant was a family affair. There's a sense of solace to the place, togetherness. And something more, a safe feeling, but Harriet isn't sure what that means. Only that it feels right. If she could drag Ev here, the girl would likely put her finger on it in a moment.

"It's a good space."

Harriet's heart stops. She blinks into the light shining through the door. It's Ev. She has a talent, this girl, for showing up out of the blue whenever Harriet wishes for her, like a frowning, disheveled fairy godmother. Harriet opens her mouth to speak, but her brain calls up an image of a barefoot child with blood on the hem of her nightgown, and the words on her tongue evaporate.

Luckily, Owen trundles in behind Ev, hauling a box of cleaning supplies and a mop.

"Morning, Harriet. I brought us some company. I hope you don't mind."

"Of course not." She nods at Ev, half-determined not to startle her again, half-hoping she'll spook and dart away, bounding off through the traffic and disappearing into the tangle of downtown forever. *Be careful what you wish for,* she thinks.

"I thought you might have some boxes for me to carry in." Owen smiles mildly.

"I didn't get to it last night." A lie. Harriet intended to bring over a box or two each time she visited, to start relieving her apartment of its burden. She spent several hours last night trying to decide which things to start with. In the end, she brought only two bright items with her, and even those were not deliberate. The bird stone and Frédérique still hide in her jacket pockets, one in each. They are fitting treasures, she realizes, like bookends for her vision for this place. Peace and love. Comfort and joy. She'll do her best to leave them here at the end of the day.

"If you like, I can help you retrieve some later."

"No, not today."

Owen nods. "Well. Plenty of time for that."

There isn't. Only three weeks remain until she has to be out of her apartment. Owen has boxed up as much as he can, given the lack of available packing space. She can't put off the move much longer. But having him in her space, moving things around and hiding them away, has been more difficult than she anticipated.

"I'll get started on the cleanup." Owen vanishes into the kitchen, an ugly renovation at the back of the building, furnished in stainless steel, where once, Harriet imagines, brisk tellers in skirts and pantyhose counted out bills on polished oak counters. Ev circles the empty room, staring up at the molding on the ceiling, the chandelier that is still blessedly intact.

"It's huge. You could fit three apartments full of stuff in here." Ev glares at her. "I told you I'm not going to help you collect more."

"I won't ask you to do that." True, if somewhat misleading, but that's a conversation for later. Right now, she only needs to get Ev on board. "Your job is to sort through what I already have. To choose the right items to populate this space."

To bring Harriet's mess to order. To create something beautiful out of the chaos. Harriet can picture it now, the objects ordered by their particular resonance, items hanging on walls and even mounted from the ceiling, shelves partitioning the rooms to create a maze with purpose, drawing people into nooks of discovery. It will be a participatory museum. She sees people moving through the space, touching the treasures, interacting with them, joy inducing more joy, beauty begetting more beauty. Her collection would grow more alive every day instead of languishing in a dark storage container somewhere, its life slowly leaching away. Harriet owes the world a little beauty.

A wave of dizziness passes over her as she speaks. She's never let anyone touch her bright things. The idea terrifies her. But she presses on. She needs to let go. She doesn't have the talent to build what she imagines, not on her own.

She pulls the bird stone out of her pocket and places it on the windowsill next to the front door. It seems to belong there, although it may seem that way only because of where she found the stone. Two weeks ago, on the way to her favorite lunch spot, she noticed it tucked in the corner of a pharmacy window. She almost left it, thinking whoever had brightened the curves of that stone might come back to find it. Except it seemed to have been placed deliberately, as though its owner had decided it should move on, soften the edges of another's life, or as if the stone itself were looking for a new pocket to warm.

Ev's voice interrupts her thoughts.

"You said you want me to curate your collection."

"Yes. Your choices will dictate what energies exist here."

"And you really think we can help people by doing this?"

"I do. We'll offer our visitors a place to feel hope, confidence, courage, or whatever it is that they need."

Harriet wills Ev to think of the implications of this. It could be bigger than individual healing, even. The right energies seeping through the walls of this building could revitalize a neighborhood rather than poison it. The more Harriet thinks about the potential for transformation, the more excited she gets. This building might only be the first. There could be others, each with its own personality. Each of them a gift to the city. Of course, she knows better than to suggest such a thing. Too soon for that.

"This place kept someone safe, someone who needed it," says Ev. "Someone lived here."

"It was a bank, once upon a time. A

restaurant. I don't know about apartments. Perhaps on the second floor." She knew there were offices upstairs, but she hadn't fully explored.

Ev shakes her head. "The someone who lived here wanted to be overlooked. Where's the vault?"

The vaults are another reason why this is the perfect place.

"There are two." She points at the room behind them, a small space to the right of the kitchen. "They opened up this one to use as a private dining room. Still has reinforced concrete walls. The other one is in the basement."

Harriet rises, slowly, and leads Ev down a hallway, past the washrooms, to the stairs. The stairs lead down to a storeroom and the vault. Four hundred square feet, with walls three feet thick and a forty-ton door, still in working order. The door is propped open. Ev isn't looking at it. She points to the corner of the storeroom.

"There. Someone lived right there." Harriet imagines it, a cot and a lamp on an empty crate. A safe haven for someone who needed it. An undocumented immigrant, maybe, or a battered wife, or a dishwasher without a home. Harriet doesn't generally like basements, not at all, but this one Ev is right about. It has a good, safe feeling.

Ev's gaze flicks to the vault. "That will come in handy."

"I thought we could use it for items you think need more containment."

"I get to choose which things go in there."

Harriet says nothing, just nods. Out of nowhere, the girl reaches out a hand — no glove — and plucks Frédérique from Harriet's pocket. Harriet can practically see the tremor that runs through Ev's body, although the girl's face remains expressionless. Her breathing intensifies, though, drawing in and out noisily through her nose. Ev stands with Frédérique in her hand for a full minute. Sweat beads along her hairline, and still she doesn't move.

Imagine being so terrified of that little bit of velvet and joy. Harriet is no fool. She's seen the damage done by hateful things. She knows bright things are anything but benign. There's a reason she wants the vault in working order. She's seen objects destroy lives. But to fear them so much as to avoid all contact — it can only make a person more vulnerable. You have to be strong in order to keep your soul intact.

As Harriet watches, Frédérique comes awake in Ev's palm. One soft paw stretches up, and his tail winds around the girl's pinkie finger. Ev's breath grows shaky, but she holds, letting the monkey speak to her. Another minute and Ev opens her eyes. Tears there. And something else. Hope. Harriet swallows her envy of Ev's talent and allows her own hope to flare up and meet the girl's.

"We go at my pace. I don't touch anything with a bad vibe. I don't touch anything I don't want to. If I need a break, I can go out, get some air. I choose my hours. I get to wear gloves if I want to. You pay me in cash. This ends when I say it ends."

"Yes," says Harriet. And it is done.

BEFORE

Evelyn stands outside of her father's work-shop, frozen. It's Sunday, and Daddy has come home with a truck full of things. For a while, they went together every weekend. Then business slowed down, and they switched to every second Sunday. The last time they went out together, Daddy wanted to buy some things that Evelyn didn't like. They felt happy at first touch, but underneath they had less happy feelings, ones that would muck up the shop and make customers feel bad. When she tried to convince Daddy not to bring them home, he said they couldn't afford to be so picky. After that, he stopped inviting her.

This is the first load he's brought home in weeks. Until a moment ago, Evelyn was excited to see what he'd found, and hoping there was a new furniture project for them to work on together. Mama made her finish folding laundry first, so by the time she ran outside, the back of the truck was empty. As she got close to the barn, her stomach began to turn somersaults. She slowed down, then stopped. Now, for the first time she can remember, she does not want to go inside the barn. There's a very bad feeling in there, and Evelyn is afraid.

She stuffs her hands into the pocket of her hoodie, pressing her stomach to hold it steady. Then she takes a deep breath, thinking about her lessons with Daddy on how to approach a new object. There's no need to be afraid. The feelings objects hold are only impressions from people who came before. They can seem ghostly and even frightening at times, especially if the feelings are sad or angry, but they can't hurt her.

Evelyn's ability to sense the feelings is stronger than ever, stronger even than her father's. She doesn't need to touch the objects anymore. She can sense them from several feet away. When she does touch, sometimes she sees pictures, flashes of memory, visions that can be confusing or startling. She takes a moment to listen now, to pay attention to the feelings coming at her from the workshop. Anger, the kind when you think something is unfair, and blame. The feelings seem weaker than when she first approached. Her tummy knots ease a little. Maybe putting words to them helps. She steps inside.

The angry feeling comes from an old sewing machine set in a wood table with an iron base. The machine is black and beetle shiny. Evelyn thinks for a moment that it dislikes her as much as she dislikes it, before she remembers that it's not a beetle. It's not alive. It's just a hunk of metal. She ignores it, putting an imaginary wall between herself and the machine, and then scans the room for her father. He stands in the darkest corner of the workshop, his back turned to her. There is a metal filing cabinet tucked away there, where he holds small objects of value that need repair or refinishing. One of his hands rests on the front of the cabinet, the other dangles at his side. He is motionless. From within the cabinet, Evelyn can feel another object. It's worse than the sewing machine. There's a big knot of feelings there that she doesn't want to untangle. It makes her throat dry and her palms damp. She can't imagine why her father is still standing so close to that knot, still not moving. Her stomach clenches again.

"Daddy?"

He jerks away and turns to her.

"Evelyn," he says sharply. "What are you

165

doing here?"

"It's Sunday," she answers in a whisper.

"Of course it is," he says more softly. He moves out of the shadows. His face is red and sweaty, but he smiles at her kindly. "Did you see what I found?"

Evelyn doesn't speak. She doesn't understand why he would bring home an angry object like the sewing machine, or whatever he has just locked in the filing cabinet. He strides over, eyes alight.

"This," he announces, "is a Singer Blackside Featherweight."

It has a beautiful name, yet she can't help but flinch when he runs a hand over the top of it. "See the dark faceplate here?" He taps the side of the machine. "Black oxide finish. This machine was made during World War II. It's very rare and very valuable." His voice is high with excitement.

"But," says Evelyn. She's not sure what to say next.

"You're concerned about the feeling," he finishes for her. "But you don't need to worry. This piece won't be here long." He pats the top of the machine with satisfaction. "I have a customer who's been looking for one of these."

"But," says Evelyn again.

"But what?" snaps Daddy. Then he smiles

again. Evelyn sees that he removes his hand from the machine and wipes it, without noticing, on his jeans. "I know what you're thinking. You're worried about the customer."

Evelyn nods.

"Can objects hurt you?"

"No?"

"No." Daddy kneels so he can look her in the eye. He appears calm again, more like the Daddy she knows. "Remember that you're growing more sensitive, my special girl. What you feel is not the same as what my customer will feel. I promise you, she will be fine."

"I don't like it."

"No, I don't suppose you do." He rocks back and forth on his heels, thinking, then slaps his thigh. "I have just the thing." He leaps to his feet and jogs away.

"Come, come," he calls over his shoulder.

Evelyn follows. As she passes by the corner where the filing cabinet keeps its secret, her heart speeds up. Daddy heads to the big wardrobe beside his desk where he keeps the holiday decorations. He pulls out a box and rummages inside.

"Ah," he says. "Here."

He's holding a large glass Christmas bauble. He wipes away the layer of dust on

167

the surface. Inside is a pristine scene: white cotton snow, little pine tree, tiny plastic fawn with tiny white spots.

"Do you remember how we talked about keeping our minds separate from the objects we feel?"

"The object's feelings aren't my feelings." That's why sometimes Evelyn imagines a wall between her and the object.

"That's right. When you get worried about an object, put a bubble around your mind just like this ornament. Then you will be like the baby deer, safe and protected. Do you understand?"

Evelyn nods. A bubble is better than a wall. There's no over or under, it's protection all around.

"Try it, right now." They close their eyes together, and Evelyn pictures the bubble. Her heart slows down. The feelings in the workshop become distant, disconnected from her. After a few minutes, she opens her eyes to find her father studying her face. He smiles at her.

"Good," he says. "This is how your mind has to be. The glass keeps the dirt out. Keeps the inside safe and clean." He passes her the bauble. "Keep practicing. You'll see. Everything will be fine."

Evelyn smiles back. She wants to believe

what he's telling her, even though those bad feelings haven't gone away. They press ever so slightly at the back of her head, pushing against her bubble. She hopes that Daddy is better at making bubbles than she is.

15

Ev leans against the chipped gray outer wall of her new workplace, willing it to hold her upright. She's finished her first day just as the dark summer clouds hanging over downtown let loose. The pavement is too wet to sit on or she'd be on her ass, maybe even curled up on her side having a nap right there. But the building's narrow eaves don't offer a lot of protection from the rain. Another few minutes and Ev's hoodie will be soaked through.

She scans the sidewalks on either side of the street. No Noemi. Twenty minutes late already. Owen is long gone, home to his latest project with some antique sink fixtures they found in a cupboard in the kitchen. They aren't stained, so Harriet doesn't care about them.

Ev's shoulders will be sore in the morning. They spent the day cleaning — sweeping, scrubbing floors, washing windows, and hauling away the junk they found in the second floor rooms, mostly scrap wood and cardboard. Hardly a stain in sight, which suits Ev fine. Despite her exhaustion, Ev's stomach tingles with excitement as she pats the bulky envelope in her backpack for the hundredth time. Harriet's not messing around. She showed up this morning with enough cash to cover Ev's rent plus groceries for a month.

"Call it your signing bonus," she said in the flat tone Ev has begun to recognize as humor. She hasn't signed a thing. But she's happy enough with the wage Harriet named, along with the promise to pay Ev in cash at the end of each week, that she's not about to complain. If Noemi ever shows up, they'll have pannekoeken for dinner to celebrate.

A cab pulls up. The driver looks at Ev. She shakes her head, waving him on, but he stays. Beside her, the door opens with a scrape. Harriet. Ev hurries to help her pull the metal gate shut and latch it.

"You still here?" Harriet raises her eyebrows at Ev.

"I'm waiting for someone."

"Want a lift?"

"No, thanks. My sister will be here soon."

"Your sister."

"Yeah." Ev bites her lip, embarrassed by

her compulsion to say those words out loud. *My sister.* As if to make Noemi real.

She realizes Harriet's eyes are watering.

"That's lovely. I'm so happy to hear it." Small talk words, but her voice quavers as she speaks, as if they are talking about something entirely different, something of greater importance. The woman has all kinds of ways of making Ev uncomfortable.

The cabbie honks.

"You'd better go." Ev yanks on the heavy padlock holding the gates shut, anxious for Harriet to leave. "See you tomorrow."

Harriet stares at her another moment, nodding, not at Ev's words but at whatever is going on in that wiry-topped head of hers, before shuffling to the cab without a good-bye.

Ev watches the traffic rush past, the occasional huddled figure hurrying down the sidewalk, head bent and umbrella raised. After another ten minutes, she gives up on Noemi and heads toward the bus stop, wishing she'd brought her bike. She should know by now not to count on her sister. She has one foot on the number 20 bus when she hears Noemi's cry.

"Ev, wait." She turns, bumping into a sour-faced man with mean eyes and a grudge stain in his jacket pocket. She edges

172

aside with a muttered apology and sees Noemi running up the street.

"Sorry, sorry, sorry, sorry."

"Hurry up." Ev climbs onto the bus, giving the grudge man some space, taking her time plugging in quarters. Noemi tumbles inside, breathless and soggy, black T-shirt clinging to her torso.

She flashes a smile at the driver. "Thanks. It's a mess out there." To Ev she says, "Do you have any change?"

The driver waves at her. "Go on."

Noemi takes Ev's arm and pulls her to the back of the bus.

"Where were you?" Ev wants to be mad, but stupid relief drowns out all traces of annoyance.

"Chinatown. I thought I could walk here, but it was farther than I realized."

"Why Chinatown?"

"To see a friend about a job. And you'll never guess who I ran into. Remember the guy from the market?"

"What guy?"

"The one I punched in the face."

"Hangdog?"

Noemi looks amused. "Yeah, I can see that. His name is Michael. I let him take me for coffee, to apologize for being a dick and making you lose your market table."

"You went for coffee. With Hangdog."

"He's actually quite nice. He wanted you to know he's sorry for overreacting. He feels pretty bad about the whole thing."

Ev's mind whirls as she thinks of what to say. "I don't want you hanging around him" is what comes out.

Noemi laughs out loud, dismissing her words with a wave. "I'm a big girl, Ev."

"He's got some weird issues."

"Everyone has weird issues. Anyway, ugh. It was nothing, just coffee. Tell me about your day. How's the new job?"

Ev wants to say more about Hangdog, but she backs off. "So far, so good."

"So, what kind of spooky stuff does your boss have? Did you learn any cool tricks?"

"No tricks. No stuff. The building's still empty. Today, we mostly cleaned up the space and made plans." And listened to Harriet changing her mind about the plan every five minutes. "Owen's going to start bringing boxes over tomorrow."

Ev gets flutters in her stomach at the thought of the stains arriving. Except this time, she realizes there's some excitement mixed in with the fear. She has to admit, Harriet's ideas are . . . inspiring. She wants to use the stains in a positive way, combine them like music to create harmonies. Visitors will take in the curated emotions and they will come away changed. Harriet makes it sound beautiful. Ev wishes she could believe in the plan the way Harriet does. She wishes she could see the world the way Harriet sees it. Like Owen sees it too, as much light as darkness. Both of them have a talent for turning their faces to the light, a cool trick Ev has never quite figured out.

The grudge man passes their seat on his way off the bus. He pushes harder on the doors than necessary. They shudder loudly as they part, spitting the man out onto the street. Ev watches him carry his pocketful of spite away. That's what she sees. People holding on to their pain. Seeking it out, even. Like Hangdog.

"Hey." Noemi's elbow jabs into her side. "Did you hear any of what I just said?"

"Sorry."

"I said you look exactly like Mom." Ev stiffens at the mention of their mother, but Noemi doesn't seem to notice. Or decides not to notice. "You even wear your hair the same way she did, with the side-swept bangs. Ev?"

Ev braces herself. She hoped she could get some food before the conversation took this inevitable turn. But she owes Noemi. She promised. She sees a flash of Noemi's flushed face looming over her, tears welling. *Liar.* The throbbing of her cheekbone. Ev always maintained she remembered next to nothing about the night their world fell apart. It's mostly true. What comes back to her in nightmares and flashbacks is so fractured she can't make sense of it. Not that she tries.

She also told Noemi that everything from that time in their life, from before foster care, was a total blackout. That she had no memories to share. Then, six months ago, she let one slip. They were curled together on Ev's single bed, like when they were kids. Noemi writing words on Ev's back in slow, looping curves. Ev, almost asleep, in a whisper so soft Noemi almost could have missed it.

Mama used to do that.

It kicked off their last, worst fight. Noemi has always believed she has a right to every shred of memory Ev holds from that time. Every detail Ev fails to share is a slight against her. So exhausting. Ev didn't want to have the argument anymore. She thought Noemi leaving would be a relief. In that moment, she believed they'd both be better off apart.

"Earth to Ev."

Ev turns to look into her sister's eyes. She

wants Noemi to know she's got her attention.

"Yes?"

For once, it's Noemi's gaze that slips from hers, a flutter of vulnerability showing in the twitch of an eyebrow.

"Do you think it was bad for her, before the end? Was he terrible?"

The memory comes to her out of nowhere, blowing her back in her seat with its force. Little Evelyn, six, maybe seven years old, tiptoeing to the bedroom door. Following the pattern of the tiles beneath her feet, white square brown square white square brown square. A SpongeBob sticker on the door just below the handle half-scraped off. Shrieks coming from the other side of it. She pushes the door open. Inside, on the bed among rumpled blankets, Mama laughing helplessly as Daddy nuzzles her neck with his beard. *Tickle fight,* roars Daddy, turning wide eyes to Evelyn. *No one is safe.*

Ev lets out a breath and pulls the stop cord.

"No," she says. "Not terrible." She makes herself look into Noemi's questioning eyes, swallows the tremor in her voice as best she can. "That was the worst part. They were in love."

She lunges for the door, not checking to

177

see if Noemi is following, and steps off the bus, stopping suddenly to orient herself, the stream of downtown pedestrians parting around her. This isn't their stop. They are ten blocks at least from the apartment.

"You promised." Noemi is there, right behind her.

"I know. Can we walk?" It will be easier if she keeps moving. Noemi takes Ev's arm and pulls her southward, past bars and cheap pizza joints, past a busker singing Johnny Cash. It's true what he says about love.

"What are you laughing at?" Noemi's little fingers press too hard into her bicep.

" 'Ring of Fire.' This way." Ev veers left into a quiet alley. She doesn't need to go on salvage missions anymore, but somehow the act of scanning bins and boxes soothes her.

"So, you're saying he didn't beat us?"

"No."

"And he didn't keep Mom locked up in the basement?"

"Where are you getting this information?"

"Just stuff I heard over the years."

"Rumors."

"I guess."

"It wasn't like that."

"So what?" Noemi's voice turns, its edges hard. "Everything was sunshine and roses?"

178

Ev counts her breath along with her steps, sneakers slapping on wet pavement. One . . . two . . . three . . . four. She spies a slick, wet crow's feather in the gutter and, just like that, she knows what to say.

"Mama liked to work in her garden. She grew peas, lettuce, tomatoes." Ev can almost catch the scent of fresh tomato leaves. "We spent a lot of time outside, you especially. You loved digging in the dirt, collecting pretty rocks and feathers. You liked to chase the crows."

She sees Noemi running through the garden, crashing through the zucchini plants, waving a stick at the crows. The stick. Ev's mouth dries up. The stick was brave and fierce. Noemi brought it alive. It was her wand, and she used it to protect the squirrels and rabbits from crows. They cawed so rudely and dug up the yard with their grub-pecking. All crows feared Noemi. She turned them into butterflies, *poof.* She yelled at them *POOF POOF* until they fluttered away.

Ev finds she can't finish.

"We were a normal family," she tells Noemi. "Happy. Then he got sick."

"Yeah, I've heard this before. The stains made him sick. See, this is the part I don't get. Your new boss, she lives with all kinds

179

of stains. From the sound of it, she's been living that way for decades. How many people has she stabbed to death?"

"Her stained objects are mostly harmless." At least she hopes so.

"Mostly. How many people have you stabbed?"

Four . . . three . . . two . . . one.

"I know what you're going to say. He was weak." Noemi puts air quotes around the word *weak.*

"Yes, he was weak. Maybe he had a mental illness that made it worse."

"Or maybe he was a violent, controlling asshole. I mean, you were eight and Daddy's little sidekick. I understand why you defend him. I just wish you'd stop."

"I'm not defending him."

"Well, that's how it sounds." They walk in silence, coming to the end of the alley and darting between cars to the next block. Ev passes dumpsters one by one, counting them off like she used to count the kitchen tiles: *green black black blue green.*

"What did he use?"

"What?" The pavement falls sideways. Ev sways into Noemi's side.

"They never found the murder weapon. That part of the story's true, isn't it?"

"Yes."

"And the other night you said you saw it happen. So I want to know."

This is usually when Noemi sees she's pushed Ev too far, when she puts her arm around Ev and they breathe together. But Noemi doesn't do that this time. She just waits for Ev to speak.

"Why that?" Ev stops to search her sister's face, genuinely curious. "Why would you want to know that?"

"Because it's something no one else knows. I want to know what you've refused to tell me until now. I want to know everything that you know."

She promised.

"Scissors," Ev whispers. "A pair of sewing scissors."

Noemi has the grace to flinch, a shadow crossing her features. "Stained?"

"So, so stained."

Noemi softens her voice. "I know this isn't easy for you. It's just I can't stop thinking about it. I've been going through that box."

"I don't want to know."

"I know. It's just so weird. How is it possible? How can four lives leave only one lousy box behind?"

Ev shakes her head, unsure of what Noemi wants her to say.

"It's not," Noemi says. She stares at Ev, as

181

though she's meant to understand something unsaid. "It's not possible."

"There was an estate sale. To pay off the debts. You know this."

"But what about the personal stuff? Where are the diaries and the letters? Our childhood toys? Your school projects and artwork? Mom was a painter, but there's only like three watercolors in there. No one would buy any of that stuff, so what? Did someone throw it all away? I mean, I even went to the house, but there was nothing there. It was a shell."

"The house?" Ev's voice falters, and the skin on the back of her neck crawls. "You've been there?"

"Ages ago. It was just sitting empty. Graffiti and crushed beer cans. No murder weapons to be found. Don't worry; I'm not going to make you tour it or anything gross like that. It's gone. It was bought and sold a bunch of times, and then some property development company demolished it and built some condos."

"I can't believe you did that."

"Why not? Why is it so awful to want to know my past? Why can't I want that? Why can't I want different things than you do?"

"Why the obsession, though? Why do you need to know every detail?"

"Because it's my story. My family. My genetics. You've spent your life afraid that you might turn into him, guarding against the signs. Well, he was my father too."

"But Noemi."

"She was my *mother*. How can I not want to know everything I can about her? Even the hard stuff?"

Ev tries to think of an answer that won't make her sound like an asshole. Nope. Nothing.

"Just go easy on me, okay? I'm trying."

Noemi slips her arm through Ev's. "Baby steps," she says, and Ev can tell by her tone that the interrogation is over for now.

"Yeah," says Ev. "Baby steps."

16

Ev drains the last of her coffee and tries to ignore the ripples of anxiety threading through her stomach. Again, she leans against the outside wall of her new workplace; again, waiting. The building was locked up and dark inside when she arrived an hour ago, and still there is no sign of Harriet or Owen. She was glad to leave the apartment this morning, to put some space between herself and Noemi's relentless curiosity.

There's a photo of me with a dog. Did we have a pet?

No. It belonged to a neighbor.

Was Mom left-handed like me, or right-handed like you?

Right-handed.

Her questions hang like choking perfume in the air. Even the ones she doesn't speak aloud in her effort to give Ev the time she needs. Especially those.

Disappointment at finding the building shut up, empty, has long since given way to impatience and frustration, then worry. It's almost ten, well past their agreed-upon start time. She should demand a set of keys. She doesn't even have Harriet's phone number. Owen's not answering his, so her only choices are to keep waiting or ride over to Harriet's apartment and see if they're there. She might miss them, but at least on her bike she'll feel like she's doing something.

She has her leg over the crossbar when she sees an unmarked white van approaching. It pulls into the right lane, slows down, and beeps twice at her. She sees two hands waving, and she lets out a sigh, part relief and part exasperation. Nothing is wrong. They're simply late.

It's strange to see Owen behind the wheel of the van and not on his bike. Once, at the beach in the early morning, she saw three raccoons swimming. Raccoons are her scavenger companion creatures. They share the same hunting territory. She scans dumpsters for signs of their masked eyes before hopping inside. She crosses paths with them in dark alleys. She's always associated them with the grittier corners of the city, so the sight of three sets of black paws paddling through light-dappled water that day struck

185

her as both odd and beautiful. She feels the same incongruity watching the van pull up beside her, except in reverse. Owen spends his life serenely paddling. Now he's the one inside an ugly metal box. His smile is the same as always, but there's a strain around his eyes as he steps onto the sidewalk.

"Sorry we're late. Harriet was still asleep when I arrived at the apartment this morning."

He opens the passenger door and extends a hand to help her out. Harriet's face shows a matching strain.

"Are you all right?" Ev asks.

"Bad night," says Harriet. "It won't happen again, but we should exchange phone numbers in case."

"I should have a set of keys. I could have been working."

"Owen's got some furniture in the back. He needs help unloading." She turns away.

"We can't work together if you don't trust me."

Harriet's back stiffens. "My life is in your hands. Isn't that enough?" She continues to the door, fumbling with the lock on the gate.

"Speaking of hands, Evelyn," calls Owen. He grips the top end of a large bookcase, its bottom still resting in the back of the van.

Ev lets Harriet go, moving around to help Owen.

"You might want to go easy on her today," Owen says in a low tone, once Harriet has propped the doors open and vanished inside. "She had a difficult time removing things from her apartment."

"Seems like you did okay." Behind the bookshelf, the van is stacked with close to a dozen boxes. Ev's stomach turns over at the sight of them.

"Every box was a fresh sorrow."

Every box oozes stain, making Ev's skin prickle. She hardens her mind against them, a flexing made effortless from years of practice. She doesn't need to be vulnerable quite yet. Ev slides her end of the bookcase out, grunting under the weight of solid wood.

"This thing's a beast. How did you get it loaded?"

"One of Harriet's neighbors. She was so delighted to see some of the clutter go, she offered to bring over another carload." Owen pauses. "It didn't help Harriet's mood."

"All right, I get it. I'll be nice."

The bookcase has a faint stain, something close to pride, barely detectable even at close range. Ev and Owen ease it inside.

Harriet is nowhere to be seen, so they lower it to the floor against the closest wall.

A box lies on top of a table in the middle of the room, a tangle of emotions bleeding through the cardboard. The table, along with three folding chairs, belongs to Owen, as do the ladder and the toolbox next to the kitchen door. Those arrived yesterday. The box was not on the table when Ev left at the end of the day.

Ev moves closer to take a look at the old cardboard flaps bent out of shape from being folded in on one another again and again, the labels scribbled over with black marker. The address catches her eye. An address with Harriet's name on it, but not the location of her apartment: 10 Angel Place. Harriet has a knack for finding spaces associated with magical things. Owen has taken to calling this building "the Dragon," after the smashed sign out front. He refers to Harriet's apartment as "Woodland" after its street name. Forests, dragons, and angels. The city turned into a fantasy landscape. It almost makes Ev smile.

"Where'd that come from?"

Owen shakes his head. "It wasn't here last night."

Ev pulls apart the flaps. She counts five objects. A baby blanket. A photograph of a man standing on a beach. A wooden spoon. A pair of worn-out velour slippers. A four-inch-tall brass Buddha. The items radiate calm and tranquility. Comfort. They've been handpicked for Ev.

"What is it?" Owen comes over for a peek.

"Peace offering," she says.

17

Harriet holds the wooden spoon at eye level, studying the sway of its handle, bent from the pressure of thousands of rotations. Her finger follows its rough edge around the blackened, notched tip and up again. She strokes the spoon's back, its surface soft and grainy, and remembers. Five years ago, January, in Paradise Valley, Arizona. The last time she saw her last lover. Theodore begged her to come away from the northern gloom and spend some time with him at his family's cabin. She had been withdrawing from him for some time, and he knew it. It wasn't the weather he lured her away from, but her apartment. He was losing her to it.

The "cabin," a three-thousand-square-foot Tuscan-style rancher with a pool, nestled against the dusty corpse of a mountain with a handful of other safely gated homes, most of them with darkened windows; all of this surrounded by five-star resorts. She spent her days wandering the mountain trails, her fingers exploring the spiny skins of cacti, while Theodore golfed with his business associates. Dull landscape, dull people, dull house. Everything in Theodore's house was new and hardly used — the furniture, the unread books, the crisp linens. What should have felt cleansing, freeing, only oppressed her with its loneliness. She hated living in that vacuum. She drifted through empty rooms, a wild-haired tumbleweed in a caftan, knowing she would last no more than a week.

She found her solace, finally, in the kitchen, a gleaming granite-and-chrome expanse that seemed to serve no other purpose than to store sparkling water and fruit. The refrigerator still had protective tape on its corners. She suspected the stove had never been turned on. Despite this, someone had made a halfhearted attempt at stocking its cupboards with cooking tools — a well-seasoned cast-iron skillet, a set of dented stainless-steel pots, a blue ceramic tart dish with a chip on the edge. Things that had lived a life before this place. Things with souls.

The spoon was a revelation; every particle of it soaked in comfort, in the nurturing bliss of hands that had found joy in preparing food for loved ones. Harriet spent an entire day carrying the spoon in her pocket. She asked Theodore about it, although she knew it would anger him. She needed to know its history. She needed to learn where these few living objects had come from.

"Those?" He shrugged, wiping post-golf sweat from his graying brow with a white hand towel. "Likely Aunt Mindy's things."

She pressed him for details, ignoring the darkening of his face and the curt edge in his voice. The unspoken plea beneath — *Don't do this again. Don't ruin us.*

What happened to Aunt Mindy? How did her things come to live here?

"She went to a home last year. My sister is sentimental. Like you," he added, in a tone that suggested this was not a desirable trait. "She probably couldn't stand to get rid of that stuff."

Harriet imagined a house full of children, a husband who wore a hat to work, a plump-cheeked wife in braids and an apron.

Theodore snorted. "Aunt Mindy had no children. She's a spinster." *Like you.* The words unspoken, the judgment hanging in the air between them all the same, leaving Harriet more perplexed than upset. Poor Teddy. He didn't understand her a bit, never had.

"And what about Aunt Mindy? For whom had she cooked?"

"No one. Herself. Her old crone roommate. Jesus, Harriet. What does it matter?" His incomprehension now matched hers, the fissure between them cracking wide open, Harriet holding the wooden spoon next to her heart, as though it might protect her. How could it not matter?

She left the next morning, and they never spoke again. But the spoon. Possibly the kindest thing Theodore did was to tuck the wooden spoon in the front pocket of Harriet's suitcase, a farewell gift for her to discover upon her return home. She wonders if the rest of Aunt Mindy's kitchen treasures still lie untouched in that empty house.

"Have you given any thought to those paint samples?"

Harriet blinks. Owen blinks back at her. The paint samples are fanned on the table in front of her, squares and squares of whites.

"I never did get the story on Aunt Mindy."

Owen smiles at the spoon. "Sometimes imagining the stories is more fun."

Harriet scans the huge, empty room. Sunlight pours in through the front window, illuminating dust motes in the air. The walls are dirty, the paint chipped and flaking.

"The walls are fine as they are."

"Perhaps I could wash them down."

Harriet nods her assent. "Where's Ev?"

"I sent her out to pick up some lunch."

"It's only ten."

"It's eleven. I told her to take her time."

"You're the boss now?"

"You were distracted. She was getting too quiet. I think she needed a breather."

"She's always quiet."

"A different kind of quiet." He nods toward the stack of boxes against the wall next to the bookshelf. "Those are making her anxious."

Those boxes represent the bulk of the contents of Harriet's front hall. It's hard to imagine that they once towered on either side of her door, turning her entrance into a dark tunnel. In here, they sag in a lonely little huddle, a harmless assortment of dusty nostalgia and faded minor dramas.

"Move them into the kitchen for now." If Ev feels uncomfortable, she'll have Owen bring them in one box at a time. One object at a time, if that's what it takes. "So, tell me. What's the story on you and Ev?"

"Ah." Owen smiles and pulls on his ponytail, inching the elastic closer to his scalp. "I met her at a thrift store a couple of years ago. I was browsing through a box of table linens and spotted some hand-crocheted lace. Perfect for the fiber-art project I was working on. When I pulled on it, it kept coming, a handmade runner, eight feet long at least, with a two-dollar price tag."

Harriet recognizes the mixture of exhilaration and disappointment in his voice, the regret of a good find long lost.

"But?"

"But Ev was holding its other end. You know that look she gets when she wants something. I knew she'd win. I don't have her fight."

"And then?"

"Then she tipped me off on a truckload of fabric she'd seen next to a donation bin. That's how I knew she was hiding a kind heart."

Harriet snorts. She's not sure about kindhearted. "I'll agree she's not as fierce as she pretends to be. And what about you? You can't be as altruistic as you appear."

"You are paying me," Owen reminds her.

"I mean, why are you so interested in Ev's well-being?"

For the first time, Harriet sees a shadow pass across Owen's face.

"She reminds me of someone."

There's a finality to his words that warns

Harriet from pressing further. In the silence that follows, Harriet turns her attention to the boxes near the door. Best to move them before Ev returns. Someone has pulled a few objects out and stacked them in an odd manner on the floor. Harriet studies the arrangement, picking out a pair of wire-rimmed eyeglasses, a yo-yo, a silver belt buckle.

"What's that?"

"Oh," says Owen, a hint of shyness in his manner. "It's a dragon." He bends and picks it up gently. "I promise nothing's been damaged. It's only held together by a bit of wire."

"I want to see."

Owen places it on the table, and Harriet leans into it. The objects do form the shape of a dragon. A rudimentary, lopsided dragon, the bulk of its body formed by a child's tin watering can, the spout a tail. It has only one wing, fashioned from a paper fan. He's used twisted wire to fasten on a brass eagle door knocker, the belt buckle and yo-yo and glasses giving the dragon a bug-eyed face. Still, it has character. It holds an odd charm, its brightness a mix of playfulness, curiosity, and pride.

"This is the sort of art you make."

"Would you like to see more?"

"I would."

He holds up a finger and jogs outside the building, to where the van is parked. He pulls something from the glove box and carries it inside carefully, cupped in his hands, over to the table where Harriet sits.

"Normally, I break down my materials in order to create something new. Of course, I wouldn't do that with your things." He sets the object on the table. It's a bird. An exquisite bird, with a twisted wire skeleton, scrap metal feathers in blues and browns, and silver button eyes.

"This is lovely." Harriet regards the dragon and the bird sitting side by side on the table. She strokes the folded edge of the dragon's paper wing, thinking. "Could you make a big dragon?"

"I usually work small . . ." Owen trails off, gazing around the open space. "I'd love to try."

"It would be a marvel." She imagines items handpicked by Ev and sculpted by Owen, a real-life luck dragon. She gathers the little bird in her hands, and offers it to Owen.

"You don't want to lose this."

"You can have it. I brought it for you."

"Oh. Thank you."

"I thought it would fit in well with your

collection."

"Not really," she says. The smile falls from Owen's face. He doesn't understand, of course. She tries to explain why it doesn't belong. "It's beautiful, but it's not alive."

"Ah." He looks away, gestures toward the boxes against the wall. "I'd better move these before Ev gets back."

She's said the wrong thing again. It's a talent she has, another reason she prefers to spend her time with objects rather than people. To atone for her sin, she picks up the scrap-metal bird and places it on the windowsill, where the bird stone can keep it company.

Poor inanimate thing.

18

When Ev returns with sandwiches, she's relieved to find that Harriet's boxes have been relocated. She knows she has to get used to the stains, but for now, one box is plenty. The peace offering still sits on the table, untouched. Owen kneels on the floor, a jumble of objects spread out in front of him. Harriet is nowhere to be seen.

From downstairs comes a heavy slam. Ev flinches. Owen straightens up, blinks down the shadowed hallway.

"Harriet?" he calls.

"Fine," comes the muffled reply. Ev hears the stairs creak as she mounts them one by one. Owen heads down the hall to meet her.

Ev drops the lunch bag on the table and peels off her gloves. Barely, just barely, she lays her palms on the nubby surface of the baby blanket. It's pink and lacy, the kind you'd tuck around a newborn in a stroller. Its softness extends beyond itself, makes everything around it soft too. It blurs the edges of the world. Ev wants to bury her face in it, see if it still has a bit of that milky sweet baby smell, but she settles for lifting it out of the box with bare hands, allowing its gentle protection to seep into her skin. To influence her.

She drops the blanket on the table and rubs her hands on her jeans, as if she could wipe them clean. That's the problem with stains, even the nice ones. They get inside you.

Owen and Harriet enter the room, speaking in low tones. Ev pulls out a chair for her, and Harriet eases into it. She still looks tired, but the creases in her face aren't as deep. Owen takes a sandwich from the bag and heads for the door.

"Thanks for lunch. See you later."

"Where are you going?" Ev tries not to sound dismayed. It's less awkward with Owen around.

"Owen has an errand to run," says Harriet.

"Back in an hour," Owen calls, already out the door.

It only takes three bites of sandwich for the silence to get to Ev. Harriet's not eating. She stares at the front window, eyes glazed over, far away.

"What were you doing downstairs?" Ev asks, too brusquely, remembering a moment too late that she promised Owen she'd be nice. Harriet's eyes flick toward Ev and back to the window.

"Checking the vault. Make sure the door works."

"You were here last night." Ev nods at the box on the table.

"Couldn't sleep."

"You brought those things for me."

"I did." Harriet leans forward, gathers up the blanket, and lifts it to her face. Eyes crinkling shut, a deep inhale. "I thought they would be good things to start with." Blue eyes raise to Ev's over a fold of delicate pink. "I want this to be a safe place for you."

"Even sweet stains can be dangerous. Even that." Ev waves at the blanket, sees Harriet taking in her bared fingers.

"Explain."

"They change you."

"Life is change. Experiences change you. People change you."

"I know."

"The things we surround ourselves with change us too, but not any more than the others."

"Maybe."

"So, when you pick up an item like this"

— Harriet tucks the bundle of blanket beneath her chin — "you hold yourself apart."

"Yes."

"How?"

"Aren't you supposed to be teaching me, not the other way around?"

"I'm curious. I don't know how to do what you do."

"I breathe," she says. "I meditate."

"Yes. And that allows you to disconnect?"

Retreat. "I guess."

"So, you create barriers inside your mind. A protective wall."

"A bubble." She always imagines it as a bubble, nothing so hard and inflexible as a wall.

"Who taught you this?"

Ev shrugs. She learned the meditation and breathing techniques from a child psychologist, a warm woman who wore rainbow-striped socks and cat-eye glasses, and sat cross-legged on the floor of her office so she could look up into Ev's eyes. The bubble, though. The bubble is much older; old as a glass Christmas bauble with a baby deer standing in cotton snow.

Keep the dirt out.

"I've been doing it forever," she says.

"And when you make items move with

your mind? How does that work?"

Ev shivers involuntarily. "I don't do it on purpose."

"But you could."

"I don't want to."

"Of course," says Harriet breezily, although Ev is sure she'd like to know more. She's caught Harriet staring with a clenched jaw at her toy monkey when she thinks no one's watching, her eyes bugged with desperate intent.

"So, what do you think is more potent? This blanket, or your friend Owen?"

Ev frowns at the question.

"You've known him for how long? Two years?"

"Yeah." He bought her a burrito after she tipped him off on a bin full of fabric. He's been feeding her ever since.

"Surely this friendship has changed you, one way or another. Do you consider him dangerous?"

"Of course not," Ev says, but she hesitates too long. Because she holds him at arm's length, doesn't she? Has always done so.

"Ah," says Harriet. "Is that your plan, then? A life without experience? Without people or things?"

"I don't have a plan."

"You're surviving."

"Yeah," Ev snaps. "I'm surviving." Better than a lot of people.

"And your sister?"

Ev wishes she'd never mentioned Noemi. "What about her?"

"Is she dangerous?"

She doesn't say so, but of course it's true. Ev stands up and begins pacing the room. She likes how her footsteps echo in the space. She wishes it could stay like this, empty.

"But you keep her close, all the same," Harriet says, taking Ev's silence as a *yes*.

Because I have to. Because I'm her sun. She picks up the wooden spoon to distract Harriet. She's tired of these questions, worded as though meant to help Ev, but seeming more and more like Harriet fishing for information.

"This is interesting," she says.

Harriet, unable to resist falling into her memories, smiles, her eyes softening.

"A lot of love in that spoon."

"Secret love." She can see from Harriet's expression that she's surprised her boss. Curiosity overcomes her. She holds the spoon a moment longer, lets the under layers of emotion come out. Already, it's easier than that first time, with the dried flower. She doesn't want to admit that Harriet might be right, that the spoon holds no danger beyond its ability to touch Ev in a way she hasn't allowed anyone, anything to touch her. She reminds herself why she's here. To heal. To help others heal. To build a future for herself and for Noemi.

"The kitchen was a safe place for her." Ev squeezes her eyes shut to hide their sudden glassiness. "For them. A place where they could be themselves."

"The roommate." Harriet's eyes light up with revelation. "Spinster my ass."

Ev makes Harriet tell her what she knows of the spoon. Together they tell the story of Aunt Mindy and her lover, all their years together kept secret from the outside world. Then she touches each of the other objects in turn, sharing her impressions. In the stitches of the slippers, the remembrance of friendship cohabits with the sleepy contentment of a furred creature and the simple comfort of ritual at the end of a long day. Worn into the photograph, acceptance of change and talismanic faith in the future. Together they tease out secrets, round out histories, and re-create lives, half-imagined, half-intuited.

She's surprised when Owen returns, jingling his keys in one hand and balancing a tray of coffees in the other. An hour has passed in a blur. She feels energized, not weakened. She's been having fun.

Owen drops the keys on the table in front of Ev. Three of them, heavy, fresh cut, and shiny. Ev looks over at Harriet.

"Front and back doors, plus the gate."

"Thank you."

"Can't have you loitering around the building, attracting attention."

Harriet makes a production of fumbling with her coffee lid, as if it will cover her discomfort. But Ev can see, in the shaking of her hands, in the bow of her head, how much this trust has cost her. For the first time, she has a glimpse of the magnitude, the immensity of Harriet's vulnerability, in allowing Ev to share what she has so carefully sought out and preserved over the years. What should a person say in the face of that kind of sacrifice?

Ev tucks the keys into her pocket without another word.

19

"Would you just tell me where we're going?"

"That would ruin the surprise."

Ev hates surprises. But Noemi bounces in her seat like a kid, humming under her breath as the bus rolls up Fourth Avenue, past boutiques and organic cafés and overpriced condos. She let her sister's close-lipped excitement carry her out the door and onto the bus. She can't back out now. She also can't resist the lure of a whole afternoon hanging out with Noemi. This normality, like old times, before the past clouded every conversation — she wants it. They haven't seen each other in days. Noemi's been out a lot in the evenings, and Ev, exhausted from the mental exertions of her new job, has been passing out by ten.

"At least tell me what you've been up to all week."

Noemi pauses. For a moment, Ev wishes

she didn't ask. The upside of Noemi and Ev constantly missing each other is there haven't been any uncomfortable conversations lately. Although she's certain Noemi has spent plenty of time poring over the contents of the family box during the last few days, she doesn't want to ruin a blue-sky Saturday with another fight.

Luckily, it seems Noemi feels the same.

"Oh, you know," she says with a mysterious smile. "Job hunting, mostly."

"When are you going to come visit? I want you to meet Harriet and Owen."

"Are you kidding? I'm dying to meet new Mom and Dad too! Next week, I promise."

"Don't call them that." Ev can't keep the edge from her voice. Noemi notices, catching her lip in her teeth. She knows she's hit a nerve and doesn't continue the joke.

"Sorry. Here." Noemi yanks the stop cord and pulls Ev toward the door. They've passed the busy shopping district. Another bend in the road, and the bus will be heading out to the university. They step onto the sidewalk next to a grassy park. Past a parking lot and the duck pond surrounded by willow trees lies a sandy beach and, beyond that, the ocean. The sight of the expanse of deep blue peaks dotted with sailboats makes Ev's chest expand.

"This way." Noemi cuts across the grass, heading toward the water.

"Let me guess. We're going on a picnic. French fries and ice cream at Jericho."

"Nope."

"We're going to feed the ducks."

"Nope."

"You have a Frisbee in your bag?"

"Nope."

"You're not making me play beach volleyball."

At this Noemi laughs. "I wouldn't dream of it."

They reach the gravel path that follows the water all the way up to Spanish Banks. But instead of hanging a left or a right on the path, Noemi crosses it, heading through a small gate in a chain-link fence. On the other side of the fence, rows and rows of boats thrust their empty masts skyward. The breeze picks up, and a musical clanging, like wind chimes, lifts around them.

"This is the sailing club," says Ev. "Don't you have to be a member to go in there?"

"That's the yacht club, silly. This is a public facility. Everyone's welcome, even riffraff like us."

Noemi strides to the beach, where a few people are gathered around five small boats with plain white sails. Seeing Ev and Noemi approach, the group watches expectantly. A knot forms in Ev's stomach.

"What did you do?" Ev stops. It takes Noemi a few more paces to realize she's not following anymore. She spins, flashes Ev her most winning smile, and takes her hand. Ev doesn't budge.

"You signed us up for sailing lessons?" She doesn't know whether to be furious or elated.

"I signed *you* up for sailing lessons."

Oh God. Noemi launches into her pitch before Ev can take in a breath, before she can react.

"This is gonna be perfect for you. I know you've always loved the ocean. Remember that time we went fishing with Mikey and his buddy James? That was a lake, but still. The way you looked that day, on the water. You didn't even touch a fishing pole. You just . . . drifted. It was the closest I ever saw you get to happy."

"I remember." She remembers everything about that day, the way the sunlight sparkled on the water, the sound of the water slapping against the side of the boat, dipping her fingers into the cool lake. The fact that Noemi remembers too makes her heart hurt.

A shadow crosses Noemi's face. She

squeezes Ev's hand.

"I think I was thirteen. I promised myself that someday I'd buy you a boat so you could get that feeling whenever you wanted. And, well, I don't know if I'll ever be able to buy you a boat, but renting one's pretty close, right?"

Ev suddenly wants to weep, but she's aware of their audience down on the beach, clearly waiting for her arrival. She bites the inside of her cheek hard enough to draw blood.

"How did you pay for this? You can't afford it."

"I've got a bit saved." Noemi's eyes shift sideways in a way Ev doesn't like. "Also, I got a job yesterday. Server at the Platypus. Tips are supposed to be great there. So, I wanted to do something to celebrate."

"You couldn't just buy some new shoes?"

"I did that too. Anyway, it's not as expensive as you think." Noemi tugs on her hand, pushing her lips into a pout. "Come on. Don't be such an Evelyn. You're changing. You're taking risks. Living more."

"But sailing lessons? Look at those people down there," Ev hisses. "Look at their healthy complexions and their toned arms and their, their fleece vests."

"Trust me, I'm looking. Check out the

toned arms on the dude with the locs. I'd get on a boat with him."

"I don't belong here."

"You'll be fine. Anyway, what are you going to do with your weekends now that you don't have to spend them rooting through garbage? Time for a hobby, right? Time to start working on your own healthy complexion. Fresh sea air, breeze in your hair." Noemi pushes on the small of her back impatiently. "It's going to be amazing. Think about it. Six weeks from now you'll be able to come out here, rent a boat, and spend the whole afternoon on the ocean. Just you and the water and the snap of the wind in your sails."

"You can do that?"

"You can." Noemi's grin widens, seeing the spark of excitement Ev can't hide. "You know you want it."

Does she? One of the things Ev's always loved most about Noemi is how she sees Ev more clearly than anyone, even Ev herself. She can never hide completely from Noemi. It's also one of the things she hates, because it's not enough to see. Noemi likes to push. Sometimes in the wrong direction, like her frequent misguided attempts to ease Ev's loneliness with surprise blind double dates. Even if Ev could manage a normal relationship, Noemi's not any better at picking dates for Ev than she is for herself. This thing with the boats, though. It could be that this time Noemi is on the right track.

"Are you sure you can't come with me?"

"No can do. I'll be working weekends. This is my last Saturday of freedom." Noemi gives her another nudge before skipping away, leaving Ev to face the class on her own.

"But I'll totally watch from the beach," she shouts over her shoulder.

Ev trudges forward. The dude with the locs waves enthusiastically, a whole body wave.

"You must be Evelyn." He offers his hand and a toothy smile. "I'm Brett. Everyone, say hello to Evelyn."

A round of awkward greetings follows, and Brett launches into the class. No one looks askance at Ev. No one suggests she doesn't belong or recognizes her as the girl who raids their alley on garbage day. The class starts off slow, beginning with the parts of a boat, safety equipment, and basic sailing terms. While Brett talks, Ev studies her classmates. Two middle-aged white women in large hats and arm bangles. A young Chinese couple in matching windbreakers. A trio of golden-haired teens, possibly siblings. One quiet kid hanging out in the back, like her. Then they're picking out life jackets, Brett outlining the rules for their first mini-sail.

"Now, I want you to break up into partners."

It's like high school all over again. Ev does what she used to do back then, avoiding eye contact, pretending to be distracted by her shoelaces while the others pair off. The shortest of the blondes takes possession of the other class loner. With any luck, she'll score a boat to herself.

"Evelyn, you're with me," says Brett. Well, at least she probably won't drown.

Things get better once they set out. A lot better. Ev feels lighter the moment her feet hit the water, as she and Brett push the boat over sand and rocks until it floats freely. Brett holds it steady while she climbs in, her heart lifting as she floats too, swaying, carried by the swell of gentle waves.

Ev pulls the lines off their winches and lets out the boom while Brett shouts instructions to the others. He does have nice arms, not too bulky, long smooth lines beneath dark skin. She curses Noemi silently for making her notice.

Ev doesn't date. Her early attempts, mostly instigated by her sister's interferences, were awkward and brief. By the time she finished high school, she'd decided that life was complicated enough without the burden of a relationship, romantic or otherwise. Even friendships come with expectations of sharing and intimacy that Ev simply can't offer. Except Owen. Owen doesn't expect anything from her, and she's grateful for that. A sudden shadow passes over that thought.

I can't wait to meet new Mom and Dad.

What if she's wrong about Owen? Maybe he does have expectations. Is she some substitute kid for the family he messed up with?

"Watch your back."

Ev turns and grabs the swinging boom before it hits her.

"Great, Evelyn." Brett beams at her. Nice smile, too, if you like the wholesome, sunny type. "You're a natural."

"We haven't moved." The sails aren't even hoisted. They're bobbing over knee-deep water.

"I can tell you'll be good at this. You're comfortable aboard. Ethan and Vanessa, one of you needs to move starboard or you're going to tip over. Starboard. To your right. The other right."

They watch as the boat capsizes, spilling

215

the couple into the ocean shallows. Brett hops out. "Think you can keep this thing afloat?"

"I got it."

Then Ev is alone. There's peace on the water and she finds it for a moment, shedding all the doubts and negativity she brought with her from shore, the breeze raising the flesh on her arms, the sway of the boat lulling her into contentment. It's the same feeling she gets from skipping stones at Crab Park, times a thousand. Out here, the stains are few and far between. She can come fully out of her bubble, stretch her mind wide, relax. She looks up the beach, where Noemi sits on the sand with a basket of fries balanced on her thighs, and feels a rush of gratitude for her impulsive, presumptuous, sweet, wise sister.

AFTER

Ev follows the narrow trail through the brush to the river's edge, a slushie in each hand and licorice stuffed in her coat pockets. Behind her, Noemi talks in a continuous stream, one of her long stories about middle school drama.

"And then Ms. Ward blamed *me* for disrupting the class, when Jayden was the one trying to draw poop emojis on our science poster."

"Did you tell her that?"

"Yes. She said I need to be less *reactive.*"

Ms. Ward's not wrong. At thirteen, Noemi is articulate and curious and a leader in her class. She's also easily distracted and prone to dramatic outbursts.

"She hates me."

"No one hates you. Ms. Ward expects more from you because she knows how smart you are. She sees your potential and she's trying to motivate you."

217

"Well, it's the opposite of motivating." Noemi skips ahead of Ev the last few steps, hopping up onto the top of their favorite log and back down on the other side.

"Hold on," says Ev before her sister sits. Someone's left a bottle cap on the log. It buzzes with aggressiveness. Ev whips a glove out of her pocket and uses it to pick up the cap. She tosses it into the water. Noemi looks at her sideways.

"What?" says Ev.

"Nothing." Ev passes her a slushie and they watch the river's slow current for a few minutes. It's early spring and everything's brown: the water, the naked trees, and the brush all around them. "I'm tired of school and this place. I can't wait to finish and get out."

Ev knows how she feels. Things are better than they've ever been, since before. They've lived at Joan and Mikey's for three years, longer than at any other foster home. Joan and Mikey are reliable caretakers with a cozy house, stained with kindness and good humor and only a few hints of sadness. It's as good a place as Ev could hope to be until she's on her own. But it's not their home. Ev will never feel truly comfortable there, not as long as she has to hide her secret. And school's worse. High schools are hotbeds of stains. So much emotion, it's exhausting. Ev has gotten through by being the loner kid, which suits her fine.

"You're almost free," says Noemi. Ev turned seventeen a week ago. She graduates next year. "Have you figured out what you're going to do?"

What *will* Ev do? She has to start planning for their future. They've agreed that Ev will move into the city and get an apartment so that Noemi can move in when she's finished school. The question is, how will she pay the rent?

"I'm thinking some kind of outdoor job. Landscaping, maybe. Or construction."

"Is that what you want to do? What about university?"

"So many people, so much sitting still. You're the one who should go to university."

"What about retail? New stuff isn't stained."

"Like a mall job? Yuck. What's wrong with my ideas?"

"Nothing. It's just, no offense, but I have a hard time seeing you as part of a crew. You're more the independent type."

"Independent? That's diplomatic of you." Ev bends to pick up a flat stone near her boot. "I don't hate people. I just like being alone. And I like being outside. *And* I need

219

a job with minimal stain contact."

"Not necessarily."

"Are you kidding? Of course I do," Ev insists. "I need to focus on safety. Stay vigilant."

Noemi laughs out loud, at the same time throwing an arm around Ev and squeezing her. Her nails are coated in gold glitter.

"Vigilant? You're such a Dark Knight. Oh hey, maybe you can wear a cape and fly around the city on your bike, rescuing people from evil bottle caps."

"Ha ha."

"Too bad we're not billionaires." Noemi picks up a stone and flicks it at the water. It skips once and vanishes beneath the surface. "Have you ever thought that maybe you're *too* careful?"

"I don't even know what that means."

"Like, couldn't you just notice a stain and move on?"

"Most of the time I do."

"Right. So how about all the time? No gloves. No avoidance. No needing to constantly keep your spaces clean. Just . . . living your life. And if you happen to touch a stain, shaking it off. I mean, they're not *your* emotions."

"But I experience them like they're mine."

"Huh."

Ev can tell she doesn't understand. Noemi's more happy-go-lucky than Ev. That's why people are naturally attracted to her. Ev doesn't even know how a person goes about "shaking things off." Then again, Noemi doesn't remember what stains can do. She doesn't have to worry that there might be a monster lurking somewhere inside her, waiting for the right stain to come along and unleash it.

"What if it's like antibiotics?" Noemi asks. "If you take them every time you have a cough, eventually you build up a resistance. Then they don't work when you need them. Maybe you need to build up your stain immunity. Be less careful."

"It's not the same thing. And it's not worth the risk."

"Isn't it?"

"No."

"Fine." Noemi throws a rock in the water overhand, revealing her frustration. Waste of a good skipping stone. "How about this? Instead of taking a job you don't really want, why not use your super senses to make money?"

Like our father did, she thinks but she doesn't say it aloud. She doesn't have to, because Noemi can guess what she's thinking. She stands, stretching, and then bends

221

to pick up two more flat stones.

"There's nothing wrong with using your specific skill set to your advantage. It's what everyone does. If I were you, I'd collect things that attract money and influence. I know that's not your style."

"It's deceptive."

"Or a tool in the arsenal." Noemi shrugs. "At the very least, you could find things people want and then sell those things to them. You'd be good at it, *and* you'd be your own boss."

"Maybe."

"Honestly, Ev? If you keep coming up with reasons why a normal existence isn't going to work for you, you might not have a choice."

Ev throws one of the stones. It hops across the water two, three, four, five times.

Behind her Noemi whoops. "Nice!"

Ev stands on the bank, thinking about what Noemi said. Could she make money from stains? If she were careful about it? If she did it responsibly? She strokes the last rock in her palm. Maybe she can.

20

Ev rolls another rock over with the toe of her shoe and watches a handful of tiny crabs skitter across the pebbled beach. The last of the sun's light warms her shoulders. Across the water, on the North Shore, every window reflects burning gold. The sky over the mountains is tinted pink. Behind her, Owen and Harriet perch side by side on a log, sharing sips from a flask. She can hear their low voices murmuring, interrupted occasionally by Harriet's bark of laughter.

They didn't mean to work until sunset. Owen brought over several boxes of toys in the morning, and Ev began work in the small room off the main floor, the one that used to be a vault, the one they decided would be devoted to play. While Harriet told stories, Owen dug out other pieces from the kitchen to show them, watercolor landscapes, a blue-and-gold silk brocade coat, strings of old Christmas tree lights. Harriet and Ev argued over where each one belonged.

Harriet's enthusiasm has infected Ev, and she's glad. For the first time in fifteen years, she isn't afraid of her own skin, afraid of touching things. For the first time, at least on good days, like this one, she can imagine a life outside of day-to-day survival. It hasn't been seamless. Sometimes, Harriet moves too fast. Some days, the emotions seem to rush at Ev from every direction, and she needs a long walk and some fresh air. Other days, it's Harriet's story spirals that drive her away, one object after another sending her down a rambling, never-ending path of loosely connected memories. Thankfully, Owen has more patience for Harriet's reveries than Ev does. He's happy to listen in Ev's stead whenever necessary while she assembles shelving. There are always plenty of shelves to work on.

They've separated the main room into zones; objects are gathered in loose piles according to their dominant emotion. Owen has taken to the system with cheer, despite not having a clue what makes one pair of shoes fall under courage and another under desire. He's declared the system charming, made signs for each of the piles using cardboard and a black marker, and delivers items as ordered without question. Harriet refuses to part with a single thing, but has kept her promise to Ev, dutifully placing any objects skewing toward the negative in a box for Owen to deliver to the vault downstairs.

The only exception to their system is Owen's dragon. Its massive head lies in the front corner next to the window. Owen spends an hour or two each day adding to it, and Harriet seems not to mind that he picks freely from her objects, so long as he doesn't damage them. The challenge of holding the dragon's head together without permanently bonding the pieces has consumed Owen for several days. He finally settled on a sculpted wire frame into which he tucks objects lovingly one by one. If he continues adding to it, eventually it will dominate the room.

Today, however, the dragon slumbered while Owen unloaded and presented objects one by one. The landscapes went to gratitude, all except the one with the ducks, which clearly belonged to affection. The coat went to delight. The Christmas lights stayed in the play room. Owen spent the better part of the afternoon stringing them up beneath the wide molding around the ceiling. None of them noticed the time passing until the sky outside began to darken.

Ev stretches her bare fingers wide. She squats, runs them over the tide-polished beach, slick pebbles, and barnacled mussel shells. The motion reminds her of the way Harriet touches each of her objects as she lays it out on the sorting table. What's the word on the tip of her tongue? Reverence.

"Ev. Time to pick up the food."

She stands and turns to them. Owen sits spine-straight, legs crossed, smile angled at the sun. Next to him, leaning into his side, Harriet tips the flask to her lips. She wears a wide-brimmed straw hat with an explosion of silk flowers around the band. She has a brown-and-yellow crocheted afghan wrapped around her middle; she even trundled into the cab with it. They look so content.

Noemi's voice interrupts her warm thoughts.

I can't wait to meet new Mom and Dad.

Shut up. She pushes her sister from her mind. Appearances can be deceiving. To an outsider, they could be a strange little family unit. But it's not like that. It's a job, nothing more. And Harriet's game face doesn't fool either Ev or Owen. The work has been taking its toll on the woman. She impedes them at every step, finding excuses to slow down the flow of objects from her apartment to the new space, getting lost in stories attached to various items, dragging Ev and Owen down memory lane with her. The way she leans on Owen isn't a sign of affection. She's exhausted. The flask, a necessity. She's using it to dull the pain of sudden and overwhelming change.

The afghan trails behind Harriet across the beach as they make their way back up to the street where Harriet instructed the driver to wait for them. Not for the first time, Ev wonders who she is, this woman with wads of cash folded and tucked in her thrift store clothing. But warmth and heavy eyelids and the smell of dal makhani filling the back seat of the cab melts the questions away.

It's dark by the time they pull up to the Dragon, so it takes a moment for Ev to recognize the shape of the person standing outside its door as Noemi's.

"Isn't that your sister?" Owen asks, at the same time that Ev blurts out, "She's here?"

"Oh," breathes Harriet.

A queer combination of emotions rises up in Ev, surprise, relief, and irritation. For two weeks she's been asking Noemi to come, every time she sees her, as infrequent as those occasions have become. In a stroke of luck, a one-bedroom with a den came up in the building, two floors down. It took Ev and Noemi an hour to move in. The den is more of a nook, no door and barely big enough to wedge a single mattress into, but Noemi is plenty happy with it. Ev folded two dozen gold paper cranes and strung them over Noemi's window, and they mounted a set of curtains across the entrance. Since they settled her into her tiny space, Noemi has all but vanished from Ev's life.

She barely noticed at first. Noemi works late at the restaurant and sleeps in late. They're rarely home at the same time, and their overlaps tend to be short, punctuated by Noemi rooting through Ev's closet or foraging in the kitchen before heading out again. Ev declines her sister's invitations to join her late at night for drinks, and Noemi finds excuses to stay away from the Dragon. It's only been the last day or two that Ev has begun to wonder if Noemi is avoiding her. Seeing her here, finally, means they're still okay. So why the irritation?

Maybe she's afraid they'll like Noemi better. Most people do. But she wanted Noemi to come to the Dragon. She needs her to meet Harriet, to see what they're doing here, to confirm that Ev's new work is positive, that it's good. That it's not dangerous. So, she greets her sister with a smile.

"You came."

"I did. I figured it's the only way I'll ever see you. Sorry I'm so late." Noemi tilts her head and shrugs, her tone as light and friendly as always, but her smile not quite reaching her eyes. They're shadowed, Ev notices, underscored by quarter-moon slices of purple. Beneath the streetlight, she sees the color in her sister's hair has faded, leaving the ends a bleached-out orange.

"You're right on time." Ev holds up the take-out bags. "Have you eaten?"

"Hello, Noemi." Rather than extend a hand, Owen bows to her. "It's nice to finally meet you in person."

"This is Owen," says Ev. "And Harriet." She looks around for Harriet, who stands two paces behind Ev, out of the streetlight's halo.

"Hello." Harriet removes her hat slowly, approaching Noemi as if she's a deer in the wild. Noemi stares back at Harriet, sullen faced, chin tipped up in defiance. It's a cooler introduction than Ev expected. After all, Noemi convinced her to take the job in the first place. She begged Ev to introduce her to Harriet. Ev realizes it's up to her to break the silence before it gets any more awkward. She rattles the take-out bags.

"Shall we eat?"

The spell broken, the words burst from Harriet in a rush.

"Of course. Welcome, welcome. Come inside. There's plenty for everyone."

Owen swings the door open for them, and they file in, Harriet, then Ev, with Noemi trailing behind, still mute.

"Everything okay?" Ev whispers behind her. She tries to meet Noemi's eyes, but Noemi looks over Ev's shoulder, into the dark building.

"Just tired," Noemi whispers back with a faint smile. She's always been this way, running hot and cold. Ev can't keep up, has never been good at figuring out what triggers Noemi's distant spells. She decides to say yes to drinks next time her sister asks. Owen hits the lights at the same time that the door shuts behind Noemi.

"Whoa," she says.

Ev studies Noemi's expression for hints of fear. She lets out a breath she didn't know she was holding when she sees only wonder there. It's the confirmation she needs.

The room is alive. It doesn't look like much, not yet. Boxes and piles of junk are loosely organized into sections, pushed up against bare walls. Stacks of wood lie near the center of the room next to Owen's table saw, where they work on building the massive shelving units that will compartmentalize the space. Sawdust scents the air and coats the tile flooring.

Some of the piles of junk have taken interesting forms, thanks to Owen. His model dragon isn't enough. He can't resist "artifying," piling objects into interesting shapes, stringing them from wires along the walls and across the ceiling, gathering others on shelves and furniture to create miniature scenes.

Owen never says anything about the magic that exists here, maybe because Ev has made it plain she doesn't want to talk about it, or maybe because Harriet has explained it all to him when she's not around. But she can see the glow in Owen's eyes. It matches Noemi's. They can feel that the Dragon is something incredible.

The magic doesn't live in the appearance of the collection. It grows from the careful arrangement of energies. Harriet calls it "curating emotions." There's a flow to the space, and as Noemi walks around it, Ev can see it in action as it plays out in her expressions, each section evoking a different feeling. Compassion, awe, wonder. Calm, comfort, safety. Protection. Maternal love.

In the back corner, at the entrance to the play room, Noemi pauses. This is where curiosity and joy meet. Plush animals and wooden toys sit on blankets and beanbag chairs and old tire swings. Paper dolls hang in zigzags from one end of the room to the other and back again, wound in and out of the twinkling lights Owen strung earlier that day.

Ev doesn't need to ask Noemi what she thinks. She's following the path of the childhood she deserved. Ev's eyes fill as she watches her sister wander through the toys with her arms outstretched, touching everything, her face lit up. She smiles suddenly, picking up a deck of cards with blue and red backs, softened at the edges from decades of shuffling.

"Skip-Bo! Hey, remember this?"

"Nope."

"Sure, you do. We played it every day for a whole summer. At what's-her-name's house. Elsie. Elsie and Jack. They had a gazebo in the backyard."

Noemi always remembers the good parts. When Ev remembers that foster home, she thinks of liver, squishy and cold on her plate, and the missing fingers on Jack's left hand, and the fear she couldn't shake that somehow those two things were related. She thinks of the picture of a bloody, tortured Jesus on the cross that hung above the dining room table. She thinks of that big rug, the purple one that made her avoid the living room at all costs, the true reason she convinced Noemi to hang out with her in the gazebo instead of inside the house.

"Spite and Malice," says Owen, as though he's read Ev's mind.

"Huh?" Noemi wrinkles her nose at the cards.

"Spite and Malice. It's an old card game. I used to play it with my grandmother. That's all Skip-Bo is, really." Owen nods at Noemi. "Shall we?"

"Definitely." All traces of Noemi's bad mood have vanished. Ev leaves her sister in the play room with Owen and puts the takeout on the sorting table. Harriet sits in her armchair, her brows furrowed, the only person in the room who seems to be unaffected by its uplifting energies. Exhaustion hangs around her eyes.

"I'll fix you a plate. You must be starving."

"When I came to the market that first time," Harriet says, "you told me there were no others."

"There aren't." She spoons some palak paneer over rice and passes it to Harriet with a fork. "Noemi's my sister, but she's not like me."

"You sure about that?"

"Of course." Ev stifles her irritation. No one knows Noemi better than she does.

Harriet nods absently and says nothing more, but Ev notices that for the rest of the evening, the lines around her boss's mouth never soften.

21

For the first time in five years, Harriet can see her living room floor. She sits on one of the bare spots, her fingers tracing the wood grain, documenting the scratches and dents that tell the story of this room; a landscape hidden only a few weeks ago, now exposed. So many exposed places. This apartment has been her home for a dozen years, but it's become unrecognizable. Harriet's skin stretches tight across her forehead. Boxes shield her to the right, but on the left, empty space looms between the sofa and the window. She shivers, imagining cold air seeping between the cracks around the windowpane. She reminds herself that it is July, but the cold eats at her anyway.

All morning she has sat in this spot, trying to put the pieces of herself back together. The landscape of her collection has been so drastically altered. She used to know each item's place. Her treasures existed in two places simultaneously, both in their physical home and in the catalog within her mind. Now the pages of Harriet's catalog have been torn out and scattered. She's not sure if she will be able to put it back together again.

This is only the beginning.

Her fingers graze a red rubber ball resting against the leg of the coffee table. It sends out tiny sparks of playfulness, as though to remind her to lighten up. She hasn't seen the ball in years, but remembers all the same, how she found it half-buried in the gravel beneath the swings at the playground down the road. It almost crackled with buoyancy then. The ball's energy has faded since, though not as much as Harriet would expect. Children impress their emotions into objects so easily, as easily as they forget and abandon their little treasures. She lets her hand hover near the ball and tries to speak to it the way Ev speaks to objects, so that they speak back, revealing their stories or even moving beneath her touch. The ball doesn't respond. She can glean nothing of its history. She can't cause it even to wiggle, much less to roll. She thought she might learn to inspire life and movement from her treasures the way Ev does with so little effort. Instead, as Ev grows more powerful, more confident, Harriet disintegrates. Ev builds her muscle memory, while Harriet's mental muscles atrophy by the day.

She hears Owen in the hall, carrying another box away. In ten minutes, he will come and load her into the van too. Enough self-pity. She's wasting valuable time. Her knees crack as she pushes to her feet, using the coffee table — now mostly bare — for support. Her trousers are coated with dust, and her brain feels similarly fuzzed. As she walks down the hall, she uses the wall for balance. She can do that now, touch the wall. Cobwebs cling to it in places. She lets her palms skim through them. She stops at the door to the left of the kitchen, the one that always stays closed. They haven't tackled this room yet, except for the single items Harriet has been extracting one by one at night, the ones she doesn't want Ev to see. But the rest of the apartment is almost finished. They'll start the second bedroom tomorrow, and she's not ready. She needs to move more quickly, and anyway, she's not sure how much longer she can keep working at night. A good night's sleep would likely go a long way toward curing her constant headache, confusion, and slowly creeping sense of dread.

It's not until she hears Owen's footsteps

in the outer hall that she realizes she's been frozen in place, her hand resting on the doorknob. She waits until he's taken another box before she opens the door.

The mingled energy of the room releases into her face like a ghost's sigh, making her shoulders and her heart drop another two inches. The door only opens a foot, just enough for her to wedge her body in sideways. That's all she needs. The box she wants waits just inside, a perfect cube and small enough that she can hold it under one arm while she shuts the door with the other. Its wrongness presses into her side, making her flesh crawl.

"You're quiet this morning. Are you all right?" Owen says as Harriet shuffles past him, leaving him to lock up the apartment. He wears his forehead wrinkles, as he often does in the mornings. His gaze falls to the box. The wrinkles deepen.

"Bad night," she says.

"Shall we stop for tea on the way?"

"Later." The sooner she deposits the box into the vault, the better. Owen rushes ahead to get the front door for her. He tries to take the box, but she turns away.

"I'll hold on to this one," she tells him.

It sits heavily between her feet on the floor of the van. Harriet feels queasy and she can tell it's bothering Owen, too. He jerks from lane to lane, twice laying on the horn.

"Take it easy," Harriet snaps. She reaches into her pocket, feels for Frédérique, holds him tight, takes deep breaths.

"Sorry." Owen fills his lungs, blows out his breath. He gives Harriet a sidelong glance. "It's that box, isn't it? I don't like it. What's in there?"

"Something for the vault."

"Something you don't want Evelyn to see." He presses his foot on the gas. "Why didn't you take it over last night?"

"I was too tired last night."

"That's what you're doing, isn't it? Filling the vault with things she won't like when she's not around to stop you?"

"I'm protecting her."

"Are you? Or are you protecting yourself?"

Harriet bites her lip, hard. *Get to the Dragon, deposit the box.* The tension will fade. She says nothing.

"How many more of those do you have?"

"In my apartment? Only a handful."

Owen throws her a sharp look, which she ignores. They arrive at the Dragon, and he hops out without a word, rubbing his temples. He throws open the back doors. Harriet waits until he's brought in the first load. Ev usually comes out with him then, to check out the van's contents and help Owen unload. She opens her door and looks busy digging through her purse until they're both occupied. Then she grabs the box and heads inside, down the hall, down the stairs. Straight to the vault.

If she could run down the stairs, she would. Instead, she takes them one at a time, feeling the aggressive energies of the box's contents bleeding through the cardboard into her chest. Her hand shakes on the banister.

"What are you doing?"

Harriet stumbles at the cold tone of Ev's voice. Her foot skids off the last step, and she clings to the banister for support, the box almost slipping out of her hands. She composes herself and turns. Ev stands silhouetted at the top of the stairs.

"I'm delivering this to the vault."

"What's in that box?"

Harriet doesn't answer. She knows damn well Ev can feel what's in the box. The object it contains is unimportant.

"I don't want that in here." Ev's tone is flat, final.

"I knew you wouldn't." Harriet backs toward the vault door. "That's why I brought it straight down here. Go help Owen. I'll take care of this."

Ev begins to descend the stairs. "I don't want it in the vault. I don't want it in the building."

"I can't take it back to the apartment. The vault is the best place for it."

"No. Get it out of here." Ev's voice shakes. "Owen!" she yells.

"Don't bring Owen into this. These are my things."

"It's a bad thing," Ev whispers. Then, loud again, "You promised. I get to decide."

"You *are* deciding. You're deciding every-thing." Harriet's fingers clench against the cardboard. "They're my things, not yours. I pay for all of this. I pay your wages. You listen to me."

"No, you listen to me!" Ev screams. The box flies from Harriet's hands and smashes against the wall before clattering to the floor. A dark blur rushes toward Harriet's face. She lets out a hoarse shriek. The object abruptly stops in midair and drops.

"What's going on? Everything okay?" Owen's voice floats down the stairs. He flicks the light on.

Ev and Harriet both stare at the object now lying inert on the stairs between them. It's a child's toy, a plastic shark.

Ev's voice comes out ragged. "Get it out of here. Burn it."

Harriet squats. There are tears on her cheeks she didn't notice shedding. She picks up the shark gingerly and tosses it into the box.

"You heard her," she says to Owen. She passes him the box. "Take this outside and burn it."

"I'm sorry," Ev says in a low tone. She sounds as shaken as Harriet. "I didn't mean to."

Harriet turns away. She hobbles past the vault. She scraped her Achilles tendon when she slipped on the stairs and needs the vault wall to keep her upright. She keeps on, to the corner in the back of the basement, the one that feels safe. She lowers herself to the ground among cobwebs and spider carcasses. A nap, that's what she needs. She's too tired for this work today. She hears raised voices on the floor above and then a clatter like a hailstorm raining down over her head. She bends, puts her head on her knees, and covers her ears like a child.

She's back in her childhood attic, curled up tight, face pressed into a dusty blue blanket, stiff black dress straining across her hips. A floor below, her mother breaks apart her bedroom. Shattering glass, beads, and bangles hitting the wall.

Everything she does is bad and wrong.

She likes this corner. Maybe she'll stay. Maybe she'll stay curled up in a ball just so, until she's joined the spiders. She imagines the story of the person who lived here. A dishwasher from the restaurant, a teenager perhaps. A regular at the bottle depot across the street, befriended by a kindhearted cook and given a home. He put posters on the walls. There are loops of old masking tape still stuck to the concrete. She could put pictures up too.

Footsteps on the stairs pull her back to the present. She braces herself for a confrontation, but it's only Owen.

"Did you do it?" she asks him.

"It's gone." He looks sad. He sits down beside her.

"And Evelyn?"

"She's gone too. Why did you keep that shark?"

"It's alive." She struggles to say more, but can't. Saying it aloud only makes it seem stupider.

"All life is sacred?"

Yes. She tries to explain. "Who am I to judge which lives are worthy and which are not? I carry hostility in my bones. Anger. Judgment."

"We all do."

"You don't."

"Some of us carry it on the surface, some of us bury it. Or turn it on ourselves." There's a hitch in Owen's voice that makes Harriet pause. What has Owen buried? Or whom?

"Who is it? Who does she remind you of?"

He says nothing.

"Do you have kids?"

"A son."

His shortness tells Harriet that she's poking around the edges of something, that she should let it lie.

"Are you close?"

He stiffens. She half expects him to lash out, but after a moment his shoulders slump.

"No," he says. "We haven't spoken in some years."

"How old is he?"

"Please. I'd rather not."

"Well, we all have regrets. Mine is my brother." Why is she still talking when Owen clearly wants to drop the subject? "I'm an idiot," says Harriet.

"No." Owen sounds tired, as though the effort of speaking is all he can manage. "You're wonderful."

"Ev doesn't think so."

"Honestly? She's happier than I've ever seen her."

Harriet tries to laugh, but the sound that comes out sounds more like a whimper.

"She needs some time. She's frightened. But the best things in life are always the scariest, don't you think?"

Perhaps. Then again, Harriet has never been a particularly courageous woman.

"Bunny and Irma are going to the moon."

Evelyn looks up from her coloring book as Noemi picks up her two favorite stuffies and flies them up to her windowsill.

"What are they going to do there?"

"Dancing." Noemi bounces them up and down. "I'm glad you're here today, Evin."

"Me too." She's been spending more time in Noemi's bedroom lately, coloring or playing games with her little sister. Many of Noemi's things have feelings, all of them good. It's the nicest place in the whole house.

Evelyn doesn't bring her homework to the shop anymore. She only goes there when Daddy asks for her. The workshop feels scary now. He never sold the sewing machine. It's still there, in the middle of the floor, and he has added more bad things since. He doesn't take Evelyn with him on Sundays. He goes out alone and comes back hours later with one or two objects at a time, things that feel sad or angry. Instead of selling them, he leaves them to collect dust in the workshop. He's been refinishing the same sofa for weeks, an ugly fearful thing. Few customers come to the shop anymore. Evelyn has seen how people go in and then come out a few minutes later with their faces changed. They look ill or frightened and leave quickly. Daddy doesn't seem to notice or care.

Evelyn now knows that the bad thing in the filing cabinet is a pair of old scissors. At first, he kept them locked up, but he stopped that, and now they sometimes sit on the worktable, where he can see them. They hurt her head and her stomach, so she only goes to the workshop when he comes to the house and asks for her. Then they have a lesson. They practice making bubbles in Evelyn's mind, and Daddy tells her that, even with poisoned things all around them, their minds can still be safe and clean.

"Keep the dirt out, Evelyn," he tells her, over and over. Once Evelyn tried to point out that Daddy's mind didn't seem safe anymore.

"Don't be ridiculous," he snapped at her. "I'm testing myself, getting stronger. Building resistance. You will too. Now, focus."

Even the rest of the house feels wrong. Daddy spends most of his time in the workshop now, but when he comes into the house for occasional meals, he brings his unhappy energy with him. The kitchen is heavy and tired because of Mama's sadness, and the dining room crackles with tension. Still, it's better in the house than in the shop. She'd rather be in the house, and best of all she likes to stay in this room with Noemi.

Mama appears in the doorway. "Girls? Time to eat."

"Is Daddy coming?" asks Noemi.

"Not tonight."

"Good," says Noemi. "I don't like him."

A crease appears between Mama's eyebrows. "You mustn't say that," she tells Noemi, but there's no anger in her words, only sadness.

Noemi refuses to look at Mama. "He's a bad guy," she insists.

"No, Noemi. He's not a bad guy." Mama sits down on the floor between them. That means they're going to have a talk. Evelyn doesn't say anything. She doesn't want to tell Mama she's wrong. Noemi only sees Daddy at mealtimes, and then he's quiet and mean-eyed. He doesn't say anything, but you know the thoughts inside his head are not good ones.

"I know your father is acting differently than usual. Sometimes people's brains get sick. They're not bad people. They just need help."

"Can you help him?" Evelyn asks her mother.

"I'm trying."

Evelyn can help. If she makes the scissors go away, everything will go back to normal. But it will be hard. When they're not locked away in the filing cabinet, Daddy keeps them close.

"It's not his brain," she tells Mama. "It's the bad-feeling things."

Mama takes Evelyn's hands. Her deep brown eyes meet Evelyn's, searching for something. "Tell me what it's like. How do you know when things have feelings?"

Evelyn tries to explain. "Big emotions stick to objects." She points at Bunny and Irma. "Noemi's stuffies feel good."

"And Daddy has objects in the workshop with big, bad feelings?" Evelyn nods, and Mama nods along with her, but she can tell her mother doesn't believe it. Daddy says she shouldn't talk about her way of sensing things because other people won't understand and might even be frightened. It's true. Even her own mama doesn't understand.

"We need to make opposite feelings," Noemi says. She has her magic wand out and she swishes it in the air. Ev can feel it from where she's sitting, brave and daring. "Until Daddy isn't mad anymore." She points the stick at Mama. "*Poof.* You're happy."

"That won't work," says Evelyn, frowning at Noemi. "You can't wish people better."

Noemi ignores Evelyn. She points the wand at Bunny and Irma. "You're happy. And you're happy."

Mama watches Noemi thoughtfully. "No, you can't wish people better," she says slowly. "But being sad and making more bad feelings won't help. Making happy feelings, maybe that could help." She looks at Evelyn. "Maybe you could change things."

"I can change things!" yells Noemi. "All of you are happily ever after. *POOF.*" Then she throws her wand on the floor and starts to cry.

"Oh, sweet pea." Mama gathers Noemi up in her arms. "We're all worried about Daddy. But for now, it's very important that you both stay quiet and out of his way."

Mama's afraid. Evelyn can hear it in her voice. Fear is worse than sadness. It makes

Evelyn's stomach turn over. Noemi sobs with her head in Mama's lap, and Evelyn's heart breaks for her.

"*Shh,*" says Mama into Noemi's hair. "Dinner is getting cold." She picks up Noemi and stands. Noemi is almost too big to be carried. She's half as tall as Mama already. "Let's go wash our hands. Evelyn, come along."

Evelyn lags behind, staring at the discarded wand. Noemi has made a handle for it by wrapping Disney Princess Band-Aids around one end. Evelyn likes the stick. It makes her feel strong. She wishes more than anything that she could actually use it to magically fix everything.

The wand twitches. Evelyn blinks, stares harder. It twitches again.

It's a sign. Evelyn knows the wand is one of Noemi's favorite things, but she needs it more than her sister does right now. She grabs it.

Mama's right. It's up to Evelyn to change things. She has to do something.

22

Ev can hear Owen calling after her as she rushes for the front door, distant and echoing as if they stand at opposite ends of a tunnel. The skin on her hands crawls, and she yanks a pair of gloves out of her back pocket to hide them from sight. She only meant to take the box from Harriet. She didn't expect the stain to fly out like that. It took all her strength to pull her mind away, to let it drop. She feels the effort of it dragging her down even now, as if she's just run ten miles. She might collapse, except she needs so badly to get away.

On the sorting table lies a bag of marbles, some mixing bowls, and a lamp. Also, an axe. It's a good axe, stained with the tranquil hum of quiet labor and the promise of warmth. She stops, imagines taking it and hacking at her wrists, cutting the poison away. Look how strong she's gotten. If she works at it, she can probably use her mind to lift the axe, bring it down on both hands. But it won't make a difference. The stain on Ev bleeds far beyond the place where her hands connect to her body.

If it wasn't a toy. If it was something worse. She's stopped short by a sudden flash of memory.

She waits in the dark until the house is quiet, then fumbles down the path to the workshop, barefoot so as to make less noise. She lets herself in oh so quietly, if she opens the door too far it will squeak. She's following the call of the scissors. The sickness in them has grown. The thought of touching them makes her tummy do somersaults, but she has no choice. She reaches out. Instead of cold metal she brushes against hot, rough skin.

She gathers what's left of her courage and says aloud what she's been too afraid to say for days.

"It's the scissors. They're changing you."

"You don't understand."

"You have to let them go. Keep the dirt out, Daddy."

"The dirt's not on the outside. It's in here."

He puts a finger to her chest, pushes the spot where her heart is.

"We're the stains."

"Evelyn." Owen's warm hand on her

shoulder makes her jump. "What's going on?"

Ev shrugs him away. "I gotta get out of here."

"You can talk to me."

"No. Work out your family shit on someone else. You're not my father."

She almost regrets her words when Owen pulls back as though she's slapped him. But the need to get away, to get some headspace, wins over her conscience. She turns to the door.

"I'm your friend," Owen says. Quiet words soaked in sadness. She cringes at the hurt in his voice. "I know you're afraid. Let me help."

The anger returns. She can say anything to him, and still he speaks to her with pity, with the quiet patience of a disappointed parent. Fuck that. She'll show him why she can't talk to him. Why she can't stay. Ev reaches out with her mind, connects to the closest thing that's safe. Not the axe, something else. She lets her mind fill up with spirited rivalry and possessiveness. A rattle fills the room. Dozens of marbles burst from the velvet bag on the table and fly into the air like a swarm of colorful insects. Owen's eyes widen with shock as he watches them circle the room. Ev lets the marbles fall.

They rain down on the floor, rolling in all directions.

"I'm not afraid," she tells him. "I'm terrified. And you should be too."

Ev leaves him standing there, lost for words. She grabs her bike and rides away. She feels weak, but she pushes herself, staying high on her pedals, pumping down to the seawall and following it around the park, past the beaches, keeps going, going, as though if she rides far enough she can escape the memory of the fear on Harriet's face, the shock on Owen's. From time to time, she pauses long enough to pull her phone out of her pocket and fumble out a hasty text to Noemi. At her sister's urging, Ev has replaced her old flip phone for a smartphone ("because no one but you actually makes phone calls anymore").

Where are you? I need to talk to you.

In person. It's important.

Please?

Despite Noemi's insistence that texts are the best way of reaching her, she doesn't reply. Ev doesn't think about where she's going, doesn't even realize the path she's following until she's up and over the bridge and coasting toward Vanier Park. She's so accustomed to calculating garbage pickup days across the city that she's automatically

255

drifted to the neighborhood that has its bins out for pickup. She doesn't have her trailer, isn't in that line of work anymore. But she continues, tracing her route through the quiet residential streets behind the park, glancing idly inside blue boxes, letting the comfort of old routines help her catch her breath.

A radiant vibration tickles her brain. Now that she's become even more tuned in, she can feel stained objects from a long distance. She peers down the street. Whatever bit of discarded emotion is there, it's in the blue bin at the end of the road. She heads to it instinctively, the chase still exciting, despite everything. Soon she can see it too. A tin can with holes punched into it in a starburst pattern. Melted wax drips down one side. An uncomplicated happy stain. It's not pretty, but she could get a few bucks for it, in her old life.

She leaves it where it lies. Something else keeps tugging at her, not an object, but a thought. She gets off her bike, walks it along the street to slow it down, give it time to finish forming.

It is this. Even frightened, even angry and betrayed and cornered, Ev was in control back at the Dragon. The shark dropped to the floor because she made it drop. The marbles, she could've driven them through Owen's skull if she'd wanted to. She catches a flash of what that would look like, all those colorful little balls turned to bullets, pulverizing Owen's head, bits of brain splattering on the freshly painted walls. She squeezes her eyes shut, trying to force the image out of her mind. Her head spins and for a moment, she can't breathe.

A hand on her shoulder. She's spun around. There is blood sprayed across his face. His spit flies into her mouth when he speaks.

"Go get your sister."

Ev shudders, leans her forearms on her knees, and counts her breaths until she's back in the present. She's here. She's okay.

Despite the pain of intruding memory, Ev really feels okay once she breathes herself back to the present. Better than okay. She didn't hurt Owen. That didn't happen. It didn't happen because Ev made sure it wouldn't. Harriet kept her promise. She has made Ev strong. She has freed her.

Struck by sudden giddiness, Ev rolls back to the bin with the tin can lantern. She scans the street for onlookers and, finding it empty, reaches her mind out. She takes her time, lets its joy fill her up, warm her chest. She can do this. She can do it while protecting the part of her mind that is Evelyn, the cool, silent bubble, the snow globe place. She floats the lantern up, up, toward her outstretched hand.

The rattle of wheels on pavement breaks her concentration. The lantern falls, rolls toward her toes. Ev swoops down to grab it and hangs it by its wire handle on the handlebars of her bike before straightening to see who's intruded on her moment.

Up ahead, a shopping cart, piled high with plastic bags full of cans and bottles, rounds the corner. Ev recognizes the hunched back, the small frame trundling behind the cart, draped in black even on a hot summer day, ball cap perched on coarse gray hair. Owen knew his name, that day when they picked up the mannequins. Eddie. He stares in her direction, his eyes focused on a point behind her shoulder. He mutters something incomprehensible.

"You won't find much down there," says Ev. "This block's been picked over."

Eddie turns up the volume on his rambling. " 'It must nestle everywhere, settle everywhere, establish connections everywhere.' "

Something, maybe the way he keeps on searching behind her for something so far away he won't ever find it again, prompts her to unhook the lantern and reach it out.

"Found this. It's got a good amount of wax left in it, if you could use a night-light."

"No," he says.

Ev suddenly wants him to have it; it seems to her at that moment that she's found it for him.

"It'd do you good."

"I don't want it," he snaps. He backs away, shaking his head, eyes flicking cautiously toward the lantern and away, as though he doesn't want it to notice him watching it.

"Sorry."

"That's not for me."

"Okay."

Maybe he's right. Maybe you can't force happiness on a person. But you can build a place where a person could find happiness when they're ready for it.

Harriet's museum suddenly makes a lot more sense.

She feels a buzz in her pocket. Noemi.

For sure, honey. Meet me at the apartment in an hour?

The last few stones of heaviness in her chest melt away.

"See you around," she tells Eddie, before she throws her leg over the crossbar and heads home, the lantern swinging next to her right fist. It will make a nice gift for Noemi. Her sister deserves a little joy.

23

Ev wakes alone to an empty apartment, no sign of Noemi having kept her promise. She waited all evening, finally passing out on the couch, the lantern on the floor at her feet. A quick check of her phone shows a message sent at two in the morning.

I suck. Sorry. Catch up tomorrow?

Ev doesn't bother to reply. She needs to wait until the lump of disappointment and resentment subsides. At least Noemi is still alive, still somewhere in the city, still planning to return. But where did she spend the night?

Another Saturday already, which means another sailing class. Ev thinks about skipping to spite her sister. Except she wants to go. She actually craves more time on the water. She's even the first student to arrive. As she coasts down the bike path and through the gates of the sailing club, she sees Brett alone by the shore, checking the rigging on one of the small crafts. She presses the brakes, intending to turn around and ride up toward Spanish Banks to kill some time, but Brett sees her first. He waves that full-body wave and calls out to her.

Ev puts her foot down, stops rolling. She's deciding if she should wave back when he starts jogging up the beach toward her. She's lost her chance to escape. She busies herself with locking up her bike instead.

"I think I saw you yesterday. Over by Kits Beach."

"Could be."

"It was definitely you." Brett shows all his teeth when he smiles. "You cruised right past my house. Looked through my blue box."

"Ah." Ev drops her gaze, making a show of digging through her backpack for the key to her bike lock. Her cheeks are hot, and it makes her angry. When has she ever cared what people think of her?

"Oh, I don't mind or anything, if that's what you're worried about. As far as I'm concerned, anything that's out on the curb is fair game."

"I'm not worried." It comes out sharper than she intended.

"It's shocking what people throw away, don't you think?"

261

Ev uncaps her water bottle and drinks, letting the awkward silence stretch out. She doesn't want to have this conversation. He seems nice enough, but she just wants to get on a boat. Ev's unfriendliness doesn't seem to particularly faze her teacher.

"You've got enough time for a walk. I saw some seals off the end of the dock earlier."

"Thanks," she says, grateful for the excuse to get away. "I'll check that out."

Brett is as enthusiastic as ever in class, and when it comes time to launch the boats, she again finds herself knee-deep in the ocean next to him. The absorbing work of raising the main sail and navigating the bay chases away any awkwardness, and Brett keeps busy shouting instructions to the other students, leaving Ev free to keep quiet and watch the boat slice through the water. Eventually, Ev realizes Brett is shouting instructions at her.

"Earth to Evelyn!"

"Sorry."

"No worries. Being on the water does that to a person. Can you move the tiller to starboard? We're going to head back."

"Already?"

"Easy there, I'd like to stay dry. Yes, already. We've been on the water for an hour."

It can't have been an hour. Ev bends to check her phone. Something catches her eye. A sheet of ruled paper, torn from a notebook and folded into a neat square, tucked under a coil of rope. She grabs it. Written on the outside of the square are the words "30 Things I Want to Do Before I'm 30." The paper is damp at the creases, and the ink has bled, but it feels like promise, like adventure.

"What'd you find?"

Ev holds the note up so Brett can read the words on the outside. His eyes light up like a child's.

"Nice. Is that yours?"

"God, no." Ev laughs. "I just found it."

"Why is that funny?"

"I don't plan for the future." She's never dared. She tries to imagine what her list might look like. *Get Noemi in college. Don't go nuts.* That's about it. But that was her old life. Before, all her energy went into protecting herself. Protecting her sister. She never imagined she could hold down a normal job or learn how to sail.

At least, I never used to plan for the future.

"And now?"

Did she say that out loud?

"Things are changing."

Like Noemi said. Maybe it's the way that

263

paper feels in the palm of her hand, or maybe it's the snapping of the sail or the wind boxing her ears that sends electricity down her spine.

"Sounds like you've got your feet in two different boats."

"What's that mean?"

"Something my dad says. Imagine your life as two boats. One's your past. The other's your future. If you try to keep one foot in each boat, eventually you're going to fall in the water. You need to pick a boat. Allison and Grace, we're turning around, let's go!

"So. Are you going to read that list? Maybe you'll get some ideas for your own."

"No." Ev unfolds the paper without reading the words and begins to manipulate it into another shape. A paper boat, its hull and sail decorated in black ink. The occasional word pops out at Ev as she lowers it over the edge. Scuba. Tokyo. Babies.

She sends the paper boat skimming across the waves. It's easier this time, like she's been building a muscle. There seems to be a quality to each object, the emotion it holds dictating the kind of response she can draw from it. She practiced with the lantern last night, lifting and floating it gently above her bed. She lit the candle inside and used the lantern's joy to control the flame, brightening and dimming its glow. She lasted only a few minutes before her head began to ache and her limbs grew heavy, sending her into a deep, exhausted sleep.

This object is lighter than the lantern. It takes little effort to connect with it, to bring it alive. The list wants to move, so she helps it along. It takes flight, spinning and whirling with the wind until she can see only a speck against the navy blue of the ocean.

"How did you do that?"

She's forgotten Brett completely. *Oops.* Ev shrugs, keeps her back turned.

"Wind must have caught it just right." She squeezes her eyes shut, hoping he'll accept the lie and move on.

"You are a very interesting person, Evelyn."

"Am I?"

"You are. I'd like to know more about you."

Ev can feel her face heating up. But better this conversation than having him question her ability to make paper fly.

"I'm hard to get to know."

"I'm patient." He lets those words hang in the air only a moment before he changes the subject. "You know, I think of all the students in this class, you're the one who's

265

going to stick with sailing."

"I hope so."

"If you really want to learn to sail, you should go to the Greek Islands. Paros."

"I don't know about that." Ev tries to imagine herself in the heart of one of the oldest civilizations in the world. Surrounded by stains going back thousands of years. The thought fills her with terror, but underneath the fear runs a current of excitement. To explore, to move freely through the world — isn't that why she loves riding her bike? Why she loves sailing? What if she could leave this city? What if she could travel?

"There's this little sailing school in the Bay of Naoussa," Brett continues. "I still dream of that crystal-clear water. Paros, Evelyn. You should put that on your list."

I don't have a list, Ev thinks. But she can't quite say it out loud.

A dot on the beach catches Ev's eye. A pink dot. She waves at Noemi, but Noemi doesn't wave back.

As the class wraps up, Ev thinks about how to talk to her sister about her growing power. She wants to show Noemi the lantern, but the lantern is hard work. Something smaller, maybe. Something made of paper.

As she walks up the beach toward Noemi,

she has second thoughts. Noemi's gaze falls past Ev to the water. No eye contact. She's in one of her funny moods. A tray of half-eaten French fries balances on one of Noemi's knees. Ev scatters a half dozen hungry seagulls on her approach.

"You came."

"I promised, didn't I?"

A promise doesn't mean much to you. Ev sits down beside Noemi. The seagulls settle back to the sand, eyeing up Noemi's lunch once more.

"Where were you last night?"

"Work," Noemi replies evasively.

"After that. Is there a guy?"

"There's a guy. Look, something's been bothering me, and I can't keep quiet about it anymore."

Ev's stomach drops. She knows where this is going.

"I've been trying to give you your space and all, but —"

"It's okay." It will be okay, she tells herself. Maybe if they can get past whatever's been eating at Noemi, things can be normal with them again. Whatever *normal* means. She steels herself. "Go ahead."

"It's about the scissors. What happened to them?"

Ev struggles to speak. It's not that she

doesn't want to talk. It's like her throat closes up, like the words can't come out, even if she wants them to. All she can do is shake her head like an idiot, and when words finally do fight their way out, they're inadequate ones.

"I don't know."

"They never found them. And they can't just have vanished. Unless you did something with them. Did you? Did you hide them?"

"I — I don't remember."

"It's just me," Noemi presses. "I'm not going to tell anyone."

"I don't remember!" Ev's shout raises heads along the beach. She glares down at the sand. It's like being in therapy all over again. How many hours did she spend staring at the carpet, unable to speak, or sitting with a crayon in her fist, a blank sheet of paper glaring at her. As though telling the story, or spilling it in red on paper, would somehow lessen its power. Bullshit. Reliving it doesn't help. Breathing helps. Noemi knows this. But Noemi has waited so long for Ev to answer her questions, to help her make sense of their past. She has breathed with Ev a thousand times. It's not her fault she's grown impatient.

"I was eight, Noemi. There are massive,

gaping holes in what I remember. I swear to you, if I did know, I'd tell you."

"Okay." Noemi shrugs, not looking in her direction.

"You don't believe me."

"I didn't say that."

"But you're mad. Do you think I'm lying to you?"

"What if there was a way to help you remember?"

"You're not hypnotizing me."

"I wasn't suggesting that," Noemi says, a little too quickly. "Just, if we could find a way to bring some of it to the surface."

"No."

"Think about it. It might help you to heal."

Ev doesn't reply. This isn't about her healing, and they both know it. After a moment, Noemi offers her the tray of fries. Ev takes one, even though she's not hungry.

"So, what's up? You were desperate to talk to me."

Ev has changed her mind. She doesn't much feel like talking anymore. "It's no big deal," she says. "Just this thing that happened at work."

"What thing?" Noemi shoots her a sharp glance, her brow furrowed. It definitely isn't a good time to bring up the shark incident.

"Nothing. A minor disagreement. I was pissed off yesterday, but I'm better now."

"Are things going okay with Harriet?"

"Yeah. I mean, other than yesterday, they've been great. You were right. This job is what I needed."

"I'm not so sure."

"You were the one who told me to work for Harriet. You pretty much ordered me to take the job."

"That was before."

"Before what?"

"Nothing. Forget it."

"Before you met her." Ev takes Noemi's silence as a yes. A shadow of doubt chills her skin. What does Noemi see that she doesn't?

"You don't like her. Why?"

"I don't trust her." A whine has crept into Noemi's voice. Ev recognizes the tone. She waits. "She doesn't like me."

There it is. Not fear. Jealousy. Ev relaxes.

"Can you blame her? You didn't exactly charm her the other night."

"She kept giving me stink-eye every time I touched anything. Like I was going to steal something."

Ev doesn't point out that Noemi is prone to stealing. When Noemi was twelve, Ev saw her pocketing a tube of lipstick at the

270

drugstore. She made Noemi apologize to the store manager, but she couldn't convince her sister she'd done anything wrong besides getting caught. Over the years, Ev has noticed a lot of nice things appear in Noemi's closet or makeup bag, always "gifts from friends." Ev can't prove that Noemi is a thief, but she knows from experience that Noemi's sense of ownership is . . . fluid.

"She's protective of her stuff," she says to Noemi, trying to keep the conversation light. "I don't think she has any family or friends. Her collection is everything."

"It's weird."

"Everyone's weird, remember?"

"Quit making sense." Noemi picks up a fry and smacks Ev's arm with it, leaving a greasy smear.

"Everyone loves you. Harriet will too. It's inevitable."

"So, I should try again?"

"Yes," Ev says. "Try again."

24

Ev rolls up to the Dragon with a paper bag full of scones in her front basket. White chocolate and blueberry, Owen's favorite. Fresh even, purchased and not scavenged. She still has a hard time forking over cash for things she knows she can get for free, but she does like the freedom of getting what she wants when she wants it. She knows Owen will forgive her for freaking out, shooting marbles everywhere and bolting, but it feels weird to face him again, knowing he's seen the root of her fear. Also, there's the thing she said about daddy issues. She wishes she hadn't brought it up. It will be easier to walk through the door with something to deflect the attention away from her anxiety. It's late, past eleven. She spent the morning riding, intending to go to work but not ready to show her face. She's glided past the building three times already.

She dismounts, peers through the glass doors. Harriet sits in her armchair next to the sorting table. She has an open book in her lap and appears to be asleep. Probably, she's reading — not reading the words, like a regular person would, but the other stories the paper holds. Her lips move. Abruptly she throws her head back and cackles. The laughter bolsters Ev's confidence. All is well inside the Dragon. Best to get this over with.

Ev pulls open the door and wheels her bike inside. She steels herself against the energies of the Dragon. Pleasant as they are, she can't allow another slip like what happened with the shark. She will be more guarded from now on, more responsible. She's unprepared for the sight of Noemi sitting cross-legged on the floor next to Harriet.

Try again, sure. But already?

"Where've you been?" Noemi clasps her knees and arches her spine in a contented cat stretch. She's dyed her hair again, blue on top with pink still showing on the ends of her pigtails. Ev wonders when and where she did it. She didn't come home after her shift last night. Again. Her mystery guy, Ev supposes. She hasn't yet been able to extract any information on him.

"I might ask you the same question."

"Poor Harriet's had no one to keep her company except me and the dragon." Owen's creation looms behind Noemi. He's turned an orange chiffon dress into a lick of flame.

"Sorry I'm late." *No one?* Ev glances through the door of the kitchen, looking for Owen.

"Owen's taking a day off." Harriet remains nestled in her chair, chin up, face composed, although her tone is low and quiet. Ev's heart sinks at the news. She places the bag on the table.

"Is he okay?"

Harriet's gaze meets hers. "He's fine. He'll be back tomorrow."

Ev nods, her shoulders relaxing. Noemi watches the exchange with raised eyebrows. Ev ignores the question in her sister's eyes, opens the paper bag, and tosses a scone at her. Noemi catches it and brings it up to her nose.

"Mm, blueberries. At least you did something useful while you were slacking off." No trace remains of the sullenness Noemi displayed during her first visit to the Dragon. She seems as comfortable folded up at Harriet's feet as if they were old friends.

"I can't believe you're here so early," she

says to Noemi. "Did you sleep at all?"

"Sleep is boring." She speaks around a mouthful of scone. "Anyway, I'm quitting the restaurant."

"Why? What happened?"

"Nothing. I thought I'd work here instead."

A hot flush spreads across Ev's face. Her first instinct is to shut Noemi down. She doesn't want to share the Dragon with Noemi, not that way. She stops herself only because she has to question her motives. Why can't she share? Why so possessive?

"That's not going to happen." It's Harriet who says it, not loudly, but firmly. Ev glances at the woman's face, surprised. She's misread the situation. Harriet's eyes have narrowed. Noemi might have confessed to not trusting Harriet, but the feeling clearly goes both ways.

"Why not? You could use the extra help. I'd rather haul boxes around than serve overpriced drinks to creepy-ass execs."

"This work is not for you," says Harriet. "You need to find your own way."

Noemi presses her lips together. Ev recognizes the expression. She isn't prepared to take no for an answer.

"You don't need to pay me as much as Ev. I just want to help."

"We don't need your help." Even Ev cringes at that.

"But I like it here." Noemi turns to Ev, confused. She isn't used to her charms not working on people.

Ev breaks in. "But Harriet, isn't this what the Dragon is for? Helping people who come looking for it?"

"When it's done. It's not ready yet."

Ev translates in her head. *You mean you're not ready yet.* She turns to Noemi. "You can always come visit. Have dinner with us." She doesn't look at Harriet to see what she thinks of that. Noemi opens her mouth to speak, but Ev ignores her. "Anyway, Harriet's right about finding your own way. Now that we're okay for money, you should be thinking about school."

Noemi looks as though she wants to argue, but instead, she scans the room, her eyes calculating.

"So, what do you do with the bad things?" she asks Harriet.

Rapid change of subject. One of Noemi's favorite tactics. It doesn't throw Harriet off. She doesn't even bother to reply. Noemi tries Ev next.

"The bad stains. You said Harriet's stuff is 'mostly' harmless. What about the things that aren't?"

276

Noemi always knows exactly how to make Ev uncomfortable. She hasn't had a chance to talk to Harriet about the vault since their fight over the shark. It still weighs on Ev, that accumulation of dark emotion below them. Her growing power makes her less afraid, but it remains unfinished business between Ev and Harriet. Still, it's not a conversation she wants to have with Noemi present. She waits for her boss to speak up. But Harriet's gaze falls on Ev, as if she waits for the answer to that question as well.

"Harriet has a plan," Ev says finally. "She's taking care of it." She hopes Harriet can read the message between her words. *I trust you.* From the way the old woman's eyes mist, Ev thinks she understands.

"Does Harriet know what's at stake? Have you told her?" Noemi addresses Harriet directly. "Do you know what our father did?"

"Noemi." Ev freezes in her chair. Her sister has done it again, caught her off balance. The one weapon she's never used. All these years, she's respected Ev's wishes, kept the past their secret. Noemi knows it, too; knows she's crossed a line. She won't look at Ev. And she doesn't stop.

"Did she tell you what the bad things made him do?"

277

"That's enough." Harriet shuts her book with a slap and slams it on the table. Even Noemi jumps at the sudden violence of the noise echoing against the walls. No one speaks for a moment. Harriet stands up slowly.

"Evelyn and I have work to do."

Ev takes Harriet's cue.

"Come on," she says to Noemi. "I'll walk you out." Ev stalks outside, not waiting for Noemi. She needs some air. Harriet will make sure Noemi gets out the door.

She barely has time to catch her breath. She sees a man shuffling down the sidewalk away from the Dragon, head down, moving quickly. Ev's skin prickles at the sight of him. She knows that walk. That round-shouldered posture. Hangdog. Ev breaks into a run to catch up with him. He glances backward slyly and picks up his pace.

"Hey!" Anger makes her careless. She rushes forward, yanks at his arm. "What's up? Are you stalking me now?"

Hangdog blinks at her. He's less greasy than usual. He's clean-shaven, and he's washed and combed his hair.

"I'm sorry," he says, "I wasn't. I wasn't looking for you, I swear," and he sounds sincere enough that Ev actually believes him. He seems different than when she last saw him. It's not just the grooming. He seems less desperate somehow. His gaze doesn't roam the way it once did. His eyes meet hers steadily. She steps back.

"So, you just happened to be in the neighborhood?"

Hangdog rubs his head and glances from side to side, as if hoping for a rescue.

"He's looking for me."

It's Noemi's voice. They both turn toward it.

"Michael. I thought I told you to meet me at New Town," she says. He blushes and hangs his head, his moment of poise gone.

"Go on," she tells him. "I'll be there in ten."

Hangdog scuttles away. Noemi smiles crookedly at Ev, as though she hasn't just betrayed her, not once but twice.

"I guess I'm busted."

"Noemi. Why?" She can't form words around her anger, not only this, but the way Noemi brought up their past with Harriet. Especially that. "Why would you let that loser touch you?"

Her smile fades. She adds a warning tone to her next words. "I like him."

"Is this some kind of revenge? What did I do to deserve this?"

"Oddly enough, Evelyn, it's not about you."

"I don't understand."

"I know you don't. You'll never understand. You're so stubbornly set on a life of celibacy."

"Have you forgotten that he attacked me?"

"It won't happen again."

"You sure about that?"

"I'm an adult. I can look after myself."

Ev shivers at Noemi's cold gaze. "I just don't think it's a good idea."

"It doesn't matter what you think," Noemi says before she walks away. "This is a decision you don't get to make for me."

Owen has repaired Harriet's mug. Sometime in the last few days, its three pieces were glued back together, the seams now almost invisible. She left it on the towel, broken, intending to fix it ever since Ev's first visit, but never getting to it. Harriet lives in the realm of good intentions. Owen, on the other hand, makes things happen. Harriet moves through her apartment, taking stock of all the other marks he has made: cobwebs swept away from corners and light fixtures, the last of the boxes stacked tidily down the hallway, kitchen tiles and appliances scrubbed down. Not only will she vacate in time, she might even get some of her damage deposit back. It's been a long time since Harriet has felt so cared for. So understood. She strokes the mug, trying to rekindle the burst of warmth it gave her when she first discovered it whole. Her chest remains cold. This is the push and pull of the last few weeks, fear and joy in equal measure.

She picks up her evening's burden and locks the door behind her. Night hangs heavy on her shoulders as she sits outside on the concrete steps, waiting. She aches all over. In her head, from the press of a million memories and the weight of the secrets she carries. At the base of her spine, from too much bending. The grinding, relentless change is wearing her down. For days, Harriet has felt wrong. Wobbly on the inside. Unbalanced. She was so snippy with Evelyn's sister earlier. She's not sure why, exactly — perhaps because she's easily irritated of late, perhaps because she doesn't trust Noemi's motives.

She glances at the small shopping bag next to her, wiping her hands on her thighs, grateful to get some distance from it. She doesn't need any additional agitation. The soft weight of Frédérique at her hip reminds her of his hiding place in her jacket pocket. A tiny swell of calm settles Harriet's shoulders as she strokes his velvet head. She waits and wonders. Will she survive the change she's forced upon herself? The Dragon is a marvel. Ev is imposing order on the collection, and it's working. Harriet can feel how the energies flow more freely, how the bright things Ev chooses seem to sing together. The Dragon thrums with joyous harmonies, and there's space for each treasure to *be.*

At the same time, she feels as though she's losing them, and as a result, she's losing herself, coming apart, breaking open from the inside. It's taxing work. Every day, she reassembles her mental catalog, remembering where all her treasures live now that they have transitioned. This is the hardest part. Though her apartment was a health hazard, at least she knew where everything lived. Now she can't be sure that every item is accounted for. She trusts Owen and Ev. Noemi less so, not with those hungry eyes and wandering fingers, but she's watched the other two enough to believe in them. Mostly. She can't help feeling as though things keep falling through the cracks. All day and night, her mind scrambles back and forth across her collection, looking for missing pieces. She can't stop it.

The cabbie pulls up, slowly, headlights trapping Harriet in their glare. Harriet threads her wrist through the handles of the shopping bag and stands up.

"Can you pop the trunk?" She waves to indicate the bag, a bright blue paper bag with the name of a famous jeweler printed in small black letters in the center. It's just the right size to carry a pair of diamond earrings. Or an angry little pistol.

The cabbie stares at her, raises his eyebrows. She stares back until the trunk door rises. She drops the bag inside and then settles into the back seat, ignoring the shake of the cabbie's head. He doesn't know it, but she's sparing him a bad night. The rage in that gun has a way of digging under the skin, leaving anyone who gets too close itching for hours, prone to easy agitation and explosive outbursts.

The day she found it, she felt it from twenty feet away. She knew she should keep walking past that carport, but she didn't. Anger that noisy, she couldn't ignore it. She stopped instead, pretending to look in blue boxes across the alley, until she felt reasonably certain no one was watching. Then she did something careless and irresponsible. Something dangerous. She trespassed, edging past garbage bins until she reached a stack of old paint cans, grabbing a bundle wrapped in paint-spattered canvas and hugging it close to her chest despite the heat of it roaring up at her. She stuffed it in her cart and rolled the length of the alley on quaking legs, sure someone would come chasing her down at any moment. No one did. It took a day for her to get up the nerve to unwrap the bundle, and another to discover the gun was loaded but hadn't been fired, the anger pent up in it still latent, germinating. Harriet liked to think that her theft had perhaps prevented a crime. That she'd walked past that particular carport on that particular day for a reason.

The pistol's influence has lessened in the years she kept it buried in her spare room, but she still feels its heat on her palms and the back of her neck. She keeps quiet as they drive. Best to avoid conversation when she's itching like this.

She always goes in the back door of the Dragon at night. She doubts she'll run into Ev on the street, but just to be safe. There's probably a more expedient way to complete this work, but Harriet's too tired to figure it out. She has thought of asking Owen for help, but he doesn't approve of the deception. Not that she's been outright lying about the vault, she hasn't. But there are things in there that Ev would certainly order her to destroy. Owen might not rat her out to Ev, but she knows better than to ask him to get involved. And she certainly isn't about to put some of these objects into the hands of a stranger. She has to do it herself. That means one or two objects at a time. Slow work. Difficult work, some nights.

The back door is tucked in a small loading bay. Harriet's night vision isn't the best, so she always leaves the light on, a single bulb that hangs over a small wooden sign: *Szechuan Dragon Deliveries Only. Violators Will Be Towed.*

The gun glowers through the side of the bag as she fumbles with the heavy dead bolt. Warm against her thigh. Should she destroy treasures as dark as this one? She's been thinking about it ever since the incident with the shark. Like Owen said, all life is sacred. What right does she have to snuff out the pistol's life? Over time, the anger will fade further, and the gun will grow less volatile. It will complete its life cycle, as all living things do. Harriet is not about to interfere with that. The vault is a fine place to house such things, to keep them safe and to keep them away from those who might be influenced by their energies. In time, Ev will understand. At least, she hopes Ev will understand why she has had to keep some secrets from her.

Harriet lets the door slam shut behind her and feels for the light switch. Down the hall, something clatters to the floor. Harriet wonders what treasures are on the move. They've grown livelier, responding to Ev's energy and the flow she's created within the space. A muffled whisper wipes the smile from her lips. Someone is here. Panic flutters at Harriet's insides. She freezes with her fingers on the switch, feeling her heart speed up. There are three options. It's Ev or Owen, neither of whom can see her here with a dark treasure, especially a weapon. Or it's thieves.

Harriet panics. Desperate for a shot of courage, she reaches for the closest substitute at hand. Anger will have to do. She puts her hand into the bag and touches the pistol's hot little barrel. It stings, but only for a moment, like a shock of static electricity that zaps up her arm and right into her amygdala. She lets the heat spread, welcomes it.

Another whisper. A female voice. The anger she's invited in surges across her forehead, flushes her face, her throat, her chest. What if her worst fears are true? What if she's been wrong to trust Ev? What if she's been taking her things, stealing them to sell? Playing Harriet for a fool. She removes her hand from the bag and heads down the hall. Not trying to be quiet anymore, the heat of the pistol still burning the pads of her fingers.

And what does she spy? Candles, lit in a pretty circle in the center of the room.

Blankets piled between. The remains of someone's dinner on the table. An empty wine bottle.

And a girl, the backside of a blue-haired girl, pushing open the front door without a glance backward. The gate clanging as she bursts outside, footsteps clattering down the sidewalk.

Not Ev. Her sister.

AFTER

Ev rolls her bike into Joan and Mikey's backyard. A kid of about five stops lining up toy cars on the back step and stares at her. He's barefoot and wearing a yellow sun hat Ev recognizes; it used to be Noemi's. Joan yells from the open back door.

"Hey, hon. Come on in."

Ev steps over the cars, unclipping her helmet and running a hand through her sweaty hair.

"Smells good."

"Lasagna, your fave. And fresh bread, if I can get it into the oven in time." Joan's hands are buried in a pile of dough. She blows her bangs off her face and gives Ev a tired smile. "How're you doing? You want a glass of wine?"

Ev is still catching her breath from the ride. She kicks her shoes off and tucks them to the side of the door. "Just water, if you don't mind."

"Help yourself. You know where everything is."

"Where's Noemi? She told me she was going to help you cook."

"Did she?" Joan snorts. "News to me. She's not home yet."

Ev buries her disappointment. The only reason she rode her bike all the way out to the suburbs was to see Noemi. It's been a month since her sister came to stay with her in the city. Ever since she got a boyfriend, Noemi's been scarce, her visits to Ev dwindling to the point that now Ev has to come to her.

"I'll help you," she tells Joan. "I just need to change out of my cycling clothes."

She heads down the hall to Noemi's bedroom and stops short in the doorway. It looks the same as Noemi's room always has: clothes and schoolbooks piled on the floor, dresser top cluttered with bottles of nail polish and costume jewelry. Ev's glad to see her old string of paper cranes still hanging across the window, their colors faded from the sun. But the room feels different. There are unfamiliar stains here. She tosses her backpack on the bed and surveys the space. They're the stains of the wealthy: prestige, self-indulgence, and pride.

Noemi has always had stains around her.

She's a girl with big feelings. Ev has had to accept this. But these aren't the playful, curious Noemi stains that Ev is familiar with. She nudges a pile of clothing with her toe, uncovering a black sequin dress, seductive and persuasive. She catches the brash swagger of something overconfident in the top drawer of Noemi's bedside table. She peeks inside and sees a money clip bulging with bills on top of piles of old receipts and makeup. She hears voices in the hallway and shuts the drawer guiltily, turning just in time to meet her sister's startled gaze.

"Ev. What are you doing?"

"Hi to you too." Ev sits on the bed, trying for nonchalance. "I can't find your hairbrush anywhere. Can I borrow it?"

Noemi shakes her head at Ev and shuts the door. She's changed her hair again, this time an angled bob with a side shave. "I meant, what are you doing in my room?"

"Changing for dinner. You forgot I was coming, didn't you?"

"No, I didn't." Noemi grabs the sequin dress off the floor and yanks a hanger out of her closet. "I just wasn't expecting to find you invading my privacy."

Ev presses her lips together to avoid riling Noemi up more, despite the hypocrisy. Noemi is constantly invading Ev's privacy

291

at her apartment. She never asks before borrowing any of Ev's things. She doesn't even knock before barging into the bathroom while Ev's in the shower.

"Sorry," she says. Should she ask about the stains? Is this who Noemi is now? Someone who values money and influence?

"It's Jonathan's." Noemi stuffs the dress into her overflowing closet and sits down beside Ev. "The cash. I'm sure you're wondering."

"Okay."

"He stays over sometimes. I sneak him in through the window. Don't tell Joan and Mikey. They wouldn't like it."

"Are you using protection?"

"Of course." Noemi leans against the wall with her arms crossed. She's still mad. Ev unzips her backpack and pulls out a clean T-shirt.

"So, when am I going to meet this guy? It sounds serious."

"It is." Noemi tries to bite back a smile and fails. "He asked me to move in with him."

Ev's stomach drops. "Are you kidding? Well, that's ridiculous."

"Why is it ridiculous?"

"Because you're seventeen and he's . . ." Ev realizes she has no idea how old Jonathan is. She waits for Noemi to fill in the blank, but she says nothing. "You've only been dating for a few weeks. You barely know him."

"Actually, it's been six months."

"Six months and I haven't met him yet? Why didn't you tell me sooner? Do you think I won't like him?" She already doesn't like him. She doesn't like the feel of his money clip, or of the stains he's left behind in her sister's bedroom.

"It's not that," says Noemi, but she doesn't explain further.

Ev pulls her sweaty cycling tank over her head, fighting outrage. When did Noemi start keeping secrets from her? She's always told Ev everything. Ev has grown to expect it. But that's not fair, is it? Because Ev has never done the same for Noemi.

"Anyway," says Noemi, after the silence has stretched out too long, "it's just an idea. I haven't said yes."

"But you're thinking about it."

Noemi breaks into a goofy smile. "Yeah. After high school, obviously. But I'm thinking about it."

Ev can't keep her face from falling. Her eyes meet Noemi's, and her sister's expression softens.

"Oh, Ev." Noemi lunges forward, wrapping her arms around her sister. "I'm sorry I've been avoiding you. I was afraid to tell you. I know we always talked about moving in together. And of course that's still Plan A."

"Yeah?"

"Yes," says Noemi with certainty. "At least, in the short term."

"Oh."

"Because it's not like we're actually going to live together for the rest of our lives, and have a tree house in the backyard, and eat Pocky for dinner every night. That was just kid talk."

"Sure," says Ev.

"Eventually, we'll both meet people, right? I know it's not a priority for you now, but surely you'll want to date someday?"

"Maybe."

"Of course you will. We'll want to live our own lives. I mean, I can't look after you forever."

Ev stiffens in Noemi's arms and pulls away. "We look after each other." Those were Noemi's words. It was their promise to each other.

"Always," says Noemi, refusing to let go of Ev's arms. "But sometimes that means we let each other grow, right? Look at you. You've got your own business, your own place. We almost never have to breathe together anymore. You're finding your way."

"I guess so."

"You are." Noemi gives Ev's arms one last squeeze before releasing her. "Now it's time to let me find mine."

26

Ev wakes stiff-necked and hot. She crashed fully dressed, the blinds cracked open, letting in bright morning sun, a book flattened under her elbow. After fuming over Noemi for most of the day, Ev decided she needed to make peace. Whether Noemi will admit it or not, Ev knows she's partly responsible for her sister's actions. She's been neglecting Noemi, avoiding her, driving her to seek attention in the wrong places. Getting angry won't help. Last night, they exchanged another flurry of text messages and promises, to no end. Noemi never showed.

Ev pads into the living room, hoping for a note, another text message, something. Instead, she finds a naked man. Okay, not completely naked. Hangdog at least has the decency to wear boxer briefs in her kitchen.

"The hell are you doing here?"

"Shit," says Hangdog. He scuttles behind the counter. "Sorry, I thought —You're usually gone to work by this time."

Usually. Ev breathes.

With red-tipped ears, Hangdog opens the cupboard next to the sink and pulls out a water glass. *He knows where we keep the water glasses.*

More breathing. She would like to run away from this situation. At the very least, she should retreat to her bedroom to allow Hangdog to put some clothes on.

Or not.

"Could I have one of those too?" She nods at the glass Hangdog holds under the faucet.

"Um. Sure." The red on the tips of his ears has reached his face. Good.

"Where's Noemi?"

"Still sleeping."

Ev glances at the curtain acting as Noemi's bedroom door, tempted to wrench it aside and drag her sister out of bed. Noemi promised to come home last night so they could talk. To wake Ev, if she'd fallen asleep. She reframes her sister's messages in her mind, seeing them now for the noncommittal, vague brush-offs that they always have been.

She lets her gaze fall back to the countertop, not quite in Hangdog's direction, and becomes suddenly aware of an absence. The tin lantern she brought home. She left it on the counter next to the fruit bowl. Now it's missing. An emptiness stretches inside Ev's chest. Noemi took Ev's gift, not knowing it was meant for her but taking it all the same. She didn't give Ev the chance to show Noemi what she can do with it. Ev has spent hours practicing with the lantern, experimenting, finding the limits of its emotion, the limits of her connection to it. Harriet was right after all. Like working out a muscle, it grows easier the more she practices, less draining. Less frightening. The more control Ev has, the more she understands that the control belongs to her, not to the object. She's learning. Growing. But the moment of magic she anticipated, the awe she pictured on Noemi's face, has been stolen from her.

She should have saved the lantern for Harriet.

"I'm sorry about that time at the market," Hangdog says, misinterpreting her silence as anger or awkwardness directed at him. "I was in a bad place. I promise I've changed. Noemi's changed me." His voice takes on a simpering tone when he mentions her name.

"You seem different," Ev allows grudgingly. She decides to try to be nice to him, for now. With Noemi barely speaking to her, Hangdog might be her only connection to her sister. Maybe he can give Ev a clue to what's going on with her.

"She cleaned me up. Made me healthy. Made me whole. Now it's my turn. Noemi's got a hole in her heart, and I'm helping her heal it."

"Um. Okay."

"I know you don't like me. But Noemi and me, we need each other. She's going through a lot right now, sorting through all that bad shit that happened when you were kids, you know?"

Needles of anger prick her all over. Now she does back away, some physical distance to allow her breathing space. Is there anyone left who doesn't know all her family's secrets?

"Noemi said you don't like to talk about the past. I get it. More than you know. But you can't run away from it forever."

There's a hint of something in his tone, condescension or arrogance. Or warning. As if he knows more than he's letting on. As if he knows anything at all about her. No. Nope. Any friendly intentions she may have had toward Hangdog evaporate. She doesn't have it in her. Not today.

"I'm late for work." Never mind that she's still wearing yesterday's clothes, or that her mouth tastes sour and her hair's unbrushed.

She's too angry to care. She cracked open the vault of her past for her sister's sake, but she never consented to letting anyone else in.

Hangdog stands in the kitchen with his water glass to his lips, watching her lace up her boots.

"You don't need to worry about running into me tomorrow," he says suddenly. "Yeah. We'll be out of your hair for a couple of days." Hangdog smiles, nodding to himself with satisfaction. "Going on a road trip."

The words *road trip* hit Ev like a double punch in the stomach. Hangdog pauses, eyebrows raised, as though he expects Ev to ask him about it. Challenging her, practically. She almost does ask, her hand hovering over the doorknob as her fury battles with her fear. Why would Noemi be going away? With this guy? And where? And for how long? Will she come back this time?

Fury wins.

"Great," Ev says, or more like shouts. "Have fun."

She takes the stairs down to the parking garage because she needs to stomp. She rides out into pale morning sun, crossing a plaza that contains more pigeons than humans. Her wheels send them scattering in waves, a dance that gives Ev an idea,

300

another gift for Noemi, a better gift than the lantern. Although it's probably too late for gifts. She rides faster.

She doesn't slow down until the Dragon's in sight, and then she skids to a stop, because something's off. The gate is open. The way it sits ajar, a newspaper flapping against its bars, makes dread creep up her spine. She leans her bike against the wall and approaches the door quietly, ready to run if she has to. Inside, she sees a lump behind the sorting table. Harriet, curled in a ball on the floor, unmoving. The waxy remains of candles encircle her. She could be hurt, or sick. Ev fumbles in her pocket for her cell, in case she needs an ambulance. The inner door is unlocked. Ev yanks it open, races toward Harriet's still body. She stops short. The energy in the room feels wrong. Ev looks from side to side, trying to identify the source of the anger she feels, then realizes it's coming from Harriet. The woman's eyes are open. A bag lies on the floor next to her, and she has her hand inside it. Ev's breath grows shallow.

"Harriet?" she calls in a low voice.

"Thief," says Harriet.

"What happened? What's in the bag?" But Ev already knows. It's something angry and hot, and it's been twisting at Harriet all

301

night. Harriet remains on the floor, coiled like a snake, mean-eyed. For a moment, Ev is eight again, barefoot in the wet grass, goose-pimpled, exhaling clouds. She can't look down in case she sees bare bloody feet.

Except Ev isn't eight anymore. She isn't defenseless. She can handle this. She breathes. One . . . two . . . three . . . four . . .

"Harriet," she says. "Whatever you're holding on to there, it's gotten in your head. Let it go."

"Thief," Harriet says again.

"No. I'm not. You know I'm not."

"I don't know." Her face twists, and tears glisten in her eyes. The anger inside the bag has sharp edges to it, suspicion and insecurity.

"You know every one of your treasures down to the last detail," says Ev. "If something were missing, you'd realize it in a heartbeat."

"I wouldn't." Tears spill down Harriet's cheeks. "I'm losing them." Her eyes grow hard again. "It's your fault. All of this is happening because of you."

"Remember when you asked how I protect myself? Breathe, Harriet. That's what you need to do right now. Let go and breathe."

She's not getting through. Ev swallows. What she needs to do, she doesn't know if she can. *It's no different than the lantern.* If she can touch that and keep safe, she can touch what's in the bag too. If she has the courage.

Four . . . three . . . two . . . one . . .

Reluctantly at first, she allows her mind to seek out the object, connect to its edges. The power in it sharpens her consciousness, slices around the cool outer shell of her soul like a skate on ice. She holds it steady, lets the anger in, bit by bit. It fills her like fire, but the core of her remains Evelyn, strong, unchanged. Her entire body tenses, waiting for Harriet to make a move. If it comes down to her or the old woman, Ev won't lose.

She breathes in calm. She's stronger than this object. She is calm, peaceful. She opens wider. A white-hot flash pierces her center like a lightning bolt, and with it a sickening jolt in her gut, and a vision. A pair of hands, knotty pale hands, dirt under the nails, chewed-up cuticles, white knuckles clenched around the grip of a gun. The barrel's pointing down at a stack of old paint cans, and a voice echoes inside her brain. *How do you like me now?*

The connection breaks. Ev bends over at the waist, dizzy, disoriented. Her mind tumbles over the implications of what she's just seen. It's more than a teasing out of the nuances of the stain left behind. It's a direct memory, experienced through the eyes of the person who created the stain. That hasn't happened to her since before. Also, the stain in the bag is a gun. Jesus. *Now's not the time to lose your shit, Ev.* She straightens, arms folded across her stomach, and refocuses on the woman with the weapon.

"Harriet." Both Ev and Harriet flinch at the sound of Owen's voice. Ev stands frozen, unsure if she should shout a warning or avoid any sudden sounds or movements. She doesn't have time to decide.

"Catch," he says. Harriet's eyes flicker. She yanks her hand out of the bag to cover her face as something whizzes toward her. It hits her wrist and falls to the floor. Harriet stares down at the object, silence stretching taut in the room. Ev registers the size and shape of it. It's the bird stone, sweet and peaceful. Waiting quietly on the windowsill all this time. Harriet places her palm on top of it. Her shoulders begin to shake. Ev hesitates. *What now?* She's never been good with tears. Then she realizes Harriet is laughing, a wheezing, hoarse giggle. Only Harriet would find this funny.

Without a word, Owen enters Harriet's circle, picks up the bag, and leaves with it.

As soon as he's gone, Ev's shoulders relax. She moves to the table, pulls a chair out, and sits down. Sweat prickles at her temples, and her heart races. She counts down her breath, lets her eyes stray down to her feet, still in sneakers, not bare, not sticky or splattered.

Neither of them speaks. After some time, Harriet struggles to her feet, stretches, shuffles down the hall, shuts the bathroom door. Ev breathes some more, wondering exactly how close they came to violence. Was that gun loaded? Thank God for Owen. She barely has time to chase the next fleeting question — what on earth is Owen doing here so early? — before she is distracted by something shiny on the floor, nestled among the blankets where Harriet was huddled a moment before, right next to an empty bottle of wine. A tin can with a starburst pattern punched into it.

Understanding dawns, slowly at first, but as she squints at the candles, the blankets pooled in the middle of the floor, and the lantern, it grows. And with it grows the anger.

27

Back on her bike. Back to the apartment. Back into the elevator, shoulders tensed at the anticipation of a fight. She left immediately, Harriet waving her on, too exhausted to care if she stayed or left. She can't let Noemi go on a road trip without confronting her. Without making her see how damaging her behavior has been. Even if she knows Noemi won't understand.

She punches the elevator buttons too hard, thinking of the way Hangdog's stare faltered as she grabbed her keys off the counter. She assumed he was startled by her sudden exit; now she translates his expression into one more familiar for him. At least if Noemi refuses to see, Ev knows that her new boyfriend will be ashamed enough for both of them. She makes plenty of noise at the door, fumbling with her keys more than necessary. She might be mad, but she's not keen on surprising them. She's seen enough of Hangdog's skin for a life-time.

What assaults her instead, when she swings open the door, is her mother's face. Serene smile, eyes fixed forever in a faraway glaze, focused beyond Ev's shoulder at something in the distance. Bangs swept to the side, just like Ev's. Baby Noemi on her lap, gape-mouthed and chubby. Little Eve-lyn frowning, looking away from the others. And him.

Stop making that sound.

She flinches from his face, hating the tremble in her hands. More photos are spread across the carpet, and papers — the entire box is dumped out, its contents stain-ing her space. She steps back, hits the corner of the door. A man's voice comes from her right, and she hears herself cry out.

"Ev?" Her sister's voice, soft in her ear. "It's okay. Come here, sit." Small, strong hands guide her away to the sofa, dissolving her resistance.

"I'm fine," she insists, though she lets herself be led. "Can you just . . . ?"

"I'll put them away. Michael, could you get us some coffee?"

Ev hears him shuffle obediently out the door without a word. Behind her, she can hear Noemi stuffing things back into the box. She puts her head between her knees and breathes, grateful for the reprieve but also pissed that she lost her composure.

"What were you doing with that stuff, anyway?" Ev yells at her sister.

"Shut up and breathe." Noemi stomps off into her room. She's gone for several minutes. When she returns, she picks up the conversation where they left off.

"I was looking for something. You gave me the box. I assume that means I'm free to do what I want with it."

"You are," Ev admits.

"I didn't know you were coming back. I try to be respectful, to save it for when you're not around, so I'd appreciate it if you wouldn't use that tone with me."

"Sorry. It's not about the box. It caught me off guard, that's all."

"Of course it's about the box. It's always about the box, about me and my creepy obsession with the past. But it's not creepy. It's important. I'm tired of pretending we come from nowhere. We must have other family out there somewhere. Don't you want to find them?"

"No. I don't." They have no family, at least on this side of the world, no one willing to take them in. They're children of immigrants. In all these years, not one family member has tried contacting them. Anyway, you never know with family. Sometimes you're better off without one.

"Okay, fine. But maybe I do. Why's that so awful?"

"It's not."

"Exactly. It's not. So why am I always the problem? What about you? What's your problem?"

"My problem?" Which one to pick? Ev's stomach flutters. They're edging on uncomfortable territory. She remembers why she flew back to the apartment in the first place, uses the opportunity to veer the conversation away from Ev's Many Problems.

"My problem is you breaking into my workplace in the middle of the night."

"Oh." Noemi rubs the side of her head and leans back against the sofa. "That."

"What were you thinking?"

"I'm sorry. It's just so beautiful. I wanted to explore."

Ev studies her sister's face, the light in her eyes when she talks about the Dragon. A needle of doubt pricks Ev's heart, but as quickly as it stings her, she dismisses it as ridiculous.

A pout creases Noemi's forehead. "Why

can't I be a part of it? She hates me, you know."

Ev opens her mouth to protest and finds she can't. "It's hard for her to trust people," she says instead. "She thinks you're going to steal from her."

Noemi snorts her disdain, but Ev pushes more.

"You didn't, did you?"

"Of course not. Jesus, Ev." Noemi turns away. "I just wanted to show Michael."

"Harriet's not ready to share the Dragon yet."

Noemi starts to speak, stops herself. "I know. That's why I had to sneak around."

"This process is hard for her. You need to give her time, build up trust. I need to know you understand. If she thinks you or I are stealing from her, I don't have a job any-more."

"I fucking get it, all right?"

"All right."

"I'll give her a couple of days to cool off, and then I'll drop by."

"No."

"She's upset, I get it. I'll explain."

"It would be best if you stay away."

"I don't want to stay away." Ev is surprised to see Noemi's eyes fill. Noemi never cries.

"Hey. Just . . . give it some time. I'm sorry

I accused you of stealing."

"I hate it when you get all suspicious."

"You did break into my workplace."

"I borrowed your keys. It's not like I smashed the windows. I'm not some stranger. I'm your sister. Both of you are acting like I'm some criminal. I know I'm not perfect, but I wouldn't steal from you."

"I know that."

"And I'm not going to mess things up for you." Noemi bites her lip, thinking. "But Ev? Could you do something for me?"

"What's that?"

"Keep an eye on your boss. I'm no longer convinced she's as immune to the crazy as she insists."

"Yeah." Ev decides to keep that morning's incident secret. "Okay."

"I mean it. If she starts going off the deep end, you've got to quit. Promise?"

"That's not going to happen."

"Promise."

"Why the change of heart?"

Noemi studies her hands. "I mean, what was she doing there at two in the morning anyway? Doesn't she sleep?"

Ev isn't about to get into the vault and Harriet's late-night activities. "She's having a hard time letting go. It keeps her up."

"Is it doing you good? Be honest."

"The job? Yeah. Yeah, it is."

"Please tell me we made the right decision."

"I told you. You were right."

"You're in closer contact with the stains than ever. Is it okay? Does it bother you? Do they — do they speak to you?"

Ev knows the question beneath that one. Noemi wants to know if the objects speak to her the way they spoke to him. A chill creeps down her neck and arms. Did her father receive visions like the one she'd seen with the gun?

"It's not like that," she tells Noemi. "Not like voices in my head."

"Are you sure?" Noemi's words so low Ev almost doesn't hear them.

"I'm sure." She tries to sound definite. "It's more like . . ." *What is it like?* She tries to think of a way to reassure her sister, of lightening the mood. She remembers the pigeons earlier that morning, the trick she thought up. It already seems so long ago. "Let me show you something."

She goes to Noemi's room, doing her best to ignore the box at the end of the bed. She stands on the other end, on top of mounds of dirty clothes and blankets, and lifts the string of paper cranes off the curtain rod, hoping they hold enough stain. It's subtle but there, a delicate lacing of sister love. She gathers the cranes in her palms and brings them to Noemi, who still slumps on the floor against the sofa.

"Watch," she says. She lifts her hands high and opens them. The cranes burst outward in a wave with a soft rustle, spreading apart until the string pulls them taut. She hovers them there for a moment before bringing them back to rest in a neat line along her arm. She looks down at Noemi, expecting bright eyes, hands clasped in excitement. Her sister's face has lost all color.

"Is that what she's teaching you?"

"I figured it out myself."

"Please don't." Noemi leaps up suddenly, backing toward the door.

"It's okay," says Ev. She feels the cranes slide off her outstretched arm. "I'm in control."

"I don't like it," Noemi whispers. She bends down without taking her eyes off Ev, her hands fumbling for a pair of shoes.

"Where are you going?"

"Get rid of those." Noemi waves at the floor around Ev's feet, where the cranes have settled. "I don't want them anymore." And then she's gone, leaving Ev alone with the cranes and her unanswered questions.

28

"Okay, class!" Brett yells over the water. "I hope you're all ready to get wet. Since there's no wind today, we're going to practice capsizing our boats."

Ev hears tiny groans from her classmates floating nearby. Beside her, Rafael mutters "Yay" under his breath. Michelle, one of the golden-haired sisters, is sick today so Ev is paired with the quiet kid.

Their lack of enthusiasm doesn't faze Brett a bit. If anything, he looks even more excited. "These two-person lasers flip easily, so you need to know how to get them upright again. This is something you should all be able to do by the end of the course, and ideally, before we go for our first long cruise next week. It looks like this."

Brett steps to one side of his boat and tips it over. As the sail crashes into the water, he jumps over the side and onto the keel. He grabs the ropes and leans back, slowly pulling the sail back up and righting the boat. The whole thing takes less than a minute. Brett climbs back into his boat and surveys his silent class.

"Come on, folks. Take turns on the keel so you all get some practice. You got this!"

Ev looks over at Rafael. "You ready?"

She isn't ready. She's still reeling and confused from yesterday's fight with Noemi, and she's finding it hard to focus.

"Nope," says Rafael, as he tightens the top clip on his life jacket. "But let's do it anyway."

They lean to one side, trying to take it slowly, but the boat lurches sideways and they both fall face-first into the water. The cold water is a shock, bringing her fully into the present moment. Ev makes sure she's aware of where the sail is and pulls herself to the surface. She checks that Rafael is clear of the boat and then swims around to the bottom and scrambles up onto the keel. Then she grabs the ropes and leans back until she can feel the sail pulling against the tension of the water. Not as graceful as Brett's demonstration, but within a few minutes of fumbling she has the boat upright.

Rafael is heavier than Ev, so when he gets onto the keel and leans out, the sail snaps out of the water and the boat rolls right over onto the other side. It takes him another two tries before he gets the balance right, while Ev treads water and shouts encouragement. When they finally climb back into the boat, panting and victorious, she offers Rafael a weak high five.

"Looks like we're doing better than those two." Ev follows Rafael's gaze over to Grace and Allison's boat. It's completely upside down. Grace has swum back to shore, leaving Allison treading water next to the overturned boat. Ev scans the water. Ethan and Vanessa are still practicing, and Brett is busy helping Judy and Caroline.

"I'm going to see if I can help." She slips back into the water.

"What happened to your sister?" she asks Allison. She squints at the beach, spotting Grace wrapped in a towel, huddled and scowling.

"She got tired of me failing." Allison rolls her eyes, but Ev can tell she's been crying.

"Let's get this upright."

"We can't. We just need to wait for Brett to rescue us."

"The hell we do. Come on." Ev starts pulling up on the edge of the hull.

Allison shakes her head. "It's too hard." Her eyes brim with tears. Her eyeliner, winged at the corners, is smudged and runny. Ev guesses they are about the same age, but at this moment Allison looks very young. "I'm too tired."

"Take a minute to rest. It's hard work."

"Not for you. God, look. Even the moms are doing it." Ev glances over at Judy and Caroline's boat. They're upright again, flopped in the boat side by side with their arms dangling over the water. "I suck," groans Allison.

Ev thinks, keeping one hand on the hull and letting the life jacket do the rest of the work of keeping her afloat. There's a stain vibration coming off of Allison, a little glow of optimism and strength. It's her earrings, tiny gold seagulls in flight.

"This might be a strange time to say it, but I really love your earrings."

"Oh." Allison furrows her brow. "They were my grandmother's." She touches one of them, as though she forgot she was wearing them. "Granny would've turned the boat over by now," she mutters.

Ev says nothing but watches as Allison idly twists her earring. She doesn't know it but she's reconnecting with her grandmother's energy. Her chin raises, and her eyes grow clear and determined.

"If I get the boat on its side again, do you

want to give it one last try?" Ev asks.

Allison drops her hand, and the spark leaves her eyes. "I don't think I'm strong enough."

"It's more about patience and balance than strength. Take your time, don't pull too hard. If your granny could do it, so can you. Or as Brett would say, 'You got this.' "

Allison nods. The spark flickers in her eyes again. "Okay. I'll try."

It takes forever. Ev pulls until her arms are rubber, but she gets the boat sideways with the sail lying flat along the top of the water. By the time Allison is on the keel and pulling the ropes, everyone is watching. When she gets the boat upright, there are cheers all around.

Back ashore, Judy insists on a celebration. "That was the toughest workout I've had since Caroline made me try spinning. Nachos are on me. Who's in?"

"Can't say no to nachos," says Brett. "Evelyn, you coming?"

Evelyn hesitates. She scans the beach. She's not expecting to see Noemi, but that doesn't stop her from hoping that her sister might have come by wanting to reconcile. It doesn't stop the wave of disappointment when she's not there.

"She's coming." Ev feels Allison take her

by the arm. "I owe you a beer."

Ev allows herself to be steered along, up the stairs of the sailing center to the pub's wide patio. They push two tables together, and Ev takes a seat next to Rafael. Allison slides a beer over to Ev. Ev takes the glass but doesn't drink. She perches on the edge of her chair, wondering how long she should stay to maintain basic politeness. She's never been good with group dynamics.

Rafael leans toward her.

"Shouldn't you be sitting next to Brett?" he says in an undertone.

"Nope," she replies reflexively, watching Brett, Judy, and Caroline talk loudly over one another. "If I'm ever stuck at a party, you'll find me in the corner farthest away from the action."

"Introverts unite." Rafael bumps his fist against Ev's. "I'm just saying, if a boy that cute was into me, I'd be on the other side of the table."

Ev's cheeks flare with heat, but before she can think up a reply, Judy claps her hands and calls for a toast. Ev raises her glass, offering a silent thank-you for the interruption.

"I'd like to offer a toast too," says Allison. "To Evelyn, for the great coaching today." Everyone turns to Ev, whose cheeks burn hotter as the group cheers for her.

"You were really great today," Caroline gushes.

"She's great at everything," Judy declares. "Did you see her last week with the knots? I had to get her to show me the bowline three times, and I've already forgotten."

"Amazing," says Caroline. "You *must* have sailing experience."

"She must," Judy agrees.

"No." Ev shakes her head. "No experience."

"Amazing," says Judy. "How is that possible?"

"I don't know. I guess I'm just good with my hands," Ev tries.

"You really are," says Caroline.

"She really is," Judy agrees. "I bet you're an artist."

"Oh," says Ev. "No." She glances at Brett, hoping for a rescue from the attention. He grins at her as if to say, *Isn't this fun?* She looks over at Rafael and gets no more than a sympathetic smile.

"Are you sure?" Judy presses. "I'm quite intuitive, and I definitely get artist vibes from you."

Isn't she, in a way? Isn't the Dragon, Harriet's museum of memory, a work of art?

"Not really," Ev replies, but Judy picks up

on her hesitation.

"You're holding back on us. I'm intrigued, tell me more. What do you do for a living?"

Ev feels everyone waiting for her to answer. Now she sees Brett drawing a breath, ready to interject. He's probably thinking about how he saw her digging through his recycling. She feels a mixture of gratitude and annoyance. It's kind of him to think she might be embarrassed about her work, and that she might want the subject changed, but she's not embarrassed, and she shouldn't be. In fact, she's curious to know what people think of Harriet's idea. So she waves him off. She finds herself explaining to the group about Harriet's collection and the exhibit they're building.

"What kind of objects?" Judy listens particularly intently, her chin resting on her hands.

"All kinds. It's pretty eclectic, but every item has had real meaning for someone in the past, and you can kind of feel it, you know."

Everyone's quiet for a moment. Ev is suddenly aware again of how many faces are turned to her.

"Things like Granny's earrings." Allison smiles at Ev, touching her ears.

"Yes, like that. There's a story in each

object. When you walk through the exhibit and see it as a whole, it feels kind of magical. Like an enchanted forest built from loved objects." She trails off, feeling uncomfortable. "I guess it's kind of weird."

"It's not weird," says Brett. "It's wonderful." He holds her gaze until she's forced to look away. There are nods all around the table.

"I love it," gushes Judy. "I absolutely believe that objects have power. Especially the objects that are the most important to us."

"Absolutely," says Caroline.

"So, you're basically like a magical Marie Kondo?" asks Grace with a hint of sarcasm. She seems less convinced than Judy and Caroline.

"Uh. I guess?" Ev laughs at the thought. "I mean, I don't know how tidy the place will be."

"A whole museum for sparking joy!" cries Judy. "I have friends who will go nuts over this. You must let us know when it's open."

She feels a rush not unlike when she's on the water, a fleeting, exhilarating sense of what it might feel like if she had both feet planted firmly in her future.

"Thank you," says Ev. "I will."

29

Harriet clings to the baby blanket, curled on her side so it acts as a pillow. It's the same blanket she offered up to Ev at the beginning of all this, and one of the first things she brought downstairs to add to her nest. Perhaps if she lays her head on its fine stitches long enough, her mind will reknit itself into some semblance of a pattern. On other days, the blanket has brought her the ease she seeks, but not this day. On this day, every treasure she touches seems to lead her backward. Whenever she closes her eyes, she sees another blanket, long lost. Her first ever treasure. That blanket was blue-gray, the blue of a newborn's eyes, a tidy basket-weave knit, neatly folded in an otherwise empty white wicker bassinet. Both of these items tucked in a crawl space in the attic room across from Harriet's childhood bedroom. A little half door, locked, its key tucked out of sight on a dusty picture rail.

The blanket so drenched in a familiar grief and longing it sparked something in Harriet's senses. It woke her up.

A loud voice interrupts her thoughts.

"Harriet."

Her spine straightens, and her fist reflexively pushes the blanket away. She's halfway to stuffing it under her pillow when she remembers she's not in her attic bedroom. She's down below, in the Dragon. The voice is not her father's but Owen's, sharp with concern, not anger. It occurs to her that he has been calling for some time.

"Yes, I'm fine," she calls up, but she's waited too long. He's already coming down the stairs. "Just waking from a nap."

His footsteps pause. "I have that cup of tea you asked for."

She forgot. "Thank you. Please, come down." She wipes at her eyes and cheeks. One side of her face feels bumpy, the pattern of the baby blanket impressed into her skin. She pats at it uselessly, settling on smoothing her rumpled dress instead. As an afterthought, she stuffs the blanket under her pillow all the same.

She didn't mean to move into the basement. There are rooms on the second floor with windows, former offices that would have made sufficient bedrooms. She simply hasn't left since the episode with Ev and the gun. The solace and comfort down here are too appealing. So she began building her nest in the basement. Here is one place Ev hasn't touched, the dark little space outside the vault, the one that was a sanctuary for some stranger in times past. Harriet has been sneaking treasures down, soft and sweet objects, her favorites. Things to bring counterbalance to the vault. She pushed a crib mattress down the stairs, a cozy thing, even if it's far too small. Already, she knows this is home.

She can feel Owen's gaze sweep the dim room as he approaches.

"I was thinking," Owen says, as he passes her the mug, "if the second floor doesn't suit you, I could make you a space on the main floor. We could partition off a corner quite easily."

"It's comfortable here."

"You don't strike me as a creature of darkness. I keep thinking you'd be better off in the light."

"This spot feels right."

Owen nods, accepting the explanation without question, as he always does.

"Will you at least let me build you some shelves? Maybe a proper bed?"

Harriet looks around the dark space.

Already the treasures she brought down here — just a few, for comfort — are stacked against the walls in untidy piles. She doesn't have Owen's knack for making things beautiful.

"Have you heard from her?" It's Tuesday. She hasn't seen Ev since Friday morning.

"Give her some time. She'll come back." Owen bends and picks up a baby food jar packed with pennies. "Why these? Lucky pennies?" he guesses.

"Wishing pennies."

"May I use them?"

"You want to make some wishes?"

"I've been working on something."

A few weeks before, she would have snatched the jar away from him. But she's seen how he works, the reverence he uses when handling beautiful objects and the care he takes to ensure that not one of her things is misplaced. Yesterday, Owen turned all of his attention to his dragon sculpture, building out its long, winding neck with a hodgepodge of treasures — old shoes and Christmas ornaments and bicycle parts. Each item placed with the utmost care.

"Take them," she says. Instead of reaching for the jar, she reaches out to the lampshade beside her bed, running her fingers along its amber beaded fringe, allowing the soft *clickety-clack* of it to hide the tremor in her voice. "Make something stunning."

Owen smiles at the pennies. "How does it work?"

"Wishing?"

"This relationship you and Evelyn have with objects."

"Objects contain energy. We leave our attachments behind."

"And you sense those energies. Can you do it with people, too?"

"People are too muddled. Always changing. Holding so many thoughts and emotions all at once. If I understood people, I would have had a much different life."

"We're complicated."

"You understand people."

Owen laughs. "Sometimes." He's quiet for a moment. Then, "What about telekinesis? I've seen Ev do the impossible."

"So have I."

"How does it work?"

"I wish I knew."

He trails his fingers along the fringed lampshade, following the same path her fingers took a moment ago. They are long and fine-boned, beautiful hands. A bubble of sudden amusement wells up in her. It's been some time since she's been alone with a man in her bedroom. Footsteps cross the floor upstairs. Harriet's laughter dies before it has the chance to escape her throat.

"I'll go," says Owen. "You take your time."

"No." Harriet sets her mug aside and pushes to her feet. "I need to talk to her."

As she climbs the stairs, she thinks on what she can say that might smooth things over. What will convince Ev that Harriet isn't losing her mind? No words come. So when she enters the dining room, she is, in part, relieved to find that the footsteps were not Ev's.

"Yeah. It's me," says Noemi. "The door was open." The girl lifts her hands in supplication.

Owen pokes his head out of the shadows of the hallway, covering any wariness with his usual mild smile.

"Hello, Noemi. Would anyone else like a cup of tea?" he asks, despite the fact that both he and Harriet have only just finished one.

"We're fine," Harriet tells him. Owen nods, disappearing into the kitchen, no doubt to allow them some privacy while remaining close, in case.

To Noemi, she says, "Ev's not here."

"I know. I came to see you."

"Do you know where she is? Is she coming back?" The words escape before Harriet can stop them. She knows she sounds too worried.

Noemi cocks her head. "Why would you think she wasn't coming back?"

Harriet keeps her mouth shut. The silence drags out.

"Well. I came to apologize," Noemi says finally. "I shouldn't have come here at night without asking."

"Did Evelyn send you here?"

"No." Noemi's jaw clenches. "In fact, she told me to stay away from you. But I know I owe you an apology. So. I'm sorry. I didn't know how much it would upset you. Ev told me the last few weeks have been hard for you. I didn't realize. And I didn't come here to steal your shit or anything. It's just . . . this place is amazing." Longing sweeps across the girl's face. "I want to be a part of it. But for whatever reason, neither you nor my sister want me involved."

"It is amazing," Harriet admits grudgingly.

"There's no place like it in the world. And I just want to be able to come and hang out without feeling like I'm some big jerk getting in the way."

"Apology accepted."

"Does that mean I'm not banned for life?"

"I haven't decided."

"Harriet?"

"Mm."

"Why don't you like me?"

Good question. Which answer to give? "You're hiding something."

"We all hide things." The girl narrows her eyes at Harriet. "You hide things."

Harriet has spent her life hiding things. But what Noemi's hiding — it isn't the same kind of secret.

"Why haven't you told Evelyn that you have the gift?"

It's a guess. Noemi only hesitates a fraction of a second, but it's enough to confirm the uneasy mistrust that Harriet has always felt around her.

"Because I don't. Why would you think that?"

Harriet settles into her chair and stares for a while out the front window. The bird stone has come down to the basement with Harriet, but Owen's little scrap-metal bird still perches on the windowsill. She feels a twinge of guilt for thinking, yet again, that it doesn't belong.

"I was thirteen when I began to feel the brightness on things," she tells Noemi, who's turned her attention to Owen's dragon, tracing its lines with her hands, moving from its open jaw slowly along its

330

massive neck. "We had a large attic. I used to hide there. My great-grandmother's furniture lived in that room. I uncovered a torn divan and I'd lie there for hours with a flashlight, reading the books my father didn't approve of. Henry James. Harlequin romances. Spider-Man comics. When I wasn't reading, I'd explore. One day, behind my mother's winter trunks, I found the door to a crawl space. In the crawl space lived secrets. Dark secrets, but they spoke to me all the same."

The baby blanket. A lost child, more cherished than Harriet ever was.

"I uncovered them all, and once I'd done that, I began to pick out the secrets living elsewhere in our home. There were many. In my father's closet. In my mother's jewelry box. My collection began then. I rooted out every bright object I could get my hands on, feeling for them room by room, drawer by drawer.

"There was a particular expression I wore when I searched for treasures. I only know because I got caught out so many times with my hands in some cupboard or other, touching each teacup and creamer. Geordie called it my listening face. Ev does it too." Harriet pauses. "And you."

"Who's Geordie?"

"Geordie?" The question jars her enough that she falls for the distraction. "My brother."

"You have a brother? Is he like you? Does he have the gift?"

Did he have the gift? Harriet doesn't think so, although he would never have admitted it. Collecting was considered an affliction of the Langdon women. When it came to Harriet's weird hobby, Geordie always maintained a safe distance. An image bubbles up in Harriet's mind, one that threatens to crumble her composure. A ball of amber glass; inside the ball, a picture of a pinup girl, glossy black hair, red swimsuit and heels, long white legs.

"He's dead," Harriet manages. "You remind me of him, though."

"Is that the real reason you don't like me?"

"No." The parts of Noemi that she dislikes most are the parts she despises in herself. The selfishness. The calculation.

"He had your charm," she tells Noemi. He also had the arrogant expectation that things should go his way, that people should bend over backward to please him. *And we did, we always did.*

"What happened?"

Another sharp image. Geordie running a comb through his long hair, tucking it in the back pocket of his jeans. Rubbing the stubble on his chin. Grease under his fingernails.

Come on, Harry. Let's go for a ride.

"He died young. Broke all our hearts."

"You're wrong about me. Ev's the gifted one. I've always been your typical no-talent little sister, following big sis around like a shadow. I know you don't believe me. But if I had my sister's gift, I wouldn't hide it. I wouldn't be afraid."

Wouldn't you? Harriet is certain Noemi is lying. But why? Is it fear? Or something darker? Harriet felt Ev's will enter the gun, felt it changing, responding to her energy.

"Ev's not afraid anymore," she says to Noemi.

"But you're worried. What happened?"

"I'm not worried." She can lie too. Until she figures out Noemi's motivations, she's not giving away a thing.

Noemi's brow furrows, but she doesn't persist. "Can you do what she does? Move things with your mind?"

"I've never been powerful that way." Not for lack of trying.

"Does it frighten you?"

"A little. And you? Are you afraid?"

Noemi looks away, betraying herself. "You know, don't you? About our family."

Harriet hesitates. Noemi is the sort of person who files away information for later use. A collector, not of objects but of intel. But for now, she wants to appear to trust Noemi. She decides to tell the truth. It wasn't hard to figure out Ev's identity. Anyone with a bit of curiosity and a knack for research could put it together.

"I do."

Noemi stares at her for a long moment, not speaking. Harriet can hear Owen whistling in the kitchen. "Blue Skies." She's always liked the Willie Nelson version best, has a *Stardust* cassette tape somewhere drenched with the freedom and meandering spontaneity of a long road trip.

"Thank you for helping her."

The words surprise Harriet. She thought the conversation was heading in a different direction. Some help she's been, threatening Ev with a weapon, forcing her to relive childhood traumas.

"She's happy, you know," Noemi continues. "At least, as happy as she knows how to be. Happier than I've ever seen her."

It's the second time she's been told this, yet she still wonders if it's true.

30

Ev lifts another stiff rag from the box on the table. An entire box stuffed with old rags, full of holes, stained with rust and who knows what else, tainted with resentful obligation or resoluteness or sometimes shame. They don't belong in the Dragon, but they don't merit a spot in the vault, either.

"I've got another box for the kitchen," she calls out to Owen, who is mounting another shelf along the wall opposite the windows. He pauses, screwdriver in hand, and turns to face her. His tone is as mild as always, but he raises his eyebrows at Ev.

"I'll get it in a moment."

She knows what he's thinking. They've been storing these uncertain objects in the kitchen with the intention of finding a place for them once the sorting is complete. But the piles of in-between things keep growing. Unused skis and tennis rackets and paintbrushes, their ambition tarnished with guilt. Old wedding albums turned bitter by divorce. The stainless-steel room is filling up with everyday sorrows.

"Where's Harriet?"

"Downstairs having a nap."

She's been doing that a lot. Ev has barely seen Harriet all week. It's been her and Owen, keeping busy with their heads down. With all the Harriet and Noemi drama, Ev never got around to apologizing for her outburst and the marbles. Too much time passed, and they never spoke of it, and now Ev feels awkward bringing it up. Owen's been quieter than usual, but otherwise he seems okay. He's the least of her worries at the moment.

After her last sailing class, Ev spent a couple of days at home, her happiness and sense of freedom slowly draining away with each lonely hour. All the quiet with nothing to do finally drove her back to the Dragon. Working is better than stewing about where Noemi has gone, if she's coming back, and why she freaked out about the cranes. Ev isn't sure what to say to Harriet about the gun, so she hasn't said anything. Neither has Harriet.

"We need to talk to her about the kitchen," she says to Owen.

"Perhaps she could rent a storage unit."

"We should haul it all to the dump," Ev grumbles.

"She wouldn't allow that."

"I know. But she hired us to help her get all this shit under control."

"On *her* terms," says Owen.

True, but that doesn't make it right. "You know there's no value to any of that stuff."

"Harriet sees value in it." Owen's gentle refusals only irritate Ev more.

"I don't get it." She shoves the box of rags away from her. Ev's phone buzzes — a text message — but she ignores it.

"Those objects contain life," says Owen. "Who are we to decide which lives to preserve and which ones to discard?"

"Since when are you on her side?" Her phone buzzes again. She glances over. Noemi.

I need to see you.

She hasn't talked to her sister since she made the cranes fly. If she wants to see Ev, she must be back from her road trip. Ev can't decide if she's relieved or afraid.

When?

Now. I'm at Pat's.

Ev has never been inside Pat's Pub. She doesn't drink, never has. Too risky to lose control. The pub's interior is dark and soaked in guilt and melancholy. She squints in the gloom, spots Noemi sitting at a table next to a piano. A couple of men hunched over pints in the corner eye up Ev as she crosses the room. Noemi clasps her hands in her lap, her own pint glass full. She's shredded her coaster into a tiny mountain of paper fragments. She stands up when Ev approaches, her chair scraping on the floor, not quite meeting Ev's eyes.

"Hey, you want something? You have to order at the bar. No, I'll get it, sit down."

"Coffee. Thanks."

Noemi pauses a moment as though she's about to say more, her lip caught between her teeth, muscles tensed, eyes a bit too wide. A wave of anxiety hits Ev. She knows fear when she sees it. Before she can ask what's wrong, Noemi bounds away without a word. Ev bends her head, ignoring the stares of the men in the corner, and breathes herself calm.

"Coffee." Noemi puts a mug in front of her. "Right back."

She returns with a bowl of creamers and two packets of sugar.

"I wanted to say I'm sorry," Ev tells her sister, before she sits back down. "About the thing with the cranes."

Noemi flashes her a perplexed little smile. "Never mind that, I'm over it."

She doesn't look over it. She looks as if she hasn't slept since Ev last saw her. "I scared you. I didn't mean to."

"I need to talk to you about Harriet."

"Okay." Ev dumps creamer into her cup and swirls it with a wooden stir stick. If Noemi notices that Ev has put gloves on again, she doesn't say anything. Just as well. Ev doesn't want to explain why — how she's afraid to receive more memories the way she did with the gun, how she still feels raw from the experience.

"How much do you know about her?"

"Enough." She knows almost nothing about Harriet. Still. That's her business, not Noemi's. She feels oddly protective of her boss, though she can't pinpoint the reason.

"She has to be loaded, right?"

"I guess." Of course Harriet's loaded. Ev has figured this out already, between the quick purchase of the Dragon and the wads of cash Harriet has stowed away throughout her treasure stash. She and Owen have recovered over two thousand dollars in tens and twenties, rolled up and stuffed inside ornaments, folded under paperweights or between the pages of books. They've returned every single bill to Harriet. Ev can't decide if this is another of Harriet's oddities or if she's testing them for their trustworthiness. She isn't going to take the chance.

"Do you know if she has any other properties?"

Ev shakes her head. "The apartment was a rental. I think she got kicked out because she's moved into the Dragon. If she had somewhere else to go, I'm sure she would."

"You don't think she has any other hoards?"

"No," Ev says shortly. "No way." The skin on her neck crawls at the thought.

"Ev, this is important." A pleading note enters Noemi's voice.

"Okay."

"So could you please stop being so fucking dismissive?"

One . . . two . . . three . . . four . . .

"I don't know about any other properties."

"Me and Michael drove up the Sunshine Coast this week. I went to see Anna Martin."

It takes a moment for Ev to make the connection. Noemi misinterprets her blank stare.

"Our next-door neighbor?" she prompts. "The one who found me on her front porch?"

"I know."

"It wasn't hard to track her down. She was quoted in some of the old newspaper articles, and her daughter still lives in that house. She was eager to talk to me. Asked all about our lives. She was especially curious about you." Noemi pauses, as though considering what to say next. "Anyway. She spilled, big time."

Ev doesn't want to know what Anna Martin spilled. Not at all. Fear of the spillage finally loosens her tongue. She asks the question she's been wrestling with.

"What does this have to do with Harriet?"

"I wasn't looking for dirt on Harriet, honestly. I only wanted to find out —" Noemi stops and looks away. "I just wanted someone to tell me about our mother. But something else Anna said kept nagging at me. Our family's stuff was all sold at this big estate sale. Everything — his antique shit and all the stuff in the house."

"Yeah." This isn't news.

"Right. So, Anna went to the sale. She told me there were a couple of pieces in the shop she'd had her eye on, but I think it was more gross fascination. She tried to act all casual, but she knew a lot about us. About him, especially. I think she had the hots for him."

341

Ev shoots her sister a warning glare.

"Anyway. Anna walks in, and there's a handful of creeps lurking around, looking for a deal or a piece of murder-house treasure — You okay?"

"Yeah." That word, *treasure*. Harriet's word. A sick feeling washes over her. "Keep going," she says, even though she really wants Noemi to stop.

"Then this one woman, she bought every single item. I mean, she literally pulled out a checkbook and said, 'How much for all of it?' "

Ev's stomach turns over. She leans against the wall for support.

"You're thinking what I'm thinking, aren't you?" Noemi stares at Ev, who can only nod. "So the question is, if she's got all our family's stuff, where the hell is she keeping it?"

Ev remembers the box Harriet brought to the Dragon back at the beginning of all this. The one with the unfamiliar address. Angel Place. A sour taste fills the back of her throat, and dread creeps up her spine.

Noemi's eyes grow glassy in the silence that follows. She draws in a breath, as if to continue, then shakes her head.

"You know something, don't you?"

"I need to think." She needs to know for

sure. And she needs to get her feelings under control. She's too angry to talk.

"Evelyn. Tell me."

"I have to do some research first."

"We need to confront her. Make her return it."

"We can't do that."

"It belongs to us."

"Not if she bought it."

"Jesus. Whose side are you on?"

"I need some time. Give me some time, okay?"

"How much time?"

"I need a week. What do you want with it, anyway? What do you think it's going to give you?"

"Her." Noemi's outburst echoes in the quiet bar. Ev flinches. "I have no mother, Ev. I have no family."

You have me. She doesn't say it aloud. Maybe she doesn't want to hear Noemi deny it.

"Did Anna tell you?" she asks softly instead. "About our mother?"

"She knew about as much as you do. Didn't talk much, always in the garden. Everyone remembers Allan. Loud, expressive, arrogant Allan. Chunlan, not so much. Anna called her a 'fade into the background' type." She rolls her eyes. "I'm guessing what that really means is she never bothered to get to know her." Noemi's mouth twists. "She remembered you."

Ev doesn't like the way Noemi says that. She clutches her coffee mug, leans farther into the wall. Both of their drinks sit untouched.

"You want to know what she said about you?"

"Not really." *But you're going to tell me anyway.*

"She said you were a weird kid, his little shadow. Followed him everywhere. She said you liked things more than people. That she went to the workshop once and you were sitting alone in a corner, talking to a broom."

"I was eight."

"She said that morning, when you came out of the woods covered in blood, the first thing she thought was, 'What did that little freak do?'"

"Stop it."

"She said . . ."

"Don't."

"She said you were in on it. Daddy's little helper. That all these years, you've gotten away with murder."

I need your help with something.

Yes, Daddy.

344

Ev can't react. She's frozen to the spot, her emotions threatening to reveal themselves not through words, but through the objects surrounding her. The piano looms heavily at her back. Some regular player has pounded regret into its keys; they *thunk* suddenly in a discordant expression of sympathetic horror. She withdraws from it, wraps her mind up tightly, and breathes.

"Say something." Noemi is whispering now. "If you don't say something, what am I supposed to think?"

"What? Say what?" She can't stop her voice from wobbling.

"Come on, Ev. Obviously, she's full of shit. She's an asshole."

"She didn't know us. She didn't know me. I was a *child.*"

"I know that. I don't believe it. Of course I don't." Here's where normally Noemi would wrap her hands around Ev's. Except she doesn't. Her arms remain crossed.

"Don't you?" Ev draws in a shaky breath. "Isn't that what you've been looking for all along? Isn't it the dirt you've been trying to dig up?"

Keep the dirt out.

"I'm looking for the truth. You're not telling me everything. You hid those scissors, didn't you?"

345

"I told you, I don't remember."

"Why would you do that? What were you hiding?"

They're hurting you. You need to let them go.

"They were dangerous," Ev cries out. "I had to hide them. I had to put them in a safe place."

"See?" Noemi runs the tip of her finger around the rim of her glass. "You do remember."

The satisfied smile on Noemi's lips makes Ev want to slap her. She pushes her chair out and stands up.

"Come on. Don't be mad."

"This isn't a game."

"I'm trying to help you."

Ev can't. She shakes her head and walks away.

"Are you going to ask Harriet about our stuff?" Noemi says to her back. Ev keeps walking. Her next words hold a veiled threat. "A week, Ev. If you don't, I will."

31

Ev knows she's getting close when the low buzz of a hive full of stains begins to seep into her pores. She stops pedaling and coasts down the empty road, watching for Harriet's other house to come into view. The one Harriet has been hiding from her. The one that might hold her past. Her thighs burn; sweat trickles down her spine. She's never been to this part of the city, a secret world tucked behind Granville Street and bordered by the river. It's like riding into another country, all fields and barns and horses in pastures. And the houses, God, they're huge.

She knew, of course she did, the moment Noemi said it. *Where's she keeping it?* She never considered the possibility that Angel Place might still be a part of Harriet's life, not until that moment.

Ev can't remember the street number she saw on the flap of that box, but a quick search reveals that the street is a single block, a dead end on the edge of the river. And Google Street View shows Ev the only house at the end of that street, mostly obscured by trees, an iron gate across its driveway and, peeking out from behind, the gabled roof of a Tudor-style mansion.

Ev doesn't want to know how much stuff a rich old lady can fit in a house that big, but she's about to find out. She exhales a nervous laugh. She never imagined she would be in this place, actively on the hunt for relics from her family's past. And what if it's true? Then what will she do? She thinks of the light in Noemi's eyes, frantic and desperate. Will it help Noemi to uncover these objects? Will she get the answers she seeks?

Perhaps she should burn the house to the ground rather than find out. The thought brings a hard smile to her lips. She's been stifling her feelings toward Harriet, holding off until she can confirm the betrayal, but they surge up then, causing her to bear down on the pedals and pump a few more times, until she can spy the tip of the highest roof peak between trees.

She slows down as the house comes into view, at least its rooftops. Overgrown trees and grass obscure much of it. No landscaper has touched its acres in years. She'll have to coast up the cracked pavement of the driveway in order to see it clearly. She doesn't want to, wants to turn around and pump like mad back to the city she knows, but she's come this far already, and anyway, another part of her surges forward, driven by morbid curiosity or fury or something.

The gate appears to be locked, but Ev is glad to have a reason not to go any farther just yet. She feels the presence of the house first, above and over the noise of the rest, its structure stained with wilted loneliness and regret. If she were someone else, she'd probably imagine it empty and abandoned, but for a handful of mournful ghosts gliding through its attics like floating cobwebs. But she's not someone else. And this house belongs to Harriet.

The closer she gets to the gate, the stronger she can feel the presence of the other vibrations within, bulging and pressing against the walls. Ev shivers; it feels as though a sac of spider eggs has hatched on the back of her neck, and little spider babies are exploding across the skin of her back. That's what the house feels like too. Like a nest stuffed with eggs, all of them jiggling and rocking, hairline cracks splitting their surfaces, ready to burst open. The windows are curtained, but Ev can see the dark fabric pressed up against the glass by the weight of things and things and more things, packed from floor to ceiling.

Does her family live here? Echoes of her past, of Noemi's past? Stains collected by their father over the years, those benign and those less so? More important, are there treasures in this house that have been left behind by her? Ev whispers her name under her breath for the first time in years, breathing her back to life.

Mama.

She never wore gloves in the garden because she liked feeling close to the earth, the tickle of roots and leaves on her skin. Her hands were rough and calloused but warm. She wore a thin gold ring on her pinky, with a little red stone. Once, when she was planting pumpkins, she slid it off and gave it to Ev for safekeeping.

What happened to Mama's ring? Is it in there somewhere? Did Harriet bring pieces of her to this house?

Ev rubs the tears off her cheeks with her forearm. She wasn't aware of getting off her bike, but here she is, standing in front of the gates, scanning the grounds for signs of danger. No electric fence. No dogs. She stows her bike in the bushes. Then she wedges her foot against the rough stone of the wide pillar on the left side of the gate, grabs an iron bar, and vaults herself up. Straddling the top of the pillar, she stops breathing long enough to wonder who she's become. Old Ev wouldn't be doing this. Old Ev would be running the other way. Then again, old Ev's skin would be split open by the force of so many stains straining against old wood. She swings her leg around and jumps into the yard.

She heads wide, following the fence line as best she can, dry grass and dandelions whipping against her shins. She watches the windows for cracks in the curtains, a place to peek inside, half-hoping she won't find a reason to get any closer.

The backyard hasn't been touched in years. It's an overgrown mess of dandelions and rosebushes. Willow trees trail their branches into long grasses. A concrete fountain sits dry and full of weeds. In the middle, an angel has been knocked off its base and lies facedown, its chipped wings jutting toward the sky. Weeds have sprouted through the cracks in the concrete. At the back of the yard, on the other side of a wrought-iron fence, Ev can see the river. A little gate at the back leads down to a rocky beach. The whole scene is beautiful, like she's wandered into a secret garden, wild and fairy-infested. Under other circumstances, she would like to explore, but the weight of the house at her back is too heavy. She has to turn and face it.

The windows at the back are covered, and like the front, the curtains are pressed up against the glass. She realizes that, given the size of the house, the energies inside are oddly muted. How else could she stand to get so close? Is it because the objects within have lain fallow so long, forgotten, slowly losing the stains that have been imprinted on them? Maybe. Or maybe the house itself muffles them, permeating the air so thickly with sorrow and longing and loneliness that it's difficult to sense the stains behind its walls.

Some instinct takes her a few steps closer, to the cracked pavement of the patio, and a trio of French doors with sun-faded blue curtains flattened against them. *There,* she thinks, though she can't pinpoint exactly why. Only the whisper of memory, a slight familiarity, like coming across a children's book in a box in an alley and remembering the cover but not the story inside. Knowing the book only by the way the story makes you feel. That's the certainty Ev feels now.

With shaking hands, she pulls her phone

out of her pocket and takes a photograph of the patio, the squashed curtains. Then she spins around on her heel, crashing through the weeds back to the gate, back to her bike, itchy with the need to get moving again. She feels as though the house is watching her go, as though it wants her. She can feel its longing, feel it sighing out a moldy, rotten sadness as she scrambles up and over, grabs her bike, and pedals away, as fast as she can. Except this time, she knows she's not running away, not for long. She'll be back, whether she likes it or not.

32

Harriet sleeps in fits and starts, plagued by dreams of rats. She stands in the heart of a maze, walls built of newspaper and furniture teetering on all sides of her. She listens to the skittering and rustling as the rats squeeze their little bodies through cracks and crevices, disturbing the balance within the walls, causing subtle, dangerous shifts, while she stands frozen, terrified to move. They have to stop, or they will bury her.

Something wet touches her toe. The rat at her feet is the size of a terrier. Its pink nose snuffles against her skin. She gasps, kicks at it. Loses her balance. Her arms jerk out, and she grabs at the walls for support. Her fingers catch on something soft. She pulls and falls, pulls and falls. The blanket in her fist becomes a rope to cling to as she drops. Its knit is gray-blue like a newborn's eyes, like a rat's pelt. It frays and rots away beneath her hands, and she crashes onto her bed in the dark.

She's awake, safe inside the Dragon, blankets pulled up high over her mouth and nose. Shuffling and noises above her head. She squints at the glowing numbers on the clock next to her bed. 7:17 A.M. Another visitor at odd hours. She untangles her limbs from blankets, fighting anger and distress in equal measure, regretting ever having made copies of her keys. She clicks on the lamp, blinking and squinting in the yellow light, and stuffs her feet into slippers. She pauses at the foot of the stairs, frowning.

The sword. Yesterday she looked for it, wanting it for her nest. It's not a dangerous thing like the items in the vault a few feet away. Sharp, of course, but its spirit holds pride and challenge rather than anger or fear. She swears she saw it leaning against the wall in the mastery corner, but she couldn't find it. One of several items she's lost track of recently.

Perhaps it's for the best. She imagines the sword's previous owner would cringe at her intent to use it for a walking stick, grinding its point into the concrete to keep her balanced in those stiff moments right out of bed. Still, its absence worries at her. She must remember to ask the others.

Light spills under the door at the top of the stairs. Her intruder-du-jour isn't trying for stealth. It's probably Owen. He's been arriving a bit earlier each day, then disappearing in the late afternoon, mumbling about some personal project. Sure enough, in the middle of the big room, she sees Owen on his knees next to the sorting table, bent over an enormous jumble of wire and color. Harriet blinks to assimilate the heap into some order in her mind.

Buttons. Hundreds of buttons. Also assorted beads, smooth pebbles, surf-polished glass, tiny silver spoons, and pennies. Wishing pennies.

"Ah, you're up," says Owen. "I hope I didn't wake you."

"What have you done?"

"I made you something. It was supposed to be a surprise. I was going to lay it out on the table for you to discover." He's tied his hair in a ridiculous little knot at the nape of his neck, which he scratches at as he rises and turns to face her, smiling as always. "But it was noisier work than expected. Don't worry."

Does she look worried? Perhaps.

"If you decide you don't like it, I can dismantle it easily enough. I promise no pennies were harmed in the construction of this piece."

He plucks a heavy chain from the center of the heap, lifting the entire contraption as its pieces clink together softly like hundreds of tiny bells. It's a chandelier. Made from bright things, the smallest treasures. Long sparkling tendrils loop in layers around and around. Harriet can no more stop herself from rushing to touch it than she could leave a lucky penny on the sidewalk once she's spied it. Each piece is held in place with wrapped wire, fully intact.

"You like it. I'm so glad." Owen tilts his head toward the ceiling. "It's built so as not to disturb the original. May I?"

"I suppose you may."

Too tired and perplexed to argue, Harriet heads to the kitchen. She takes her turn fixing tea while Owen drills holes in the ceiling. She tries not to dwell on the subtle uneasiness his gift has stirred in her, instead putting thought and care into preparation of the tea. She chooses gunpowder green, his favorite, and the best mug, the heavy, speckled one with the thumb-crater at the top of the handle. She watches the leaves uncurl.

The chandelier may explain why Owen's dragon hasn't grown much over the last few days, why he's been disappearing for long periods, leaving Harriet and Ev to avoid each other. Yesterday, Harriet woke from an afternoon nap to find them both gone. Rather than track them down, she used their absences as an excuse to indulge her nest-building urges, picking through the piles for treasures to brighten up her basement corner.

Things are missing. She's certain of it, though she can't prove it, can't keep track anymore. The sword. She looked for the Buddha yesterday too. It was no longer in the peaceful pile. Did it get categorized elsewhere? Has it been incorporated into Owen's dragon? The lost treasures itch at her. But she can't point fingers, not yet, anyway.

By the time she comes out with the mug, Owen's new piece is already up, supported by four hooks placed around the existing glass chandelier. The tendrils drape almost to the floor, a sparkly curtain.

"I'll hang these, too. I need more hooks. What do you think?"

"It's beautiful."

He must hear the hesitation in her voice. "You won't know for sure until you're under it, of course. It's meant to be experienced from below."

"Indeed." Harriet hands Owen the mug

and slowly stretches out on the floor. A thousand hopeful little souls shine down on her.

"How does it feel?" She notes his use of the word *feel,* his astuteness in recognizing the importance of this over the appearance of his creation, however grand, however astonishing.

"Marvelous," she tells him, truthfully. "I would prefer, in future, if you would ask me before you make changes to the space and my collection."

"I asked about the pennies."

"But not the beads or the stones or the spoons."

"My apologies. I can take it apart if you . . ."

"Of course not. I only want you to remember that the collection belongs to me. I decide how the objects are to be used." She'd like to say more, but she's interrupted by the familiar scrape of the outside gate opening and the lock turning over in the door.

"It's Evelyn." Harriet reluctantly rolls to her side. She and Ev still haven't exchanged more than a few words since the morning of the gun. It's well past time to clear the air.

"Guess I'm not the only one who couldn't

sleep," says Owen. "I'll go pick up some breakfast."

"Before you go. Have you seen my sword?"

He doesn't turn around, but his shoulders twitch, just a bit.

"Which one?" There are three.

The proud one, she's about to say, but he won't know. "Gold, with the twisty hilt."

"I'm sure it's around somewhere. I'll have a look about when I return."

She'd like to say more, but by the time she makes it upright, Owen has already slipped out the door. Almost certainly to give them privacy, but Harriet wishes he hadn't when she sees Ev stalking the floor. Enough avoidance. Clinging to the lingering glow from the chandelier, she confronts the girl.

"If there's something eating at you, best come out and say it."

Ev looks up from the floor with a sharp glance.

"You're coiled up like a packed-away jack-in-the-box. Speak, or I'll be forced to wind you up more."

"Why didn't you tell me there's another house?"

Harriet doesn't move. The joy drains from her body. She puts her hand out to find some steadiness via the wall.

360

"What's that mean?" she stalls.

"I know, Harriet. I went there. I saw it."

Well. She knew they'd come to this eventually. She hoped to come to it in a different way, but from Ev's tiger posture, she guesses denial won't get her anywhere.

"It's my mother's house." Coward, trying to pin the blame on her mother. She corrects herself. "Was my mother's house."

"But it's your house now."

"Yes."

"Why didn't you tell me?"

"And give you another reason to run away? I was going to tell you when you were ready."

"So, what? You're telling me your mother was responsible for what's in that house?"

"No," says Harriet. "It was me." This is the time to come clean, to own up to what she's responsible for. Still, the words won't come. Shame seals her lips.

Ev stops pacing and closes her eyes. Harriet can almost hear her counting.

"It's not all treasures," she tells Ev. "Like I told you, my mother was a collector too. A sensitive, like us, but she didn't restrict her collecting to bright objects. She loved anything that sparkled. Clothing, shoes, jewelry. Ornaments and bob-bits and doodads. Later in her life, she grew less . . .

361

discriminating."

"She was a hoarder."

A loaded word, that. Harriet hates the implications of it. People who fill jars with shit and have cockroaches for carpet. People living in squalor, surrounded by garbage, their walls rotting around them. Harriet's mother wasn't like that. For a moment, Harriet sees her, the way she was before all the heartache, glossy hair and bright eyes, draped in jewelry and Shalimar. Her passion for beautiful things stemmed from her passion for life. It never felt compulsive or unhealthy, back then.

On the other hand, of course her mother was a hoarder. Absolutely, without a doubt. As is she.

"My mother was ill for most of my life." How much to tell? That she blamed Harriet for her despair? First for the loss of one child, and later, a second? "She existed in a fog, helped along in good part by the pharmaceuticals that made my family rich. We were all surprised when my father died first. Heart attack. My mother lingered for some time after that." Harriet, the last, the least cherished child, left alone to care for her. "Collecting was the one thing that brought her joy, even as it ruined her."

"I want to see it."

"No." Harriet barks it out in panic. "Not yet," she amends.

"Why not?"

"It's not just that you're not ready. I'm not ready. And . . ." She chokes on the words. The things, Ev's family's things. Harriet hasn't had an opportunity to explain to her, to make her understand. Harriet considers what to say. She can see the resolve on Ev's face; see she won't win this argument, at least not for long. Will Ev understand why Harriet preserved those things? Why she took them all?

Say it. Tell her.

Everything she does is bad and wrong.

She can't. She needs more time.

They were the last items she brought into her family home, packed into the great room through the back doors, the ones that once opened out to the river. Stuffed in, and the doors locked forever. And Harriet, as soon as she did it, knew she'd gone too far. Knew either those things had to go, or she did.

"I can't face it," she finishes. "Not yet."

"Why? What are you afraid of?" A challenge in her voice, as though she's daring Harriet to say it. Does she know already?

The truth sits on the tip of Harriet's tongue. *Your past lives in that house.* But some greedy, fearful darkness deep inside of her snatches it back, stuffs it down her throat. She couldn't face the weight of Ev's past when she fled twelve years ago. Can she do it now? Can Ev?

"My past lives in that house," she says. A half-truth. Ev hesitates, thinking. "I don't know if I'm strong enough," Harriet adds. She doesn't bring up the gun, but Ev seems to understand what she leaves unsaid. She nods in agreement, although the tension in her jaw remains.

"Then Owen and I will go."

"It's dangerous. It's not like my apartment." Worse, so much worse. "You need me if you don't want to get buried." An image from last night's dream resurfaces, the cool wetness of rat nose on her bare foot, the walls around her trembling. She shivers.

And yet, wouldn't it be something to lay her hands on some of her estranged old friends? To bring them to the Dragon, where they'll have new life? To transform them from lonely ghosts to lively spirits, members of the Dragon community?

"If we do it together," Ev says, "we'll both be strong enough."

Tackling the house was part of her plan all along. To excavate all the beautiful things whose lives have been wasted, treasures buried rather than cherished. They deserve better. And to clean up the less beautiful things, the ones she fears still. She thought she'd have more time to prepare both of them, but is it really too soon? Are they strong enough?

She thinks of all the treasures she hasn't seen since she left her childhood home. Treasures older still, ones that have been buried since her mother passed. The cast-iron owl. Those gold-and-black bone china teacups. Ah, her favorite piece of driftwood! She can see it in her mind, lying in a bowl full of seashells, and worn, buffed sea glass in shades of blue. A layered and complicated treasure, like an old, complex bottle of wine. Ev and Owen can help her recover all of these things and more.

The only safe route through that house is via the front door. It will take weeks to clear out enough things to gain safe passage to Evelyn's past. Finally, Harriet considers her greatest fear. Ev grows stronger while Harriet continues to weaken. What if she's as strong now as she'll ever be? What if she only continues to decline? What if there is no better time than now?

"All right," she says. "We'll go."

33

Ev mounts the steps up to the Platypus, following a string of fake tiki torches. Their plastic flames glow orange, despite the fact that the sun is still high overhead. The restaurant is quiet, caught in the lull between the lunch and dinner rushes. Ev pulls off her bike helmet and shakes out her damp, salt-crusted hair. They finally went on a real cruise in sailing class, around English Bay and looping back to Spanish Banks. Ev's face feels chapped from the wind, and her arms ache from trimming the sail, but she holds on to the sensations. They remind her of what happiness feels like. Not someone else's happiness, left behind on an object, but Ev's own, particular happiness.

After class, she went for a swim with Brett.

"You can't tell me you're ready to leave the water," he teased. She thought about making some excuse, but he was right. The water tempted her, and she wasn't ready to return to the real world. She imagined herself a raccoon, stealing a moment of pleasure, cooling her fur, bobbing over softly cresting waves. She dived under the surface over and over, shutting out the world. For a while, she left all her heaviness on the beach. Until Brett brought up Noemi, that is.

"Your sister hasn't been around lately." They stood chest deep in the water, letting their arms float in front of them.

"She's working." Ev couldn't hide the shadow that flickered across her face.

"Everything okay? You seemed a bit distracted in class."

"Do you have siblings?"

"Two sisters. One older, one younger."

"You're a middle kid."

"Why do you think I'm so easygoing?"

"Are you close to them?"

"Yes and no. My older sister's taking a different path in life. We don't see eye to eye on a lot of things. She's conservative, religious, dropped out of college to get married young."

"What's your path?"

Brett laughed. "The opposite of that. Travel. Grad school."

"I didn't know you were in grad school."

"Of course you didn't. This is the first

time you've asked me a single thing about myself, Evelyn." He softened the comment with a smile, but Ev flushed anyway.

"Sorry."

"It's fine. I know you're not a people person."

"I'm trying."

"And I appreciate it. I'm studying biomedical engineering." Seeing Ev's blank stare, he added, "Basically, I design and build medical tools."

"Wow. That's so . . . useful. And important."

"What you're doing with your museum is important too."

"I'm not saving lives."

"You don't know that," he said, his eyes serious. "You want to help people. So do I."

"Are you trying to convince me we have things in common?"

"Absolutely. Here's another thing. I chose engineering because I like to build things. Tinker." He raised an eyebrow at her. "Just like you, I'm good with my hands."

The way he said it made Ev's ears burn. She felt the sudden need to change the subject. "So, what about your younger sister?"

"She's a spitfire. I love her to pieces. But she takes up a lot of space, you know?"

"Sounds familiar." Ev paused. "My sister and I aren't getting along."

"Family is complicated."

"Yep." *You have no idea.*

"I'll always be there for my sisters if they need me. But that doesn't mean we need to be besties."

Ev's throat stuck on her next words.

What if they are the only family you have left?

"Anyway." Brett gently splashed water in Ev's direction. "I know you're only asking me questions to avoid talking about yourself."

This was her cue to open up. She wished she knew how, that she was better at talking to people. She wanted to tell Brett how she always thought she knew Noemi inside and out, but that somehow she's become a stranger. Instead, she swallowed and looked away, and let the moment pass.

Now it's nearing Saturday evening. On Monday, she and Harriet and Owen will go to the house on Angel Place. And she has to tell her sister. All that urgency over Harriet and the estate sale, and now Noemi is ignoring Ev's messages again. She shouldn't give her sister the satisfaction, should make her wait at least the full week she claimed she needed. She should make Noemi come to her. But the old fear keeps gnawing at the pit of her stomach. Why isn't she replying to Ev's messages? Where is she? What if she runs off again before Ev can explain herself? Before Ev can finish telling her story? Despite everything, she wants Noemi's support.

She managed to keep her anger toward Harriet hidden through the rest of the week, wanting to give the woman an opportunity to fess up to owning Ev's family estate. They've never talked about Ev's past, not even after Noemi brought it up at the Dragon. At first, Ev thought Harriet was being kind, respecting her privacy. Now she's not sure. It's clear Harriet is hiding something. They circled around it the day she confronted Harriet about Angel Place. Maybe she's afraid to come clean to Ev, or maybe the hoarder in her wants to keep the estate items secret so that Ev can't lay claim to any of them. Maybe Ev's wrong about it all. She won't know for sure until they get inside that house.

Since that conversation, Harriet has been hiding down by the vault, where Ev refuses to go. The Dragon is quiet and tense with only Ev and Owen upstairs. Owen's turned cold, but Ev isn't sure why. Or maybe she does know why. Maybe she hasn't done the right thing by Harriet. She already seems so scattered and fragile. What will going back to that house do to her? She wishes she could talk to Noemi about it, even though she knows exactly what Noemi will say. She knows Noemi will push her to take back what's rightfully theirs.

Maybe she wants that too, a little.

"Welcome to the Platypus," says a perky voice. "Are you meeting someone?"

The hostess wears black except for a large purple silk flower pinned into her hair. Beneath her clothes, between her breasts, something — a charm tucked away, perhaps — radiates a lusty confidence.

"I'm looking for Noemi. Is she working today?"

Stopping at the Platypus was a whim. If she can't get Noemi's attention via text, she can always pull a standard Noemi trick and drop in on her unexpectedly.

The hostess purses her perfectly lined lips. "There's no Naomi here."

"Not *Naomi. No-mi.* She's new. A server."

"*Nuh-uh.* Still doesn't ring a bell."

Ev gets that tingling feeling, the feeling that something isn't quite right. People don't forget Noemi.

"Are you sure? Pink or blue hair? Big voice?"

371

"Oh." The girl's eyes grow wide. "Yeah, I remember her. She came in for like, three shifts, and then she just stopped showing up. Left us short-staffed on a Saturday — no phone call, nothing. Alex was pissed. She hasn't even bothered to pick up her pay-check. Oh my God. Is she okay? You don't think something bad happened to her, do you?"

"She's fine."

"Oh." She sounds disappointed. "Well, if you see her, tell her Alex wants his apron back."

Ev waits until she's turned away to allow the anxiety to bubble up in her gut. She takes the steps down, two at a time. If Noemi isn't working, what is she up to these days? Where does her money come from?

She pulls out her phone and punches in a number from memory. Mikey answers.

"Hey, Ev." He sounds genuinely happy to hear from her. "We missed you the other night. Hang on a sec."

She can hear the baby fussing in the background, Mikey cooing at it. She pictures him settling into his oversized recliner with the baby in the crook of his tattooed arm, burp cloth slung over a shoulder, Jays cap perched on his balding head, a formula bottle and a beer on the end table next to him. A wave of sudden warmth passes over her, something close enough to homesickness that it closes her throat for a moment.

"So, what's up? When are you coming to visit?"

"I can't talk long," she says. "I wondered if you've seen Noemi."

"Not since she came for dinner." A pause. "She take off again?"

Did she?

"I don't think so. I'm sure she'll turn up. But will you let me know if you hear from her?"

"Only if you do one thing for me." Ev waits, straddling her bike, stifling impatience. "Tell me honestly. How are you?"

"I'm fine."

"Fine, huh?"

"I'm good." She softens, relents. "Better than usual. I've got a job that pays the bills. And I took up sailing."

"Get the fuck out. Sailing?"

Ev smiles. "Seriously."

"That's awesome, Ev. I remember you always loved the water."

"Yeah. Anyway, I'm on my way to work," she lies. "I'd better go."

"Okay kiddo. Listen, Noemi's gonna do what Noemi's gonna do. You can't change her."

"I know."

"Do you?"

Ev doesn't know how to respond. The baby gurgles in her ear.

"You're a good sister. You've always looked out for Noemi, and that's great. She needs you. Just, sometimes I think you're so focused on who you want her to be, you don't see all of who she is."

"What does that mean?"

"It means, make sure you look after yourself, too."

Ev finds herself pedaling toward Chinatown. She has no idea of Michael's last name, much less where he lives, but she knows where he likes to hang out. She has to do something. Sitting around an empty apartment all night isn't an option. It's a market night, and already the tents are coming up. Vivian and Ken will be rolling up with their truck at any moment. She wonders if she should drop by, maybe when Ken isn't around. Would Vivian be happy to see her? She remembers the look on Vivian's face when she was picking up the pieces of her broken bells and decides not to find out. She skirts around the block and coasts along the sidewalk until she reaches the New Town Bakery.

No sign of Noemi or Michael. She walks

up and down the block a couple of times, trying to figure out what to do. She looks for apartment entrances and scans the names on their intercoms. She passes the convenience store where she saw him watching her on that last night at the market. Not in front of the store but standing in that doorway to the left. There are three buzzers next to the door, no names next to any of them. Ev considers pressing each of them. She considers pressing all the intercoms in a three-block radius. Not the best strategy. Surely there is another way.

An old woman shuffles past. Something hidden in her purse holds the memory of her husband. Love, duty, fear. Not a kind man, but she feels adrift without him. Ev watches her continue down the sidewalk. She felt the stain so clearly and without effort. Ev is stronger. A lot stronger. More often lately, she's caught not only the emotion attached to an object, but specific memories, flashes of story encapsulated in the molecules, perfectly retained. These moments seem only to reveal themselves through physical touch, but their vivid clarity shocks her every time.

She turns back to the glass door and the dimly lit stairs on the other side of it. She reaches her mind up the stairs, searching.

There it is, faint but familiar. Shame-stain. She's found Hangdog.

The first two buttons receive no reply. The third button rewards Ev with static and an incomprehensible mumble.

"It's Ev."

The static cuts off. Nothing happens for a minute or two. If they think they can ignore her and she'll go away, they are dead wrong. She presses the button again. It beeps once, twice, three times. Then a shadow appears on the stairs.

Ev hangs up. Michael opens the door. He looks more like Hangdog again, unshaven, red-eyed.

"I'm looking for Noemi," she says. "Is she here?"

"You'd better come in."

Michael's apartment is tidier than Ev expected. The tiny living room is lined on three sides with shelves full of books and movies. The movies are mostly old kung fu and anime; the books, classics and poetry. They sit side by side on the only piece of furniture, a cheap futon covered with a fleecy blanket. Ev perches on the edge, as close to the door as possible. She doesn't see any sign of Noemi; no stray articles of clothing or open nail polish bottles drying out on the coffee table.

"She's obviously not staying here."

"I haven't seen her in three days," he tells Ev. "I thought she was at your place."

"You brought me up here to tell me that?"

"I'm worried about her. I mean, I should've guessed she wasn't with you, since, you know."

"No. I don't."

"Since she's afraid of you."

Ev shakes her head, swallows the flash of anger his words produce.

"That's not true."

"It's only because she's so wrapped up in her past. She's so deep in it she can't think straight anymore. I tried to tell her, but —" He breaks off, starts picking at a loose thread at his knee, where the denim has worn thin. "I guess you'll be happy to know she broke up with me."

"Sorry."

"No, you're not."

She is, a little bit. This is what Noemi does. She's perceptive enough to know her effect on people, but it doesn't stop her from leaving them. She makes people love her and then she moves on.

"Let me guess. You're too dependent on her for your happiness."

Michael makes a noise in the back of his throat. It might be a laugh.

"I suppose I'm not the first."

"Nope."

"I disappointed her. She tried to help me, tried to clean things up around here. We rounded up a bunch of the stuff I bought from you and threw it over the Burrard Street Bridge. But I couldn't let go of it all."

Ev nods. She can feel it, of course. On the chiding brass clock on the wall. In the rug on the floor, a reproachful kilim in blues and golds. He did not purchase these from her.

"She actually told me I'm too stuck in the past."

They both laugh.

"Where do you think she went?" asked Michael.

"She's got other friends in the city." Ev makes her voice unconcerned, but in fact, she has no idea. Who are Noemi's friends? She met one or two back when Noemi was still living with Joan and Mikey, but she can't even recall a face, much less a name.

"She'll turn up soon enough." She isn't sure of this either, but she isn't going to admit that to him.

"I won't see her again," says Michael. "She took some stuff when she left."

"Stuff. What stuff?"

"Some money. What was left of my mom's

378

jewelry."

"Shit." Ev squeezes her eyes shut. "I'm sorry. How much? I can pay you back." She can't replace the jewelry, though.

"I don't want your money. And if you see her, tell her I'm not mad."

"How can you not be mad?" Ev is mad. She's furious. "She used you."

"Yeah." Michael shrugs. "That's just Noemi. You know what she's like."

"I don't know if I do."

"It's how she survives. Besides, she made me feel good. Being with her, I was the happiest I've been in years. I knew it wasn't going to last. Is it so terrible that I wanted to enjoy it while it did?"

"I don't know."

"I do," says Michael emphatically. "Maybe I paid her way for a while, and maybe she helped herself to a parting gift, but she *helped* me. I feel different since that emotional baggage went over the side of the bridge. Lighter. She did that for me, and I'll always be grateful."

Meanwhile, Ev has spent the last year adding to Michael's burden by selling him objects she knew were hurting him. So who's worse? Noemi or Ev?

Michael stands, and Ev takes the cue. She follows him to the door.

"You know, I think you're brave. I mean, what you did that night, saving Noemi."

Why does her sister have to have such a big mouth?

"I know you don't like talking about it. Noemi told me. I just thought you should know that whatever she thinks about it all, I know you were brave. There's nothing harder than standing up to a parent, especially one you admire. I couldn't." In a lower tone he adds, "I didn't."

She hates him more than ever in that moment. Fuck him for thinking they have something in common. Fuck him for pointing it out. She makes herself stop and turn to him.

"Do you still have the brooch you stole from me?"

He has the grace to flush. Then again, shame is his specialty.

"Noemi was right. You don't need to hang on to the past," she says. She thinks of Brett. A foot in each boat. "You should get rid of it. All of it. The brooch and everything else that's still weighing you down. At least about that she was right."

34

Ev peers into the dark undergrowth of the tree, up and up, trying to spy the knotted hammock hidden among the dense, slick needles. She knows Noemi is there before she calls out. There's energy emanating from above. Fear, confusion. Whatever stain Noemi's holding on to, Ev will have to convince her to let go of it.

"Hey," she calls. "You up there?"

"I'm here," comes Noemi's voice, small and reassuring.

She finally promised to meet Ev, the silence broken only after Ev made a promise of her own. Desperation set in after her visit with Michael, her desire to lure Noemi out of hiding overtaking every thought. So she did it. A single sentence, delivered by text.

I'll show you.

The reply came at once. *Meet me at the tree.*

Ev climbs. Her muscles ache from yesterday's sailing class, plus hours of biking around town. Not to mention the worrying. She moves clumsily, grateful that a tiny bit of daylight remains. She arranges her words carefully as she grows closer to the top.

She finds Noemi curled up in a little ball in the back corner of the hammock. She looks disheveled and unwashed. She faces away from Ev as she scrambles in, the hammock wobbling under her movements. Ev can't pinpoint the object that's staining the treetop with fear. Noemi appears to be empty-handed. Then she realizes, her stomach lurching, that there is no stain. The energy Ev senses is coming from Noemi. Noemi's fear. Noemi's confusion.

Ev takes a moment to digest this new development, a whole new terrifying ability, turning her head away so that Noemi can't see her matching fear and confusion. Through the treetop, she can see a few pale stars. She pulls a plastic bag out of the pocket of her hoodie.

"Licorice?"

Noemi shakes her head. "I can't stay long."

Ev shoves the package back in her pocket, unopened.

She wants to ask where Noemi is sleeping. She wants to ask Noemi if she plans to get another job. She wants to beg her to come home with her. Instead, she digs into her pocket again, this time pulling out her phone.

"You were right." She passes the phone to Noemi so she can see the photo she took of the house at Angel Place. "She has a house. A mansion. It's busting at the seams."

"The estate sale stuff?" Noemi's face glows, ghostly from the light from the screen.

"It's in there."

Noemi fixes her gaze on Ev's for the first time. It has grown too dark for Ev to make out her expression, but she can hear the urgency in her sister's voice.

"I want to see it."

"You will."

"Let's go now."

"Not yet. I need to go with her first. There's probably an alarm system and stuff."

"I can take care of that," Noemi says dismissively.

Ev decides not to question that comment, not now.

"It's a hoard house. We could get crushed, not knowing our way around. For all we know, she's got it rigged with booby traps and shit. I need Harriet to show me first."

"When are you going?"

"Tomorrow. As soon as I can, I'll take you, too."

"And if I want something?"

"If it's ours?" Ev stares into the tree branches. *Sorry, Harriet.* "If it's ours, you can take it."

A long pause. "Can I have some licorice now?"

Ev fishes it out of her pocket, tears open the package, pulls apart two long strings.

"Come home."

"Not yet."

"Noemi."

"It's not about you and me."

"What is it about?"

Noemi shifts, the hammock creaking beneath her weight as she tries to put another inch of distance between them.

"I just need some time alone to figure some things out."

"I saw Michael."

"Can we not talk about this right now?"

"Do you have a place to sleep?"

"Ugh, I'm fine. Stop making concerned-parent eyes at me. I'm staying with Jonathan, okay?"

"Ex-boyfriend Jonathan?"

"Who do you think? More licorice, please."

Ev closes her eyes. She lets the swaying of the hammock lull her into pretending this is all going to turn out okay.

A few hours of fitful sleep later, Ev paces the sidewalk outside her apartment. Harriet has insisted on an early start. Maximum daylight hours, she said, but Ev suspects she's as anxious as Ev about returning to the house. Farther down the block, where Ev's quiet side street meets the clogged artery of Georgia Street, the day has already begun, cars streaming into the city from the north despite the fact that the sky is tinged dawn pink. Down here, Ev has a lone crow for company, pecking at a fast-food bag in the gutter.

She plucks the bag up, sending the crow fluttering a safe distance away, and dumps out its contents: a crumpled napkin, half of a soggy hamburger bun, four French fries. She steps back again to allow the bird to feast. Scavengers help one another out.

The van approaches. Only Owen is inside. Ev pulls the passenger door open.

"No Harriet?"

"She needed a few extra minutes to prepare."

"Isn't she the one who insisted we leave at the crack of dawn?"

Ev keeps her tone light, but Owen doesn't smile. He waits until she's buckled in before pulling a three-point turn in the street. They head back toward the Dragon. Ev doesn't usually mind silence, especially with Owen, but on this morning, it feels like a solid substance within the confines of the van. Like he's waiting for her to say something, but she doesn't quite know what.

"I said I was sorry for freaking you out with the marbles, didn't I? I haven't seen you much lately. So, if I forgot, I am. Really sorry."

"You told me. It's okay."

"Oh. Okay."

She's used to Owen carrying the conversation. Without his help, she's at a loss, so she lets the silence press in again. They don't speak until they've pulled up outside the Dragon. Ev reaches for the door handle.

"Evelyn."

She turns to Owen. His placid expression has been replaced with creases of worry.

"Are you certain about this?" he asks.

"Yeah." She says it like Noemi would say it, like it's the obvious truth. "Why wouldn't I be?"

"I'm not sure that returning home is the best thing for Harriet."

"We're helping her."

"Are we?" His eyes search Ev's. "I'm surprised you want to go there so badly. Why is that?"

For a second, it's on the tip of her tongue, the real reason, Harriet's lies and Noemi's desperation. Owen would understand. He might soften again; stop holding his shoulders so stiffly around her. But what's in that house belongs to her and Noemi. Much as she likes Owen, it's none of his damn business.

"You haven't seen it, Owen. It's like the apartment times a thousand."

Owen says nothing, but it's clear he expects more.

"Look what we've done so far. She needs us."

"I think it may be too soon. She's tired. This work has been difficult for her."

"It has to be now." Ev knows she sounds sour and petulant, but she can't think of a reasonable argument. Why now?

"I need this," she finally admits.

Owen nods as though he's known all along.

"Do you need it at Harriet's expense?"

"We can take it slow. I don't expect her to tackle it all at once. This is just a scouting mission, an assessment."

Owen is driving her nuts with the way he's

looking at her, as though everything that comes out of her mouth is exactly what he expects, but as though he's disappointed by her words all the same. He knows she's being selfish, that this has nothing to do with Harriet. But he opens the van door and steps out. Ev exhales a breath and follows.

Owen waves her back inside.

"No. I'll go. You wait here."

Owen never makes commands. She studies his face, reevaluates the concern lined there. He's more than worried. He's angry and trying to stifle it. Hell, she's stupid sometimes. While she's been trying to salvage her relationship with Noemi, a shift has taken place at the Dragon. She's been too busy to notice the loyalties realigning. Ev, losing her only allies. She's become the outsider. She watches Owen walk away and feels truly, completely alone.

35

Harriet shrinks down inside the van as her childhood home comes into view. Somewhere along this journey, she's lost her place as the wise old witch, the teacher. She's become the nervous apprentice. Ev sits spine-straight and composed next to the window, her face revealing nothing. Meanwhile, Harriet prepares for what's ahead by practicing the protective techniques she told Ev to abandon. Breathing and bubbles seem awfully attractive at the moment. All the fear that drove her away from this place and into the safety of her little apartment, it claws at her insides again. It was easy, over the years, to distance the memories, to imagine that house as no more than an oversized storage unit. When Ev tempted her into coming back, she only thought of those lost treasures, so many stories to experience all over again. A house full of old friends into which to breathe new life via the Dragon. A rescue mission.

In truth, didn't she abandon Angel Place? Will the house welcome her? Or will it lash out in anger?

Stop. She's getting ridiculous, bordering on hysterical. Too much time spent with Ev and her paranoia. She doesn't fear the house. She fears facing the vastness of the mess she helped to create. She fears coming home to all those old memories. She roots in her pocket for the bird stone, an after-thought she brought along to keep her calm. She cups it in her palm and strokes it gently with her thumb. Much nicer than a bubble.

She's already decided she will go in alone first. As strongly as the emotions swell within those lonely walls, she can tell they have become muted over the years. Her presence here will awaken some of the treasures that have gone to sleep, excite those that still live. She needs to greet the house and prepare before allowing others to enter. Especially Ev.

Harriet passes Owen a set of keys. "This one opens the gate," she says. "Make sure you close it behind us."

Owen hops out. The gate scrapes along the gravel.

"Go around the side," says Harriet, when he's returned to the truck. "There's a garage

to the left. You can park in front of that."
She wants the truck out of sight. No reason
to attract the curiosity of neighbors. It's
unlikely any of the old families still live
nearby. The poisonous energies of Harriet's
house certainly drove away more than one.
Others left out of greed, selling their properties for outrageous profits during the most
bullish years of Vancouver's real estate
boom. However, if any are left to remember
Harriet, she doubts they will be happy to
see her.

They bump slowly over the driveway, such
as it is. Nature has reclaimed it, for the most
part. Weeds creep up the lower windows and
push up through the pavement of the patio
out back. She says nothing when Owen
turns off the engine. She simply waits for
Ev to open the door and slide out. Then she
follows, planting her feet among the dandelions.

"Wait here," she says. "I'll call you when
it's time."

"I'm coming with you." Both Owen and
Ev speak at once.

"You'll wait until I'm ready."

Ev begins to argue, then seems to think
better of it. She kicks at a clump of grass.

"Take these, then." Owen hands her a
surgical mask and a pair of white cotton

gloves just like the ones Ev wears. She notices he won't look at the house, as though it's dangerous to make eye contact. "Call us if you need anything. We'll be right here."

Harriet's breath heats the air under the mask. She winds around to the front of the house and takes the three steps to the front door. The pane of frosted glass on the right has been smashed, presumably a break-in attempt. But naturally, upon meeting a wall of newspaper pressed so tightly against the glass that it leaves no gap to even slide a hand in, the would-be robber gave up. She made sure to buffer all the windows that had easy access in a similar way. She unlocks three dead bolts and pushes the door inward cautiously. It opens just enough to allow Harriet to slip inside.

The smell hits her first, the sweet, damp mustiness that clings to all old West Coast homes, amplified over time and mixed with dust, newspaper, and roses. Still roses, after all this time, the lingering memory of every bouquet her father sent home in apology for another missed dinner. For a moment, she envisions the foyer as it once was, the cut glass chandelier and polished wood floors. Geordie at the bottom of the wide, sweeping staircase in a gaudy blue tux, holding a rose in his teeth and posing like a toreador. All her most vivid memories are of him.

The tunnel through the foyer lies before her, narrow and dark, muffling the energies behind it. She designed it that way; building walls around a pathway using ordinary objects she pulled from the garage. A deceitful tunnel, made to trick intruders. Anyone who gets past the door will see a hoarder house, stacked to the ceiling with junk. A house not worth anyone's time or skin.

There is an alarm panel to her left, as advertised by the stickers on every door and window. Lost now, behind stacks of newspapers bundled tightly with string. She still remembers the code: 1-12-1996. The day of her mother's death. It's not armed, of course, the power was shut off long ago. She relies on the survival instinct of thieves for security. And if survival instinct fails, there are always the booby traps.

Her ears detect no cockroaches or rats scuttling away from the door. She spies no droppings on the small patch of bare wood at her feet. A good sign. Not that she expects the house to be vermin-free after all this time. But they shouldn't have taken over the place. It's always been important that the collection be preserved. Even at her worst, she was meticulous about food scraps and garbage. The worst came after her mother died. A decade with only her treasures for company. She got lost, used collecting to fill her time and ease the loneliness. She became indiscriminate, careless, driven by need and greed. She's embarrassed to show Ev and Owen. Even now, at the very doorstep, she's putting it off. This house is a monument to all that Harriet lacks, the vast hole inside that she's been trying to fill for her entire life. She wants to keep that void hidden. But they're here now. Her reckoning has come.

Harriet's scalp begins to prickle. From the inner reaches of the house, she can feel some of the more vibrant treasures reaching out already, searching for her. Some have been so long buried she hasn't touched them in years, can only brush her consciousness up against theirs. There, the proud brass elephant that lies somewhere in the den. And there, a compact mirror, cracked and desperate for attention, in a drawer in the master bath. She shakes it away.

She hasn't moved a step beyond the alarm panel. Her eyes have grown accustomed to the dark, so it is time to do the real disarming. She scans the narrow space in front of her, searching. There, a foot in front of her, at ankle height.

"Harriet?"

The voice startles her. She flinches, steadies herself with a hand gently placed next to the alarm panel, the only spot of wall available to her, old habits keeping her from putting weight on any of the objects around her.

"I told you to wait," she says to Ev.

"It's been half an hour. We were worried."

Half an hour. Harriet blinks. Her head feels stuffed with wool, like she's just woken from a nap.

"Can I come in?"

The mask muffles Ev's voice, but Harriet can hear the gentle respect there. She feels a rush of gratitude.

"Not yet. Give me a minute. It's not safe."

She reaches into her pocket and pulls out the pair of nail scissors she tucked inside that morning. Then, slowly, gently, she kneels and snips the wire stretched across the narrow path.

"Okay. Come."

There isn't a lot of room to move, so Ev steps into the doorway, her arm pressing against Harriet's. She draws in a sharp breath, but her face remains calm. She is quiet. Listening.

"How long did it take to find all this

stuff?" She speaks in a hush, as though she's worried the house is listening back.

"My mother collected for twenty years before she became too ill. I've been collecting since I was a teenager." Still she tries to diminish her role, as though they can't see through her. She doesn't mention how she's the one who filled up the bulk of the main floor in the frenzied years after her mother died. Harriet reaches out to touch the leg of a stacking chair to her right, gently putting pressure on it until she feels sure it is a safe weight-bearing spot.

"You haven't run away screaming," she says to Ev.

"Not yet."

"Where's Owen?"

"Exploring the gardens. I think he's a bit spooked."

"There's so much. I don't remember it being so much." But of course, she knew. Why is she lying?

"Can we go further?"

"Soon. I need some time. Please."

Ev exhales loudly under her mask. Harriet doesn't budge. When Ev finally realizes Harriet isn't going to press forward, has no intention of moving an inch, she steps outside. Harriet wonders if the girl is ready for this, strong as she's become. While Ev has made a huge amount of progress, there are things in this house that will trouble her. Treasures as toxic as the shark or the pistol. Not just the objects from her family's past. They could work for months without uncovering those, and Harriet will ensure this is the case. It's too soon yet, is the refrain she repeats to herself. She must protect Ev until she's ready. She buries the other reasons, fear of Ev's reaction, fear of what will happen when those old secrets are let loose, and worst of all, the grubby, greedy, Gollum part of her that knows she has no right to Ev's inheritance but wants to keep it anyway.

When she's sure she's alone, Harriet burrows her way toward the front stairs and the entrance to the great room. She stands at the crossroads, where the path offers three choices: left, toward the kitchen, the breakfast room, and the dining room; right, toward the sitting room, the library, and the stairs to the second floor; and straight ahead, into the great room. Before she can change her mind, she clicks on her flashlight, ducks around the barstool, and weaves left, past the service stairs and into the maze that was once a kitchen. She wants to make sure the long path through the dining room is still intact before she makes her next move. She gingerly steps over the wire stretched taut at the entrance to the break-fast room. Everything appears to be in place, including the cluster of fear-soaked plastic snakes and spiders she tucked in the crevices of an armchair on the edge of the path, a psychic deterrent in case her physical one fails. She weathers the skin-crawl they inspire, edging forward a bit more so she can peer through the doorway of the dining room. A crack in the thick curtains at the back of the room has allowed a thin slice of sunlight to pierce the dusty gloom. Tears spring to her eyes at the sight of long-unseen friends.

They are in various states of decay. Many of them have faded into plainness, no longer treasures. Others remain brilliant. The glass fisherman floats she found on the beach, charged with secrecy, piled up in an old vase of her mother's. A violin turned to grief and guilt but made beautiful by the daily devotions of the one who laid bow to strings. As she grows accustomed to the darkness, she begins to notice differences. The rubber dinghy has drifted across the tops of stacks and now rests near the window. And toward the entrance to the sitting room, she sees other items out of place. A wooden rocking horse tipped over on its side. An overturned bag full of yarn ends scattered on the path ahead. What else has changed? What tricks does the house have waiting for her?

Best to head back outside, before someone comes looking for her. Harriet turns and winds back through the kitchen and into the hall. She ducks back around the bar-stool, and then quickly, before she loses her nerve, grabs two of its legs and yanks hard, pulling the stool out from under all that it supports. She scuttles backward as a hor-rible clatter fills her ears and the walls in front of her crash inward.

Something hits her shoulder. She bows, throws her arms over her head. This is it. The house is claiming her. She should have known it would. The noise stops. Dust tickles her nose, even under the mask. She isn't dead. Her shoulder aches dully, and her knee stings where it hit the floor too hard. Other than that, she's unharmed. But she does appear to be stuck.

She hears Owen yelling.

"I'm here," she calls.

She waits for him to find her, ass up in the air and pointing in his direction.

"Don't move," says Owen from behind.

"Wasn't planning on it."

"Are you hurt?"

"I'm fine. Just stuck."

"You've got a chair on you." Owen whistles. "You're lucky. It wedged on some boxes and kept the other stuff from burying you." She feels the weight lift from her.

"You shouldn't have come in this far," she tells him. "It's dangerous."

"No kidding," he says. "Back out. Carefully."

Harriet wiggles backward, pressing up against Owen's legs in order to get past him. Owen sets the chair back down gently. The path into the great room has been blocked. Perfect. Now the only way to the back corner is to take the long and winding path. And Harriet plans to send them in the opposite direction to start.

Owen helps Harriet to her feet. His hands cup hers. "That could have been much worse. From now on, no wandering around in here by yourself."

"It's my house," Harriet says crankily. "I got careless. It won't happen again."

"No," says Owen. "It won't. You're right, it's too dangerous."

He says it kindly, but it rubs her the wrong way. Even if he's right.

400

36

Ev heaves another stack of newspapers onto the recycling pile. She feels jittery, impatient. She's been sorting for hours, the sun baking the back of her neck. They have to start at the beginning, clearing a wider, safer passage through the front entrance. That means hauling out all the boring stuff — old magazines and newspapers and telephone books, stainless and dull. Shit that should have been dumped in a blue box years ago.

They've pitched a tent in the backyard and rolled a big tarp out underneath to keep everything protected and dry. The day is hot, but there's no telling how long this process will take. They're settled in for the long haul, Ev stuck with the job of sorting outside while Harriet helps Owen navigate inside. Secretly, she doesn't mind. Her first steps in the door left her breathless. And after, when she quietly followed Harriet underneath the barstool, noting the path that curved into darkness ahead, the one that would lead her to her past, was worse. She didn't stay inside long. Only long enough to see where Harriet went, to watch her avoid the trap she'd set, to witness her standing motionless at the dark doorway to yet another room. Then the fear set in, and she retreated. This was before Harriet sprang one of her own traps and narrowly missed getting buried alive.

As the hours pass, she knows she can't put it off much longer. She should be thinking about this evening, with Noemi. She needs to learn her way around. Besides, the longer she stays outside in the shadow of the old house, the more bored she gets. Bored and curious.

Harriet isn't bored. Since she recovered from her fall, she has displayed renewed energy. She's been fighting with Ev all day, pulling stuff out of the discard pile and back into the keep pile, stained or not. Owen floated the idea of hiring some extra help with the sorting and heavy lifting. He knows plenty of binners who'd be willing to take some of Harriet's cash. Harriet vetoed that quickly. Too tempting. They never know when they might find a pair of diamond earrings in a box with a bunch of *Star Trek* novels.

Ev stares at the house. Owen has run out to get some lunch. She makes up her mind.

"Harriet."

"Mm." She's lost, sitting nearby under a willow tree with magazines fanned out all around her.

"I'm going inside."

Harriet's eyes flick up to meet hers. "Now?"

"I want to see." Ev puts on a surgical mask and stalks toward the house, not looking behind her. She hears Harriet sigh and scuffle.

"Hold up. I'll go first," Harriet calls after her. "Can't have you getting crushed."

Ev builds her familiar protective inner walls as they near the front door. Breathe and center. It's become so easy, like throwing a cloak over her shoulders. Stepping across the threshold, she promises herself she won't let the stories in. Right now, she needs to focus on navigation, not discovery. Later, she might need to let those walls down, but she doesn't want to think about that yet.

They wind their way through the front hall, flashlights in hand. Ev tries not to panic at the walls of junk towering over her.

It gets dark fast. Ev's unease grows. There are things ahead that hold bad energy. Things that threaten to find any hairline cracks in her walls.

The passage hits a fork. Harriet predictably veers right, away from the room where Ev sensed the energies of her past. She has to twist sideways to fit through, moving toward the huge staircase.

"What's down that path?"

"Kitchen and dining room. We'll get to that later." So that's the way she and Noemi have to go. Harriet gestures in the other direction. "We're starting in the sitting room and library."

Ev stops. She stares straight ahead, squinting. It's like one of those artworks made up of thousands of tiny photographs. The longer you stare at it, the more incredible it becomes. Boxes holding up sofas and dining room tables. A harp on top of a bookshelf on top of an ottoman. Two, no three pianos. A suit of armor. Silk fans. A basketball. The closer Ev looks, the more she sees. Mardi Gras beads draped around the neck of a mounted stag head. A single wooden oar. A clown mask. A set of poker chips. There's the little wooden boat that goes with the oar, propped on top of a dining room table and filled with books. Half of the stuff buzzes with low-grade stains. A few things radiate powerfully, reminding Ev to keep herself buffered.

She's no more than twenty feet into the house. Somewhere up ahead lie the boxes containing her family, what's left of them. Her breath comes faster.

"Is there only one path?"

"There are others. Hard to see them if you don't know where to look."

"But you'll show me."

"In time." Harriet turns to Ev, frowns over her flashlight beam as though she can read her mind. "You mustn't come in alone. I've built in safeguards."

"Traps."

"Safeguards. Watch for trip wires. Don't put your weight on anything unless I tell you. There are structures that are stable enough to climb on, but . . ."

"But you need to show them to me."

She's so busy taking it all in that it takes her a while to register the dread that has begun to overtake her body. She realizes, slowly, that she's become rooted to the floor. Ev feels the deep-down gut fear of something bad beneath her feet. It reaches up through the floorboards like a tentacled creature, winding around her ankles and pulling down, pulling her heart into her stomach.

"Harriet, what's in the basement?"

"We're not going into the basement."

Ev can't breathe. She needs to escape but is stuck, trapped by an oily hatred that whips its way up her calves and thighs.

"You okay?" Harriet is suddenly right there, her face close. "Ev?"

Ev manages to shake her head. "Get it off me," she whispers.

"Snap out of it. Breathe."

"Can't."

"It's in your head. Remember, you're in charge." A sigh and a rattle in her throat. "Well, I can't pull you out. I can't get around you. You gotta move."

"Can't." The mask clings to her mouth, moist and hot. Ev wants to claw it off, but she's stuck, trapped. She tries to empty her mind, ignore the pull of the hate.

"Here." Harriet presses something cool into the palm of Ev's hand. The tension releases. Ev's breathing eases. The tentacles slide away and back through the floor. Good old bird stone. Ev clutches it as she retreats, weaving back through the path as fast as she can, pressing her arms to her chest to try to quell the shaking of her limbs. She feels suffocated, objects pressing in all around her. How will she stay calm long enough to guide Noemi through those pathways? How will they extract the things they find?

Outside now seems a fine place to be. Ev spends the afternoon sorting mechanically and preparing for her next entry. She made a promise to Noemi so, like it or not, she has to find a way. She'll do it alone this time, challenge herself, see if she can hack it. The opportunity comes when Owen finally convinces Harriet to take a break and walk with him to the back of the property to look at the river. Ev pleads exhaustion and lies down under the willow tree to nap. When their voices sound suitably distant, she steels herself and goes back into the house.

She keeps moving, not allowing any one thing to take hold of her. She winds through the foyer and left into the kitchen. She spots the wire and steps over it carefully, muscles tensed, limbs pressed tightly to her body. A creeping sensation invades her flesh, something nasty hidden along the wall of this path, but Ev saw Harriet pass by it unscathed so she presses on, to the door of the dining room, where the path curves to the right. Only a little light filters in through the curtained window at the front of the room. The air is heavy with dust. She's glad for the mask, even though it's moist and hot against her nose.

She shines her flashlight on the path. A grandfather clock is lodged across it at waist height, a few feet to the right. The path to her past, barred by time. She grins at the clock. Ev ducks under, before she can change her mind. She crawls a few feet, gloves tacky on old wood, watching for other signs, triggers like the ones Harriet pointed out. The wood gives way to carpet of some unidentifiable color, beige or pink or dust. Here the towers of clutter narrow, leaving a space just wide enough to slide through sideways. Just past the opening, Ev's flashlight catches a glimmer. Another wire stretched taut a few inches from the floor.

She aims the flashlight deeper into the room. Its beam illuminates the edges of boxes and the curved legs of chairs. The path tunnels at an angle, veering right and out of sight, surrounded on both sides almost to the ceiling. She tries to spot something familiar.

She's still for too long. That awful oiliness from below begins to seep and pool around her knees, drawing her downward. She scuttles backward in shock and revulsion, her toes bumping the corner of something

408

solid. The oiliness recedes, and Ev, recovering her wits, decides it's best to keep moving. The flashlight has fallen to the floor, rolling almost under the wire booby trap. She shuffles to it, wraps her hand around the barrel, freezes.

The beam shines into a narrow hole on the left side of the path. A miniature tunnel, created by the frames of three bicycles. Behind the bicycle frames is a box. On the side, written in black block letters, is a name. *Marchand.*

Ev's head swims. The name, more than anything else, more than the oiliness below or the probing neediness of the house itself, makes her knees buckle. Not only are they here, they are in reach. There are cemetery plots outside of the city, flat granite slabs with names and dates. Ev saw them once, has never been back. They never seemed real to her. She could never connect those slabs with the names etched into them. But here. That box. The objects hidden in this room. This is real. This is her family's burial ground.

37

Not much later — too soon — Ev hurtles toward Harriet's house again, this time in the dark. Noemi is a careless driver, drifting between lanes for no apparent reason, coasting through intersections as yellow flicks to red, sharing her musical taste with the world through open windows. The Ramones seem too upbeat for a night like this, at least for Ev, who clutches the cracked vinyl seat of the ancient Civic Noemi showed up in — borrowed from a friend, she explained vaguely — unsure if her hands clench in reaction to the driving or to the speed at which they approach their target. Noemi sings under her breath, determinedly chipper. It seems she's decided to treat the break-in as some grand adventure, all black clothing and headlamps and midnight-snack Pocky. But Ev isn't fooled. The gulf between them continues to widen, she can see it in the faraway look in her sister's dull eyes.

They're playing at sisterhood. This is a re-enactment.

They turn off busy Granville Street, the instant quiet changing the tone.

"Slow down," says Ev. "And kill the music. We don't want to attract attention."

"Thanks, Captain Obvious." Noemi punches a button on the stereo and they wind toward the river in silence. The closer they get, the farther apart the houses spread.

"The lights are all out. It's like no one lives here."

"No one does." Half of the houses in this corner of the city are owned by foreign investors. The neighborhood is dying.

"And you're worried about attracting attention? Check that out." Noemi slows down in front of a sprawling modern rancher, all darkened glass in a sea of perfect lawn marred only by a *For Sale* sign. "Maybe I'll move in. Claim squatter's rights."

Ev tries to smile, but her facial muscles won't obey. "Next right. We're almost there."

She spots the gate. The house takes her breath away. She feels it reaching out, more awake than ever, its energies simmering. Even Noemi falls solemn. She instructs her sister to stop and pulls the gate open. She

411

left the padlock unlocked when she volunteered to close it as they left with Harriet earlier. They roll around the side of the house, the only light from the car's headlights, the half-moon over the river, and in the distance, across the water, blinking airport lights.

Noemi stops the car. They sit without speaking for some time — a minute? Ten?

"It's really big." Noemi's voice, hoarse, sounds frightened for the first time.

"You still want to do this?"

"It's the only thing I want."

Ev opens the car door, steps out into the night, and faces the weight of the house. It seems to lean over her, shadows on shadows, eager to welcome her back, hungry for her attention. Noemi slips across the grass with a snaky rustle, heading straight for the big, dark windows off the patio. It chills Ev to see her place her hands on the glass, then her forehead. Noemi stands motionless that way until Ev can't stand it a moment longer. She imagines the glass melting and the house swallowing her sister up, her body vanishing behind the curtain.

"Noemi." She speaks in a whisper. "Come away from there."

Noemi lifts one hand from the glass and knocks on it, a series of rapid-fire blows like shots being fired into the silent night. Ev swallows a shriek.

"For fuck's sake. Stop it."

Unrepentant, Noemi turns to Ev. "Just making sure no one's home. It's in there? Somewhere behind those curtains?"

"Yeah."

Noemi begins running her fingers along the seams of the doors. She jiggles the door handle.

"Not that way. It's not safe. Over here." Ev indicates the path alongside the house, a narrow trail of tamped-down grass. Noemi takes a last look at the dark window before drawing away, back toward the car. Ev takes the headlamp Noemi offers her and stands silent while her sister hauls out the toolbox she stowed in the hatch. She leads the way past the piles of garbage under tarps, past the garage, around to the front door. Then she watches her sister proceed to pick the locks like she's been thieving her entire life. While she works, Noemi's face relaxes into self-satisfied concentration, her frenetic energy temporarily soothed by the task at hand. Another thing Ev didn't know about her sister.

Noemi opens the door, and they file in. Noemi immediately gravitates toward the bottom of the grand staircase.

"Don't touch anything."

Noemi runs her fingers down the dark wood, then plucks a fedora off a coat rack next to the staircase and perches it on her head.

"I mean it." Ev grabs the hat, getting a jolt of self-centered petulance as she hangs it back up. "Come on — this way."

Emotions bubble up from all directions. She remembers the beginning of all this, the jar of buttons Owen found and how it overwhelmed her. Now she stands in the middle of thousands of stains, still whole, still strong. She decides to take comfort in this.

She leads Noemi through the foyer and steps over the threshold into the kitchen. She has to admit the headlamps are handy, even if they shine a ghostly blue light and cast sharp, strange shadows. Behind her, Noemi catches her breath when she enters the kitchen. Her arm brushes Ev's, and she can feel the tremble in her sister's limbs.

"We need to keep moving." She doesn't want to explain about the thing that tends to ooze up from below, so she keeps creeping, slowly, steadily, making her way to the clock. Noemi lags only a little behind, anxious to see the box Ev described. Ev kneels and crawls under the clock, Noemi

414

close at her heels. When they reach the doorway, Ev tilts her head to shine the lamp on the little wire that stretches across.

"Can you see it?" Her voice comes out as a wheeze. Her chest feels tight, like a hand clenches her heart.

"Yeah."

Ev stands and carefully steps over, sliding sideways past the bike frames. Noemi follows. When they're both in, she kneels again, pointing her light into the little tunnel, so that Noemi can read the name printed on the box.

"Oh my God." Noemi reaches her hand in, snaking through silver aluminum tubes, fingers splayed wide despite the fact that the box is too far away to touch.

"How do we get it?"

"I told you, it's going to take some time. We have to be careful."

Ev can feel the greasy tendrils pooling beneath her boots. She steels her mind again and shifts, moving deeper inside the room, slowly winding toward the middle. Her heart stops at the sight of a spray of roses on silk fabric, the arm of a sofa she recognizes at once.

"There's more," she tells Noemi, squeezing the words out. But Noemi hasn't followed. She's out of sight, and Ev suddenly feels too alone, too compressed.

"Noemi?"

Her sister comes to her at once, warm hand on her arm.

"Breathe with me," she whispers, and they count down together, Ev letting Noemi hold her weight, just for a moment.

"I can't do this."

"But you are. You're doing it. Ev, this means so much, you bringing me here. You don't even know. I thought you wouldn't. I was sure you wouldn't."

"I promised."

"I found something. I think we can get it out. Just this one thing for tonight. Then we can go."

Tonight. How many nights will Noemi make her endure?

Noemi tugs her back gently. She shines her light up to the top of a bookshelf, where a squat yellow wicker basket rests on top of a stack of *People* magazines.

"That? Why that?"

"I dunno, it looked familiar to me. Do you recognize it?"

"No." Ev tries to isolate it, searching out its vibrations. She ignores the other voices competing for her attention. Her skin prickles all over. The basket wants to slide away from her, but she keeps at it, narrowing her focus. There. The basket itself holds no stain, but an object inside it does, something faint, soft and comfortable.

"There's something inside," she says, relieved at its relative safety.

"Can you tell if it's ours?"

"Maybe." She stays with the object. A flash of memory grabs her, vivid and saturated with light, the bars of a white crib, green curtains floating in the breeze, afternoon sun, sleepiness. A voice in the room.

She breaks away, her breath gone ragged.

"Are you okay?"

"It's ours." She blinks away the tears.

"Can you reach it?"

"Not quite."

"If I could get up on your shoulders?"

"God, no. Too risky. I need something to stand on. One of those folding chairs against the wall in the foyer."

Noemi darts away.

"Watch the wire," Ev cries, but Noemi hops over expertly.

Ev is alone. Surrounded. She shudders, pacing in the narrow spot between the trip wire and a pinch in the path, keeping her eyes averted from the basket and the place where she saw that sofa. She can hear the house, little squeaks and groans and murmurs, maybe rats or insects, maybe objects

417

on the move. To distract herself, she lays her hands on the smooth corner of a black piano bench, trying to glean its history, playing the game she often plays with Harriet. Nothing. No, there. A snatch of fumbled music and laughter, shoulders touching, dizzy infatuation, scent of candle wax. Unasked questions: *Could we? Should we?* She pulls her hand away.

"Ev."

She flinches. She didn't notice Noemi's approach. Noemi stands on the other side of the wire with a folding chair tucked under her arm.

"Can you take it?"

Ev lifts the chair over the wire and unfolds it. She puts one foot, then the other, on the chair and slowly straightens. Harriet's collection stretches out beneath her, a wasteland of discarded hopes and dreams. A graveyard of memory. She reaches over, takes hold of the handles on either side of the basket, and lifts it down. Her throat closes, and her vision blurs.

"What is it?"

Blue wool, smiling eyes. Cool fingers brushing her scalp. The sweater smells musty, but it holds her in its fibers, hints of garlic and lavender.

Mama.

Wool presses against her cheek and nose.

You don't have to help him anymore. You can stay here with me.

Mama used to speak to her in Cantonese, but all of those words have since vanished, swept out of the corners of her brain. She remembers these words because her mother spoke them in English.

It's okay, Mama. I want to.

You can change things.

She tried to change things, but she was too late.

"Hey." Noemi has a hand on her calf now. She can't. She thrusts the basket at Noemi, sits on the chair, and lets the sadness take her.

38

The house speaks to Harriet, and Harriet listens. It confirms what she feared: She has rats after all. She knew for sure when she arrived this morning and found the piece of cardboard she wedged in the front door yesterday lying on the floor, a silent alarm. She found other signs, too. A chair out of place. A hat hanging on the wrong hook. Owen mistook her breathless anger for a panic attack. He dragged the offending chair over to her, sat her down, and placed a water bottle in her hands. She couldn't trust herself to speak, so allowed the misunderstanding. It gave her time to think. To plan. Now that she knows she has rats, she needs to set better traps.

She waits until they're busy out on the lawn. The weather has turned, so the other two are huddled underneath the tarps. Despite the rain, it's more comfortable outside than in, and there's plenty out there to sort. She should be safe to slip deeper inside and extract a few helpful items.

She heads into the kitchen. There's a second path there, harder to see but easy to navigate if you know where to find it. It skirts the large island and winds into the back of the room. The basement door waits in the darkest corner, gray and solid, its sliding bolt resistant. As she wiggles it slowly free, her stomach knots itself in anticipation. She runs through her mental catalog, hoping the items she remembers are still close at hand, on the topmost steps.

The bolt edges free with a loud snap. Harriet tenses, and then as she finds her breath, feels the surge of adrenaline course through her body. Her fingers tingling, she cracks open the door. A sour smell wafts into the room. Harriet recoils from it, even with the mask covering her nose. The door hits the corner of a box at the halfway mark and shudders to a stop. She points her flashlight into the dark. A face looms, cracked white skin with one wide eye, one empty socket. Harriet expected it, but still it causes her to gasp and suck the paper mask against her mouth. She reaches down, jerking the closest box and the doll along with it, out into the open. There's a clatter, but she doesn't stop to find out what she's knocked down.

She slams the door shut and shoves the bolt back into place. Over the pounding of her heart, she hears a faint voice. It's coming from outside the house. She hurries back along the kitchen path, grateful for a reason to leave the box behind. She reaches the back stairs just as Owen appears in the foyer.

"Everything okay?"

"Fine. I knocked over a lamp. No harm done." She pushes her hair away from her sweaty forehead.

"Are you ready for some lunch? It's wet. I thought perhaps we could get some soup, sit in somewhere."

"Wonderful idea. Why don't you and Ev do that and bring something back for me." Owen hovers, looking as though he'd like to argue. She brushes past him, heading toward the library. "That box by the door is ready to go out," she calls over her shoulder. *Go away.*

When she's certain he's gone, she marches grimly back to the kitchen. The box of dolls waits. There are a dozen or so, each of them steeped in childhood terror. Not dolls that were cherished, but those that inspired fear. Awful little things. She reconsiders her plan only for a moment. A nagging doubt, telling her it's past time to come clean, to communicate. Stop the sneaking around. She shakes the thought away. She must protect the house. No, that's wrong. She must protect Ev. As quick as she dares, Harriet tucks them one by one into the cracks and crevices of the walls lining the path into the dining room.

That's one set of rats managed. The last rat, she's put off too long. Shivering and sniffling back tears, she escapes upstairs for some cleansing. The path up the service stairs is barely visible, but Harriet knows how to squeeze in. It's tougher making her way up than she thought, not because of the path, but because she's getting closer to the more familiar voices of her own past. These were the stairs she used until the end, when she finally gave up and fled. Downstairs is where other people's memories live. Up is different. Up is Harriet's past, her stories.

The relief she's after lies halfway up on the tiny landing. A laundry basket perches on top of a stack of boxes, all full of plush. From that pile, a friendly voice nudges her. Sparkles the Octopus, sweet thing. She gave him the name for the pink glittery felt covering his beanbag head. He probably never had a name before she found him, only a feeling. He was a friend to some long-gone pup. Not her dog; she was never allowed animals as a child, and as an adult, never wanted to subject an animal to her living conditions. She has always been drawn to objects loved by animals; and this one, a chewed-up thing with matted fur and two missing tentacles, still feels rich with simple joy.

She basks in the warm spot of Sparkles's companions, balls and squeaky toys and matted, torn stuffed animals. It's like stepping onto a sun-drenched square of carpet, the perfect spot for a winter's nap. She thinks of settling in, of wrapping her tail snug around her body and curling into warmth. But more memories call out to her. She sets Sparkles down with his playmates, moves on and up. A multicolored pinwheel spins as she passes, *flick, flick, flick*-ing against the side of a plastic crate full of glass soda bottles.

"Harriet."

They are looking for her again. They are always looking for her. A surge of nervous energy sends her scurrying forward. Not too far, though, or she'll run into one of her traps.

"Harriet."

"Not yet," she calls. "I'm fine."

"It's time to eat."

The hallway path narrows past the first

door. On the left, her mother's room is blocked; she hasn't been inside in fifteen years. To her right is the guest room. She still calls it the guest room, though she used it herself in the last years, spent more years in it than she did in her childhood room down the hall. The door swings open more easily than she expects. The room, dark within, welcomes her.

"Harriet."

The voice has grown closer. Resentment bubbles up. She ignores it, sneaks inside, and places her hand on the spine of a book poking out of a nearby box. *Anne of Green Gables.* A Christmas gift from her parents. She remembers the day. Geordie received a chemistry set. She wanted one too, but instead received the set of books. She was so angry she didn't read any of them until she was an adult and her mother fell ill. She read them aloud at her mother's bedside and felt cranky at the realization that she liked Anne Shirley.

The oblique memory of her brother draws her gaze up to the chest of drawers, and the glass gearshift knob resting next to a music box. It's too dark to see the pinup girl trapped under the glass. She can only make out the shape of the knob. Maybe, if she concentrates, she might be able to feel the

425

reckless rush of it, still lingering. Funny that for so long she kept a treasure steeped in recklessness as a reminder to be careful. She kept it always within sight, so she wouldn't forget. She'd never given another treasure as a gift after that day.

A hand on Harriet's shoulder startles her. She shrugs it off.

"Get lost, Geordie."

"It's Owen."

"Of course it is." Harriet blinks at the face attached to the hand. "What are you doing here? I didn't invite you. Didn't I tell you I was coming down?"

"Twenty minutes ago. Your soup is getting cold."

"I'm not hungry."

"Come anyway."

"I'm not ready."

"Harriet." She turns at the darkness in his tone. Her flashlight casts sharp shadows across his face, giving it the lean lines of a hungry wolf. His eyes plead with her, but she doesn't buy his concern.

"Where's my Buddha?"

A momentary squint of confusion, and then something else that causes his eyes to flick sideways. As she thought.

"Harriet, please." Changing the subject. He told her he found the sword knocked onto the floor and buried under a rug. Misplaced, he said.

"Did you take it?"

"We'll find it later. It's time for a rest. Come with me."

"Get out of my house." She presses the book to her chest.

"Harriet."

"Get out," she yells, "and don't come back!"

She can't trust any of them. Only the house is loyal.

"Harriet."

39

Rain pelts the tarp above Ev's head, rolling off the staked edge in a steady stream. Spread out at her knees, dozens of watches are lined up in various styles and colors. They blur before her eyes. Only three hours passed between Noemi dropping her at home and Owen's morning pickup. Between that, perhaps a few moments of anxious sleep.

Owen works as quietly as she does, moving between the indoor and outdoor realms with detached steadiness. Harriet, she hasn't seen since they arrived, although Ev wonders if she could pinpoint her location if she tried hard enough. She could sense Noemi up in the tree the other night. Why not Harriet, too? She focuses her attention on the house, cuts through the scramble of energies, imagining Harriet inside, burrowing and burrowing. She roots out her presence, a bright spot in the darkness, a heartbeat in the center of the house, her emotions whittled down to a sharp tip. Possession.

Ev shudders, shaking her head to rip away the connection. The static takes over for a moment before reassembling itself into another form. She senses a big, simmering emotion, hot and close. It makes her stomach clench. What is that?

"Help me with something?" She didn't notice Owen standing at the edge of the tarp. His boots and rain pants are spattered with mud. He's drawn his hood up. The shadow of it hides his eyes.

"Sure. What's up?"

"Uncovered a wingback chair in the library. If we can get it out, it'll open up the path a fair bit."

She stands, waiting for Owen to lead the way, but he doesn't move.

"It's difficult, isn't it, seeing so much wealth accumulated in one place? The excess is astonishing. The disregard for the value of things. It's easy to forget that this all belongs to Harriet."

Ev's stomach lurches. She says nothing.

"Are we here because you mean to take from her?"

She can't look at him. She clutches a paperback book, stares blankly at the back cover.

"I'm helping her."

"This." Owen slaps the tarp, sending water spilling over the edge. "This is not help."

The force of his words knocks the breath from her. She understands, suddenly. That seasick feeling, that rage rolling over her, it comes from Owen. She caused it.

"She's not okay." Ev can hear the anguish in his voice and clutches the paperback tighter. "If she stays in there any longer, I'm afraid we'll lose her."

"I'm sorry." These words she breathes, or perhaps she only thinks them. The heat presses into her temples. She wants to run. But this is Owen, not her father. This anger has truth behind it. She breathes, hearing Noemi in her head again, counting her down. Four . . . three . . . two . . . one . . .

"Do you hear me? It's making her sick."

Keep the dirt out.

Her Pocky-and-coffee breakfast threatens to come up. She keeps counting. The heat recedes, and Ev senses something else around its edges, something very familiar. Not anger but guilt. It lingers as Owen's anger ebbs.

What did you do? She wants to ask him but is afraid to bring the rage rolling back.

430

Instead, she asks, "What do you want me to do?"

"Get her out."

Ev nods, too queasy to talk. She gets up, her head spinning, points herself in the direction of the house, lurches toward it, lets the press of it wash over her. Lets its opening swallow her up. Quick as she can, she retreats into her head, breathing her bubble around her. She holds the house and all its lonely souls at bay.

Ev can hear Harriet muttering from somewhere above. The main staircase is still blocked, so Ev follows the sound to the back stairs. She creeps up the narrow path on hands and knees, grateful for her gloves and mask. The carpet, once ivory, is coated in dust and ground-in debris, tiny black dots that looks suspiciously like mouse turds scattered throughout. Harriet appears at the top of the stairs, her mask pulled up to her hairline to keep the frizz out of her eyes. She cradles a worn, fringed leather handbag in her arms.

"She took the bus out of town."

"Harriet, it's time to go."

"Not you, too. I told you I'm not hungry."

"The Dragon needs you."

She blinks at that, the moment of clarity encouraging Ev to continue.

431

"Owen's bringing a load over, and you need to help us find new homes for the treasures we've recovered."

"You can't take things from here."

Electric dread travels the length of Ev's spine. She knows.

"The house doesn't want us to take things away." Harriet squeezes the handbag closer to her chest. Ev relaxes.

"The collection belongs to you. Not to the house."

"It's not safe here," she says, her voice small as a child's.

"Come." Ev reaches out and takes the handbag from Harriet, setting it gently on the top step. She takes Harriet's hands. It's the first time they've ever touched. Harriet's palms are damp, her skin soft and fleshy. She doesn't fight. She holds on tightly as Ev eases her from the house's grip, one step at a time.

40

"Come."

Noemi's cold, bony hand slides into Ev's, pulling her away from the dense tangle of darkness that hides the riverbank. On the other side of the wall, a stretch of water waits, sluggish and silted but still cool, still quiet, still a place Ev could float, spread-eagled and alone. She wishes it were Saturday. It's Tuesday night. Has it really only been three days since her last sailing class? It feels like months.

Another yank.

"I'm coming."

"The night's already half over."

Is it? Ev stumbles through the grass. She doesn't know how day has become night, can't remember what occurred between joining hands with Harriet and this moment, her hand now clenched by her sister's, Noemi shrouded in black a half-step ahead of her. She can hardly feel the house, though it looms over both of them, over the hot static of Noemi's trembling fear and excitement. She doesn't like this new facet of her ability, this reading of people the way she reads objects. Noemi's focused emotion overwhelms her, hitting her in waves like nausea.

She needs sleep. She can't bear another night like this, another night like the last one. Whatever Noemi hopes to extract from Harriet's house, she'll have to find it tonight. Guilt eats at what's left of Ev's nerves. But Harriet is deceiving her too. She's refused to come clean. She leads them away from Ev's past, into the library and upstairs. She keeps them from getting too close.

Ev tells herself all these things. It doesn't stop her from feeling she's betrayed the woman. A foot in each boat, like Brett said. And mistake or not, she's gone ahead and stuck both feet into Noemi's boat, into the past and not the future. She holds on tightly while Noemi steers them home.

Noemi lets go when they reach the threshold, allowing Ev to take the lead. Their lamps wobble weak beams into hanging dust, catching the leg of a chair here, the corner of a box there. Ev's guts twist, but she refuses to hesitate. As she nears the kitchen, the twisting grows more savage.

Sweat pricks her hairline. Something pinches her elbow. She cries out.

"It's just me," says Noemi, right in Ev's ear. "Slow down."

"Can't." If she loses momentum, she'll lose her nerve. She's barely finished this thought when she crosses the threshold into the kitchen and stops short. Her guts unwind, loosening to jelly and pooling at the base of her spine. Noemi crowds against her back, huffing loudly under her mask.

"What's going on?" she asks, but from the tremor in Noemi's voice, Ev can tell she feels it too. The queasiness infecting her has a source outside her own anxiety. Outside of Noemi, even. It's here, in the kitchen. Something's changed.

"She knows." Ev's mouth clicks drily. She scans the room with her headlamp, but she can't find what she's looking for. She'll have to let her guard down.

"What do you mean?"

"She's planted objects to keep us away." *And I can't find them without cracking open my shell.*

"Is that why I feel like I'm going to heave?"

"Yes. Quiet for a minute. I need to concentrate."

She grabs the hand clutching her elbow for support and opens her mind outward.

That first rush of noise fills her head, blinding her for a moment. She breathes as steadily as she can, searching out the bad stains. That oily stain in the basement seeps through the floor, winding up her ankles.

"Ev. Are you okay?"

She can't talk, so she nods instead. Okay. She can do this. The new stains prickle like static electricity, pinpricks of terror barbing the walls leading to the dining room. She steps forward, ignoring the slippery pull from below, and roots out the first one, stuffing her hand into the front pocket of a piece of carry-on luggage and plucking out the stain. It's a doll with matted blonde hair, a beanbag body, and empty sockets instead of eyes.

"Let's go." She drops the thing and backs into Noemi.

"What are you doing?"

"Leaving. I'm done here."

"No." Noemi grips her shoulders. "Don't let her win. She's trying to manipulate you."

And you're not?

"Let me help." Noemi pushes Ev gently to the side and slips around her. She picks up the doll and winds past Ev into the depths of the kitchen. She returns empty-handed.

"What did you do with it?"

"Stuffed it in the oven. Where's the next one?"

Ev laughs, a strangled sound, half-amused, half-horrified. But she grabs another one, a porcelain head missing its body, cracks marring its rosy cheeks. By the time she's extracted four or five, the process has become mechanical. They work in silence, Ev rooting out the stains and Noemi vanishing them one by one. It's oddly empowering, even if the effort leaves Ev's head pounding and her nerves raw. Noemi appears to be suffering too. She doesn't complain, but her face grows more drawn, and Ev catches her flinching every now and then from the touch of the dolls against her skin.

Finally, they're through the kitchen and standing in front of the grandfather clock, and Ev is able to hide inside her bubble again, safe.

Ev mentally gauges the space beneath. She won't attempt to move the clock. It's too well wedged in. Anything they take with them will need to fit under or over. Last night, they managed to burrow deeper into the great room and pinpoint a stack of small boxes not far off the path. She heads straight for them, then stops short when something else tugs at her attention. Something familiar. She directs her lamp to the left, scanning.

She spots a stack of plastic bins stuffed with blankets and towels. She knows they belong to her family, not because she feels it, but because of the toy trapped against the clear plastic sides. A Raggedy Ann doll. Not one of the horrors she just dealt with, but her own childhood doll. She stares at it, leaning in as close as she dares. Dust has gathered in the red yarn of her hair, and one cloth arm hangs by a thread, stuffing poking out of the hole. Her dress has a green marker stain on the hem.

Laughter unexpectedly bubbles up inside Ev. She knows what she'll find if she can get into that bin and extract the doll, if she lifts the yellowed apron and the blue ruffled hem of her dress. A pair of circular breasts with big green nipples and a scribbled thatch of green pubic hair. Her doll made anatomically correct, thanks to three-year-old Noemi. She was so mad when she discovered her sister's artwork, she threw the doll in the garbage, declaring her ruined. Someone must have rescued her from the trash can under the kitchen sink. Someone cleaned her up and put her to rest in the linen closet. Not her father. He only dealt in antiques, in the memories of strangers.

The person who preserved Ev's doll had different ideas about the value of things. More than the sweater they found last night, more than the memories it unearthed, this salvaged toy brings Ev's mother rushing back to her.

"Hey," she says to Noemi, when she's able to speak. "Check this out." She turns, eager to share the story. Except Noemi isn't behind her. The towers looming on either side seem to grow taller, and the laughter extinguishes in her throat before it has time to reach her lips.

"Noemi?"

No answer. She follows the path backward, over the wire, under the clock. There. Noemi stands in the kitchen, her back turned to Ev. She's found a narrow opening between the island and the refrigerator and has made her way to a table near the back wall. Ev avoids looking in the direction of the oven. The table is covered in silver teapots and tiered tea trays, stacks of china plates and cups.

"Hey. Can I get some help over here?"

Noemi turns. She holds a ceramic cookie jar shaped like a clown.

"Sorry. I got distracted." She pulls off the clown's grinning head and looks inside the empty cavern of its body. "This is the stuff of nightmares, huh? It's enough to put a girl off snickerdoodles for a lifetime."

"I thought you wanted to get this over with."

"Sorry," she says again. "This place is not ADHD-friendly." She replaces the clown's head with a dull clunk and sets it on the table. Her hands linger over the stacks of dishes. "A lot of cool stuff here."

"Yes."

"A lot of expensive stuff."

"Don't even think about it."

"I wasn't," Noemi lies.

"We're only taking things that are rightfully ours."

"God." Noemi mutters something else as they wind their way back through the dining room, too low for Ev to hear. Ev chooses to ignore her.

"Those are ours." She points her forehead at the stack of boxes in front of the linen bins. "We need to shift everything to the right to get in. See that table behind you?" One of the few surfaces left with enough space to stack a few things.

"Yeah."

"I tested it earlier. I think it'll take some weight. There's a bit of space under, too. I'll move some of this stuff into the path and pass you the rest."

440

"Got it."

To Noemi's credit, once they start working, she stays focused. It takes less time than Ev expected to get within reaching distance of the boxes. She uses the mechanical nature of the work as a meditation, keeping her bubble impenetrable. She keeps her mind blank as she pulls the first box off the stack and passes it to Noemi. Noemi immediately drops to her knees and starts pulling the packing tape off.

"No," Ev says, a little too much panic in her tone. "Not now. We don't have much longer to work. Put it in the car. You can look later."

Noemi furrows her brow, but doesn't argue. She disappears down the path, leaving Ev to extract the rest of the stack and pile it up on the path behind her. Five more boxes. Now she's walled in on all sides. Bubble, she tells herself. Breathe.

Noemi takes far too long to come back.

"Could you move a little faster?" Ev asks when her sister finally drifts into view. "I'm kind of stuck here."

"Right," Noemi replies, making no effort to change her pace. She pauses with her hands on either side of the next box, her head tilted as though she's listening.

"What's wrong?" A horrible thought oc-

441

curs to Ev. "Did you hear something? Is someone here?"

"No. It's nothing."

"Do you want those, too?" Ev points at the linen bins, which are now within reach. "I think they're just full of old sheets and towels."

"I want them."

Noemi lifts the box and wanders away like a sleepwalker. Ev gingerly edges her way around the newly formed stack, leaning on the top box for support. If she doesn't help load the car, they'll be here until sunrise. She meets Noemi near the front door to pass off the next box. The night air seeps into the foyer, deliciously cool. Ev wishes she could run out onto the lawn, down to the river.

Once they've cleared some space, Ev steps into the cavity she's created so that she can extract the linen bins. These will fill the back seat. Then, surely, they can leave. She shifts left around the arm of a leather chair and inches deeper into the crevice. Something prickles at her arms and cheeks, a familiar sensation. Dread creeps under her skin, turning it cold and clammy. She breathes against it. The effort of extracting Harriet's dolls, plus keeping her defenses up, has made her bubble feel weaker, its walls thinner and more fragile.

Something buried behind the bins threatens her composure. She grabs the top one, too roughly, bumping a lamp with a heavy ceramic base with her right elbow. It teeters on the edge of a box. Ev wedges in closer, stopping it from falling over with her shoulder before escaping with the bin. Her hands have grown slick inside her gloves. Only three more. She wants to tell Noemi that they have done enough, but she worries her fear will only make Noemi more curious, encourage her. So she keeps on. She ignores the creeping of her skin every time she goes back into the gap. In and out with the bins. In and out with her breath.

She picks up the final bin. Shivers run up and down her back as she retreats, but she doesn't look back, keeps her face composed in case she runs into Noemi on the way. Over the wire. Under the clock. Through the kitchen, dread chasing her all the way. Into the foyer where the clean air taunts her. Noemi meets her at the door.

"I'll take that." She reaches out, but Ev turns away.

"I need some air."

Noemi watches her for a moment. Ev thinks she might argue, and if she does, then Ev will lose it, her act will crumble, and she'll fall to pieces.

Noemi steps aside.

Once she's made it out, Ev gulps down mouthfuls of fresh air. She blinks back tears, refusing to let them come. The car's hatchback is full. Noemi has left the passenger door open, the seat flipped forward. Ev dumps the bin in the back seat, peels off her gloves, and lies down in the grass. You can see stars in this part of the city. Ev tries to pick out constellations, but the only one she knows is the Big Dipper. She traces its outline in the sky. She'd like to be a star, even if it means she's in the process of dying, of slowly burning out. Being human isn't much different, really. At least the stars have space to burn in peace.

The sky has turned from black to navy. Ev needs sleep. She can't face another day here with Harriet on a two-hour catnap. And Noemi. Noemi has been inside too long. Which means she's gotten distracted again. Ev's stomach contracts. She's left an awfully tidy gap for her sister to explore.

Now the panic slips in, poking pinholes in her defenses as she lurches back into the house. No Noemi in the foyer. No Noemi in the kitchen. Ev knows what she'll find. She keeps going anyway, pinholes cracking wider. Under the clock. Over the wire.

Noemi in the gap, hunched over something. Ev averts her eyes, not ready to see.

"What are you doing?"

Noemi doesn't flinch. Doesn't even look Ev's way. She has a box between her knees. Ev clenches her fists, fingernails digging into wet palms. She's left her gloves outside. Her pulse beats between her ears.

"What is this?"

Noemi holds up a hand broom, round and wood-handled, like a tiny witch's broom. Her headlamp shines in Ev's face so she can't see Noemi's expression. She doesn't need to lay her hands on the broom to know the secrets it holds, but Noemi thrusts it at her all the same. Blood roars through Ev's head as her walls crumble.

Wood and varnish fill her nostrils, and in her ears, the dry scratching of the broom's bristles on the floor. Yellow light and shadow. The lights are always off, except for that one bulb above the worktable. The other lights are too bright, he says.

Scritch scratch.

Stop making that sound.

Evelyn stops her work, makes sure the little stick is hidden beneath her knee. She's been practicing something with the stick that she doesn't want him to see. It makes her brain hurt, but she's getting better at it.

445

She dips her finger in the pile of sawdust in front of her, pretends she's drawing pictures in it. She has been drawing pictures in the sawdust, but not with her finger.

Those terrible eyes are still on her, she can feel them. He doesn't blink anymore. His eyes just stare and stare. She pretends not to notice. She takes courage from the hidden stick, her sister's magic wand. Evelyn shouldn't have stolen Noemi's wand, but it was exactly the right thing to practice with. A safe thing. The stick listens to her when she speaks to it. It scratches swirls into the sawdust when he's not looking. A happy face. A heart.

Evelyn picks up the broom again and sweeps the sawdust into a little pile, taking care to be oh so quiet. She's afraid to leave and afraid to stay. A sharp tang of fear has bled into the wood grain of Evelyn's little broom. Fear, but also anticipation.

You can change things.

Evelyn will change things. She knows what to do.

A clatter brings Ev back to the present. She lets the broom drop and blinks tears into the darkness. A kitchen chair has overturned next to her, the wooden spindles of its back inches from her hip. The box still lies on the floor, where Noemi opened it. But Noemi is gone.

41

Harriet lies awake, rubbing her hands absently along the baby blanket. It soothes her some, but the hum of the house at Angel Place has gotten under her skin, and she can't shake her rattled discomfort. Ev's word pops into her mind — *stained.* Hours later, she still hasn't washed the feeling away. She glances at the sword leaning next to the stairs. She let Owen drive her back to the Dragon, but demanded his keys from him when they arrived. He didn't fight. She wishes he had tried, at least a little.

The phone jolts her fully awake. She picks it up, only because of the lateness of the hour, which means it's unlikely to be someone trying to sell her insurance or a cruise. A glance at the display shows an unfamiliar number.

"Harriet?" A hoarse whisper. "It's Noemi."

Harriet sits up, instantly alert.

"Where's Evelyn? Is she okay?"

She hears only static and heavy breathing. The static seems to reach through the phone, burning her eardrums and prickling the skin of her palm.

"Speak up," she says. "I can't understand you."

The girl's voice twists as though she's close to tears, but she raises her voice enough so that Harriet can follow.

"I don't know what to do. You have to help me."

"What's wrong? What happened?" *What did you do?*

"It was supposed to be a secret, but I feel so awful about it, and I'm worried about Ev. It's the house. The big house? She wants us to go there tonight."

"You mustn't go there." A queer sense of inevitability fills Harriet and, at the same time, a distant curiosity. Why would Noemi call her? Caution keeps her from giving away too much. "It's dangerous. Evelyn knows that."

"She does, but her mind's made up. She's going with or without me."

"You're there already." She keeps her tone even, but the tightness in her voice gives her away. She knows it's true and, despite her best efforts, feels the red rise in her stomach, flooding her chest and head.

The girl doesn't deny it. "She thinks there are objects from our family's house inside. She's obsessed with finding them."

"Is she?" Suspicion curls the edges of Harriet's words.

"For me," Noemi hurries to explain, the words now tumbling out a little too smoothly. "She's doing it for me, to help me find some peace with the past. She thinks she's trying to help me, but I don't want it. Not this way."

Liar.

The door to the vault seems to jump out at her then, cold and dark on the other side of the room. The image of the pistol flashes in front of her eyes, making her shiver, breathe to regain control. Did Owen put it in the vault? Or did he make it disappear? She never asked. Never mind. She isn't about to let this girl crack her. Everything she says is a lie, in the same way that Evelyn can only tell truths.

Not that Ev hasn't deceived Harriet. Of course she knows Ev's motives for convincing Harriet to excavate the house. It's been written on her face and in the wringing of her gloved hands all along. But she doesn't blame Ev for hiding her reasons. Her reasons are good ones. It's clear how much she

450

fears becoming her father. Noemi's reasons, however, Harriet can't figure them out. All she knows of Noemi is deception and sneakiness, a self-serving craftiness that she recognizes, because it lives inside her, too.

"What would you have me do?"

Noemi chokes on a sob. Whatever else might be going on, the girl's panic seems real. She says something Harriet can't decipher through the static and the muffled breathing.

"Speak up."

"I lost her."

Harriet's vision narrows to a pinpoint of light, one of the tiny yellow bulbs on the string Owen has draped along the basement's walls.

"Where is she?"

"We had an argument and she ran upstairs."

"She can't do that. It's not stable up there." Harriet begins fumbling for her clothes, pressing the phone between her ear and shoulder.

"I know. She knocked some things over. The path is blocked on the stairs. I can't get up and she won't talk to me. Please. I need to find her."

"Stay where you are. I'm coming."

She hangs up and calls a taxi. The anger

has given way to calm. She knew the house would call her back. Poor Evelyn. All night, Harriet has thought only of herself. How hard it is for her to let the house go. She hasn't had a single thought for Ev and the grip the house might have on her. On her sister. What did it cost them to go there alone in the night, to attempt to face their family's past? More than Harriet has to lose, surely.

When Noemi admitted to losing Ev, Harriet believed her. It's the only true thing the girl said. And whatever she meant by it, whatever she did, it's Harriet's fault. The house belongs to her. She created it. She must do what she can to help.

She opens the vault door, scans the scant bags and boxes lining the floor, looking for the little blue bag. Owen did keep it. She's surprised, although a gun is harder to destroy than a plastic toy. Perhaps he didn't know what else to do with it. She takes the bag. Halfway up the stairs, Harriet notices something strange. She stops, puts her hand inside. The pistol is still there. The anger, however, is gone. There's no life left in the pistol at all. It's dead. Harriet has never known a treasure to lose its emotion so rapidly, but it's just as well. It was a foolish idea to bring it. She leaves the bag and the

452

pistol on the stairs.

She follows the sinuous body of Owen's dragon as she heads for the door, tracing its lines with her fingers, greeting its various pieces: a languorous ashtray, some zealous ski poles, an exuberant trumpet. The lick of its flame almost touches the empty front windowsill. Owen's little tin bird is missing. He must have taken it, along with the treasures he thought she wouldn't notice. Before she leaves, she kisses the cool top of the dragon's head, a smooth, comforting spot on its tin kettle brow, in case it's good-bye.

42

Ev rubs her hands over and over on the damp cotton of her tank top. Her legs have gone wobbly, she can do no more than sit on the floor and try not to curl up into a fetal position. Memories slither around her, from the inside of the open box, from the depths of the room. From the chair Noemi tipped over as she ran away. One of theirs. Ev remembers the curlicue pattern carved into the back, how Noemi used to trace the grooves with her chubby fingers.

Noemi.

She calls for her sister. Noemi has gone out to the foyer, she can hear her moving around, footsteps creaking on floorboards, and now she's talking to someone, maybe to herself, like Harriet was doing earlier. Ev strains to hear Noemi's words, but she can only make out the urgent rise and fall of her voice.

Something is wrong, she can feel it. She

can practically smell the fear and panic Noemi left behind. What sent Noemi away? The kitchen chair. Her mind snags on something then, the edge of the connection she's been missing. Before she can change her mind, she grasps the chair's arm.

Mama, standing at the dinner table, hands gripping its edge. Noodles sliding down the wall behind her. *No more. Evelyn stays with me.*

This is Evelyn's fault. She's being too noisy again. She scraped her chair on the floor, and it made him angry.

It's okay. I want to help him.

No, says Mama. *I will not allow it.*

Ev lets go of the chair, drags her mind back to the present and her body back onto the path. She stumbles forward, her past biting at her heels. She bites into the flesh of her forearm in response, to keep her mind in the now, to keep from screaming.

Daddy needs me.

She veers off course, the horrible suspicion growing as she winds past the refrigerator and over to the table where she found Noemi with the clown cookie jar. She takes hold of it by its white-glazed neck ruffle. Anxiety sharpens into fear. The yawning black mouth of a red-eyed clown looms overhead, poised to bite off her head. A hint of cinnamon. Snickerdoodles. A child's recurring nightmare.

This is the stuff of nightmares.

Enough to turn a girl off snickerdoodles for a lifetime.

Noemi knew the exact experience attached to this cookie jar. She knew that the yellow wicker basket belonged to their family, not because she remembered it. Because she could feel the vibration of the sweater tucked inside it. Harriet was right. Noemi shares Ev's affliction. She can feel stains.

All the other signs come rushing back to Ev, the clues she brushed aside because she was too stubborn to see the truth. Noemi's fascination with the Dragon, and Harriet's suspicions about her. The look on her face when Ev was telling her about meeting Harriet. *What if there are others? I bet there are.* Noemi helping Michael clear out his shame-stains. How could she have done that if she couldn't also sense them? She thinks even further back to the way Noemi's bedroom was always filled with stains. Ev thought the stains came from Noemi's own feelings, but what if she collected them? Noemi used to try to convince Ev to use stains to influence people. Is that what she did, surrounding herself with items of wealth and persuasion, the sequin dress and the money clip that Ev stumbled upon? Then there's Noemi's growing fear. *It's my history, my genetics. He was my father too.* Noemi's not just afraid of Ev. She's afraid of herself.

Worst of all, if she saw the nightmare attached to the cookie jar, that means Noemi can see other memories attached to objects, just like Ev. Which means she experienced the same memory Ev did when she pulled the broom out of the box.

I need your help with something.

Yes, Daddy.

The hard edge of anticipation bordering on excitement as little Evelyn decided what she needed to do. Did Noemi also feel what was left behind on the kitchen chair? That sick, fearful tension? The determination? The decision?

Daddy needs me.

She has to explain. Without the context, without Ev's side of the story, Noemi must be thinking the worst. That the things that woman, their neighbor Anna, said about Ev are true. That she's a monster, like he was. A shriek followed by a sudden crash from upstairs punctuates that thought.

"Noemi," Ev yells.

No response. Ev plunges into the dark with only the cold, teetering glow of the headlamp to guide her. Why would Noemi

457

go upstairs? She wiggles into the gap on the stairs and pounds up them expecting to find a cave-in, Noemi pinned under hundreds of pounds of newspaper, but the hallway at the top stretches like a tunnel, farther than her light can reach. Noemi has gone silent.

"Where are you?"

Ev inches forward. Upstairs feels different somehow, but Ev can't stop to examine why. She scans the floor in front of her, looking for signs of a trap. Her light catches on something. Inches from her shins, a wire stretched across the hallway. She tries not to think about how close she came to burying herself. She steps over, resolved to slow down. There are gaps in the walls to the left and right a few paces in. Doorways.

"Noemi." Her voice comes out a cracked whisper. She suddenly wishes she had some water. She clears her throat and tries again.

"I know what you saw. It's not what you think. You don't know the whole story. And I know that's because I never told you. But there were things I couldn't explain, because I couldn't remember."

Still nothing. The house seems to hold its breath, all its inhabitants quiet, leaning in, listening. Ev ducks her head left and right, peering into the dark cavities of the doorways. No Noemi. The doors both closed.

No. The right one is slightly ajar.

"But I remember more now. I can explain."

She jabs at the door as though it might burn her. It swings open a few inches and stops. Something stops it.

"Noemi?"

She points her light into the crack between the door and its frame, but no shadowed figure hides there. She moves in closer. She sees the dark form of a bed in the far corner, a narrow path leading to its foot. The rest of the floor is covered in boxes and bags. A lump forms in her throat. This room, it bleeds sadness. Everything in it seems stained with regret, loneliness, or grief.

Worse, the stains hold a familiarity almost as strong as those of Ev's family's relics. This is Harriet's bedroom. The objects stained by Harriet herself, not collected from strangers like those on the first floor. The pain, Harriet's pain. Ev backs out, tears clouding her vision. She can't bear to get closer.

She hears a scuffling sound nearby. It came from farther down the hall. She moves slowly, watching for more wires or loose furniture, heading for the next two cavities down the hall. Her throat feels thick when

459

she tries to speak again.

"I know you can feel stains, Noemi. And I know you're scared. You saw the memories, didn't you? You think that woman is right about me. But she's not. I didn't do what she said. I thought I could save all of us. Dammit. Where are you?"

"Liar."

Ev's heart jumps. She spins. Noemi stands near the end of the hallway. Somehow, she's gotten past Ev, and now she blocks the way to the stairs.

"Don't move, Noemi. There's a trip wire right behind you."

Noemi takes a step backward, as though she hasn't heard.

"All I want is for you to admit what you did. Tell me the truth."

"You tell *me* the truth. How long have you been able to feel the stains?"

"You first."

"I stayed up late that night. I waited until the house was quiet and I snuck out to the workshop."

"Are you a murderer?"

Ev's head swims. "I had a plan. But he was already there, sitting in the dark. I was too late."

"If you're lying, I'll find out." Noemi squeezes something against her chest.

"How long, Noemi?"

"Always."

"That's impossible."

Noemi laughs. "Why, because you'd know?"

"Yes."

"You didn't want to know. At first, I hid it, because I didn't want you to be afraid of me like you were afraid of yourself. All those times we counted together, did you really think that was only for you? Later, I realized you refused to see it. You didn't want me to have what you had."

"No. I didn't. I don't." Ev wouldn't wish it on anyone, least of all her sister.

"Because you were afraid? Or because it made you special? Better than me."

My special girl.

"No." *I never thought I was better than you,* she thinks, but she doesn't say the words aloud. She's not sure if they're true.

"I was never like you. I liked my power. And after you moved out of Joan and Mikey's I was free to explore it."

The dress and the money clip. Like Ev thought.

"Is that why you were having second thoughts about moving in with me?"

"I didn't want to spend my life being afraid. Like you. But you were right. I get

461

that now. This thing we have is dangerous."

"No, it's not. I'm sorry I made you think that."

"Stop making it about you!" Noemi shouts. "It changed. *I* changed. I started spending time with Michael, and he had so many shame and fear stains in his house. I could feel them changing me, the shame seeping into my mind. It was awful."

"So you made him throw his things off a bridge."

"Even after they were gone the feelings lingered. Then I started spending nights in the Dragon, and my power changed. I started feeling more. You know what I mean, don't you? The complexities. The memories. And the more I felt, the more I understood how easily a mind could be poisoned."

"I can help you, Noemi. The same way Harriet helped me."

But Noemi's not listening to her.

"Then you did that thing. You made the cranes move with your mind. It was the scariest thing I've ever seen. I knew I had to stop you from getting any stronger. What if you got poisoned? You were right. We're dangerous and we need to be contained."

Ev tilts her chin down, trying to get a better view of Noemi. In her arms, Noemi cradles a metal box. Ev almost didn't notice it. Ev probably wouldn't have noticed it, if the broom hadn't just shared its memories with her, if the box weren't once her box. That's the wonderful thing about it. The wonderful, horrible thing. It is a secret keeper; like the Dragon, but stronger. It defies notice like no other stain Ev has ever encountered. It can be in the middle of a room and remain invisible. In the middle of a crime scene, even. It's the perfect hiding place for the most dangerous of objects.

"Our father was right," Noemi tells Ev. "We are the stains."

43

"You want me to take you inside?"

The taxi driver peers up the driveway to where the house waits. It feels like a living thing now, all its dormant inhabitants awoken and spilling out through the front door, their energies infecting the air.

"This is fine, thank you."

He doesn't argue. "You gonna get down there okay? It's darker than the devil's soul out there."

"I know my way."

"Good." The driver moves his hand across his chest. Father, Son, Holy Spirit. "That your house?"

"That's home."

"Don't take this the wrong way, ma'am, but I think your home needs an exorcism."

"You may be right."

The driver pulls a business card from his visor. "I know someone. You need help, call Angelo. That's me. No offense meant."

"No offense taken. Thank you, Angelo." Harriet takes the card, gives him a ten-dollar tip, and makes her slow way toward the house. It isn't until the taxi vanishes around the corner that Harriet allows her shoulders to slump. Perhaps Angelo will hear about her on the news. An unfortunate woman found dead in her house, buried by her own trash. There will be photos of her home on the Internet. Of the sad state she lived in.

The gate is closed but not locked. A car is parked in front of the house, its hatch open. Boxes nestle inside, their flaps torn open and left askew. Harriet's chest tightens at the sight of the name scrawled in black marker across the cardboard. They did it. They burrowed all the way in. They worked their way around her safeguards and stole back what rightfully belonged to them.

It pisses her off. Part of her wants to yank the boxes out, steal them back. Why did the house allow the intrusion? Didn't she put in safeguards? Shouldn't the house understand what she wants and help to defend against this? They're in this together, aren't they? But even as the thought forms, Harriet discards it, as the house draws her in, invisible fingers of need and greed and possessiveness wrapping around her spine and urging her inside. They aren't in this together. The house has never been hers. It has always been the other way around.

What a terrible idea, all of this. They should never have come here. She was foolish to think it would end well. The door is propped open. She steps inside. She didn't bring a flashlight, will have to creep and feel her way into the heart of the house. Her pulse hammers between her ears, and her hands wobble. Inside, the energies swirl furiously, assaulting her skin. She beats back hysteria. Stop. She may not be in control, but she belongs here. She stands in the foyer and listens for signs of life, the kind still contained in a human body. After a moment, the house yields. She hears someone crying, a jagged intake of breath from upstairs.

"Ev," Harriet calls. "Where are you?"

"Harriet?" Ev's voice sounds faint, shocked.

"Don't move. Are you hurt?"

"I'm okay. We're upstairs. In the hallway."

"Are you near the jukebox?" She can't have gone much farther.

"Don't come up, Harriet. Get out of the house. It's dangerous."

"You don't say. Is Noemi with you?"

No reply. She thinks she hears muttered

voices, but she can't make out what they're saying. She winds past the grand staircase and toward the service stairs.

"Ev?"

"We're both here."

"Don't move," Harriet calls out again. "I'll come get you."

"No!" Ev cries. "Get help."

Harriet hears more muffled whispers, a hushed argument not meant for her ears.

"I know how to get you out. Hold tight."

She hopes she knows. She bends to her knees, the safest way up the stairs still a crawl. But it's too late.

She hears a sharp cry. "Don't!" Ev shouts, and then a crash. Harriet's heart sinks and sinks. The sound spreads. The avalanche will contain itself above, she thinks, but her heart pounds all the same. She knows the walls are closing in, and that it is her fault. She yells, but her words are swallowed up. She imagines her carefully laid paths crumbling inward, burying Evelyn, burying Noemi, as well. The house taking them. Just a little more buried treasure.

44

Ev breathes in shallow gasps, her lungs working. Alive. Not crushed. Her fingers and her toes wiggle. Not broken. How? A thousand pounds of longing, lust, regret, anxiety, and anger press against her body from all sides. Even the beautiful emotions — the bursts of old, softened joy and the occasional rub of affection — they hurt her skin. Nothing moves. The avalanche has passed, and yet she feels she is being beaten by dozens of tiny, blunt objects.

All dark everywhere, but slowly she takes stock of her situation. She's fallen forward, her shoulder and left arm jammed against an armoire. The armoire saved her, holding steady against the onslaught. Some sharp corner digs into the back of her right thigh, and soft pressure explodes against her back, radiating pain and self-pity. Her heart beats in her temples. She wants to flail, fight her way out, but she can't. She doesn't dare. A whimper escapes, and the sad sound of it galvanizes her. She clenches her jaw and then tries calling out.

"Harriet?"

Her voice is sucked up, as though she's yelling into a pillow. Did Noemi know what she was doing when she stepped backward and tripped the wire? Or was it an accident? She never got the chance to finish explaining before Harriet showed up. To get that box away from her sister. She digs her fingernails into her palms and bites her lip until it bleeds to keep from screaming.

Stop panicking.

If she can move objects with her mind, she can figure this out. She breathes more deeply, shaky at first. She closes her eyes and goes inside, shutting out all the insistent, probing emotions coming from outside. Soon her heart stops pounding, and she can think more clearly.

She could stay put and wait for rescue. She can't reach her back pocket and her phone. But Harriet will call for help. Won't she? Either way, it could take days for anyone to safely reach her. She could die of dehydration while she waits. Or she could figure out how to get out on her own. Her eyes have adjusted to the dark. The nearest doorway lies five feet down the hall on the right. If she can make it there, she might be able to make it to a window.

She takes in the objects surrounding her. Immediately, her safe place shrinks, and the armoire begins to beat at her shoulder. She can practically hear its greedy whispers in her left ear. *Mine. Mine. Mine.* She squeezes her eyes shut. She searches for the calm of Noemi's voice counting her down, but all she can hear is her sister calling her a liar. Harriet's voice saves her instead.

The objects serve you. But only if you let them.

The way out is to open herself to Harriet's treasures. They can show her. Ev opens her eyes. She draws in a deep breath. She lets the stains speak to her.

Her body burns. She feels electrified, a pulsing mass of nerves. The stories flow through her like a swift current. Pain and desire. Wild laughter, gut-wrenching fear. She lets it all wash through her. Despair and elation in dizzying waves, until she can hardly tell where one emotion ends and another begins. Suspended in the midst of it, she becomes aware of the kernel that remains Ev. A tiny bubble, a little flame. The rest of it doesn't belong to Ev. It's only feelings. Not madness. Not sickness. Not good or evil. Only impressions and memories.

She floats. Some of the stronger stains begin to flicker and transmit more clearly. Here, a dizzy rush and a hand cupping a cheek; there, a hot flash of pain and a glimpse of wet pavement. Near the fingertips of her right hand, grief radiates from a box of old photographs. She can see the face of a baby, feel the yawning loss attached to the image, the flash of another image layered over the first, an empty crib, blue blanket neatly folded at its foot. Ev lets the sadness pour through her, out of her. She lets it happen, until the next stain overtakes her, and she lets that one in too, because she is stronger than any of them. A secret song hums under flannel sheets. The giddy lurch of a swing hitting its highest point.

Soon she begins to cast her consciousness further, to explore the spaces behind doors. A full-length mirror in an ornate frame, piles on piles of clothing in velvet and satin. Covetousness and lush greed. The stain of pretty trifles. Except buried under the trifles are other secrets. Betrayal. Grief. Abandonment. So much like the things in Harriet's room, except these ones lack hope. They molder beneath, long lost to the light. It's a soft room. She could crawl over the piles without fear of injury. If she can get to the door. She senses instability there. It isn't safe to move in that direction.

In the other direction, something feels wrong too, but she can't figure out why. She can't pinpoint any particular emotion that seems dangerous or unstable, and yet. She shudders, lets go of the nagging feeling, and contracts her scope. She focuses on the relationships of the objects around her. Pull the right leg out first, the armoire will hold. Place her right foot on that box there, and then slide out the left leg. She moves, holds her breath as the box at her back crashes to the floor. She clings to the corner of the armoire. Inside, rows of authoritarian suits bark at her. It doesn't matter. She's moving. She's still in one piece.

Pressing her lips together, she stretches, grasps the arm of a sofa, and pulls her weight upward. She can see above the piles. She draws in a deep breath, thick with dust, but a full breath, her chest unobstructed, allowing hope to ignite inside it. She cranes her neck, trying to see what lies farther down the hall. Her headlamp has come off, and if dawn has broken, the sun's light hasn't cracked this part of the house. A sudden thought comes to her. If she leans against the armoire, she can reach into her back pocket now with her left hand. She pulls out her phone. No signal. Of course.

The objects around her begin to shiver ominously. She freezes as all the angry bits tucked here and there throughout the house suddenly bubble to the surface, lighting up like a string of Christmas lights. Down below, a fierce, wobbling energy rises. For a heart-stopping second, Ev thinks it's an earthquake, until she senses the epicenter of it directly below her, in Harriet's living room. Something's happening on the main floor.

She grabs hold of the top corner of the armoire and drags her body up before she loses the chance, gasping, fumbling along the dusty, varnished top while the rage builds around her. Then she curls her body into a ball and shuts her mind against the awful tide.

45

Harriet sits heavily on the little gap of clear stairway. Her calls to Ev have gone unanswered. What seemed so clear an hour ago is now a smear of muddled and confused emotions gummed across the back of her eyes. She is heavy, limp, a sack of fat and bones. It occurs to her that she might never move from this spot. Where is Frédérique? She pats at her pocket. Flat. Empty. She left him at the Dragon, same as the bird stone. Good. She doesn't deserve any comfort. She did this. She built the traps. She took Evelyn's past and hid it away in this mess. She kept it a secret. Next to her left hip, a fluttering from deep inside a banker's box reaches out to her, a math workbook with dog-eared pages.

Stupid, it tells her.

"I know," she replies. Tears soak into the knees of her trousers as she folds her body and wishes to disappear.

A sound reaches her, muffled but human. Her heart skips a beat, but of course it's not Ev. She looks up. She is not surprised to see the dark outline of Noemi lurking behind the jukebox, watching her from the top of the stairs. Alive and unharmed, the little rat. A tangle of words sticks in Harriet's throat like a knotty ball of yarn. She pulls one loose.

"Why?"

"It was an accident." Panic in Noemi's voice, bordering on hysteria, but something else, too. A hard edge. A wave of hot rage rises up in Harriet's belly, swelling over her despair.

"Why did you do that?"

The edge sharpens. "She's a liar. You're both liars."

"She's your sister." Anger gives her body momentary buoyancy. She straightens her legs, stands tall. She can't see Noemi anymore, she's ducked behind the jukebox, but she hears her hitched laughter.

"You're going to play the sibling card on me? That's rich. You know, I've been in your bedroom. I know all about your dead brother."

"You don't know."

It's never the whole story. There are always gaps to fill with the imagination.

Always. There's a click in the darkness. A white-blue glow illuminates the stairwell.

"Oh, I know," says Noemi. She steps into the open, shining her headlamp down at Harriet so she's momentarily blinded. Harriet shades her eyes as Noemi begins to descend the stairs. "I can see it all. I held that pinup girl knob. The one he installed right before he crashed his car. The one that wants to go fast."

She can sense memories, like Ev. Harriet has never told anyone that story. They went for a joyride, the two of them. After the crash, she took the gearshift knob and replaced it with the old one in the glove box. She wanted to keep it, to remember. And to hide what she'd done from her mother. Harriet backs down to the bottom of the stairs and begins to move toward the foyer, anxious to be on level ground with Noemi. She keeps her talking.

"You think you see it all. You don't." She loved Geordie. What happened was an accident, a stupid accident. He was the only person in their family who showed her kindness. But like her father, Geordie was too busy with his own life to pay much attention to her. The moments of kindness were fleeting, rare treasures. She only wanted to capture one more before he left home for university. Left her here, alone.

"It was your fault." The light swings back and forth in front of her eyes, throwing her off balance. Noemi's face remains shadowed.

Harriet feels anger building in her chest, her throat, her head. "You catch fragments of stories," she says, trembling. "You don't see the whole picture."

"I know guilt when I feel it. He died because of you. You're as bad as Evelyn."

"No." Harriet lets the rage loose. Her head and limbs and fingers bloat, the heat building from red to blue to white, and the house begins to rise with her. All of the angry things, the wronged things, the grieving things — they begin to tremble, to rattle, to shine out their tortured souls into the darkness. They howl for Evelyn, and Harriet howls with them. Shivers run up and down her spine. She imagines Ev's power must have felt this way, terrifying and thrilling. She is so close to being able to command her treasures the way Ev did. Close, but not quite there. They sing at her beckoning, but still she cannot move them.

Harriet hears a frightened cry coming from a distance. She raises her arms as though conducting a symphony, and her treasures respond in a rising crescendo of pain.

"Stop it," Noemi screams. "Stop it, please."

Harriet lowers her arms. The cacophony dulls, but the vibrations remain, an echoing horror. Deep exhaustion pulls her to her knees. She folds back into a ball, every ounce of energy sapped. The world turns black.

"Oh God, oh God." She's not sure how long she's been passed out when Noemi's moaning creeps into her consciousness. Daylight has begun to slip through the cracks in the curtains, a reminder that there's still a world beyond these walls. The mutterings are coming from somewhere around the corner, from the depths of the great room.

"Hello?" she calls. "Are you hurt?"

Noemi's next words are muffled.

"I can't hear you. Are you okay?"

"I'm stuck. There are boxes across the path."

Good.

"Harriet? Help me."

"I'll call 911."

"No. I can get out, I just need your help. Come over here."

Harriet backs away.

"Please," Noemi cries. "Don't you want to know what else I found out about Geordie?"

She stops. "You don't know anything."

"I know what his last thought was before he died."

Dammit. Despite herself, Harriet creeps down the passage toward the great room. As Harriet's eyes adjust, the girl's form appears, a metal box balanced in her arms. She wasn't lying about the blockage. A stack of boxes has shifted, tipping over the top two. They're wedged against a bookshelf.

"There's space underneath," Harriet says. "You can crawl under."

"What if they fall?"

"You have to try. It's your only way out."

"But I need to show you something. Come closer."

Harriet doesn't like the way she keeps flipping between crafty and bewildered. At least she's turned her headlamp off so Harriet can almost make out her facial expressions. She sees that Noemi's hand is inside the box. There's something awful emanating from its cracked lid. The box bothers Harriet as much as Noemi's erratic behavior. She remembers it vaguely, one of the estate sale items, but when she tries to reach out, to feel it, her mind slips away from it. It remains a fuzzy thing on the edges of her vision, like when you think you've seen a ghost, a movement behind you that you can never catch the source of. It's hiding something terrible inside.

"You need to put that box down."

"You'd like that, wouldn't you?" Noemi hugs it closer.

"It's hurting you."

"Shut up. My mother is in here." Noemi smiles then, not at Harriet but at the box.

"You were going to tell me about Geordie," says Harriet, desperate to distract her.

"She helped him," Noemi says. "Did you know that? She helped him kill our mother. She's a monster. You two are a lot alike, you know."

Harriet begins to back away, slowly.

"Better not move," says Noemi. She pulls her hand out of the box and grasps a rope that's tied around the leg of a chair. She's found one of Harriet's triggers. It will cave in the path behind Harriet. If they're not buried, they'll be trapped.

"What are you doing? You'll kill us both."

"Will I?"

One look into the girl's eyes, and Harriet knows. She means to finish all of them, to bury them here. The last lingering wisps of Harriet's righteous anger drain away.

"Go on, then," she tells the girl. "Pull it." It's no less than she deserves. Harriet closes her eyes.

"You," Noemi says from a distance. "His last thought was of you."

Then Harriet hears the walls rumbling, hears the dull roar of her fate coming for her like the tide crashing on a pebbled shore.

46

Ev crouches on top of the armoire, listening for signs of other life within the house. Her throat burns from thirst, from yelling for Noemi and Harriet. Moments ago, the rising anger abruptly settled. Ev kept her body curled up, terrified of another wave. Before she could muster up the courage to move, a horrible, gut-churning crash came from downstairs. Now silence. What happened down there? Are they trapped? Crushed? Did they escape and leave her here alone? She tries reaching out, to feel them the way she could feel Harriet's presence in the house yesterday, but the tangle grows too thick and confused.

From down the hall, the something strange nags at her again, that oddness she can't identify. Ev leans in. Focuses. With a shock, she realizes what lies behind the last door on the left. Space. Empty space. Is it possible? It doesn't seem like it can be, not in this house. Except she can feel the open expanse of it, its stark contrast against the rest of the house. That room is her way out.

She steels herself for the crawl to freedom. She'll have to take a leap of faith, stretch out over the top of the pile of boxes and shimmy on her stomach. She moves, stretching her body out and across. She grabs hold of a bookshelf and edges out. Her body slides off the armoire, landing on a soft pile of musty-smelling sweaters. Ev climbs over bouncy piles of cotton, linen, terrycloth, and denim, their stains a weak, uniform blend of hunger and possibility. Wooden hangers *click* and *clack* beneath Ev, but nothing hurts her. As she moves, her confidence grows. The house will guide her, as long as she listens.

A sudden stab of terror knifes into her gut. She cries out, loses her grip, rolls onto her back. She sinks into squishy piles of shopping bags, sliding back headfirst as she grabs at fistfuls of wool. Her skull hits the edge of a box. She stops moving. Her brain is on fire, and her chest screams. She can't breathe.

No. She isn't hurt. The hurt comes from outside. Noemi is still in the house. And she's opened the box. She can feel the sick pulse of those sewing scissors, even through the thick tangle of objects that lies between them.

I need your help with something.

Ev's survival instinct kicks in. Her legs are buried under a pile of winter coats, her cheek pressed against a bag of old sneakers. She breathes in a lungful of sweat-scented air. She wants to hide from the scissors, but the only way out is to keep her mind open to the house. The scissors can't hurt her from here. Noemi can't get to her. Focus.

She pushes and pulls and rolls, rights herself. Three feet from the door now. Her skin crawls all over with the frantic need to get away. A battle cry tears from her throat as she dives toward the door. She fumbles blindly for the handle beneath a heap of towels. It turns. She pushes it open and falls into brightness.

A crack in the curtains lets in only a slice of sunlight, but it is enough to make Ev squint. She stands frozen in the past. Blue walls with dusty movie posters tacked to them, *Jaws* and *Star Wars*. A Montréal Canadiens flag. The bed unmade, striped cover bunched at one end. The closet door ajar. On the right side, a large wooden desk with a typewriter and curled, yellowed papers. On the left side, a long dresser with a record player next to the mirror.

The room must have been left this way for forty years. Its emptiness makes it more devastating than any of the stains she's encountered. And those stains, the ones she has encountered in getting to this place, the lost and sad things in Harriet's bedroom, the dark regrets locked behind the mother's door, they reassemble into a picture. Into a story. In a flash, Ev understands Harriet's history, not the facts of it but its pain. Two dead siblings, a baby and an almost-man, two lost promises. The cold shadows of a long-absent father. An untouchable mother, trapped behind walls built of need and loss. And Harriet, trying to fill the spaces left behind.

Ev moves woodenly past the bed, over a braided rag carpet, past the dusty-topped dresser cluttered with bottles of aftershave and coins. She pulls the curtains away. The first thing she sees is the river, a flat brown expanse dissolving into clouds. Her heart leaps at the sight. She fumbles for the latch, pushes the window up. It shudders in its frame, but fresh air pours in. It smells so sweet. Ev wants to drink it like water.

There is another disturbance inside the house. The stains inside are wobbling, a tense winding up at its center. Ev doesn't know what it means, but it makes bile rise in her throat. Something bad is about to happen.

She puts a leg over the windowsill and peers out. She sees a ledge about three feet down. It's narrow, but if she can reach it, she'll only have to jump about ten feet to the grass. She can do this. The tension in the house shoots up the half of her that is still inside and twists in her belly. She climbs out and lowers herself to the ledge. She doesn't give herself time to think twice. She launches.

47

Harriet's treasures sing to her, a chorus of angels. So bright. A sky full of stars, swirling and burning, keeping her warm, lighting her afire, bathing her in a clean, white love. She loves them all, even the darkest of them. They are her children. They are her life and breath. They hold her. They are the sum of her.

Slowly the fire grows, and slowly the light diminishes. Harriet sinks back into her body. She isn't dead, not yet. Disappointment settles in the bottom of her stomach. Some sense of self-preservation must have kicked in. She doesn't remember diving under the coffee table, but there she is, her head and as much of her body as she could fit stuffed under the solid oak top.

Her only injuries seem to be her knee, which has been bashed hard by something, and her head, which throbs with pain and feels oozy on one side. It seems to be stuck to the table's thick pedestal. Perhaps her skull has been crushed, and her brains are leaking out. She tries a small movement. Neck works okay. She moves her head away from the pedestal. Tacky underneath. Some hairs stick. She lifts a hand to touch the spot. Stinging, but a bump only and some blood. No brains.

Alive then. For now.

"Hello?" she cries, but her words get lost, muffled in newspaper and cardboard. She laughs in the dark. Who's going to hear her? Her cell phone is on her body, zipped up safe in her pouch. She checks the signal, knowing full well there won't be one. Too much interference. Even if she could call 911, even if they could get to her in time, then what? She'd be labeled, her home taken away, one of her slick cousins granted control of her assets. Her treasures would be lost, and she'd be shipped off to some sterile institution for her own good.

You could live forever.

The thought comes from outside herself. It comes from the house and from the treasures surrounding her. She shivers. What happens if she dies here? Will she truly die, or will she become a part of her collection? Another voice in the choir. In the northeast corner of the great room, near the grand piano, are several nursery room items. Harriet's own baby things. They were moved down to the parlor when her mother gave up on more children. Of course, they were meant to go to Goodwill, but they never made it out of the house. Nothing ever makes it out of this house. To think she once imagined she'd escaped.

The nursery corner would be a lovely place to die. The rocking horse, the cradle, the sterling silver rattle. All of them gently vibrating with her mother's energy, the energy she had before her decline, the energy Harriet barely remembers. She only has to tunnel her way to the piano. Twenty paces, no more. She bites her lip against the pain in her knee and works slowly, carefully. The piano has a nice, empty space beneath it for Harriet to shimmy into. The baby things are just on the other side of it. She might even seek out a soft blanket or two. A nest within a nest.

She slides under carefully. Somewhere underneath the piano is a weak spot in the floorboards. She knew about it and made certain to keep its load light, the piano sheltering the spot. The weak boards will be to her left. There. She skirts to the right, dragging her bottom in a weak crab walk.

The heel of her hand sinks down and

down. Her heart sinks along with it. The spot has grown. She presses the floor around her, feeling the give of rotting wood in all directions. She holds her breath, waiting for the groan and splinter, for the old, damp fibers to spread apart and slide her through, like a baby slipping through the birth canal. Right down into the basement and into the waiting arms of the things that live there.

Harriet hangs for a moment with her bottom exposed to the basement. She feels the rags first, those oily rags that have been licking at everyone's heels, stuffed down in the corner, oozing bitter hatred onto the concrete. She feels cool air beneath her and the writhing anger of other objects long neglected. Objects heavy with jealousy and fear. She tries to reach the nearest piano leg, but her fingers only graze it. There's the groan. The floor parts, scraping and tearing at the skin on her back and thighs. She slips through, hands clawing uselessly at broken wood, as if she has any choice in the matter. The house does what it likes. It takes what it wants. She ought to know this by now. These thoughts flash through her mind as the last of her, head and feet, falls.

48

Ev hits the grass hard with both feet. Her right ankle twists, sending a shooting pain up her leg. She tumbles to her hands and knees, pausing to catch her breath and take stock of her injuries. She's bruised. Sore. Cut and scraped. Raw on the inside. But whole. She tries putting some weight on her ankle. She can stand. She can hobble without too much difficulty. The river calls to her, and she moves toward it without thinking, through the garden toward the gate that leads to the beach, toward solace and safety. Dewy grass hits her calves, and between that wet coolness and her awareness of the throbbing heat of the scissors behind her, even obscured behind all those layers of other vibrations, Ev catapults into the past.

Bare feet on wet grass, on sharp stones. Noemi's head on her shoulder, damp baby hair tacky against her neck.

Shush, don't cry.

491

He's following them, and he's faster than Evelyn. She has to make a choice. She puts Noemi down in the wet grass. "Run," she tells her sister. "Under the fence and through the woods. Go to the red house and knock on the door. I'll find you."

She tumbles into cold, rattling iron, her hands outstretched just in time to shield her from full impact. The gate at the bottom of the yard is chained shut and padlocked. She leans against the wrought-iron bars to catch her breath. The sun has barely lightened the sky. It can't be much past five. A gull picks its way along a floating log; otherwise, she sees no signs of life. But she feels it, tingling against the back of her neck. She won't find calm at the water's edge this time. She's not finished.

She turns back to the house. At the same time, she hears Owen's voice carried on the wind, panicked and urgent. Calling her name. She spots him running up the driveway, weaving around Noemi's car, its hatch still open. Ev's limbs are heavy with exhaustion, but she manages to lift her arm in a weak wave. She watches him jog toward her, thinking she should meet him halfway but unable to convince her feet to move.

"What are you doing here?" she calls.

"I went to the Dragon to check on Harriet, and she was gone." He has one of his handmade birds cupped in his hands, love-bright. "What's happened?" he asks. "The front door's open, but I can't get past the stairs."

Ev closes her eyes. "She came here to save me. It's my fault."

The bird falls from his hands. "Where is she?"

Her legs won't hold anymore. She folds.

"Evelyn." Owen is on his knees in front of her. "Where is she? Is she alive?"

I don't know, she's about to say. But doesn't she? She can still feel Noemi's tortured anger flickering through the walls. If Harriet lives, shouldn't she be able to sense her, too?

"I need to get closer." She crawls forward, too tired to stand. Her ankle is starting to swell. The wet grass soaks her jeans. She passes the scrap-metal bird, love in layers, infused with threads of gratitude, of penitence and regret. She keeps moving, sliding forward, until she's within arm's reach of the cracked concrete surrounding the dry fountain. She sits, head on her knees, and focuses the last of her energy into the house.

We're the stains.

Noemi is a red-hot pain behind her right eye. She lets the pain fill her up, blinding one side, so she can get behind it and below it, slip in deeper, zero in on another cluster of energy. This one is bile-green, a sick slither in her gut. She gags, vomits on the grass.

"Evelyn." Hands on her shoulders to bring her back.

"I'm okay. She's alive."

"Are you sure?"

"She's in the basement. Your bird. Don't lose it. She's going to need it."

"Here." Owen passes her his water bottle. She guzzles it.

"Thank you."

"Are you okay? Can you get up?"

"I need to sit for a minute." The distance she sensed between them has gone, despite all the ruin and pain she's caused, and the relief of this swells in her chest. Only for a moment, though. Only until she realizes the fear and sadness churning her insides is matched in him.

"Are you still mad at me?"

"I was never angry with you. I was angry with myself. Do you have your phone with you? I'll call 911."

Ev checks. Now that she's outside, she's getting a signal again. Even so, Ev almost tells him not to call. Harriet will be furious.

"I can find her."

"It's too dangerous," says Owen.

"The house will help me."

"There may be injuries. I'm calling for help anyway. Let me look after Harriet."

"You're right," she says. She knows what she needs to do too. "I have to find Noemi."

49

Harriet lands hard on her right side in a shower of splintered wood, but with just enough unexpected give to keep her from shattering. Something squishy and squeaky has broken her fall. She would laugh out loud if the wind weren't knocked out of her, if the skin on her back didn't feel scraped raw from the floorboards, and if her right hip didn't explode into hot pain when she tries to move.

She's fallen through the floor onto a mattress, of all things. She remembers it, an item like so many others down here that she ought not to have preserved. Ev was right. She should have released these objects from their pain rather than leave them to linger this way, their energies mingling in the dark. She can't spin it as preservation, not down here. That pile of rags and the venomous old mop propped up next to them. Why? To what end? An object scratches the top of her skull, a restless, anxious energy eager to get her attention. She twists her head to see a square of tarnished gold. She recognizes it at once. An escapee from a box near the back wall, the Zippo lighter rests on the mattress, close enough to touch. She knows better, of course. The first time she picked it up in a pawnshop on Hastings Street, she got a literal shock from its hunger for destruction. If she flips it over, she will see the skull engraved in its surface. As though it knows it has been noticed, it snaps even more impatiently at her consciousness. Harriet reflexively jerks her head away.

The mattress's fear and pain begin to seep into her bones. She's a hunk of meat that the house has thrown into a cage of hungry tigers. Her treasures will eat her alive. She thinks of how Ev copes, how she builds walls in her mind to keep the stains out. Never mind all the times Harriet berated her for it. Ev was thrown into a place darker than Harriet's basement when she should have been blowing bubbles and making mud pies in the backyard. She should have listened to her. She has to listen now. She squeezes her eyes shut, tight tight, and begins to calm her breathing. One . . . two. . . three . . .

A loud knocking startles her. She cries out.
"Harriet?"

A familiar voice. Owen.

"I'm here."

"Hold tight, Harriet. I'm coming to the other window."

That little beam of hope is the worst. Now she has to survive. But the absence of the voice makes it impossible to breathe. What did Ev say about protection? Find space inside. She tries. She searches for the space inside, where Harriet lives, but it's not there. Harriet has always been a cut-and-paste job, a collage. Harriet has no identity outside of her collection.

The sound of shattered glass and a beam of light, of actual daylight, pierces through her panic. It comes from the far side of the room, from a window painted over, now broken.

"Harriet." Owen's voice, low and urgent. "I see you. Are you all right?"

No.

"Harriet? Talk to me. Your eyes are open. I can see you. Are you hurt? Can you move?"

She can't. They're holding her down.

"Listen, I can't get in through the door. We'll have to come through the window. It's going to be all right. Keep breathing. Help is on the way."

It doesn't matter. It's too late. No amount of deep breathing or Zen meditation shit is going stop the darkness from suffocating her. The shadows come crawling up onto the mattress, smothering her.

Something hits her shoulder. The shadows shrink back. The something feels . . . wonderful. Harriet turns her head to look. She sees a bird made from scrap metal. Owen's artwork.

"Can you hear me, Harriet? I made you a gift."

The bird is awake. He has loved it alive, breathed into it bright, fierce loyalty. Friendship. Atonement. Its love chases the shadows away, holds them at bay. It even presses back the fear soaking into her back from the mattress.

"Help is coming. Hold on, Harriet."

Harriet reaches her fingers out. She touches the bird. She holds on.

50

Ev approaches the house from the back, limping tenderly on her sore ankle, following the beacon of Noemi's fear, of her father's rage. It pulses with nauseating, mechanical regularity. She wraps her arms around her body, as if to protect herself from the memories. Panting breath, wet thud of metal hitting muscle and bone. As she nears the patio with its row of French doors, flashes of memory assault her.

She waits in the dark until the house is quiet. She follows the call of the scissors. She knows they're on the table; she can feel them there. She has to do it now. Get them in the forgetting box, and then they'll all be safe.

She reaches out. Instead of cold metal, she brushes against hot, rough skin.

She doesn't want to meet with the scissors again. She doesn't want to remember all of it. She wants to run back to the river, vault over the wall, dive into cold water. Get as far away as possible.

"I need your help with something."

He steps away from the table. Metal sliding on wood as he takes the scissors with him.

"Are you coming?"

The crying won't stop. She shakes her head, trying to get back to the present, to think clearly. Except the crying isn't in her head. It's coming from inside the house. Noemi. She remembers why she is here. To save her sister, again.

Shush, don't cry.

Bare feet on sharp stones. Noemi's head on her shoulder. Damp baby hair tacky against her neck.

She lets out a shuddering breath and runs her hands along the panes of glass. She opens herself to the house once more. Somewhere, there must be a path that leads to Noemi. She lets the house show her the way.

There. She presses her palm against the glass. Behind this pane, a space created where a squat sofa cradles the remains of a bamboo swing chair, half rotted by moisture. She needs something to break the glass. She surveys the yard, spots the dry fountain, the figure in pieces at the fountain's base. The fallen angel of Angel Place. She hops inside the concrete bowl and picks up one of his broken-off legs. It makes a satisfying crash when it connects with the window. She uses rolled-up newspaper to punch out the remaining shards of glass, creating a hole for her to fit her arm through and feel for the dead bolt. It swings open, scraping aside dried leaves blown against the edges of the patio.

All the lights are on in the house, the door cracked open. Evelyn sneaks inside. She has the stick in one hand to help her feel brave, the box in the other. At the top of the stairs, the carpet is dark. She sees a foot with pink polish on the toes.

She climbs in, then worms over the back of the sofa and into the bamboo cage. She follows the path the house reveals, wiggling and panting, skin crawling as her palms connect with dust and dead insects littering the floor.

Down the tunnel until she sees her sister huddled on the floor. Noemi slumps over the scissors. Ev can't see them, but she doesn't need to. She can feel the sickness radiating from them, poisoning everything. The sight of the whites of Noemi's eyes stabs Ev in the gut. She sees her four-year-old sister in that face, reliving that night as though it happened yesterday.

"Noemi." Ev is so tired. She doesn't want

to repeat the same stupid script all over again. "Give me the scissors."

Nothing. Noemi exists in another time, another place. Ev crawls nearer, slowly, and low to the ground. She speaks louder.

"Noemi."

Her sister's eyes remain fixed on a point behind Ev.

"Let go. They're making you sick." She puts a hand on Noemi's knee. Noemi flinches, scrambling backward.

"No!" she yells.

We're the stains.

Ev lunges toward her, meaning to grab at the scissors, but Noemi suddenly slashes upward. Searing pain opens up along Ev's collarbone. She rears back. Noemi leaps on her, pushing her to the floor, stronger than Ev expected. A tear rolls from the end of Noemi's chin onto Ev's cheek. Ev wraps her hands around Noemi's, the side of her right palm making contact with metal.

Evelyn has to get the baby. But first she has to sneak past Daddy and the toes at the top of the stairs. She puts the box down and climbs the stairs. She can't look. She pretends she's digging in the garden with Mama and Noemi. That sound, it's just dirt. Dirt and rocks that sometimes make a sticky clink against the trowel. Her bare feet are wet with mud.

Just mud.

A hand on her shoulder. She's spun around. There is blood sprayed across his face. His spit flies into her mouth when he speaks.

"Go get your sister."

He lets go of her shoulder. Turns back to his work.

Evelyn moves. She can't quite believe he's letting her go, that he really thinks she's helping. She's almost past the doorway to the kitchen when she catches movement out of the corner of her eye. It's Noemi at the back door, thumb in her mouth, easing the screen door open. Her heart leaps into her throat. Smart girl. Good girl. Evelyn makes noise, helping as best she can. She stumbles, knocking over a vase on her way down the hall. She lets the bedroom door hit the wall as she opens it. Shuts it behind her. Up on the bed. Slide the window open. The screen pops out like Mama showed her, in case of fire. She can't feel her arms, but they somehow hold her weight as she climbs over the sill. She still has the stick, can't let go in case the bravery goes with it. Please let Noemi be outside.

Behind her, the door opens. It all happens so fast. She lets her body drop. Noemi's on the back stairs. She scoops Noemi into her arms and she's running, running . . .

Ev pushes and pushes, but her strength

504

can't match Noemi's. She's too tired, and her sister has the fuel of the sickness powering her. It's too much. Maybe she should give in, let Noemi finish the story the way their father meant it to end. Maybe he was right all along.

Maybe you can change things.

Mama believed she could change things. But what power did an eight-year-old have against the relentless anger of a stain strong enough to bend minds? Back then, she only thought of the box, of hiding the horror away. Now, in a flash, she understands. Finally knows what her mother was trying to tell her all along. She hears four-year-old Noemi's voice in her ear too.

We need to make opposite feelings. Poof, *you're happy.*

She was wise even back then. Ev reaches out to the house. A thousand ghosts rush in. Her grip on the scissors eases with the effort it takes to expand her mind, allowing Noemi to pierce the skin of her chest. She cries out, flails, and grabs hold in her mind of a willing object. An enthusiastic baseball bat to her right. It batters the sides of the box it's packed into until the box tips over, toppling onto Noemi's legs. Noemi gasps. Her grip loosens just long enough for Ev to scramble backward using her elbows and forearms. Noemi rolls to her hands and knees. Ev grasps more objects with her mind, pulls down two more boxes to slow her sister. Heat and pain fill her skull, and the voices of the house cry out with her. The floor seems to rumble beneath her. The walls on either side of the path wobble. She can't lose control, can't let the ghosts take them. Noemi is climbing over the boxes, coming for her. Ev backs up more, until she reaches a bend in the path, putting several feet between her and Noemi. She breathes in. She speaks to the house.

Hush.

The shaking stops. The voices cut off, as though she's hit a power switch, but they're not gone. They're still inside her. They wait.

Not yet, she tells them.

Noemi crawls over the last box in her path. Ev, still on her back, barely has time to rise to her knees to meet her sister, who flies toward her with the scissors.

Now.

The boxes on either side of the path explode. A landslide of books cascades down, flooding the space between them. Papers and photographs burst into the air in a sudden blizzard, whipping at her sister's face. Noemi stops in her tracks, covering her head with her arms, and giving Ev the opportunity she needs. She lunges and tackles her sister by the legs, pushing her over. She digs her knee into Noemi's stomach, reaches up, and tears the scissors from her grasp.

Rage and fear pummel her body. She feels a scream tearing her throat, but can't hear it over the noise of the pain attached to the hot metal. She clamps her mind shut with all her strength, beating back the stains as best she can. Then she drags her body backward until she's leaning on the pile of books.

Noemi sits on the floor too, hair over her face, hands shaking, propped up by one of the toppled boxes. The fight's gone from her. Loose papers continue to flutter down around them.

"Are you hurt?"

Noemi says nothing.

"We have to get out of here." Ev has to get out. She can't stand it much longer. "Are you coming?"

Noemi lifts her head. All the wildness has drained from her eyes. They're glassy with tears. Her voice is strained when she speaks.

"Did I hurt you?"

"I'm okay. You're okay too."

Noemi shakes her head, her mouth twisting. "I'm not. I'm sorry, Ev."

"I know."

"How can you do that?" She stares at the scissors at Ev's side. "How can you touch those without going mad?"

Ev remembers she once asked Harriet the same question, sitting on the front steps of the Woodland building.

"I got strong," she says. "Like you said I would." Still, her skin crawls. She itches to fling them into the depths of the house. "I can show you."

Noemi drops her head. "I need to know something. One more thing. Anna said you were covered in blood. When you came out of the woods, you were covered in blood."

One . . . two . . . three . . . four . . .

"But you weren't there when he did it. I saw it." She wipes her eyes, as if to erase the vision. "You weren't there. So, what happened? What happened after we left the house, Ev?"

Four . . . three . . . two . . . one . . .

He's following them, and he's faster than Evelyn. She has to make a choice. She puts Noemi down in the wet grass. "Run," she tells her sister. "Under the fence and through the woods. Go to the red house and knock on the door. I'll find you."

She turns to face her father. She still has the stick in her hand, the brave little wand.

She lets it fill her up.

"I did it," she tells her sister. "I put the stick in him. I made him stop." The stick went so fast and so hard. It stuck right into his chest. When he fell and was finally still, she took the scissors from the ground beside him and hid them in the box. Then she followed her sister's path through the woods.

"Oh, Ev." Noemi's face crumples. Ev turns away.

"You did the right thing," Noemi says, although it sounds like a question, not a statement. "You saved us?"

"Of course I did the right thing. We're not dirty, Noemi. We're not stains." *We're treasures.* "Come out of here. Meet me at the river. I'll show you another way."

Ev doesn't wait to see if Noemi follows. She has to get out. She has to try to make her mother's words true. She limps back toward the French doors, battering her hips and shoulders against boxes and furniture along the way. She needs a safe place to work, a calm place. The river. She stumbles through the yard, the pain in her ankle shooting up her leg with each step. She flings the scissors over the wall. Flings herself over the wall.

Hands and knees hit the gravel. The scissors shout their horrible voices at her, two

509

feet away. In the daylight, she can see the bloodstains and swallows back vomit. Somewhere behind her, perhaps, Noemi has found the path out and followed her. But she can't worry about that, or about whether Noemi is still a threat. Ev takes a moment to empty her mind, watching the river.

You can change things.

She picks up the scissors. She holds them close to her chest and opens herself to their vibrations. Her father's obsession is the loudest, a mechanical, illogical anger. Under that pulses the source of his illness, a sour fear turned into jealous, explosive rage. Also, there is a little girl's terror and grief and powerlessness, singing the hopelessness that Noemi heard so well. Ev's terror. Ev's powerlessness.

Except the scissors didn't change her. They never changed her. She's always been strong. She faced a monster and lived. She saved her baby sister, and she will do it again. She holds the scissors closer. She reaches way back and pulls up another memory of her father. She's lying in bed, watching him in the dark. He holds an infant Noemi in his arms, and he is singing her a lullaby. No stains, no anger. Only love.

She pours that song like water into the spaces around the scissors' rage. She sends forgiveness to her father. She sends forgiveness to her eight-year-old self. She sends forgiveness to the anonymous one who marked the scissors long before they destroyed her family. She sings all the stains to sleep and washes the scissors clean.

Ev sits cross-legged on the shore of the river and watches a tugboat glide toward the sea. The scissors balance on her knee, harmless now. Her jeans are covered in dust, and her body feels sticky all over. Her final escape from the house did a number on her ankle. It's turning purple and has swelled to the size of a baseball. She presses her T-shirt against the thin red line where Noemi scored her chest. It's long but not deep; the bleeding has already stopped. She thinks about braving the current and dipping in, clothes and all. The water looks calm, but who ever knows what's happening under the surface? Instead, she hooks her fingers into the handles of the scissors and flings them as far as she can. They hit the water with a soft plunk and vanish.

The sound of sirens approaching brings Ev back to reality. The sun has risen over the trees to her left, and Noemi hasn't emerged from the house. Is she still inside? Does she need help? Ev went in to save her and then she left her there, consumed with the need to carry out her mother's long-forgotten instructions. She runs as best she can to the gate. An ambulance has arrived, lights flashing at the side of the house. Owen jogs next to a paramedic, right past the smashed door Ev has left ajar, pointing ahead. A second paramedic unloads a stretcher from the back of the ambulance.

Let her be okay.

Something else catches her attention. Noemi's car was parked where the ambulance now flashes. In an instant, Ev knows she's left, gone without saying good-bye again. Ev ducks behind the wall, eyes blurring. She blinks against the tears and sees a flash of her sister's broken face as she held the scissors to her chest. She knows she won't see Noemi again for a long time.

51

Harriet pinches the wing of her scrap metal life buoy. Holding on. Hoping for rescue instead of death. How quickly the mind can turn. Every time the house crowds in on her, she squeezes tighter. She won't let it go. Owen talks to her, to help her stay tethered. He tells her the story of his family and how he failed them, and how Ev gave him the idea to make his estranged son a peace offering. He confesses that he stole from Harriet in order to build it. He took objects from the labeled sections of the Dragon in order to create a particular emotional impression. But it never came together quite right.

"It always felt tarnished," Owen says. "Every time I looked at it, I felt ashamed."

He promises to return every last item, if only she'll allow him to continue working at the Dragon. When she's healed, he says, they'll finish what they started. When she's healed. She holds on to the words, along with her little bird.

Something hammers at the door. Unfamiliar voices yell through the open window, and she mumbles something back. Yes, she's alive. No, her hip, she can't get up.

"Hang on, Ms. Langdon. We're coming."

Harriet hangs.

A series of mighty cracks jars her ears, followed by a splash of bright light that breaks into the basement from the top of the stairs. The door is open. More shouts and shuffling and banging as boxes and bags are cleared from the stairs. Harriet shuts her eyes and keeps holding. Time passes.

A frenzy of boots stomp down the stairs, voices shouting orders, then hands and faces loom over her. The EMTs behave admirably. She can see the tension in the grim sets of their jaws, and once the woman, a young thing with wide shoulders and a tidy bun, squeezes her eyes shut as though to block out some sudden sorrow. But the basement doesn't frighten them away. Harriet supposes they are practiced in shielding their minds from pain and fear. They have to be.

They load her onto a stretcher, barely glancing at the chaos around them, and trundle her outside, where Owen waits. The burst of joy that warms her chest at the sight of him rather surprises her. But there's no time for sentiment. The EMTs plop her on a trolley and rush her right past him. One of them tries to pry the bird from her hand, but she won't let them take it. She can hear Owen's voice as he follows her feet.

"I'll meet you at the hospital."

"Okay."

"I'll bring tea."

"Okay."

"If I can find Evelyn, I'll bring her too."

Harriet's heart stops. How could she forget? She lets go of the bird and tugs at someone's sleeve, the nearest human.

"Evelyn is upstairs. Trapped."

"She's okay." Owen's warm hand squeezes hers. "She climbed out a second-floor window."

She beat the house. Of course she did, amazing girl. Harriet gets an idea. They're about to lift her into the ambulance. Owen's hand is slipping from hers.

"What about Noemi?" she cries.

"Alive. Ev went back in to save her."

"You're sure they're both out?"

"I saw them both down by the river a little while ago."

That decides it. Harriet has only a moment before she will be carried away too far to act. Quick, before she loses her nerve.

515

She closes her eyes and enters the house one last time, in her mind, allowing her consciousness to seek out the treasure she needs. It responds immediately, as she knew it would. For the first time, Harriet succeeds in commanding an object. The Zippo, almost shaking with pent-up anxiety and anticipation, needs very little coaxing.

Heat tears from the stem of her brain down through her spine as the oily rags ignite, carrying the flames across the basement to the mattress, to the stacks of cardboard and up to the floorboards of the great room. Tears roll down the side of Harriet's face, puddling near her earlobe on the thin foam pillow beneath her head. She can feel the vibrations going still, only a few at first, but then more and more bright things blinking out of existence. Her life's work, burning away. She should bear witness, but in truth, she is relieved when the ambulance carries her away, back into the heart of the city and out of reach.

52

By the time Ev feels strong enough to stand again, the ambulance has left too. Only Ev and the house remain. She regards it through the bars of the gate one last time. Something's different. The house is changing. Is that smoke drifting across the yard? Ev steps to the top of the stairs for a closer look. Her foot hits something that scrapes against the concrete. She looks at her feet, at the box next to the toes of her right sneaker. Her forgetting box, her hiding place, the box Noemi was clutching when she brought the house down on Ev. Noemi left it behind. She left it for her.

When her skin makes contact with the cool metal, she feels the jolt of fear little Evelyn left behind all those years ago. But beneath that, she senses the lingering, feather-light breath of old pride and curiosity. She remembers standing at the table in the workshop on a stool, watching him unpack a box of items he found at a garage sale. A porcelain vase covered in dust. A piggy bank painted with little pink roses. She remembers how he would give her a soft brush to wipe away the dust. How he would lay his big hands over her small ones and let her feel the vibrations of each object, ask her to guess at the emotions in each one.

Protection, she'd whisper with her eyes closed. *Love. Joy.*

That sense of shared secrecy survives on the surface of the box. Only Evelyn truly knew and understood Daddy's secret. There was delight in this, and she can feel that, too, another vibration she left behind. But it's hard to detect. It's so well covered over by the frantic confusion and fear that colors all of Ev's childhood memories. A vibration Ev is surprised to find doesn't frighten her like it did before. Mostly it makes her heavy and sad.

Sometimes he would bring her gifts. Small, secret things. She opens the box. Broken glass litters the bottom, the curved shards of a Christmas bauble. Ev pokes a finger around a pair of rhinestone sunglasses, a ceramic kitten with a glossy ball of yarn, and a blue plastic dinosaur on a leather cord. She finds the Christmas fawn nestled next to a gauzy bag full of polished stones, rose quartz and amethyst. Some of its tiny white spots have been scraped away. But it has survived, intact. A piece of her father, kept safe from the monster he would become.

One more thing rests in the bottom of the box. A ring, gold with a ruby stone nestled in a tiny rose. Holding it makes her chest and throat constrict until she can hardly breathe. Holding it, she remembers her.

A piece of her mother. Intact. The soft layers of her mother's spirit live solidly in the gold: compassion, duty, fierce love, and a sweet thread of giddy, offbeat humor that reminds Ev of Noemi.

Ev places the ring on her own finger.

53

"Are you ready?"

"I am."

Harriet allows Owen to place a blanket on her lap before he wheels her outside and toward the park. Despite the clear sky, the air holds an early fall crispness. Harriet closes her eyes and breathes in the smell of sweet heather. She shouldn't be so content. She expected the dead cleanliness of the hospital to depress her. In fact, although the sounds and smells and the awful food lived up to the reputation of all hospitals, Harriet found her time there refreshing. The quiet was a welcome respite. So, when it came time for her to move into Owen's house, she felt ready to inhabit a space with room to breathe in.

Over the last couple of weeks, Owen and Harriet have settled in well as roommates, although it took some adjustment. At first, Harriet clung to Owen as though he were a life raft, allowing him to keep her afloat. Once she had a few days to recover, both from her injuries and from the loss of the house at Angel Place, she began to pull away. She's still working on trusting him. She's getting there, day by day. She even returned his keys to the Dragon so that he could continue their work while she heals.

Knowing she can't manage the stairs at the Dragon, she agreed to his suggestion that she move into the recently vacated main floor bedroom of his house, and allowed him to make the arrangements, thinking it temporary. As it turns out, the house with the sagging front porch holds a comfortable and cheerful brightness, and the young couple on the second floor are excellent cooks. Owen brought his handcrafted chandelier from the Dragon and hung it over her bed. She may stay awhile.

A blackberry bush spreads across the back fence bordering the park. Owen pushes her across the grass and stops next to it without asking, remembering how much Harriet enjoyed filling her cheeks with berries yesterday. He's brought a plastic container from home, and he fills it up. He parks Harriet next to a bench in the sun, and they eat berries until their fingers are stained purple.

Harriet has grown accustomed to listening to the goings-on inside her head. She is getting to know her own feelings about things, rather than relying upon the feelings of the things that surround her. As it happens, she has a lot to catch up on. Quite a lot of the time, she thinks of Ev. She has not come to visit. In fact, Harriet has only received a single text message from her. It came the day after the house burned.

We're okay. I'm sorry.

Owen hasn't been able to fill her in much more on the details. Ev is fine and will be in touch soon. Noemi has vanished. However, Harriet is quite certain she can fill in the blanks. The other day, she received a letter. Harriet's name was written on the envelope in rounded, girlish script. No name on the return address, but a post office box in Saskatchewan. Inside, she found a single sheet of lined paper folded into the shape of a crane. There were no words on the paper, but Harriet could feel the sorrow and guilt soaked into it.

She hopes Noemi will like what she sent back. She didn't include a note with it either, but she has a feeling Noemi will understand what it means. Harriet doesn't need the bird stone anymore, anyhow.

"You can take me back now. You must want to get back to work."

Owen has been spending most of his days at the Dragon, transforming Harriet's treasures into art. In the evenings, he describes his work in detail, every object used, so that Harriet can imagine the emotional resonance of each of his sculptures. His dragon is nearly complete, and besides that, he has been using items from each of the sections she and Ev sorted to create new works of art, each with a distinct vibration. When she's walking better, she will return to experience it for herself.

She also has an idea to help him with his forgiveness project for his son. When she's well enough, she'll help him get the right balance. Soon, the Dragon will be open to the public as an art exhibition. Perhaps Owen's son will come to the opening gala. Harriet can be persuasive when she wants to be.

"It's not time to go quite yet," he replies.

"Why? What's happening?" He adjusts the chair so she can see. Ev hangs back at the edge of the park, bottom lip caught in her teeth. She looks different. Younger. No, softer. And nervous. Owen waves at her cheerfully and makes space on the park bench so she can sit.

"Hello, Evelyn," he says. "You're looking well."

"You look guilty," Harriet adds. "What have you been up to?"

Ev breaks into a smile. The first smile Harriet has ever seen on that face. "Nice to see you, too."

Owen lays a hand gently on the top of Ev's head. Harriet notices she doesn't shrink away. Then he leaves them alone. Harriet, as relieved as she is to see Ev whole and healthy, feels the emotions she's been struggling with rise back to the surface. She wasn't sure how it would feel to see Ev again. She still isn't. She lets the silence stretch out.

"You're looking well too," Ev offers. A weak start, but Harriet accepts it all the same.

"Owen tells me you've been busy. A new job of some sort."

"More of a business." She pauses, drawing in a deep breath. "I'm afraid it might upset you."

"Is that why you stayed away so long?"

Ev shrugs, looking down at her lap. "I'm sorry. About the house."

"I'm not." She wants to say she's sorry too, about Noemi, about Ev's family, but she's not ready to talk about it, not yet. "Tell me about this business," she says.

Ev pulls a small black box out of her

pocket. Harriet can feel the vibration contained within it. It isn't strong, but she shrinks back all the same. She has grown more sensitive to bright things, after being away from her collection for some time. Shame is a difficult emotion to be around anyway, but right now it hits too close to home.

"You feel it, right?"

Harriet nods in assent. Curious now, she watches as Ev lifts a gold brooch out of the box. Two antlers around a piece of amber glass.

Ev envelops the brooch in her palms and closes her eyes. She sits for a long time like that, silent. Harriet waits. She doesn't have anywhere to be. Slowly, she becomes aware of another energy in the air around them. It feels like respect. Honor. Pride. It's coming from Ev.

Harriet doesn't notice her own tears until they drop onto her forearm. The energy fades. Ev opens her eyes and her hands. The brooch lies in her palm as before, but the shame vibration has vanished. The brooch doesn't have any brightness at all.

"You killed it."

"Neutralized it. But not completely. Here." Ev puts the brooch in Harriet's hand.

No. Not dead, not quite. She's left the

softest hint of familial love intact, some hint of brightness that had been hidden under the shame.

"How the bloody hell did you do that?"

"It's something I figured out." Ev tries to sound humble, but her eyes burn with excitement.

"How?"

"You have to inhabit the object. Let the emotion live inside you. Once you have the exact sense of it, you find its opposite and just kind of beam it in with all the force you've got."

Harriet remembers the pistol. Ev must have removed its anger that day when she was trying to talk Harriet down at the Dragon. She probably never even knew she'd done it. The power needed for that kind of work. The courage. It is nothing short of magic. Harriet feels breathless.

"So, you do this for people? For money?"

"That's the plan. My first customer was pro bono." She closes her fingers around the brooch. "I have some friends with objects for me to practice on. But I've taken a couple of paying gigs, and I'm hoping the word will spread. I want to work up to larger objects."

The possibilities unfold in Harriet's mind. She could heal relationships. She could unhaunt entire houses. A stab of pain stops her from speaking the words aloud. If only she knew Ev was capable of this before.

"I haven't tried a whole house yet," Ev continues, as though she heard Harriet's thoughts. "But I think I can work up to it."

"You're a goddamn ghost buster." Harriet laughs out loud. Perfect. Just perfect.

"I prefer the term *psychic restoration artist*." Ev peeks at her from behind her hair. "You're not upset?"

"It's brilliant."

"I'm only using it to wipe out negative energies." Ev seems anxious to explain. "I don't want you to think that I'm going to snuff all the life out of every bright thing I can find."

"I don't think that."

"I've realized that not all of them are harmful. Some of them can help people. Like the bird stone. Your museum of memory. Owen's artwork."

"Have you heard from your sister?" Harriet asks, the bird stone reminding her.

"No." The light leaves Ev's eyes. "I don't think I will."

Harriet wants to give her some reassurance, but finds she can't, not with regard to her sister, anyway. The girl deserves honesty. So instead, Harriet tells Ev something else she needs to hear. Not to be kind, but because it is true.

"It's good work you're doing, Evelyn. You're a good person."

EPILOGUE

It's evening on the Aegean Sea, and the lights shine on the water like submerged stars. Ev stops to peek at the view from the crest of the hill she climbed on foot, a narrow cobblestone road winding up through a village street. All around her rise white-washed, cubed houses. Her destination lies a little closer to the beach, a modern villa with a kidney-shaped pool nestled against it. An opulent oasis deserted for over two years, its only occupants the ghosts of its ugly past. She's arrived too early and has decided to view the house from above, to get a sense of its layout and of how far the vibration of its tightly coiled anger radiates.

This will be her first international client. The initial referrals came via Judy and Caroline from sailing class, as well as Michael, who turned out to have more connections than she realized. It didn't take long for the requests to begin rolling in via her Miss Cellany email address. After that, word of mouth spread about Ev's particular talents. She has plenty of work now. She can go anywhere.

She pulls off her gloves. She wears them now not out of fear, but merely to give herself a rest. A day in Greece is like a day spent in the ocean, letting the tide roll in over your body. Wonderful, but it also wears her skin down. She flew into Athens and spent two days there, where the very air is soaked with layers upon layers of emotion, a tapestry of human experience. The buildings have an almost musical vibration to them, the way their stone has absorbed the comings and goings of so many passions. Ev can stand in one spot all day and pick up hundreds of story threads. A shiver of delicious fear runs through her. This is the first place she's visited outside of Canada, outside of her young city. There are many places left for her to encounter.

Far below, she can see the small port where her ferry docked earlier that morning. Along the shoreline, tiny sailboats glow white in the moonlight. Ev has a secondary motive for choosing Greece as her first international destination. The water calls to her. She missed her last two sailing classes with Brett because she was so consumed with her new business, but she intends to make them up. Tonight, she works. Tomorrow, when the sun rises, she heads to Paros. This morning, she mailed a postcard to Brett, care of the Jericho Sailing Club. She meant it as a simple thank-you, but sometime between placing the stamp and slipping the card into the postbox, she changed her mind. Channeling her inner Noemi, she scrawled her phone number on the bottom.

The time has come. She reaches into her bag and touches each of her talismans in turn, objects she carries with her for courage: a red chiffon scarf, a paper crane, a tiny plastic deer. She strokes the gold ring on her left hand with the pad of her thumb. Then she heads toward the villa.

Harriet moves slowly through the crowd, heading toward the colorful string of lanterns at the opposite side of the street. It's the last Chinatown Night Market of the year, so despite the cold, the street is filled with people. Next to her, Owen holds a package wrapped in tissue and twine. This is the first of Owen's artworks to leave the Dragon, although it won't be the last. Ev commissioned this particular piece. Harriet helped her pick out the materials — empty wine bottles, worn coins from faraway places, and keys of various shapes and sizes, a lovely blend of conviviality, prosperity, and good fortune. As always, Owen has done a beautiful job of fashioning the pieces into something entirely new. In this case, a set of bells.

"There," says Owen. He nods at a nearby table, where a woman in a creamy woolen sweater is selling socks and toys. He passes Harriet the package, and she maneuvers around a family sharing mini doughnuts on a stick to deposit the package on the table behind a *Season End Clearance Sale* sign while Vivian is occupied with a customer. Before she sneaks away, she ensures that the Miss Cellany business card is still tucked under the knot.

"Now where?" Owen links his arm through Harriet's. Although her fractured hip is not fully healed, she's moving around better now and walks daily as part of her rehabilitation.

"Let's go to the Chinese garden." She tries not to take her walks in the same spots. Usually they take a taxi somewhere — Ambleside, Trout Lake, Queen Elizabeth Park. It's a cold October evening, the sun setting on what might be the last day without rain they'll see for a month. They wind past the street blockades and cross the sidewalk toward the round gate that leads into the garden.

Harriet's pockets are full of tiny treasures. A cat's-eye marble. A string of beads. A business card so old the print has worn off. As much as she enjoys curating experiences, choosing the right objects for Owen to work with and the right person or place to receive his finished pieces, she knows that sometimes, like the bird stone that was left to find a new home in an unknown pocket, an object needs to seek its own fortune. So Harriet lets them slip out of her fingers one by one as she and Owen follow the stone path next to the koi pond. A jade elephant. A rare stamp. A silver pen. She leaves a trail of blessings around the garden. Around her city. One by one, Harriet lets her treasures go.

AUTHOR'S NOTE

This novel is set in Vancouver, a coastal Canadian city that sits on the unceded traditional territories of the Musqueam, Squamish, and Tsleil-Waututh First Nations. I love my hometown and write it through the lens of my own lived experience, but I have tried to capture the city as accurately as possible. That said, while many of the places in the story are real, some are imagined and others have ceased to exist. Sadly, the last Chinatown Night Market took place in 2017. The Vancouver Chinatown Merchants Association canceled the struggling market in early 2018, calling it a protest against the city's neglect of the neighborhood's businesses. The market has yet to return.

ACKNOWLEDGMENTS

Thanks to the folks at Atria Books and especially to my editor, Melanie Iglesias Pérez, whose vision for this book matched mine so beautifully and whose guidance was key to bringing that vision to reality.

Thanks to my wonderful agents, Melanie Castillo and Taylor Haggerty. Your enthusiastic love for this story and its characters has been such a gift.

Thanks to Chris Anderson for sharing his sailing expertise, and to Danmei Liu for answering my questions about Chinese culture and language. Any errors related to these subjects are entirely mine.

Several people provided me with photos of shiny objects to write into the book. While not every one made it into the final version, each of them inspired me and remains forever part of Harriet's collection. Special thanks to Caryn Cameron, Jennifer Douglas and Steve Mills, Micaiah Huw

Evans, Henry Lien, Barb and Tom Hopkins, Jenn Lewis, and Carlie St. George for your contributions.

Thanks to Kim Aippersbach, Caryn Cameron, Bryan Camp, Forest Eaton, Micaiah Huw Evans, Neile Graham, James Gordon Harper, Les Howle, and Henry Lien for giving me valuable feedback on early drafts. My sincere apologies if I've forgotten anyone.

A heartfelt thanks to the Clarion West class of 2012. The seed for this novel was planted during the workshop, and your voices have been with me ever since. You are all dear to me.

Thanks to the Pegasi, for the chocolate and camaraderie.

To my mother and stepfather, Barb and Tom Hopkins, thank you for so much emotional and financial support over the years.

Thanks to my father, Roy Mills, for teaching me to be a daydreamer.

To my daughter, Cassandra, thank you for reminding me daily to be bold and curious, and never to stop seeking wonder.

And finally, to my husband, Shane, who told me twenty-three years ago, "You should be a writer," and since then has supported me in hundreds of ways both big and small as I worked toward achieving that dream: I can honestly say that this book would not exist without you.

ABOUT THE AUTHOR

Kim Neville is an author and graduate of the Clarion West Writers Workshop, where she found the first shiny piece of inspiration that became *The Memory Collectors.* When she's not writing she can be found heron-spotting on the seawall or practicing yoga in order to keep calm. She lives near the ocean in Vancouver, Canada, with her husband, daughter, and two cats. *The Memory Collectors* is her first novel.